PARADISE FRACTURED

ZANE MACKINLAY

CONTENTS

1

—— • ——

PROLOGUE

"My love... you've come back to me!" The young woman ran to her husband and buried her head into his chest. The force of her impact caused him to take a step back, but he managed to steady himself and return her embrace. Her husband held her close, lightly rubbing the small of her back. Even as she cried before him, he said nothing. "I'm sorry, I'm so sorry!" she sobbed, "I tried everything to save you from their hatred, my love! You're my heart, I can't lose you again!" she pulled herself up to rest her head into the crook of his neck, and he held her small waist with one hand to help her balance.

"Nothing lasts forever, Elnorse," he whispered darkly, letting his lips gently graze below her ear.

He breath hitched. "My heart... my Zaphon. I'm whole only with you here," she pulled back to look up at him. Her eyes begged for his touch.

"Our love is a burden to the Empire, but I'll let no one take this treasure but me," he tightened his hold on her, "My sweet, sweet Empress."

His hand slipped to his belt to pull out a knife, and in a swift movement, he pierced her lower back. Her delicate skin tore easily, and her white gown became stained red with her own blood as it seeped out of her. She gasped, but he quickly grabbed her pale face and placed a deep, affectionate kiss over her lips as he swallowed her screams. She closed her bloodshot eyes as he tightened his grip, piercing her deeper and deeper with the knife.

He moved from her lips and whispered against her ear once more. "I follow my destiny, my love. With your death, I will take what is mine to take. I will claim my title as Emperor of the East."

Her eyes opened wide with terror as he pulled away from her. She looked down in shock when she saw the amount of blood seeping through her dress. His eyes followed her small frame as she stumbled before him.

"It's mine now, Elnorse. Mine alone," he said in a choked voice as she crumbled to the ground as gracefully as an Empress should. He turned and walked out, not daring to look back. He stopped only at the open door of the palace that was once his home. He threw his head back, giving a muffled, sickening laugh. Tears streamed down his face, and he used his bloodstained hands to wipe them away, coating his face in her blood. He narrowed his eyes at the thought of his new claim to the Empire. Staring off beyond the silver seas of his planet, gleaming in the light of the blue sun, he said the two words that would turn the fate of the Realms for eternity.

"Elnorse fall,"

Three days after the fall of the royals, in the Northern empire on the planet V'rasór...

"Deny our freedom..." the young boy said in misery. "Deny our future... and now you?" he scoffed. The boy's older brother sighed loudly.

"I can't protect V'rasór and us!" he said, not daring to face his younger brother. "You had no issue denying your claim to the throne, but I will not deny mine."

His younger brother huffed in response; their little sister silently watched as they argued about their futures.

"This is my fate- I must protect my empire as Emperor, for V'rasór's sake... for the sake of the entire Realms. So run, ne'leir," the older boy practically begged his brother, hoping the endearment would convince him. "Take our ne'la and go. You don't want the crown, and our sister is too young to decide. If you stay, you are a threat to him, and if you're found he will do worse than kill you both." The older boy tried to muster the strength to order his sibling to leave but couldn't seem to do it.

"No! I am a fighter nãe'heir! I won't run and hide from him; I will fight alongside you! For our planet and for the peace and justice of the Realms!" Little blue lights danced in the markings that surrounded the eyes of the younger boy, responding to his passion.

"Do you speak for our ne'la as well?" the older spoke quietly so their little sister wouldn't hear him talk about her. Finally, the younger of the two dropped his eyes knowing, his older sibling spoke the truth. "No, ne'leir, this is bigger than only a fight between empires. This affects the entire Realms. I won't let that madman force my hand into a bloodbath that will destroy our galaxy. War is what they want, and they will have it, but not until we are ready and until then I can't let him use either of you against me," the older finally faced his brother. "Ne'leir... please, go!"

His brother finally relented at his plea. With a stiff nod, he placed his arm against his brother's chest in goodbye. The older stiffly returned the gesture.

The young boy took a step back. "I wish you all my strength, nãe'heir."

"As I wish you all of mine, ne'leir," the older responded, and then glanced wistfully at their younger sister. The small girl immediately stood, her eyes red and tired from lack of sleep. She kept blinking her eyes, refusing to cry in the sight of her brothers. The older opened his arms to her, letting her run and embrace him as she gave up to her tears.

"Will we ever see you again?" her voice cracked up as she spoke the words.

"W-We shall," he stammered, but it was a promise he wasn't so sure he could keep.

"I don't want to leave! There's nowhere he won't find us. Nowhere he won't be able to lay us in our own blood like..." she trailed off, unable to speak about her mother. His treachery had broken her when she witnessed his crimes.

"Shh..." the older said, trying to soothe her by tightening his embrace. He glanced at his younger brother warily, who returned his gaze with pleading eyes. They both knew that there was no place in the universe would keep him from hunting them. The older brother's eyes hardened, and he shoved his sister away. She stumbled back with a surprised gasp.

"Go, I've forgotten you," his voice was hard as he stepped away and turned his back from her. He heard her tears turn into sobs.

"Face me, Cronos. Please!" she said in-between sobs, but he didn't dare. Instead, he closed his eyes and waited for his sister to leave. She walked backwards, shaking her head in disbelief. His brother placed a hand on her arm.

"Come," he said tightly, and led her away by her arm. Their sister was gently pushed through the door, but before his brother followed her, he turned around to face his older brother one last time. The older- Cronos- already turned to look at his brother with shaking hands, tears falling from his eyes.

"Turn and leave ne'leir, or I will never let you go," Cronos all but whispered. His brother gave a quick nod and left without looking back again. For some time, Cronos stood there, gazing at the door where his only family vanished before his eyes. He took a deep breath and finally turned towards his own exit. Taking in another short breath of air, he stepped through it. Guards were already there, ready to take orders from Cronos, the young Emperor of the North. He looked at each of them and saw the anticipation in their eyes. He saw the hunger for revenge, justice, freedom, and most of all, a yearning for war.

"This..." he said loudly enough to gather everyone's attention.

".... This is only the beginning of their end."

2

— ◆ —

CHAPTER 1

9 years later...

When most close their eyes, all they see is the darkness that lurks there, but not me. I saw colors, heard songs in many voices, and felt the pull of phantasm dancing in my heart, connecting me to the Realms. Mother said we were special. That only we, the people born of Natarah, the soul of our galaxy, mattered. I felt its pull trickle down my veins, shimmering through the markings around my face. I wanted to tell her that I felt it. I felt the power flowing through each person born in our galaxy, and my own core, my source of phantasm. I should have.

My eyes opened. Before me was the cold floor of the Rectifier, my brother's ship. I shifted my eyes up toward the viewscreen of the bridge and saw the beautiful triplet moon planet of E'arka, our hopeful new trading partners. The ship drifted in the planet's gravitational pull, preparing to land. My brother, Rain, sat at the front controls with his co-pilot.

They tried to put on a brave front for the crew, but I knew how nervous they were for this mission, how nervous we all were. It was a miracle we had made it this far without getting detected by our enemies. I mentally scolded myself for referring to them as enemies.

They were merely carrying out our galaxy's laws. Thinking about them as enemies wouldn't help anything, but it wouldn't make it any less true. We may not currently be on terms of war with them, but that wouldn't stop them from blowing up my brother's ship if they found out we left the Realms.

They were cruel, the Union of MioTamir. It wasn't even the thought of death that was feared by us, but rather the fear they would use our traveling into the Forbidden regions as an excuse to begin war with our home planet, Eurkxo. It wasn't our fault we were forced to break the laws of our galaxy by crossing into the Forbidden regions and leaving our home galaxy. Our planet's people were dying from hunger, but no agricultural planet within the Realm's dared trade with us. Not with the Union threatening them into compliance.

I heard my brother sigh at the sight of the beautiful planet.

"Adam, you're sure no one knew that route?" My brother turned his head to the side to face his co-pilot, who sat comfortably next to him.

"Ay, as I am ever, brother!" Adam said cheerfully. He spun his chair around to face my brother, smirking. His voice was deep, with the accent of someone born on the planet MioTamir. He was much bigger than my brother, and had thick looking skin, dark eyes, and a shaved head covered in red flower-looking tattoos. I knew the man since I'd first moved to the planet Eurkxo. Though I didn't know him as long as my brother had, he was considered family to me. More than my own at times.

"Reaching our destination, planet E'arka, in half-hour time."

A voice said from Rain's panel. I assumed it was the ship's naviga-tor, who wasn't currently on the bridge but rather in the navigation room. My brother told me she was a skilled member of his crew, and though I was introduced to her upon boarding his ship, we hadn't spoken since then. I knew nothing about her except that she was an Anari from the planet Ardiamus, and that assumption was based solely on her appearance. I stretched out my arms. We would be landing in about forty minutes, the equivalent to a half-hour if we were going based on our ships time system which had been set to our home planet's time cycle.

"Noted," Rain responded through his control panel. He turned to the rest of us on the bridge. "Everyone be on high alert! Being away from the Realms doesn't mean all danger has been escaped. Fighting an enemy that is known to be fatal is treacherous, but fighting an unknown enemy is impossible."

"Then we shan't make any enemies, ay?" Adam grunted loudly, obviously trying not to laugh at all the seriousness. Rain gave him a sideways glance, clearly not amused.

"Rain is right. We understood how things work in the Realms, but in the Forbidden regions, it's as unforeseen as tomorrow." Another voice sounded as they walked to my brother's side. The man appeared to be another Anari, like the navigator. My eyes trailed over his exposed dark, almost black skin, patterned in beautiful shades of yellow. I didn't want to be caught staring and give him the wrong impression, so I turned my eyes away.

My thoughts drifted to what my brother said, and I immediately agreed with his words. We managed to survive departure from the Realms without being killed by those who hate us. That was a miracle in itself. No one was meant to leave the Realms, and no one was meant to enter.

I remembered my mother telling me something about a tragedy that happened generations ago, and a promise that had to be kept which was the reason for the law. I found it an unreasonable and unrealistic law. I hoped it would be revoked one day. However, that's an opinion not widely shared by the rest of our galaxy. Unfortunately for us, living in the Realms was a fatal life, but it was one that was more familiar. If the Union found out about us leaving to enter the Forbidden Region, they could use it to start the war within the Realms. More fighting, which is precisely what some wanted. A cold shudder ran through me at the thought of them. A people whose very name sent waves of terror through planets.

Elnorsefall...

They weren't like the Union. They were worse. They followed no law; they kept no morals. They slaughtered those who got in their way and lived for one purpose. They wanted the planet V'rasòr to belong to them, and they would stop at nothing until it did. Fortunately, they had no quarrel with Eurkxo, the planet me and my brother currently lived on. However, a war would be the perfect distraction to take out V'rasòr's last crowned royal. They were the center planet, the leaders, the voice of reason in the Realms. If V'rasòr fell to Elnorsefall, the entire Realms would soon bend a knee to them.

I was born on V'rasòr, it was my home once, but no longer is. Even though I no longer considered it home, the last thing I wanted was to become part of the reason they fell. They had enough issues being torn apart from the inside by Elnorsefall.

I sighed, pulling myself out of my own thoughts, and tried to focus on the livelier conversation around me. Being alone in my memories wasn't exactly pleasant. In fact, I would go as far as to say I hated it. Because it hurt, it always hurt.

Adam laughed, "Ay shucks! Stop worrying your heads off," he said as he slouched deeply into his chair. "That 'er energy cores we've brought with be enough to keep us friendly enough ye'see?"

"True enough, my brother. It would surprise me if they did anything less than bow down to us when we offer them the cores we've brought to trade with," Rain laughed lightly and slapped Adam on the shoulder. Even the Anari laughed, which was a rare gesture I'd noticed. Then again, not many can resist Adam's charms. Even I find myself giggling like a child most times a day by him. "Adam, send out a broadcast message, everyone is to report to the bridge." Rain told Adam, who nodded in response as he typed something on his panel.

We were joined on the bridge by the other Anari woman on board and Rain's three engineers, as well as my fellow representative, Erayame, who was also a guest on my brother's ship.

"This is all so exciting! Would you not agree, Keeper?" I smiled at the three brothers, who practically sparkled in excitement as they strapped themselves into their seats.

All three were quite young, only a bit older than me. I also met them when I first entered the ship, and immediately felt friendly with them. I was told by the oldest, Tehayo, that they were from the planet Láuran, which was known to be a rather peaceful planet. Most, like the brothers, had fair smooth gray skin, and a tall, learn-like appearance. He also mentioned to me that he and his siblings were banished from their planet because they wanted a different way of life. Unlike their people, who valued family above all else, the brothers wanted to be free to explore and live life on their own. According to Rain, their planet now vowed that the siblings were dead to them.

I responded with a soft smile. "Yes, it certainly is."

Next to me, Erayame grunted, his nose tipped up in annoyance. A small smile appeared on my face in response to his annoyance. He despised the thought of landing on such an inferior planet, which he boldly stated to the Elders before we left Eurkxo. Unfortunately, he was our best diplomat, so the Elders gave him little choice in the matter.

I watched as my brother stood from his chair and walked over to where I sat. He stood over me as I gave him a curious look. He smiled tentatively.

"How are you, Keeper?" he asked while sliding down on an empty seat next to me, his hands rested comfortably on his knees. I smiled in response, not answering with my words, but rather with my expression.

He nodded in approval. "Good."

I waited patiently for him to continue; a bit concerned as he stared off.

"It's okay to be anxious," Rain finally said, looking down suddenly. I raised an eyebrow at him.

"You are correct. It is okay to be anxious, commander," I answered with a tilt of my head. I knew he was trying to more- so convince himself rather than me.

"I hadn't meant me..." his mouth tipped into a slight frown as he mumbled under his breath, but I already knew I was right. I tucked my long black hair behind my shoulder, lifted my chin slightly, and placed my hands gently on my lap. A small gesture that changed me from a younger sister to someone he would listen to.

"You are making the right choice, you know this," my eyes followed him as he slumped down, defeated.

"Eurkxo has been abandoned of trade by most all of the sectors due to the panic of angering our neighboring worlds..." he sighed in frustration, a frustration I understood all too well.

Eurkxo was a planet where many beings from different worlds came together in peace on one planet. Of course, every being in the Realms has their own planet of origin, but some, especially outcasts or half breeds, preferred a quiet life without prejudice. It's the only reason I could imagine why the MioTamir Union despised Eurkxo to the point of alienating them from trade with the other worlds. No one wanted to challenge the Union in fear of igniting the spark for a war, so instead they chose to pretend Eurkxo didn't exist. They refused trade, and refused to communicate with us, so we were forced to look beyond the Realms for trade.

"If we don't engage in this trade, I fear Eurkxo will be taken out of the Elder's grasp. You and Erayame are a part of the council, and I understand it was important to bring you both. The elders trust both of you with the fate of the planet. It was the right decision," he said with a strong nod as if he was trying to reassure himself. Yes, it was a vital mission, which was why I immediately answered yes to the Elders even though our safety was not guaranteed. I stared at him with an empty look. I heard the hesitance in his voice just now, and my stomach coiled with unease.

"As commander of The Rectifier, you have doubts. You don't trust us?" I gestured to my fellow council member sitting on the seat next to me with my chin. I brought my gaze back to him, staring intently. "Do you not trust me?"

"What?" his head jerked up sharply, his eyes widening. "No... I mean yes of course I trust you...I trust you more than anyone."

"I know you do," I said quietly, but inside, I knew the reason he hesitated. He couldn't trust me to let him protect me as my brother. He knew there was a line he couldn't cross. He may be my brother, but both of us had our duties in life, and such duties put us both in the light of fire.

As a member of the elder's council, I could easily become a target for the Union, especially if they found out I was on this mission. I worried for my brother as well. He didn't have to volunteer his ship to be the means of travel for this mission. No one would've blamed him for not risking it, but he volunteered without hesitation. There was no doubt in my mind that he would be punished with death by the Union if they discovered that he had commanded this flight.

No one expected this from us. It bothered me that they didn't expect us to help the planet we had both been raised on for so long. I suppose it was rather foolish- to risk our lives which were already in such danger from another darkness. They would not understand. They would not understand this need to fight back against the prison that has been built by such darkness.

My brother fidgeted beside me, clearly wanting to say something more. I tilted my head at him as I waited for him to speak his mind.

"Keeper... Cloverlyne, don't misunderstand me. You accepting their request means you have moved out of my hand, I worry..." he stammered out quickly, but I cut him off with a raise of my hand before he could finish.

"Enough, I understand ne'leir."

He paused at my words, giving me an irritated look. "I do not like associating status with my little sister, my ne'la," He crossed his arms, and he let his lips purse out in frustration. It was such a childish look I couldn't help but smile at him.

"Rain..." I started to say but was interrupted by the Anari woman.

"Arriving at our destination, prepare for landing," I glanced over Rain's shoulder to see her putting a control tablet away, which I assumed was what she was using to track our movements.

Rain's head shot up at her words.

"Everyone brace yourselves for landing!" he barked out, hurrying briskly to Adam's side once more. I reached under the seat to grab an extra set of belts meant for landing purposes. The others followed suit, clipping their belts and holding on to the crossed front. The front window changes into a darkened screen, blocking out the light of fire from entering the planet's atmosphere. The ship rumbled as it glided down, which caused me to tighten my grip on the belt.

I attempt to recall what we knew about the planet so far to distract myself from the rough landing. It was a trading planet of an intelligent race who had seemed friendly enough based on the information given from past scouts. According to them, these people spoke an ancient dialect that seemed to have derived from Kêva, the language of the planet D'thaya in the Realms. The scouts claimed that they mostly resemble the ancestors of the First Planet like us. I was glad for that at least. Some species within the Realms had evolved alarmingly.

DNA splicing and genetic experimentation was common in the Realms, my people being the leading researchers in such. I always found this ironic because even though we were the leading researchers, my people were proud of being the closest to the Ancients DNA and genetic makeup with only a few alterations.

The humming of the ship grows louder, pulling me out of my thoughts. I griped the belt covering my chest tightly as the ship began to shake even more than before, until finally becoming steady as it hovered above the landing platform.

"Landing!" Adam called out from the co-pilot seat. "In five, four, three, two, one-"

Before he made it to zero, our bodies were thrust forward by the force of the landing. For a moment, we all sat there in silence. I slowly released my grip on the safety belt around me and pressed the middle button to release it. I heard the clicks of the other's releasing the belts, and watched as they stood, and stretched their muscles. I did the same, gently reaching as far back as possible to rub my shoulder blades which were sore from the tension built up.

"Everybody head to the disembark chamber," Rain called out, pressing a few buttons as he stood.

"Prepare meh for death, we shan't last a fortnight 'ere," Adam said, walking over to me and offering his arm with a wink. I took his arm with a warm smile and let him lead me. Rain shook his head at Adams' comment.

"Must you be so dramatic?"

"Justa warning, mate. If y'erself get eaten alive by hunchback trolls!" Adam smirked, punching him playfully in the shoulder. Rain frowned.

"Say that in front of them, and mark my words Adam, I swear to kill you myself."

"We shall be cautious of everything we say, commander," I added, grinning in a playful way along with Adam, who kept in step beside me.

Rain threw a desperate look to the heavens.

"By Natarah, and all its power," he mumbled quietly to himself. He opened the door to the chamber where the exit to our ship was.

"Lord above, be with us," I whispered a prayer to myself. All of us walked quietly to the chamber on the near side of the ship which was where we would exit from. It was an uneasy silence, even my brother said nothing about how we would proceed. We all reached the chamber, there were about eight of us, not including myself. Surly Rain would not have all of us leave the ship?

My assumptions were correct as my brother turned to face us studying each of us intently before he nodded his head as if coming to a conclusion.

"Keeper, Erayame, Adam, and Tehayo," Rain said, looking at each of us as he said our names. "With me."

"Rihaya, Cyenvier, Vis, and Morak." They each nodded to their names.

My eyes perked up at the names of the Anari. I wanted to remember their names so I could address them later. The woman seemed a gentle sort, and being the only two women on this ship I assumed we would have some sort of conversation soon. The man, I wasn't too sure about. He had such a stoney expression on his face, which I imagined was the reason for him remaining on the ship.

"Stay with the ship, let no one come in or out unless reported by me," Rain continued while handing out brown cloaks for us to wear. They were long, especially on me, and the hoods they had looked as though they would cover most of our faces.

"By your command, commander," The woman, Rihaya, said with a slight bow.

"Ah yes 'by y'er command' indeed commander," Adam mocked, tipping his head with a smug expression "By the ancients' way of say'n it 'let us skedaddle," he raised his hand above his head and pointed it towards the door with two fingers. He continued with his dramatic flair, popping his hip out to the side. He looked as smug as ever. I giggled to myself when I saw Tehayo's confused expression as he stared at Adam with wide eyes.

"Ske-daddle?" he asked, pronouncing it slowly as his head tilted to the side.

"It means 'to go quickly,'" I answered. He stared at me and blinked, then looked down thoughtfully.

"Ske...ske-daddle..." he mumbled again. Out of the corner of my eye I saw Vis, and Morak trying to pronounce it as well, without much success.

"Dear Lord!"' Erayame moaned under his breath. "What have you unleashed?"

"Hoods up!" Rain said, and we all followed his example, tightening our cloaks and putting the hoods over our heads. My initial thought appeared right, the hoods did cover much of our faces, but the material was unique in that we could see out from under the cloaks, whereas others couldn't see in. "Remember," Rain said suddenly. "This is a diplomatic mission. Be friendly, but cautious. Answer their questions as vaguely as possible," Rain pressed his hand against the door's sensor, and it made a sound of recognition before the door slowly began lowering.

"And remember, do not remove your hoods unless I say."

We silently nodded as we watched the door completely open revealing three small beings of E'arka. Seeing them for the first time I thought back to what Adam said earlier. They really did look like hunchbacked trolls with their large feet and curled backs. They truly were an alien species. They each looked similar to each other, but upon closer inspection, I saw distinct differences in their facial structures. We stepped down the ramp, bowing our heads. A symbol of acknowledgement for our people.

"Greetings!"

They made a symbolic gesture with their hands as they spoke, their voices creaky, and deep.

"Greetings to you as well, friends," Rain said to them, friendly, but distant. They appeared to smile, though it looked more like a lopsided frown.

"I am he called Koi!" the one in the front said. He had long fingernails, painted in bright colors which he held up to his mouth. I assumed this was a form of greeting. He then gestures to a woman with short gray hair and a huge nose to his left. "She is called Toa," He then turned to his right to another man who was much shorter than the others, though they were all much shorter than me, and I was even considered small even on my birth planet. "He is called Gru."

Rain raised his hand to his heart, "I am named Rain," he then gestured to his left as Koi had done. "Adam" then brought his hand further to gesture towards Tehayo. "Tehayo," he gestured to his right, "Erayame," and then to me. "Cloverlyne."

"We have invited neighboring beings to a banquet of your honor," the one who said his name was Koi said in an excited voice. His head raised high in an obvious sign that he was proud to show us off to his 'neighbors'. My body tensed beneath the cloak, that wouldn't be good for us. Too much attention could cause... issues.

"We will be pleased to meet any friends of your people," Rain responded, and though the little trolls didn't notice, his voice was tighter than normal. The E'arka however, were ecstatic, and stood proudly by our side.

"Come!" the one called Toa said, gesturing for us to follow. We kept pace with them, letting ourselves move more slowly.

"And they w'er never seen a'gain!" Adam mumbled in Narvi-ik. Even though I felt confident that any 'friends' of these people wouldn't question us out of respect for their allies, I couldn't help but wonder if Adam was right.

3

— • —

CHAPTER 2

It seemed like they spared no expense for our visit. The banquet was in a gallant hall with dim lighting, and the walls had a kind of silver material embedded into them. They weren't smooth like they were at home, but rather chiseled into patterns of fruits and different herbs. Streamers of light greens and rich pinks hung from the grand ceiling. Giant pillars with plants growing inside of them spiraled from the floors to the top of the ceiling.

On the far edge of the hall, beautifully winding staircases painted in many colors rose to the second floor of the building, with bright jade gems decorating them. Lighting the room were wooden-looking chandeliers with a kind of hanging vine growing from inside them. Low tones of music hummed softly in the background as entertainment and sounded mostly like small forest birds. Beings were gathered everywhere around the hall, dancing and laughing together in groups, and some standing off alone gathering refreshments.

It was a beautiful sight but was also a bit overwhelming. Even as I wore the hood, the feel of stares stained my skin as widened eyes fell upon us. They were almost disturbingly curious about us, but they seemed like pleasant creatures.

We were led through the hall before turning towards a rather large doorway, which turned out to be the entrance to a balcony overseeing a large valley. Their world was truly beautiful. It wasn't as vibrant in floral colors as Eurkxo was, but rather had lush green fields of vegetation. In the distance I could see hills that seemed to have been chiseled into, making them look like stairs. I wondered if it was a natural occurrence on their planet, but instantly thought better of it. Most likely it was a specific farming trick they'd picked up since they were purely an agricultural planet with little to no technology.

My eyes turned from the balcony to follow a little E'arkan being who hurried towards us with what resembled a basket that was cone shaped with a curled-up tail. She also carried a bag on her shoulder which had something else in it. Koi said something to her so softly that we couldn't hear, and she nodded back as she let the bag slide down from her shoulder. He took some kind of cup from the inside of the bag and reached into the basket. When he pulled the cup out, it was filled with some kind of liquid. He handed the cup to Rain, who nodded back in thanks.

The E'arka wouldn't have been aware of his movements, but I noticed Rain's hesitation before he took a sip of the liquid. Unease swirled in my stomach. I knew we shouldn't offend them, but drinking or eating an unknown substance was a huge risk.

I couldn't help the feelings of suspicion at giving our commander something without telling us what it was. Part of me was annoyed at how foolish Rain could be. He should've refused it, but another part of me knew we had to prove we trusted each other. It wasn't as if the E'arkan knew how many had died from poison just from a touch to a glass to quench their thirst.

My body tensed seeing Koi smile as Rain took another sip from under his hood, and I sent a quiet prayer to the heavens. My brother paused for a minute before he gave the cup back to Koi.

"It is good." Rain said, to my great relief, but a small voice whispered in the back of my mind that it might not have been instant poison. Koi continued smiling as he called us back through the doorway and into the main room once again.

"Please!" he gestured to the surrounding area. "The banquet is yours, enjoy the banquet." My eyes darted around the room from under my hood. It seemed like it would be enjoyable enough, if it weren't for the fact we would have to be cautious of everything we said and did.

"Come!" The one called Toa, said.

She had only gestured to me, Tehayo, and Erayame, but not Adam and Rain. I reached out and brush my brother's arm in an attempt to gain a subtle answer without being rude to the little people. He answered by simply flicking his wrist, a gesture that gave us permission to leave. Without any hesitation, I led the way to follow Toa across the hall, maneuvering through the crowds.

She led us to an open area that was only separated from the main room by four giant pillars, arranged horizontally to each other. Inside the open floor, miniature pillars of different heights were positioned in a circular way with decorated foods displayed on top.

"These are some samples of our harvest from this year." Toa explained, gesturing towards the pillars of food proudly.

I smiled from under my hood. Just from looking at the samples I knew we'd made a good choice to trade with them. Their harvest was abundant and healthy unlike any harvest attempted on Eurkxo. We'd attempted to grow our own food before, but the plan failed within the first year. Although Eurkxo was wild with vegetative life, our soil was better for exotic flowers and plants then any edible goods.

My fellow council member, Erayame, walked right up to the tables and examined the harvest through narrowed eyes.

"Quite exceptional." he said, not sounding at all impressed. Toa didn't seem to mind his rudeness. Actually, she smiled at him.

"We have much!" She gestured around, proudly. "Everything grows abundantly here."

"Your people are blessed." Erayame picked up a piece of fruit and placed it in his mouth. We all eyed him warily, anticipating his reaction.

"It's not bad." he said finally, making the biggest grin appear on the little woman's face.

"The Mother is good to us with harvest!"

"It's our hope that our cores will help your people in your industrial development. A fair trade, isn't it?" I asked nobody in particular. Her eyes widened excitedly as she clasped her small hands together.

"Yes, yes! Your cores will be like magic to my people." Her eyes lit in awe. "The Mother will be pleased."

"As will our God." Erayame said sarcastically as he shook his head and sighed. I fought the urge to slap the back of Erayames' head for his behavior. I was glad the little woman was so aloof to his proud attitude, or perhaps she just didn't want to make us angry by saying something. Both were possibilities. I wondered why he was so annoyed. Maybe he was jealous of the little people? It was unfortunate that Eurkxo could not provide for itself, and the thought of relying on others wasn't exactly a thrilling feeling, but we really didn't have a choice in the matter.

Erayame continued asking questions about the details of the harvest- a conversation that bored me. I had little knowledge of such things, so my presence was not really necessary for this discussion. Instead, I found myself drifting away from them, desiring to see more of this banquet.

I noticed a smaller room a little way from the place I was previously in and decide to see what was in it. I caught sight of a brilliant flash of light coming from inside the room, and curiously made my way towards it. I stepped inside the room and almost gasped at the sight. Lights flickered through a symmetrical artwork. Some parts were vibrant, while others were dull, but it mixed so well that I couldn't pull my eyes from it. Lantern-like lights added to the effect, casting over the artwork like flames. I had no words to describe the beauty of it. I reached my hand out as if to touch the lights while breathing it all in deeply. It was so... so...

"Captivating, isn't it?" I whirled around, startled by the deep voice of another being.

He stood tall at the arch of the doorway. My gaze fell to his chest, bare except for a black vest of sorts. His skin was fair and ruff looking, with flickering gold embedded in patterns around the top of his chest. It was... pretty.

I tore my eyes away to examine his face. His hair was the color of copper, half bundled on top of his head while the rest hung down wildly at his neck. And his eyes... I was in awe. They were completely golden, flickering darker in some areas while lighter in others. I turned back to the artwork, trying to hide the fact I'd been staring, even if he wouldn't know because of the hood.

"It is very beautiful." I answered softly. He walked closer to me, making my body tense.

"Why do you wear the hoods?" He asked suddenly.

"Why do you want to know?" I asked back while turning to face him.

"Because I want to be friends. You people are fascinating and I'm curious." He flashed a mesmerizing smile which only seemed to attribute to his high cheekbones. I took note of the fact that his teeth appeared sharper looking then mine. Much sharper looking. Perhaps his kind ate more meat than mine and had developed stronger teeth for it? He was certainly attractive, and from the way he held himself, he knew it.

"Oh?" I stepped around him and let his eyes follow me. "I'm so fascinating to you? What are you curious about?" My tone almost mocked his curiosity, and I hoped he would back off a bit, but surprisingly he didn't seem to mind. He stepped even closer to me.

I swallowed nervously. It wasn't exactly a bad thing he was questioning me. If I played this right, I might be able to get more information about this galaxy. What we knew already were only crumbs of information told by others who had journeyed here, and that information wasn't always accurate. There was no better way to learn than from the locals themselves.

"Yes, you are fascinating, and I'm curious if your face matches your voice." He tilted his head to the side as his eyes dropped low before lifting to my face once more. I felt my face flush at his bluntness. For the first time I let myself take in his height.

Dear Natarah, he's tall. My head only reached the middle of his chest.

"What is it to you?" I took a step back, eyeing his face from a comforting distance. Out of nowhere, he tipped his back and laughed softly. My body stiffened further at his unexpected reaction. He certainly wasn't a very predictable individual.

"Would you not satisfy the curiosity of a friend? Your voice is sweeter than the waters of Levion." The right side of his mouth twitched as if to smile again.

My mouth parted at his boldness. It wasn't as if I was unused to compliments. People often said nice things to keep themselves in favor with me, but he didn't know who I was. He had no reason to find favor with me other than curiosity, and for that reason it must have come from a place of pure intentions.

It had been a long time since I met someone like that. I doubted his intentions were completely pure though, being that he approached me, a being from another galaxy, first. I was almost certain he had his own reasons.

Nevertheless...Was he really complimenting me? A being from another galaxy so different from my own?

I inwardly laughed at the idea.

Who would have thought?

"Your name isn't even known to me, friend." I mocked, emphasizing the word friend. I chuckled lightly while stepping away from him and turned as if to stalk him. Instead of being offended by my mocking, he followed me with a dark smile. He was quite persistent, it made me wonder what he was really after.

"My name is Xorion." He stepped even closer to me; another step and I would be able to inhale his very breath. "What is yours?"

"I am a Keeper of..." I started to say, but he gave me a suspicious look that let me know he knew it wasn't my name.

I sigh, "Cloverlyne. My name is Cloverlyne." I said at last. I stepped away from him again, but not by much. He gave me a grin, showing off his sharp white teeth.

"We know names now." He tipped his head forward and his eyes lingered on the hood expectantly while he made a twirling motion with his finger.

I hesitantly reached up to remove the hood but stop before pulling it off. Rain had said no, but he was the only one here with me, and I wouldn't want him to get suspicious of why we were hiding our appearance. It was my job to observe and make friends of sorts to work with by building trust. Even if we really didn't trust them, we had to work with them. With my mind made up, I removed the hood.

His gold eyes towered over my blue ones. Standing so close to him I was able to see the honesty and youthfulness in his eyes. He didn't seem to be one who was deceitful by nature, and his eyes were not of someone who kept his darkness hidden beneath them. Our eyes were quite different, but it was the innocence in his that strangely drew me in.

"I believed the art to be the most captivating thing in this room. I was mistaken... you are." He said suddenly and let his hand brush against mine. I looked down to where his hand had brushed mine. He looked into my eyes with a wary look, before his eyes darted down to my hand again. "May I?"

I was confused at first, not knowing what it was he wanted, but then I noticed his hand still hesitantly close to mine. He wanted to hold my hand. I nodded, letting him take my small hand into his much larger one. My eyes widened at the difference. He could cover my entire fist with just one of his hands. His eyes stared at it as his fingers brushed each of my fingers gently, as if he were afraid he would hurt me.

I scoffed at the lightness of his touch. If anything, he should've been afraid of me. My phantasm could take him no matter how strong he was physically. His strength was no match for mine. I could just imagine the surprise on his face if I ever let my phantasm pass through him. The expression he would make would be absolutely priceless.

"It is..." he hesitated, "So delicate." I fought the urge to roll my eyes.

I opened my mouth to respond, but then closed it again to think. I couldn't exactly deny the delicateness of my skin, but I didn't want him to think I am weak either. Perhaps it would be better to remove myself from this situation than to pursue it any further.

"My people will be searching for me." I pulled my hand out of his grip while giving him an unimpressed smile and lifting my chin up haughtily. He may have been... I'll admit, good-looking, but we came from different worlds. There was no point in entertaining anything more than friendship. Anyways, I wasn't looking for any relationships of that sort at the moment, maybe even never.

"Of course." He appeared as if he was trying not to laugh, which annoyed me. He stepped away, allowing me to leave. I put my hood back on and walked towards the arch-like door of the room quickly. Before I exit, I turned back to him. His expression... was that dissatisfaction? I looked forward once more and shook my head.

I wandered around the hall until I saw Tehayo standing by a white pillar, waving me over. Hurriedly, I went over to him, bowing my head at a few crowds who acknowledged me.

"Where did you disappear to?" He asked curiously when I finally reached him.

"Some art caught my attention. It was quite beautiful..." I trailed off as I thought about the being I met. Xorion... Who were you?

Oh, sure Clove, it was the art you found beautiful.

I felt my cheeks heat up and shook my head at my own thoughts.

"Art?" He asked, glancing around as if he wished to see it also. I raised my hand in dismissal, wanting to drop the subject. Thankfully, he took the hint. Both of us made our way through the crowds, back to Erayame, who seemed to be debating something with Koi.

"Our planet of origin is of no concern to you." Erayame was saying quite sternly to him. Koi looked nervous. My stomach coiled in unease. It didn't surprise me they were trying to find out our planet's location, but it still felt unnerving.

"But... to trade..."

"Our ships will be sufficient." Erayame crossed his arms in irritation at the little being's persistance. Koi, noticeably uncomfortable, bowed his head in submission.

"Don't be alarmed, our planet is very far from here, and our ships are faster." I tried to explain while also attempting to put the being at ease from Erayame's unfriendly demeanor. It seemed to work. He gave me a grateful smile.

"Yes, Mother is good to you..." He nodded, "Thank you, we are grateful for your cores." We nodded back in acknowledgment.

"We are grateful to you as well." I responded, eager to put out a more approachable front unlike some of my colleagues. I felt Rain, and Adam's presence behind me, and I turned to greet them. Rain glanced at me, his stance tense as he switched to our galaxy's universal language, Narviik.

"Others seem to be curious about trading with us." He said, looking over my shoulder at someone behind me. I turned slightly to see who the beings were and was met with the golden eyes of Xorion, and beings that were the same species as him. I turned my attention back to Rain.

"They are from a powerful dominion in this forbidden galaxy according to the locals, seen as the protectors of this galaxy." Rain's voice was calm, but he was noticeably concerned. We didn't need to deal with any suspicious predators when we already had the Union and others to worry about. I wondered if that was the reason for Xorion's conversation with me? To gain some information about us.

"They're intelligent beings. I fear they will become too curious about the source of our energy cores we brought with us to trade, or worse, of who we really are." Rain and Adam glanced at each other, both thinking the same thing.

"It'er be dangerous becoming involved in a powerful group, 'specially when their intentions are unknown. I'er don't like it." Adam said quietly as he shook his head.

I glanced at the beings again. Xorion caught my gaze and led his group towards us. I swallowed and tried to compose myself.

"We may not have a choice in that." I said softly as they approach us. We nodded to the other beings in greeting and switched to the local language.

"It's said that the cores you bring are a most powerful resource." One of the beings spoke for the others. I noticed that instead of his skin having flickering gold as Xorion's, it flickered a more rustic color, and his eyes, as well as his hair, were dark, almost black but with streaks of lighter brown.

"We take pride in our energy cores, yes." Rain responded calmly, yet carefully.

"What kind of energy is it that the cores hold?" This time it was Xorion who asked, but he wasn't looking at Rain when he asked it, he was looking at me. I shifted my weight, and kept my eyes averted even though I was wearing the hood. Rain's voice became stiffer at the question.

"We call it Phantasm energy."

"You must be a very advanced race, and rich, as you're blessed with such a powerful source of energy." The one with the blackish colored eyes said, holding his hands behind his back.

Even though it was a statement, I knew he wanted an answer. I felt a tug on my shoulder and look up. Adam must have become aware of Xorion's gaze on me, because he pulled me more behind him. Out of the corner of my eye, I noticed Xorion's eyes flicker up at Adam in surprise, but then change to a look of understanding as his mouth twitched into a smile.

I could only imagine what Adams' expression looked like in response. He had always been a bit protective of me being the younger sister of his best friend. Rain looked back at us as if concerned but didn't question us.

"We're of average scale." Rain answered the question without hesitation. I almost scoffed at his choice of words. Average scale in the Realms. Here, it would be way above advanced.

"We would be grateful if we might have the opportunity to discuss a possible trade with you as well." The same one with rustic flickers spoke for the group again.

"We will discuss it amongst ourselves." Erayame answered, most likely out of fear that Rain would act out of impulse in his state of concern and suspicion.

"Of course." he said while raising a hand over his heart as he bowed his head. "I am he called Aeis, my people are called Fehichen, and our planet's name is Vaymos." He continued, then looked at each of us expectantly.

None of us spoke for a moment, unsure what to say. We were specifically informed by the council not to reveal any information about where we were from. Thankfully, Rain did something smart, but unexpected. He slipped off his hood and set his chin high as he met the stares of those around. Hushed silence befell those around us. It was the first time they saw us without the hoods.

In a clear, confident voice, he said. "We are called Regents; our home is the Rectifier."

I smiled under my hood. He might not have given them exactly what they wanted, but he certainly gave them a truthful answer. We were technically regents of Eurkxo because we were standing in for the Elder's and our home for the time being was the Rectifier, but they didn't need to know it was just the name of my brother's ship.

"We look forward to speaking to you again." Aeis said, his mouth twitching into a smile as if he knew something we didn't.

We nodded to him and turned our attention back to Koi as the group of Fehichen's left. Before I gave my full attention to Koi however, I turned back to gaze at the group. Xorion stared at me as if he were staring into my soul. I tilted my head to the side, and he smiled with a nod before turning to leave with his companions. My brow wrinkled in confusion.

Why does he keep staring at me?

I lightly shook my head and dismissed the question. A firm hand was placed on my upper arm, and I looked to see Adam gently holding it protectively even as his gaze followed Xorion. I tugged my arm free to get his attention, and then put my focus on Koi. Adam crossed both his arms and huffed.

"You will stay here, yes? For the time being?" Koi asked with brightened eyes. His feet shifted from side to side as he waited for our answer.

"We were planning on staying on our ship..." Rain trailed off as Koi shook his head.

"Your people must not rest in your ship; we have very comfortable rooms here. We wish you to feel welcome."

"Thank you for your hospitality. We would be grateful and hon- ored to stay wherever you deem appropriate." I quickly answered for us before anyone else could protest. Rain turned to me, arching an eyebrow, and Adam switched to Narviik to voice his concerns.

"Wouldn't e'er be safer if we'd stay in our ship, ay?"

"It would be rude to refuse their request on- mind you- their planet." I shook my head in annoyance that I had to explain such a simple answer. Both Rain and Erayame seemed to agree with me, but Adam just huffed in disapproval, which was not at all surprising. He always voiced his opinions louder than the rest, making it clear when he didn't like something. Rain turned to Koi with a smile and a nod, to which he excitedly grinned back.

"Come, come, we have prepared the rooms for you." Koi said, and practically leapt for joy.

"They act like excited children." Tehayo mumbled in Narviik.

I agreed with him. These people were innocent and treated us like precious gems. I sincerely hoped they would remain this way.

4

CHAPTER 3

I lay sideways on an enormous, circular-shaped bed with cushions made of many different colors surrounding its borders. Each pillow was decorated with ruffles and silk-like material making it rather comfortable to lay on. Vegetation I had no name to was embedded into the walls of the room and poured out through holes that were punctured into them. Fragrant smells oozed out of the plant life surrounding the room, which reminded me of home back on Eurkxo.

One of my hands rested lazily on my hip and my other hand supported my head as I watched Adam pace back and forth before me. Rain leaned back in a chair, stroking the nape of his neck.

Tehayo, not wanting to be involved in the discussion, rested in his own room. I suspected his decision was largely due to the angry look on Adam's face when he'd asked for this meeting in the first place. If it were anyone else, my brother might have just dismissed the concerns, but it was Adam, who was practically our brother.

"Dis trade they'd be propose'n... Y'er considering it?" Adam asked, clenching his jaw. His eyes narrowed down on Rain.

"Well, I think they're just curious. I don't see the harm in more trading partners." I said pointedly. It bothered me that Adan was so against the idea. These people didn't seem to have ill intentions, and it was perfectly understandable that they were curious about the trade their neighbors were making with us. Any smart empire wouldn't want to be left out.

"Ay curious! 'course you'd say that!" Adam snarled while throwing his hands up in the air. My nostrils flared at his accusation.

"Your meaning?"

"A trade with them could prove to be useful to Eurkxo." Rain said, trying to calm both of us down.

"Useful!" Adam jabbed a finger at Rain. "You will regret 'dis." He turned to point at me angrily. "That'er male desires the attention of y'er ne'la! Don't y'er see 'dis?"

My eyes widened at his outburst "I can handle myself." I argued back. "I stand on my decision. They've never seen our kind before, they are curious about us and about what we can bring them!"

Adam opened his mouth to keep arguing back but was cut off by Rain.

"Enough of this arguing! Our Keeper knows the mission, Adam. We are here to trade, and if that's what these beings want then I don't see the issue with that." Rain stood up to face his friend face to face. "It's her responsibility as a council member to represent friendship. You don't need to be so worried."

"Ay, it is dis... but-" Adam voice trailed off as he sighed.

"I'm thankful for your concern, Adam, but it's unnecessary. I was born to represent." I sat up and folded my hands with a soft smile. I didn't want to continue fighting with him. Adam was silent for a minute before speaking up again.

"Ah, sorry, Keeper. Y'er know how I'er get sometimes." He bowed almost sheepishly. His hand came up to scratch the back of his head. I noticed the side of his mouth twitching into the ghost of a smile as his eyes found mine. A true smile bloomed on my face at the sight.

"Your apology is accepted, but unnecessary."

"Allow my ne'la some rest, Adam. Let's go." Rain opened the door to my room.

"Right y'er are." Adam winked at me before leaving with Rain. "G'night, Keeper."

I stood up from the bed and bowed my head to him.

"Goodnight, Adam." I nodded "Rain." Rain nodded back to me. They stepped out of my room and shut the door behind them.

I sighed, threw myself back on the bed, and stared up at the ceiling for some time. It was so... quiet. I could almost hear my own heartbeat.

I closed my eyes. I wasn't used to the silence. Back on Eurkxo, the Elders had encouraged me to live in the Serenity Tower in Cynard along with the other council members. I denied the request and asked for my own place instead. It took a bit of convincing since they thought it would be better for me socially to live with the others, but they finally gifted me a house located near the outskirts of the city. My house was peaceful, but never quiet.

I tossed and turned in my bed. The thoughts of home kept me awake. With a sigh, I finally sat up. A cool breeze ran through the room from the curtained off balcony across the bedchamber.

Perhaps some fresh air would do me good...

I slide my legs off the side of the bed and stand while stretching out my arms. I wandered towards the balcony and let my hand brush across the auburn curtain. It was surprisingly soft. I held it until I reached the white painted railing before letting it fall back.

Leaning forward, I looked out beyond the balcony. The scenery was like something from a fairy tale. From here, I could see the building we stayed in was a circular structure all the way around and made of some type of white stone. Below me, I could see a small orchard in the middle. Little lights were embedded into the trunks of the trees. It was beautiful.

"You do love to admire what you see, don't you?"

I whipped my head to the building beside mine where the voice sounded from. Standing on the other balcony with golden eyes, gleaming with mischief, was Xorion.

"You frightened me!" I hold my hand over my heart, letting it settle from the sudden surprise.

In all honesty, I hadn't expected to see him again unless we agreed to his people's request. I stepped back and tilted my head, wondering why he called out to me.

He chuckled loudly, "Didn't expect me... did you?" he asked as he moved his elbows up to rest on the railing. He cupped his chin in his hands and stared at me expectantly.

"No, I didn't." I leaned against the railing as well and tried to hide my smile by looking away. Hearing the railing squeak from the pressure he put on it, I glanced at him through the corner of my eye.

"I suppose the night does captivate a lot of beauty. Wouldn't you agree?"

I nodded my head while admiring the view of the orchard and pretty chiseled buildings.

"Yes."

He grinned and eyed me as if he was amused by something I didn't know about. I was curious but made no mention of it.

Who knew what was going on in the thoughts of this man any-ways?

He could be thinking of throwing me off the balcony for all I knew...

With that thought, I frowned. I had no reason to be so paranoid.

Perhaps I've been entertaining too many dark scenarios lately...

"I hope your people consider the trade." He said suddenly. I turned and fully faced him, raising a brow. He met my eyes, and they showed his full honesty. "I want you to come to my world."

"Why?" I asked, tilting my head again. My first assumption about him must have been true. He was bold.

"I enjoy looking at you." He said, shrugging his shoulders.

"Pardon?" I asked, not thinking I heard him correctly. How in all Natarah's power could he be so bold? My face heated up. I couldn't lie, I don't not enjoy it.

"Is it wrong to enjoy that?" He smirked at my expression as if he knew I liked it.

I smiled and looked away, trying my hardest to hide my blush.

"Not in the least."

"Are you going to remain out the entire night?" He turned to lean his back against the railing. He arched his back over it, looking up into the night sky.

I found myself unable to stop staring at the beauty of his eyes. They looked like small golden stars.

"Are you?" I asked, watching as he stretched out.

"I'm contemplating it." He said through a sigh. I laughed, and he sent another smirk my way, but then his expression turned serious.

"Your people seem almost tense here." It was a statement, but I knew he wanted an answer.

"We come from a faraway world. Everything's different here." I answered simply. He doesn't need to know any more about us.

He nodded, "The tall being that stands next to you so often..." He turned to look at me through hidden eyes.

"Rain?" I asked, standing straighter. What could he want to know about my brother?

"No, not the two male speakers, nor the private being."

A male speaker?

Perhaps he meant Erayame and Rain as the speakers. I supposed Tehayo was the private being, so that only left one other.

"Oh, are you talking about Adam?" I wondered why he was asking about him.

"Yes, who is he to you?" A wrinkle formed between his eyes, and I had a strong urge to smooth it out.

"He's a protector." I answered as honestly as I could. He continued to study me as if wanting more.

I sighed, thinking. "A brother of sorts." I finally said.

I don't really know my brothers crew members on the Rectifier, but Adam came to visit numerous times with Rain on Eurkxo. He was there for me when no one else was. Making me laugh or telling me things were going to be alright when I felt alone. From the day we first arrived on Eurkxo so long ago, he was the first one to make me smile again.

"Ah, a brother." Expression returned to his face through a smile.

"Why did you want to know?" I asked suspiciously. I wouldn't want to put a target on my friend's back.

"I... admire his protection of you." He said a little too quickly. He wasn't being completely honest. He seemed to be a quite a horrible liar. A breeze suddenly blew, and I shivered, hugging myself to keep warm.

"You should go inside." His eyes lingered on my arms hugging my body. "The nights become frigid about this time"

"Yes" I turned and walked back into my room but stopped before closing the curtain. "Goodnight" I said while turning back to look at him over my shoulder. He looked confused for a minute as he tilted his head at me.

I laughed, "It's something we say when we leave to go to sleep."

"Ah" He chuckled to himself. "Here, we say 'may you rise.'"

"My mistake. May you rise, Xorion." I corrected while giving a small bow of my head.

"May you rise, Cloverlyne." He mimicked the same bow of his head at me, still leaning against the railing.

I smiled and walked into my room. Making sure the curtains to the balcony were closed, I removed my overdress so I could sleep.

Xorion...

I thought while lying on the bed again.

Such an unusual being... Will I ever clear my mind of you?

5

CHAPTER 4

I awoke not realizing I'd fallen asleep, and my body made it clear with small pains all over because I hadn't gotten into a more comfortable position during the night.

I tried to ignore the uncomfortable feeling by stretching out and walking over to a water basin to wash my face. Once I looked slightly more awake, I redressed in my blue overdress and attempted to work on my hair.

With no small amount of frustration, I managed a rather messy side braid. Usually, I would have one of my attendants do it for me because my hair was very long, as was Soaran tradition. I was far from satisfied with the braid, but it would have to do.

I put on the hooded robe from yesterday and kept the hood over my head. Rain may have already shown them what we looked like, but I didn't feel like being stared at first thing in the morning. I was about to leave my room to find my brother when I felt his presence already behind the door. A few seconds later, he knocked on it.

"Enter." I said when he finally did knock, and Rain walked in, ready as well. I pulled the hood back to show my face and greeted him with a warm smile.

"Morning, I'd say good morning, but it looks like it was ruff." He said, giving me a grin.

I frowned, "I didn't sleep that well." I said in my defense. He looked me up and down, giving me a look that said 'clearly'. I rolled my eyes and waited patiently for him to finally start the real conversation he came to my room for.

"Erayame agreed to discuss the trade the Fehichen put forward."

"That's good news." I placed my hands behind my back and walked towards him.

"We'll withdraw from this planet, and travel to the planet Vaymos immediately." Rain left no room for question. Not that I would question it anyways.

I found myself feeling excited, as if we were off on a new adventure.

"I made contact with Aeis last night. He went ahead and gave me the coordinates to their planet. They've already left for their planet to prepare for our arrival. They should arrive only a couple hours before us." He sighed, "I have yet to discuss this with the others."

"It doesn't matter. Both Erayame and I have agreed to it already, and we're the only ones whose opinion is relevant." I paused and glanced up at him sheepishly. "And your opinion of course, commander."

"Let's go then, Keeper." He offered me his arm with a smile. I easily accepted it.

We walked down the hall into a sitting room I hadn't known was there. Tehayo, Adam, Erayame, and Koi were already there, and immediately stood as we entered the room.

"We are thankful for your generous hospitality. Unfortunately, we will have to leave your planet for now. We will continue to trade with you using our cargo ships. Those in command of these ships take their orders from us so you have no need to question them."

Tehayo nodded at us without question, understanding what it meant by leaving early, but I noticed Adam clench his fist even though he nodded. Koi looked so devastated, I almost wished we could reconsider.

"Must you leave so soon?" Koi asked. He rubbed his hands together anxiously.

"Our trade with you is quite secure, there's no need to remain on your planet any longer" Erayame said lightly, although I was a bit irritated by how pleased he sounded about leaving.

"We're merely leaving for a trade discussion, if it interferes with our trade with your people the discussion will cease." I added. That seemed to calm Koi.

"Of course, you must do as it pleases you." Koi said, looking a bit happier.

"We'll take our leave." Rain said while gesturing for us to follow him.

Koi ended up taking us through a different route that led us down a hall directly to The Rectifier. We didn't speak a word as we followed him. There wasn't anything else to say. When we did arrive at our ship, Koi seemed to become even more sad at the sight of our ship.

"I bid your people safe travels." Koi said quickly as he shifted from foot to foot.

"We thank you, and your people." I placed a hand on my heart and bow my head.

We each stepped into the ship and looked back at Koi as the door closed before us.

"May the Mother speed your way." Koi said, bowing low.

The door closed firmly.

"You've returned earlier than expected." Rihaya commented, greeting us by leaning up against the doorway and tipping her head.

"Unfortunately..." Adam grumbled.

"It's been decided that we'll go to the planet Vaymos." Erayame answered for us, stepping past her.

"Have they proposed a trade?" She asked curiously, pushing off the wall to follow him.

My eyes followed her, admiring her strong, warrior-like stature. Wearing only shorts and a tank top, all her dark purple markings were fully exposed. They were like natural tattoos covering her entire body.

They were beautiful. My people had no markings all over. We only had some patterned markings around our eyes which glowed, but only when we surfaced our phantasm energy within us. It was a small mutation that occurred naturally over time from living on the planet V'rasór. For instance, my markings lit a light blue when I chose to surface my phantasm.

"Yes, they have." Rain answered Rihaya this time.

We followed him to the bridge as he continued to command his crew. "Tehayo, head to engineering with Morak and Vis." Tehayo nodded and left to do as he commanded.

"I will go to the navigation room to inform Cyenvier." Rihaya said as she turned to walk the other way.

"I will send you the coordinates." Rain called out to her as he continued his fast pace. Following our arrival at the bridge, Rain wasted no time in sending the coordinates to Rihaya. Adam sat himself in the co-pilot chair and ran the protocols for departure.

Erayame and I sat ourselves on the side passenger seats and clicked on our safety restraints not wanting to be in the way.

"On the bright side we'll be findin' out how advanced they'd be really." Adam said through a sigh.

"Coordinates are set," Rain said, ignoring his comment and sitting down in the pilot's seat. He opened a communication line. "Rihaya, begin the countdown."

"Departure on 20, 19, 18, 17, 16, 15..."

The ship began to vibrate as it slowly lifted to hover above the ground, and I held on to the safety restraints a bit tighter.

"10, 9, 8, 7, 6, 5..."

"Ay shutters were feelin' rattle that'er bones!" Adam yelled out in excitement above the noise of the engines roaring to life.

"3, 2, 1, 0...."

"Nightmares of Elnorsefall! Never y'er could be stopin' us!" I barely made out what Adam yelled as the force of the ship's take-off pushed us into our seats. He always loved flying. He was the one who taught Rain to pilot actually.

Moments later, a screen came up. It showed the dark, greenish-gray, and blue planet below. Could it ever appear any less... magnificent?

"This is who we are." Rain said, awe sounding in his voice. He messed with his screen to set a speed for the journey to Vaymos.

"We'll let not'er no one" Adam looked at Rain who finished his statement, "Stand in our way... Ever." They both finished at the same time.

I let out a laugh. Adam had a way of brightening any situation, even the most stressful ones. I knew it would take some days for us to actually reach the planet, but it should be a smooth ride from here on out.

Once the thrusters were set, Rain gave us permission to unbuckle the safety restraints. Letting out a stretch, I let my muscles relax. The tension in my shoulders wasn't pleasant and had me frowning as I stepped out of the bridge.

Suddenly, someone grabbed my shoulders, rubbing them back and forth. I threw a look over my right shoulder only to discover that it was just Adam. He smiled at my frown as I gently swatted his hands away.

"It be 'em seats that be given' ye the pain." He nodded towards where I had been seated only moments ago.

I rolled my eyes, "Please, I'm sure it was more than mere seats."

He laughed and offered me his arm which I gladly accepted.

"Yer comin' witha me!" He pointed to himself with his thumb as he led me down the hallway.

"Where're we going?" I asked curiously as he turned down another corridor.

"After all 'dis stress we'd be going through? Some refreshments would be nice!" He nudged me softly, his mouth tilting into a smirk. "Just like old times!"

"Adam, don't you dare offer my poor sister one of your disgusting drink recipes!" I heard Rain yell from behind us. We stopped and turned around, watching as he all but ran to catch up with us. Adam leaned in and whispered into my ear,

"Ah, but thay'a make ye live longer ye see! Besides, I'er give 'em the disgusting 'uns on purpose. For you, only the best." He moved back and winked at me as a huge smile appeared on my face. Rain caught up to us, shaking his head.

He placed both hands on his hips and let out a huff. "The last thing we need is someone getting sick aboard my ship. I swear, I will put you in charge of waste duties for the rest of the trip!"

Adam mockingly placed a hand over his heart. "Y'er would never!"

"Oh, he would." I looked knowingly at my brother, who just laughed and walked ahead of us.

I started to walk after him but was stopped as Adam placed his hands on my waist, pulling me back towards him. I looked back at him, arching an eyebrow.

"Whata y'er say we'er take'a shortcut and prepare him somethin' special for 'em shall we?"

I smirked at his idea. "I say yes!" I looked back the way we were going. "But I didn't think there was another way into the-"

Adam grabbed my hand and pulls me into another corridor, running down the hallway. I picked up my dress with the hand he wasn't dragging, fearing I would trip on it.

"Adam!" I whined.

I didn't want to be seen doing such a childish thing, but he just held my hand tighter.

"Y'er can run faster than that! I've seen it with me own eyes when me, and y'er brother would race back in Cynard!" He said laughing as he continued to drag me along.

I laughed at the memory. I had beaten both of them in the race. It had just rained, and Rain fell headfirst into the mud in his brand-new uniform. Adam had tried to jump over him, but Rain had grabbed his legs so they both ended up muddy. The two wouldn't stop wrestling until I ordered them to stop, and then we had to sneak into the attendant's washroom in order to clean my brother's uniform without getting caught. It was quite a day to remember to say the least, and all of us were scolded relentlessly for it, but it was worth it.

"Come 'dis way!" He said while turning down another corridor which revealed a door. He typed a quick password which I didn't get to see because his shoulders were in the way, but it opened the door to reveal a vent-like passageway.

I pulled my hand out of his grip and crossed my arms, my hip popping out as I stared him up and down. He turned and gave me a frown, crossing his arms over his chest to show he could be just as difficult.

"Adam, son of Ledon. I will not step one foot in there and crawl through a dark, gross, vent doorway!" I argued, looking away haughtily.

"Its'a only a maintenance hall! Nothin' dark, and gross 'bout it... but if yer insist on not stepping a'foot..." He suddenly grabbed me by the hips and lifted me up.

My arms reached to grab his shirt in reflex as he carried me through the maintenance door.

"ADAM!" I screamed, picking up my dress with my free hand so it wouldn't drag on the dusty floor. Adam laughed at me while adjusting me in his arms so I wouldn't fall.

Dear Natarah and all its power, I would murder this man, brother or not.

I glared at him, wrapping the arm that wasn't holding my dress around his neck and gazed at the ground warily.

He was strong, and I didn't mean just because he could carry me so easily. I was light as a feather. I knew that, but it was because I could feel it in his arms, and through the way he walked... full of confidence.

I played being mad at him, ignoring him the entire way through the hall, but really, I enjoyed his company. He was all fun and ease, having a playfulness I'd never had. We reached the end of the hall where the exit door was, and Adam shifted me to his side, holding me with only one hand so he could open the door. Once the door opened, I wiggled out of his hold.

"Come on Clove, yer did say'a yer didn't want to step one foot in there didn't ye?" Adam said, nudging me.

I ignored him, devising a plan for my revenge in the back of my mind.

Together we walked down the short hallway that led to the cafeteria, which was sort of the wrong name for it. It was more like an overly large lounge.

The automatic doors slid open, and we hurried inside. The room had a circular table around it, each set with four chairs. On the sides of the room were pretty gray sofas placed around a large, short table in the center. Adam immediately went to the refrigeration storage to create his 'masterpiece' while I just stared around the room for a while.

My eyes stopped when I spotted three figures sitting around the sofas. I easily recognized Rihaya, and Cyenvier who sat across from one another, and Morak was seated on a singular sofa to the side of them, closer to a table where he had a drink. All three of them turned towards where we came in, and I smiled, bowing my head to them in greeting. Morak grinned at me, bowing his head back and Rihaya followed suit. Cyenvier didn't smile as he bowed his head. His lips remained in a firm line.

I tried not to feel offended by his coldness, I figured it was just his personality. Afterall, I had hardly seen him smile this entire trip.

They turned back to whatever conversation they had before our arrival, and I turned my attention back to whatever Adam was doing.

He finally emerged from the storage carrying a few ingredients I had no name for. He set them on the table and started mixing and pouring things rather quickly. Wanting to be helpful, I walked over to a table near the side of the room which had many different types of glasses. I made my choice of two lightweight glasses and carried them over to the table Adam was working at and set them down. He had pulled out quite a few things I didn't recognize, but one in particular I knew was a common drink on V'rasór as well as on Eurkxo. It was a non-alcoholic sweet drink made of many fruits and sizzled on the tongue.

I poured it into two cups and carried the bottle back to where I found it but froze. A smile came to my lips as I saw what one of Adam's ingredients were. Ianupa seeds, known to be extremely bitter and were commonly expressed as tasting like dirt after dissolving into liquids. Adam was looking the other way, focusing on his creation. I quickly grabbed the bag and pulled out a package of the seeds. I grinned as I opened the package, knowing this was how I was going to get my revenge. I picked up a few of the seeds with my fingers and placed them in the glass I would give to him.

I was about to throw away the evidence but paused once more as I glanced back at the glass.

What if Adam was used to the seeds...? After all, Myans usually liked bitter stuff...

I shook my head, walking back over to glass.

He wouldn't be able to handle it if I put more...

I was only going to put a little bit more, but in a moment of pure amusement, I poured the entire package in. The seeds dissolved in a matter of seconds.

I stepped back, and glanced at Adam, who seemed to just finish. He poured his creation into a bottle and left it on the table. He then grabbed the rest of the stuff and went to put it back into the storage. I picked up the two glasses and carried them over to the sofas on the other side of the room from where the other three were. I didn't want our little game to disturb them.

Adam hurried out of the storage, his eyes searching until he found me and jogged over. He winked at me and nodded towards the bottle on the table.

"It's labeled as his favorite. He wont'a pass it up."

I let out a short laugh,

"Is that so? Won't he be in for a surprise!" Adam laughed at his little plan, and I laughed at my own. These boys made it too easy.

It wasn't long until Rain finally walked through the main doors. He stopped in his tracks when he saw us, a frown forming on his face as he waved a finger at us. He looked back towards the doors, and then back at us.

"How...?"

"We took'a shortcut." Adam shrugged as he leaned back into the sofa, giving me a devious smile. I smiled back knowing. I would get my revenge very soon.

Rain grabbed a glass from the same table I had and walked over to the table with the bottle. He poured it into his glass, and then walked over to where we were seated, leaning an arm on Adam's chair. Adam and me both grabbed our drinks, and Rain held his own glass up.

"To the adventure of meeting new friends!" He said, and we all drink. I burst out laughing as both of them spat out their drinks and started gagging.

"What the-" Rain said while wiping his mouth with his sleeve. Adam stood up, the contents of his drink accidentally spilling all over his shirt. He stared at me in shock. I took another sip of my drink, just to antagonize them.

"Yer one spiteful woman!" Adam said as he tried to play being mad as I had, but I could see the amusement written all over his face.

"Did you seriously make my favorite drink into a disgusting mon-strosity?" Rain glared at me.

I giggled and shook my head. "It wasn't me." I said, looking at Adam with a knowing smile. He grunted.

"It was meh." He looked down at his drink. "But it'a seems my plan backfired."

"You drank your own creation?" Rain asked, looking smug as he shook his head.

"Believe meh, it wasn't on purpose." Adam mumbled, frowning at his cup.

"Oh Adam, you didn't really think I would let you off from that little stunt... did you?" I mocked, crossing my arms over my chest while staring him down. We stared at each other, eye to eye, before both of us burst out laughing once more.

"You boys better clean that up!" I heard Rihaya call out from the sofas, and I looked over to see that all three of them were staring amusingly at us. Rain faced her and threw his hands up in the air in exasperation.

"It wasn't even me!" He said before turning back towards us. He jabbed a finger at Adam. "As commander of the Rectifier, I order you to clean up this mess, and to throw out that monstrosity of a drink you created!" He said with slight annoyance in his voice.

Adam rolled his eyes, mumbling something to himself, but didn't argue.

"And Clove..." Rain placed both hands on his hips and stared down at me. I bat my eyes innocently, daring him to punish me. He sighed, "Just stay out of trouble."

"Oh, come on! That'a not even fair!" Adam whined, "I'er call favoritism!" I smiled and gave him a tip of my head.

"Of course it is. Enjoy." I twisted my dress to walk towards the exit.

I smirked to myself as I exit the room. At least I knew that this trip wouldn't be boring. I was almost sad that it would be over so soon. After we finished our business at the planet Vaymos, we would return home.

I smiled at the thought of going to Vaymos. I wondered what the planet would be like. Would it have a warm climate? Cold? Perhaps a mixture between? I enjoyed traveling to different worlds. It was a shame it was so dangerous. Hopefully the next few days would go by quickly so we could finally learn about the strange planet of mysterious beings.

6

— • —

CHAPTER 5

Thankfully the next few days flew by quickly. It took shorter than we previously thought to travel to the planet Vaymos. We could've made it there within a few hours if we'd used the ship's phantasm jump system, but we didn't want to risk being questioned about it. These people had no idea who we really were, and we planned for it to stay that way.

I filled my time by studying old scrolls about this galaxy that the little people apparently gave Erayame while we were there. He said he had no use for them and let me look through them when I told him I wanted to.

I'd never felt such soft paper before. The thought of using paper was strange to me. Especially since they were an agricultural planet. Most planets in the Realms were against such a waste of valuable resources. Plus, digital texts were much more efficient and preferred amongst our people. There were a few planets who still used paper for important books and important documents. Like on Rihaya's home world, Ardiamus, for example, but it wasn't common.

The scrolls were interesting but had the strangest ideologies. Most of them were about nature and something about the sentience of different creatures. Before I could even process the words though, I had to get past the fact that they were... well, scrolls.

I knew my people were advanced, but how could people who had space travel technology still use scrolls? Did they have no technological advancements on their home world at all? It worried me.

If the little people had no technological advances, not even to store the great details of the galaxy they lived in, I could only imagine what Vaymos would be like when we finally reached it. Perhaps the space travel technology wasn't even there's, maybe they borrowed it from neighboring planets?

We reached the planet Vaymos after two cycles, roughly the equivalent to four days according to this planet's rotation. It was a beautiful planet, full of colors. The sky of the planet appeared to be a light shade of purple, with deep yellows, grays, and light green mixed into the swirls.

It truly was a beautiful world from the outside looking in, but I knew looks could be deceiving. However, they seemed like honest beings. I hoped my instincts were right and we wouldn't encounter any... issues while we visited their world.

Rain started the landing sequence and breathed out loudly. He seemed anxious about landing, everyone did.

"Why'd it seems that'er our coming here t'was but a huge mista ke..." Adam said, exhaling into his chair.

Rain gives him a friendly slap on the shoulder. "Ease yourself, brother. What is life without a few little risks?" His mouth twitched in a smirk.

"A few little'r risks, ay?" Adam shook his head.

"This trade agreement we... might make, would be good for us. That is final." Erayame said, flicking his wrist.

Clearly, he was annoyed that Adam continued to voice his opinions about the matter. I caught Adam rolling his eyes at Erayame, and smiled even if I disapproved of his disrespect.

"We're an unfamiliar race, and our knowledge is obviously superior to theirs. They're asking for this trade only to quench their curiosity. They wouldn't dare threaten us." I added to Erayame's comment. I straightened my posture to make myself seem more qualified to make such a bold statement.

We all had our suspicions about them, Adam just voiced his concerns louder than the others.

"I knows dis, Keeper" He sighed, "I just... argh" He began typing furiously on his panel as if to distract himself.

"Adam..." I started to say, but was cut off by Rain.

"Breaching the planet's atmosphere." Rain said, not even looking up from his panel.

Me and Erayame quickly attached the safety restraints, clamping them in place. The ship started to hum and rumble as it falls through the atmosphere. After a few minutes, it began to shake violently, and I knew we reached the platform.

"Landing in 4, 3, 2, 1, 0,"

Once again, my body was thrusted forward, making me flinch in surprise.

"Good?" Rain asked while spinning his chair around. We nodded.

"Let's go to the disembark room."

We detached the restraints and followed him as he hurried out of the room. When we arrived at the room, Rain wasted no time making his decision about who would attend this diplomatic mission.

"Our two delegates of course, and Tehayo and Morak." Rain glanced at everyone else. "As for the rest of you, stay with the ship until further notice." Adam raised his hand and gave my brother an annoyed look, but still nodded his head, giving Adam permission to speak freely.

"Request to be on dis'er mission." Adam asked while crossing his arms. He tapped his foot impatiently, further adding to the tension. I bit my lip. If he was trying to irritate Rain, he was doing a great job at it.

"Request denied." Rain said simply, much to my surprise. Adam opened his mouth to argue back, but Rain pulled him aside to speak to him privately. Even though I wasn't keen on eavesdropping, I heard bits and pieces of their hushed whispers.

"I cannot risk... they will see so many different... a clear suspicion for them to..." Adam threw his hands up defensively at Rain's explanation.

"They'er intentions be clear...'ought not be trusted"

"It is not about trust, Adam."' Rain shook his head, his voice rising. "I need you here anyways... Morak, and Tehayo both.... we cannot reveal how many different beings are aboard."

"Remove yer hoods ye plan?" Adam widened his eyes in shock.

"I'm not planning... it is a precaution..." Rain sighed and placed his arm on his friend's chest. Adam finally yielded, placing his arm on Rain's chest.

He leaned in and whispered something to Rain that I couldn't hear. Whatever was said brought a smile to Rain's face.

"Right, put your hoods on everyone!" Rain places his hand over the lock which responds by opening the exit door.

"Let us...ske...ske-dad..." Tehayo started to say, but Adam cut him off with a grunt.

"Skedaddle's the word yer looking for, friend."

I smiled. Adam could be frustrated one minute, but quick to understand. The next thing you knew, he would be joking. I liked that about him. It made him an easy person to be around.

"Give 'em hell!" He said, giving me a wink.

I felt my cheeks redden, but quickly turn away so he wouldn't see. Inwardly, I cursed at my stupid cheeks. Thankfully my skin was well tanned. It would take a bit more than slightly heated cheeks for anyone to notice.

"They might not believe in our definition of hell." Morak commented thoughtfully. Erayame gave a huff of annoyance while pressing his hand to his forehead.

Adam let out a loud laugh. "Just'er expression m'eh friend!"

He turned around and left the chamber, closing it behind him before the exit door started to open.

We stood frozen, watching as their door opened at an agonizingly slow pace. When it finally did open fully, I saw Aeis and two others who I don't recognize right outside our ship, ready to greet us. Behind them, I noticed Xorion with his confident smile that shined through silver sunlit rays.

Dear Natarah... Was Adam, right? Would we survive this?

Chapter 6

Unlike on E'arka, we were immediately brought to a private discussion room upon exiting our ship.

The room was as bright as it was big and reminded me of a conference room. Much to my delight, I was able to get a good view of their planet when they led us to this room. It was surprisingly industrialized, with huge buildings in the distance shaped like domes. Purple seemed to be an ongoing theme on this planet. Almost every building was lit in different shades of the color.

I wondered if it was a religious aspect, or if they just liked the color. Maybe it was for traditional purposes? I would have to ask around if I had the time.

Only Aeis, Xorion, and two new beings who introduced themselves as Kasoir, and Sa'ak were in the room with us, but I managed to catch a glance of few others of their kind wandering around when we made our way here. They kept their distance, but were polite, giving us subtle glances of curiosity.

When we came into the room, I noticed how quickly they shut the door behind us as if we were discussing something secret. I narrowed my eyes as I took in the new surroundings. There was a huge table in the middle of the room, with chairs all the way around it. It was practical but far less cozy than anything we experienced on E'arka.

"Your energy cores are most mysterious... powerful as well." Aeis said while gesturing with his hand for us to sit.

The seats were comfortable enough, with light gray cushions coforming to the form of our bodies.

"It intrigues us." He continued, keeping his gaze on Rain. "I hope you will not take offense by not meeting our leaders in person, most trading matters are done by their speakers."

"We don't mind, but is there a specific reason for this that we should be aware of?" Erayame responded instead of Rain.

Aeis tilted his head at him. "It's our way, but- and I apologize for this, it is also for security reasons. Our leaders never greet off-worlders or leave their ruling grounds for that matter. However, I assure you, our leaders are fully aware of our dealings and have given me full authority to go through with this discussion."

We gave each other subtle glances at his explanation.

So, they were going to be honest about not trusting us. It was smart, making sure their leaders were safe, but unsettling that they weren't dealing with such a huge opportunity for their people themselves. Aeis seemed at ease though, as if he'd explained this many times, and I wondered if this was normal in their leadership system on their planet.

"We understand, do continue." Erayame said with a flick of his wrist.

Aeis nodded, "It would be good for both our peoples, our leaders believe, to discuss a trade in which we both will benefit."

"Of course," Rain said with a touch of sarcasm that I hoped Aeis didn't catch.

"You want our cores, what do you have to offer in return?" Erayame crossed his arms and tipped his head down as he locked his eyes on Aeis.

"We understand that your trade with E'arka consists of their harvest, and other produce." Aeis placed a hand on the table, tapping at it with each individual finger.

We all nodded again at his statement, knowing it was no secret what the little people were giving us in return. However, it did worry me that Aeis was bringing it up. These people were smart, whether we chose to acknowledge that or not. They knew our trade with the E'arkan beings was a sign of weakness.

"It's known that you will not reveal your own private situation about why your planet is having troubles in these areas but tell us this." He leaned forward, "Would our friends, the E'arka, and we be placed in an opposing position to your far away world if we opened trade with you?" Aeis asked, his eyes slightly darkening.

Rain stiffened, not expecting the question. He glanced back at us, unsure how to respond.

Aeis's comment was something I'd feared he would bring up when he first mentioned it. Clearly, he wanted to know why we were here, but he knew we wouldn't reveal it on our own accord, so he was trying to get around it by making us feel guilty about endangering the little people.

He was right to question us though. The Realms would wage war for even the slightest amount of evidence we traveled into this forbidden galaxy. It was why we were planning to use ships specifically designed for stealth in order to take our trades back and forth, but unless we brought anyone from here into our Realms in alliance, we'd only really be endangering ourselves.

"You're correct about our private matters being our own, but you don't need to worry about being put in an opposing position." I said as confidently as possible.

It seemed to do the trick as he locked eyes with me and nodded. Out of the corner of my eye, I noticed Xorion smiling knowingly at me as if he already knew what I would say.

I looked away from him, choosing to stare at the patterns on the table.

"That is good." He said finally, "Our planet produces a special gas which can be harvested. It can be used for many desirable purposes."

Rain glanced back at me, silently asking me to question it further.

"What kind of purposes?" I asked slowly.

"Spaceflight, and home-planet vehicles?" Erayame's asked, his eyes perking up with interest.

Aeis nodded with a smile as if he knew we would be caught in the trap of this trade.

"And if partaken correctly, it can be sub-used to give off an en-hanced adrenaline rush."

Rain shifted in his seat, and I knew he was already thinking about the benefits that could be used for if the war happened to come into effect. Our people could have an advantage where others did not.

Aeis smiled even brighter, seeing our interest. "We use it often, for many occupations that consist of hard labor, me included."

"We will have to see the medical records on the effects." Erayame said, lifting his chin haughtily, but he was clearly excited, as was Rain.

It could be vital help to Eurkxo even without the war. Our planet had been forced into sustaining itself since we couldn't trade with any planets in our own galaxy, and staying alert was difficult some-times for hard working citizens. Our phantasm easily exhausted us. Of course, we had our own tricks for this, but they weren't as effective as Aeis made this gas seem.

Although... he could easily be exaggerating on its effectiveness...

"Of course," Aeis said, not bothering to mask the pride in his voice over finding something that interested us.

I was about to suggest that we ask for a sample to test how our bodies would react to it, but my thoughts were interrupted by the entrance door opening. A Fehichen woman stepped through and bowed her head to Aeis, who smiled back at her.

"Ah, it seems the refreshments have been prepared!" He gestured for us to stand and follow him. "Come"

We followed him out of the meeting room and into a hall that led to a much larger room where tables of foods and drinks are set out. Many Fehichens gathered around, giving us many warm smiles. The room wasn't grand, but it was comfortable and decorated in light gray cloth that hung round the low, modern-looking tables.

"Please, rest and enjoy!" Aeis said in a merry voice, but his eyes lingered on our hoods.

He was wary of us; of the way we acted like strangers to this galaxy. I didn't blame him one bit. Had it been them who came to our galaxy... well, they'd be treated in a far less respectable manner then we were currently receiving.

I gently brushed my hand on Rain's arm, hoping he would notice their wariness as I had. He lifted his hand to his hood, and slowly removed it from his head. Me and the others followed his lead, taking ours off more quickly.

If they stared at us before, they really started staring now. Aeis mostly eyed Tehayo and Morak which was expected since they had yet to reveal what they looked like before now. Rain seemed to like the attention we were receiving. He grabbed one of the glasses from the table and gestured for us to do the same.

"A toast!" He said, switching to Narviik while lifting his glass.

The Fehichen stared at us curiously, wondering what he was doing.

"To the wellbeing of our new trading partners, and to our hopeful future lives."

We all smiled and took a long sip of our drinks. It was sweet, with a slightly bitter after taste, but was soothing to the throat. Rain turned to Aeis, who smiled but was obviously confused at what we did.

Rain switched languages. "A tradition we do that has been passed down from many generations." He explained, placing his drink back down on the table. The confusion wiped off Aeis's face, replaced by a bright smile to match Rain's.

He looked back at Tehayo and Morak and swallowed before seeming to find the courage to walk up to them.

"You are not the same?" He asked, glancing at Rain and then back at them. They visibly tensed and looked back at me for help. This was going to be tricky to wiggle out of.

"They were not born on our planet, though they live there now." I answered carefully while subtly giving the brothers the okay to talk a little about their world.

"We were born on a neighboring world, which is why we look... different." Morak added.

"I see." Aeis said, "Are there many different species in your galaxy?'

"Only a few civilized ones." Rain answered with a roll of his eyes.

I smiled at his joke before frowning when the hairs on my neck rose in response to someone watching me. I turned to locked eyes with the culprit. Xorion, was he ever not looking at me? When he saw me catch his eye, he walked towards me, and I moved over to meet him.

"I believe the discussion went well." He took a sip of his drink, but still kept his eyes on me. "Wouldn't you agree?"

"I believe we will have a trade." I answered with a smile.

He smiled brightly back at me, but for some reason he looked more nervous than the other times I'd seen him. I wondered why.

He took my glass from me and placed it on a table behind him. "I'd like to show you something." He pointed his chin in a general direction.

I clasped my hands behind my back and looked up at him suspiciously.

"Where would we be going?"

He smirked, "You had no hesitation sneaking off to look at art last time."

"Is that where you'd be taking me?" I raised a brow, "To see the art of your planet?" I glanced back at Rain.

He caught my eye before glancing at Xorion and then back at me. He tilted his head, subtly asking what was going on. I gestured with a tilt from my head that I was going with him. Erayame said something to him that he acknowledged before flicking his wrist at me to let me know he understood.

I wondered what Xorion would say when he was alone with me. I had a feeling there was more to this trade then his people were letting on. Xorion himself seemed far too invested in a relationship with me then just personal friendship. What was his motive?

I smiled confidently at him, trying not to let my suspicion show. "Lead the way." I gestured for him to take me with a wave of my hand.

He turned and led me through the crowd until we reached an empty hallway. We walked down it for some time before he stopped suddenly. He walked up to a door on the side of the hall and opened it slightly before turning to make sure I was watching. As he opened the door fully, I gasped.

The artwork was the most exotic thing I'd ever seen, even more so than before. I wasn't sure what it depicted. Perhaps an imagined paradise of the afterlife? But it was beautiful, colored in shades I couldn't describe. It surrounded the room, almost looking as if you could walk into virtual colors swirling around the walls. Xorion lets out a laugh and leaned into me playfully.

"Do you not have art on your planet?"

"Oh, we do, and it's wonderful, but nothing quite as remarkable as this!" I answered truthfully.

Eurkxo mostly had sculpture and digital art, but most of it was more of a realistic style of flowers or animals. I rarely got to see art as wild as this before. The colors were untamed, not meant to represent anything but beauty.

I was drawn out of the trance the art casted over me by Xorion's sudden sigh. I turned and tilted my head at him, wondering if he was okay. He hesitated, but with my eyes I convinced him to speak.

"May I ask you something and promise not to be alarmed?"

"I can't keep you from asking me something, but I'll promise nothing." I shrugged my shoulders. I wouldn't lie to him. He sighed once more.

"Your planet is on the verge of a war, aren't they?"

I froze at his question; my only answer was the narrowing of my eyes.

"I can see it in you people's attitude. You are cautious, but not of the unknown. You are cautious of revealing too much information." He continued as he searched body language for answers.

"My planet is not on the verge of war." I answered quickly.

It wasn't really a lie. We weren't on the verge of war per se. Those who wanted it were delicately setting up any reason to begin the war. To say we were on the verge of war was to believe that we had a chance to keep it from happening, which was false. The war was happening, the only question was when it would happen. Everyone knew it. We could only delay it for so long.

"You don't have to deny it, although I'm sure your people have told you, you must. Are the ones who oppose you so dangerous? From the power your energy cores give it seems that you'd have nothing to fear." He paused in thought, "Yet you're trading with an obviously inferior race to you." He shrugged.

I frowned at his last statement. He wasn't wrong. Us trading with them did make us seem desperate.

"You speak about things you don't understand." I said, trying to avoid the question.

His press on the matter made me wonder if he consulted his leaders about his suspicions... or if they were the ones that told him to ask me about this. Pain shot through my neck because of how tense I was. I took a deep breath, trying to relax.

"We won't use the knowledge against you, if that's what your people fear." He lifted his hands in surrender. "We only want to be able to trust each other. Your people are obviously highly advanced but aren't open to admit it which means you want to keep yourselves hidden here. Perhaps we can be of help to you?"

"You offer your help out of ignorance, it's for the best that you don't seek out any more information about us." I snapped at him sharply.

I refused to look at him and chose to hug myself and sigh while trying to think of anything I could say to make him drop the subject. Unfortunately, I couldn't.

"Why?" He asked softly as he moved to stand quite close to me.

I turned and lifted my eyes to his. "Because the deeper you dive into these waters the more likely you are to drown." I all but whispered.

Memories of the stain of red blood filled my mind as I glanced down. No being from this galaxy would ever understand the horrors that occurred in our galaxy.

He frowned at me, "It must be a pretty serious situation for you to deny answers to the very people who have the power to keep the E'arkas from trading with you."

Anger flashed through me.

How dare he threaten us with our new trade?

"Don't become involved, Xorion. Your people have yet to feel the pain of bloodshed." My hands clenched and I felt my phantasm burn angrily within me. If he continued arguing with me, I wasn't sure I would bother to contain myself.

"My people have felt this pain." He tilted his head slightly, as if confused.

"Pain from beings in this universe?" I gave a short laugh.

He wrinkled his brows at me, becoming even more confused by my laughter during such a serious topic.

"Please." I dropped my laugh, "Your people have yet to feel pain."
I let all the anger I felt show on my face.

He knew nothing of the horror the Realms would go through when
the war began. He knew nothing about the amount of destruction
it would cause.

His eyes pursued me with a new understanding.

"I can see it in you, in your eyes." He said gently. "They're not
someone raised in innocence."

My thoughts drifted back to the one person I feared, the one who
killed my mother. I remembered how he came into our home so
many years ago. I remembered watching him stab my mother with
a knife while he kissed her. I remembered my brother holding me
back and keeping a hand over my mouth to stop me from screaming
as we stayed hidden nearby. No, I was not someone who was raised
innocent.

"We know of... beings in our universe who spy on the worlds we
protect. Their masters are the same who threaten you, aren't they?"
He asked carefully.

That was news to me. I tilted my head, wanting to know more,
especially why he thought they were connected to us. It couldn't be
the MioTamir Union, out here? It went against everything they stood
for, but if it was Elnorsefall...

This was bad. If it was Elnorsefall, then we were in deep trouble.
We could monitor Elnorsefall in our own galaxy, but out here they
could do anything they wanted without our knowledge. Elnorsefall
would expose what we were doing just to ignite war.

"My people aren't one to wait. We will fight, and these beings have
threatened some of the lower evolved planets under our protection.
If someone is threatening them, then we have to stand against

them." He paused, looking at the floor. "But they have weapons we've never seen before, and their ships use the same energy cores as you. That's how we made the connection." When I said nothing, he continued. "We believe that if we ally with your people, we can stop them from taking over these planets before it's too late. I'm sure you know more about them than us."

I sighed. They know nothing about what they were planning to oppose. They could crush their planet without even one death on their side. Of course, they didn't know about our abilities or about the Realms. I wondered what he would do with the truth if I chose to give it to him?

"I trust your honesty; your eyes do not hold deceit. So, if I confide with you on this matter that is my choice, not because of your own tactful brilliance." I gave him a knowing look.

His eyes flickered with confusion, and he opened his mouth as if to protest, but I cut him off.

"You don't have to deny it, though I'm sure your people have said you must." I mimicked his earlier statement, looking him up and down before lifting my chin haughtily.

He visibly swallowed. I wondered why he continuously met with me, noticeably seeking me out. Now I knew. He was probing me. I smiled. We must have done well not giving away information. He'd completely exposed his people's plans, leaving them vulnerable to our own intentions.

"I-Yes, it is true my people wanted answers. They didn't tell me to go to you specifically. I didn't lie to you." He gave me a sly smile. "You were fascinating, and I was curious if your figure matched your voice... It's most pleasant." I ignored his comment, choosing to get straight to the point.

"If you believe the beings that are threatening you are the same who threaten us, they are very powerful." I said carefully.

He nodded thoughtfully. "So... we were right after all." He wondered out loud. His hand came up to stroke his chin. I gave him a sideways glance.

"It would be in your best interest not to become involved with them." I fiddled with my figures in front of me, no longer looking at him as I kept my eyes lowered but glanced up as he answered.

"How can we not?" He frowned, frustrated at my response.

I bit my lower lip. He wouldn't understand. I knew the look he was giving me, as if we were surrendering to them when we were only trying to keep as many from death as possible. I questioned my own thoughts.

How many could we really save?

My personal feelings betrayed all common sense.

How long could we keep the enemy at bay?

I needed to speak to Rain.

"I will not make rash decisions myself. I will have to discuss this with the others." I gripped my dress tightly and turned to go back to the main hall.

"Thanks for listening to me, Cloverlyne." He called after me.

I inhaled deeply and paused. Without even looking back I answered through my exhale.

"Do not thank me yet, Xorion."

"Still, thank you."

I continued walking without acknowledging him anymore. I finally reached the room I was previously in, and my eyes searched for my brother. It took a few minutes to feel his presence in such a large room, but I finally saw him sitting at a table near the front of the room, smirking at Erayame, who was sitting closely with a Fehichen female.

I hurried over to him. "Rain, we need to talk."

Rain flicked his wrist to show he wasn't interested and continued to stare at Erayame. Frustrated, I stepped in front of him, blocking his sight.

"Now, Rain."

He looked down at me, annoyance spreading across his face. He jerked his head to the side while giving me a look that said to move, but when I don't listen, he raised a brow at me.

"The most social activity I've got to see from him yet..." He started to say before his voice trailed off.

Realization dawned on him. He knew I wouldn't interrupt him for something trivial. He gave me his full attention, and I switched to Narviik.

"The Fehichen know about what they believe are Elnorsefall spies threatening their people and others across this galaxy. They've made the connection to us through our energy cores. They've asked for an alliance; they wish to fight this threat." I spilled everything without taking a breath.

Rain blinked at me for a few seconds before letting out a long breath he was holding.

"When I noticed he kept seeking you out this certainly wasn't the outcome I imagined." He said, staring down at the ground thoughtfully.

"Oh? And what outcome did you expect? You knew as well as I did that there was more to this than a simple trade whether we chose to acknowledge it or not." I answered more coldly than I would have liked. I was more frustrated with myself for not seeing this sooner than I was at him.

"I know, but they figured out these spies were connected to us through our energy cores... I am surprised." His face paled, and his teeth clenched together. I wanted to force the hood back over his head.

"You are displaying fear." I cautioned him. We couldn't show how dangerous this situation had become to them. Not till we knew more.

"Apologies, Keeper, I was just thinking about how big a problem this could be for us." He said, bowing his head. Some color returned and he relaxed himself.

I nodded, "It's vital that we confront Aeis."

"Noted. Gather Morak, and Tehayo, and I will attempt to pull Erayame from his entertainment." He stood but I eyed him skeptically.

After ignoring me earlier due to being distracted by Erayame's... predicament, I was hesitant in his ability to focus, but one look from Rain and my hesitancy was gone. His determination was one not to be ignored. We both knew how important this was.

Tehayo, and Morak stood awkwardly close by. It only took one glance from me for them to hurriedly come to my side.

"What is it?" Morak asked, glancing nervously around.

"Let's meet back with Rain, he will explain." I answered simply and turned to walk towards him without another clue.

The brothers don't question anything further, but both their walks became stiff with worry. The moment we reached Rain, he began explaining.

"A Fehichen has voiced their suspicions about us. Suspicions which were correct. Me and the Keeper believe it's time we confront them."

Teyhao and Morak froze. No doubt, they were wondering if Rain was being serious. Erayame, who was red with fury at being pulled away from his 'social activities' went pale.

I glanced around and saw Xorion speaking to Aeis, no doubt informing him about our talk, I'm sure. Aeis' eyes fell over us, and he motioned for Xorion to remain where he was while he walked over to face us. Rain boldly walked right up to meet him. Head-to-head, they stared each other down.

"I believe you have something you have to say to us." Rain said through narrowed eyes. Some of the Fehichen around us looked confused, although some looked nervous, and some had hope in their eyes.

Some of them knew... and they believed that we could save the m...

"Then..." Aeis said, holding his head a little higher. "Let us discuss."

8

CHAPTER 7

I could almost taste the tension inside the small discussion room. On one side, the Fehichen stood with their arms stiffly at their side while we stood with our chins held high on the other.

Aeis looked like he wanted to start, but seemed unsure, as if he didn't know what to say to us. I supposed it was fitting for him to be nervous. He did use one of his warriors to try to probe a people he knew nothing about. He was lucky we were understanding. If it were anyone else, this building might not have been standing right now.

"So..." Erayame began since it was obvious Aeis wasn't going to. "Was the trade just a means to bring us here?" He asked with no small amount of accusation in his tone.

Aeis winced. I resisted the urge to poke fun at him for being so fearful of us. It probably would've made the situation worse.

"Our leaders wanted to follow through with the trade even if it was not our first intention. They believe in mutual need." Aeis lifted his chin confidently.

I narrowed my eyes at his choice of words.

What in Natarah did he mean by mutual need?

Rain openly glared at him, "Don't hold yourselves to such a high standard before us. We may consider this trade, but we do not need you."

He was just as annoyed as I was. Although, I did wish Rain wouldn't be so blunt about his annoyance. I understood Aeis' words even if they were said out of ignorance. However, it would be better to make them understand that we didn't need them in the first place. It would only cause problems later if we weren't direct about it. Afterall, they were the ones who exposed that they needed us in order to help save those who have put their trust in them as protectors. Aeis clenched his jaw.

"We understand that, but with the alliance we propose this trade will make both sides stronger. You have to realize this." Aeis tried to appear calm when he spoke, but his body language remained tense.

I noticed him breaking eye contact with Rain. A nervous habit I assumed. He had no idea how we would react. If he thought we were going to make it easy for them, they had another thing coming.

Rain smiled sweetly "What we realize, is that you have put yourselves in a position where you are at our mercy." I watched Aeis visibly blanch at Rain's statement.

I looked down and smiled. They had a lot to learn about us.

"Your arrogance astounds us; it was you who agreed to come to our planet." Aeis said, clenching his fists.

"Don't be so bold that you'd believe that we would... lower ourselves in such vulnerability as you have. At least we have the power to back ourselves up." Erayame said, giving him an unimpressed look.

Rain smirked when Aeis's face flushed.

"We recognize you are a superior people, but you can only defend so many angles. We may not have the technology or knowledge you have, but we certainly have the willpower to fight back, and the numbers."

I tilted my head at him, surprised by his statement. He was still fighting no matter how much we tried to push them away. I couldn't deny my peoples arrogance, but he still chose not to back down.

I lifted my eyes to view his people. They stood beside him proudly, not letting themselves be intimidated by us. They truly believed that we could help each other.

"My people have been preparing for war for many years. We have held off this war for so long, but one day we will have no choice but to allow it to happen. If you truly wish to help us, then you will be going up against an enemy that is greater than anything you've ever seen. They will not surrender no matter how great your armies are. If you oppose them, they will not only vow death for your entire race, but also your planet as well. We believed you only offered an alliance with us out of your own ignorance... your galaxy is far below us, especially in technology. Do you truly want to take that risk?" The words spilled out without taking a breath.

Erayame narrowed his eyes at me, warning that I was giving out too much information, but I wanted them to know what they were proposing. Part of me wanted to see the warriors they were. The ones who would do anything for justice. The other part of me wanted them to forget this and say it was all a mistake made out of ignorance.

Aeis was silent for a moment as he looked down at his feet. No doubt he was contemplating the consequences of an alliance with us that his people suggested themselves.

When he continued to look at the ground, I sighed. Just as I thought, he would never risk his people, his planet, for another world.

He suddenly looked up, a fierce look in his eyes. "My people are warriors, we will fight. With our conjoined power we could rid their filth from every known universe."

My eyes widened.

They would really sacrifice themselves to fight this evil. I glanced over at my comrades and noticed they wore similar expressions of shock.

Perhaps they were fools, but maybe that's what the Realms needed in order to save both our galaxies. I placed my right wrist over my left and interlocked my thumbs together with my palms facing up. Once the symbol was made, I knelt on one knee.

Tehayo and Morak looked as confused as the Fehichen, but Rain and Erayame both stood deathly still, their mouth tipping into a firm line. It was an old symbol, a form of the highest respect that was taught to me by my mother. I raised my head, still kneeling.

"They wish to fight. Who are we to stop such warriors?" I answered the unspoken question I knew my brother and Erayame had.

I saw the fire in Aeis's eyes. I knew that there was no stopping them from the path they had chosen.

"You know that the decision of an alliance is out of our hands." Erayame said in Narviik as I stood.

I gave him a look that lets him know he didn't need to tell me that. Of course, it was a decision that needed to be made by the Elders, and by the other Council members of Eurkxo. I had full confidence they could be convinced though.

However, we were moving into dangerous territory. We couldn't just think of ourselves. If the MioTamir Union discovered this alliance before we were ready the threat of war could spiral out of control all too easily. There was also the issue of bringing the Fehichen to Eurkxo undetected.

"We must return to the Realms and inform the Elders. We must find a way to bring the Fehichen." I voiced my thoughts out loud in Narviik to Erayame.

"Bring the Fehichen to the Realms?" They all stared at me as if I were crazy. Maybe I was a little crazy.

"They must be allowed to announce this alliance themselves, face to face with our Elders." I answered, frustrated I had to explain. That should have been expected at least.

"Well... yes? But... the risks of this..." Rain mumbled to himself, and I caught a look of displeasure as he glanced at the Fehichen. I placed my hand on his arm, choosing to ignore the look he gave them.

"The risks are great, but you and I both know the words of the Custodian Emperor of V'rasór."

"War is what they wish, and they will have it..."

I recited in my mind as I said the words out loud. I remembered what was said as if it were said this very moment. Everyone was preparing for this war, and we should as well. My brother sighed, thinking for a moment before responding.

"To rid ourselves of their filth..." He closed his eyes. When he opened them again, a new confidence overtook him that he didn't have before. "It will always be worth the risk." He nodded to himself, and I nod in agreement.

Rain turned to the Fehichen, switching languages.

"We must return to our planet to discuss this with our Elders." Rain informed Aeis, who breathed out in slight relief that we didn't flatly refuse their requests.

"We understand. This is a decision that should be made with the agreement of all participants." Aeis said almost happily.

"Tell me." Rain tilted his head curiously. His eyes watched Aeis almost predatorily. "What do you know of... The Realms?"

"The... Realms?" Aeis's mouth dipped into a frown.

"I believe you call it the Ghost Region, a place no one comes back from." Tehayo added. "Quite fitting."

All of the Fehichen in the room paled at his words.

"You are from the Ghost Region? W-We thought it was a myth... it's a tale told to scare children." He visibly swallowed.

"You lie!" Another Fehichen shouted while pointing a finger at us accusingly. I rolled my eyes. At least the others were able to ignore the hysterical Fehichen.

"Then what does this tale tell of us?" Erayame tapped his foot impatiently. Many of the Fehichen stepped forward to answer, but it was Aeis who ended up explaining.

"The Ghost Region is said to appear only when the gods become angry. It is home to powerful entities of space with magical gifts. One look at them, and you will cease to exist." He paused, "There are stories of times these entities came to some of our worlds and performed the impossible. Some say they were not from the First Planet, that the region created itself and its inhabitants..." Aeis broke eye contact with us as he trailed off.

I wondered if it was because of the part in this tale that stated the whole 'One look at them, and you will cease to exist' nonsense. There was some truth to the tale, but it also had falsehood much like any story. It was interesting to me that that's who we were here, a story. I would've liked to know how much truth the story had, but we had no records from that long ago. Most people in the Realms cared little for historical knowledge. The past didn't matter, it was our way.

Fortunately, there was still vague knowledge about the beginning that I knew about, and I was able to make sense of how such a tale came to be. The Realms didn't disappear and reappear. It was known about for a time, I think, but anyone who knew of it was either silenced or imprisoned to the Realms, hence the 'One look and you cease to exist.'

Obviously, we didn't just form in the Realms, that was just utter nonsense. More than half the planets in the Realms were barren before artificially made to hold life. We arrived there from the First Planet. Realmers did, however, possess phantasm energy that all Realmers carried within them. It was always part of us, of who we were, deep within our cores, pumping through our veins.

Phantasm energy was the scientific name, and mostly referred to when we talked about it in regard to ourselves, but outside of us, flowing throughout the realms, most Realmers called it Natarah. It was a force, an unknown energy. It had no official name, just Natarah which meant 'entity' or 'unknown.' To these beings in the Forbidden Region, I'm sure it would seem like magical gifts.

"An interesting tale, but as all tales, it carries as much falsehood as it does truth." Rain grinned as he voiced my own thoughts. One of the Fehichen began to figit, glancing up as if they wished to speak. With his eyes, Rain questioned the young man.

"Can- are you... able to use such gifts?" The man asked nervously.

We each looked at each other, grinning knowingly. With my fingers, I played with my dress. Tehayo, and Morak stepped to the side. Unlike us, their Phantasm energy was nonvisible. Those of us with Soaran heritage, or those born of V'rasór, had a more visual representation of our energy.

Me, Erayame, and Rain stepped closer together with our heads facing down. Simultaneously, we willed our phantasm to the surface. A warmth flowed through my veins circling around the markings by my eyes. I forced my phantasm to settle softly so the shimmering light blue glow wouldn't be too bright for them.

We each raised our heads together, showing off Natarah within us. I glanced at the others out of the corner of my eye. Rain's shimmering light was a darker blue than mine and Erayame's was a dark forest green.

The Fehichen let out gasps, hurrying away from us in fear. Even Aeis' eyes widened as he stepped back, his mouth hanging open in shock.

I smiled at the scene. Their expressions were priceless. Making symbolic gestures with my hands, I willed my phantasm to circle around my arms, before moving it down as delicately as the flow of water. Rain, clearly not concerned about blinding them, made the room alight, his phantasm hoovering lusciously above his shoulders in little glowing lights.

One of the Fehichen I recognized as Sa'ak, dropped to his knees with a cry. Two younger ones followed his lead, falling to their knees as well, eyes full of fear. I almost felt bad, our phantasm must have felt overwhelming to them. Of course they would fear us.

"Do not fear, we have no desire to harm you." I raised my hands in surrender, hoping to ease their fear. Unfortunately, it only seemed to cause them to cower even further. It was quite a sight seeing such a physically stronger species fearing us so openly. Rain seemed to expect as much as he began to laugh. He even crackled his phantasm for effect.

"The energy from the cores you brought burns within you! How is that possible?" Aeis asked, trying to appear calm, but he noticeably kept his distance from us.

"Behold our truest form. Mind your words and you may not be crushed under our power!" Rain called out in a merry voice. His eyes sparkled in mischief.

"You might find this amusing, but I do not." I told Rain in Narviik, frowning deeply. If we were to forge an alliance with these people, we couldn't belittle them like this.

"Don't worry, Keeper. They have to know who they'll be up against." Erayame shrugged, clearly enjoying the sight as much as Rain was. He crossed his arms and raised his head high, which only added to the Fehichen's fear.

"Enough of this. It was only our intention to show them, and we've already done that." I said as I clenched my fists. Rain and Erayame shifted uncomfortably for a moment, but then yielded to my demand, willing their energy to settle once more.

"We did not realize..." Aeis managed to stammer out.

"Tell your people to stand." Rain said calmly. Acis turned to his people, nodding his head. Those who fell to the ground apprehensively stood up again. Erayame looked down at them.

"We've told you about our home, the Realms."

"Exposed the phantasm energy that's within us." Rain raised his head proudly.

"Do you still want this?" I asked. After seeing who we really were and what they would have to fight against, would they still choose an alliance with us? It was, after all, their choice.

"We've made our choice. We will live and die with this choice." Aeis stood firm. "You may have this magical power..."

"It's just Natarah..." Tehayo mumbled next to me. Aeis ignored him.

"But we have our intelligence and our own physical and mental strengths. We are not a people who allow our weaknesses to suppress us from delivering justice." Pride sounded through his voice.

His people stood tall behind him with a newfound confidence. It made me smile. Despite knowing they were nowhere near our level in power, they had the spirits of warriors. I knew they would not allow themselves to be looked down upon. Perhaps my people could learn a thing or two from them.

"You still believe this is the right choice?" Rain shook his head in disbelief, "There's no stopping your persistence... I admire that." He sighed.

"We must travel back to the Realms immediately. We will send a ship that you can send representatives in. Be discreet. If any of the sectors within the Realms find out about this possible alliance, death will follow." Rain spoke slowly so they would understand the importance of his words.

"You will take your leave now?" Aeis asked, surprised.

We nodded. The sooner we got back to the Realms, the sooner this alliance could begin.

"I will escort you myself." He called a Fehichen forward to escort us with him.

We turned and left the discussion room, following Aeis down the halls. Others outside the room openly stared at us, wondering what had taken place.

As we neared the docking bay, I caught sight of Xorion once more. I slowed my pace, letting the others pass me. I felt him walk up beside me.

"Well, here we are again. I heard your people caused quite a spectacle earlier." He commented, his mouth twitching in a smile.

"Stalking much?" I asked, ignoring his other comment. We stopped walking at the same time and turned to face each other.

"It seems to me, that you enjoy my company. Don't worry, you're much to my liking as well." He smirked.

This man...

I shook my head softly.

"Am I? Because you're not to my liking at all." I teased as I turned my head away, hiding a laugh.

It was a lie of course. He was certainly attractive, and I did enjoy his company. However, he hinted at things that were beyond friendship, and I couldn't have that. I was on the Eurkxo council, and he was from an entirely different galaxy. To top it off, I was a Realmer and he was from the Forbidden region. We probably wouldn't even see each other again after I returned to the Realms.

"Oh? Well, isn't that something... what is it they say? Opposites attract...?" He moved closer to me, brushing his hand against my arm. Unlike before, I didn't move away.

"Improvement!" He said happily, noticing my reaction. Instead of dropping his hand, he moves it up along my braid. He moved it along until the braid reaches my head before curling his hand around it and cupping my head.

"It seems I am to your liking, Keeper." He said, softly looking into my eyes. Amusement was written all over his expression. I matched his gaze with a look of shock, purposely leaving my mouth parted slightly. Two could play that same game.

"I-" I stammered out for effect. "Simply speaking I- I..." I stuttered the words. He seemed to buy the act, looking down at me expectantly with his alluring golden eyes.

"Oh, Xorion!" I gasped and placed my hands over my lips.

Shaking my head exaggeratingly, I gasped out again. "It seems we're the same about liking each other! How unfortunate, now we simply don't attract!" I tore myself away from him. Giggling at his confused face, I hurried towards the Rectifier.

Behind me, I heard him laughing quite loudly. "I'll see you on your planet, Keeper. Mark my words!"

Somehow, I doubt that, my silly, young friend.

When I finally reached the ship, Rain was speaking to Aeis about something.

I hurried behind them still in a cherry mood. It was a shame that my fun was over, we seemed to get along quite well.

Not paying attention to the conversation around me, I followed the others into the ship quietly, hoping I wouldn't draw any attention to myself. Before the door was fully closed Erayame called out to the Fehichen below with a smile.

"Oh, and when you come, do bring your trade goods as well! They would be... most appreciated."

The door closed, and Rain turned to me with a curious expression. I looked up at him innocently.

"So... what were you and that Fehichen man speaking so amusingly about?"

9

CHAPTER 8

I stared at Rain. His eyebrows rose curiously while he signaled to continue walking towards the bridge. I fell in step beside him.

"I'm surprised you feel it's any of your business. After all, it's my job to be friendly." I tilted my head slightly, half joking, half not.

I knew I wasn't being fair by not answering him, but when was life ever fair? His eyes narrowed slightly before just nodding in response.

I sighed, knowing this conversation wasn't over. He wouldn't drop the subject until he had the full story. I was glad he wouldn't do it in front of the others at the very least. He might be my older brother, but he knew there was a time and a place for such discussions between siblings where we could throw our titles aside.

We arrived at the bridge and Rain wasted no time sitting and starting the sequence for departure.

"Yer being awfully quiet, ay?" Adam questioned, obviously wanting to know what had taken place down on the planet.

Rain hadn't called the crew to the bridge yet. I assumed he would have a meeting with everyone later.

"Adam, after we depart keep us hovering the planet. There's something we need to inform the crew about."

As I suspected. It seemed he wanted to have the full discussion about the plan before we returned to the Realms.

"Oh? What'er might that be 'bout?" Adam asked with no little amount of attitude while gracefully managing the sequences to leave.

Rain flicked his wrist, dismissing him, "Not now, Adam."

"Ah, tis 'bout 'that' is it, ay?" Adam shook his head.

"Sequence set." Rain said, ignoring his statement.

He opened the communication line to Rihaya. "Begin the countdown."

"Departure on 20, 19, 18, 17, 16, 15..."

The ship shook as it hovered above the ground and gradually traveled up into the atmosphere. I gripped the restaurants, my muscles tensing in response to the violent shaking. I tried to let myself relax, but it was difficult.

"10, 9, 8, 7, 6, 5, 4, 3, 2, 1, 0...."

We breach the atmosphere with a jerk, forcing me forward, but finally the ship becomes steady. Adam sets the ship to hover in the planet's gravitational pull before glancing between me, Rain, and Erayame with curiosity. I'm sure the others were just as curious about why we were stopping as he was.

"We'er hovered." Adam said with a little wave of his hands through the air and arching an eyebrow at us.

"Everyone to the bridge." Rain commanded through the communication line before standing from his seat.

Me and Erayame undid our restraints and stood with him. Once everyone arrived, Rain stepped in the middle of the group, gaining their attention. He quickly ran through what went down on the planet. Of course, it didn't take long for everyone to get the gist of what was happening. Adam's voice was rigid as he loudly disapproved of the opportunity.

"What?! Yer wish to discuss an... alliance?" Adam slammed his fists against his control panel. As expected, all the crew was apprehensive about the announcement, but Adam was always more vocal.

"Calm yourself, Adam. It has been decided. This is only the announcement." Rain said flatly.

"If there is to be an alliance, how do you plan for them to enter the Realms? The Union watches the border planets. They already know we travel here; they just need proof. If the proof is found, they will be interrogated until they speak the truth about who they were meeting. And they will talk." Rihaya voiced her concern.

She wasn't rude about it, but with her arms crossed and her mouth tipped in a frown, it was obvious she wasn't convinced this was the best course of action.

"They will come in our ships that leave no detection along with the trading goods. These ships also have a self-destruct mechanism aboard which they will be informed about. If boarded by an unknown vessel, it will destroy itself." Rain said simply, which seemed to satisfy Rihaya for now.

"And how can we'be sure no spies are on that'a their planet? They'd find a'way to communicate with their ships. They've tried before and will a'gain." Adam questioned now slouched over in his chair.

"We can't be certain, but it will not be an exposed alliance. Only us aboard the Rectifier, perhaps some guards, and the Elders will know about it. They will not leave the Tower's residence." Rain reassured.

"And'a what if they'd find it in their best interest to join those against us?" Adam all but mumbled, but I still caught it.

I narrowed my eyes on him. "That is not who they are, Adam." I said, leaving no room for argument.

I turned my attention to address the others. "This discussion is over. It has already been decided, they will come to Eurkxo."

Determined to make a point, I gripped my dress and twisted it harshly with me as I hurried out of the room.

Adam grumbled behind me about his concerns being ignored, but strangely enough, he seemed to shrug it off as if he was never really that worried about it.

"As so, it tis said, it'er done."

I frowned, knowing full well that he disagreed even though he was playing it off as if he didn't. I never liked having confrontations with him, but lately it seemed that we didn't agree about anything. I missed us being carefree and open with each other. Always laughing at some inside joke.

I hoped he wouldn't keep this up over the next few days. It would take some time to finally reach the opening of the Realms even traveling at light speed. If we used our phantasm to jump through space, it wouldn't take as long, but of course that was out of the question considering we had strict orders not to do so by the Elders. It was simply too risky to attempt anything faster.

I stopped walking through the hallway, amusing myself by imagining the faces of the Fehichen when they would enter our galaxy. It would be priceless.

10

CHAPTER 9

Entering the Realms was not an easy task. It required precision and accuracy in both sight and calculations. Some stories spoke about the Realms as if it were a doorway someone could walk through but that was far from the truth.

The Realms were secret for the very reason that no one could not enter without knowing the key to entering. Special calculations were required at specific times only known to us Realmers. Even if someone discovered the calculations, they wouldn't be able to make it through. The ships had to possess phantasm within the material they were made from in order to enter the Realms, and the only way to get the material was from within the Realms in the first place.

"Adam?" Rain asked worriedly as he glanced over his shoulder at him.

Adam leaned forward to type out sequences, trying to pinpoint the exact time that we needed to move though the field of Kaintra Troin. Supposedly, it was named after one of the founders of the Realms. I didn't know if that was factual though. No one spoke about the beginning of the Realms. It just didn't matter.

"Yeah, I'er know... got it." He mumbled as he narrowed his eyes at the screen below him.

"Go ahead and put it on the visual screen." Rain casually flicked his wrist above him and within seconds the view screen above changed to reveal the field of Kaintra Troin.

The best way to describe it like a curtain of dark matter energy or pure phantasm, which made a barrier around our galaxy. Every few minutes a gateway would appear like a cloud revealing a moon for a few seconds before covering it once more. Those few seconds was all the time we had to make our reentry. Of course, it was impossible to go through without even the slightest touch of pure phantasm, but since our ships were made of metals crafted within the Realms, they already had a touch of the energy, so it wasn't an issue for us.

This was a blessing whenever an unknown ship tried to enter our Realms though. That had never happened in my lifetime though. The energy would tear it apart within seconds of a single touch. My mouth parted slightly as I gazed in awe at the sight. I'd seen it before, when we first departed the Realms, but it was still so beautiful.

Dark swirls of crackling energy moved through just the perfect amount of electric sparks which swam through the field causing miniature explosions. It was amazing to me that something so deadly, so mysterious, could be so incredible to the eyes.

I looked over at Rain and Adam and strained my senses to hear what they were discussing.

"Calculate it with the key." Rain said softly as if he was afraid any loud sound would distract Adam.

"Within'a minute or so, ay..." Adam said, leaning back. "...Er' gateway will open."

"We will have approximately twenty-one seconds to move through it before the ships system collapse." Rain said through a smile. "That's more than enough time. We're having a pretty good day so far."

"Ay, absolutely fantastic." Adam mumbled sarcastically.

"And there she is..." Rain said in awe.

All of us gaped breathlessly as the swirls of the dark matter split apart, revealing a pathway through the gateway we would travel into.

"Take us through gently, Adam." Rain said lightly as he pressed a hand onto his friend's shoulder. Adam grunted, concentrating deeply on the objective ahead.

"No pressure Adam, only our lives on the line." Erayame commented in a cherry, almost sarcastic tone.

"Oh please, it's like Rain said, we have plenty of time to move through the gateway." I rolled my eyes. Adam turned around and winked at me and I felt my cheeks heat up in embarrassment.

"Next time the council decides to send us into the next God-for-saken galaxy, I will flatly refuse." Erayame grunted out miserably, shuffling in his seat.

"I rather enjoyed the trip." I said mostly to myself as I thought back to our time on E'arka with the little people and then to Vaymos. If I were completely honest, I didn't just like it... no. I loved it in that galaxy. Everything seemed so much simpler there.

"Everyone be silent please... One small tilt and we could graze the sides of the gateway." Rain turned around to look at us as he spoke.

Both me and Erayame immediately fell silent, the only sound being the soft sounds of the ship's movement, and our own breathing.

Each second felt like a century, but we swiftly, beautifully, crossed the gateway.

"Ladies and gentlemen, welcome back to the Realms!" Rain said, breathing out heavily in relief.

I smiled. Even far away from our home planet, it still felt like home. My phantasm relaxed within me, flowing peacefully throughout my veins as if comforted by the presence of a mother. I wasn't the only one who embraced the peaceful silence of home.

The entire hour, no one spoke a single word. Words were not needed to fill our soul, but by our God's gift to us, our energy was filled as it embraced the peace of Natarah surrounding us.

My heart ached to return to Eurkxo, in a good way. This was where I knew we belonged. It felt right. Unfortunately, even if it was home, it was still dangerous. We knew the MioTamir Union would be monitoring the border planet sectors, wanting to catch anyone going through Kaintra Troin.

It was funny, really. They knew Eurkxo was sending ships through to look for new trading partners, but because they had no proof, they had no excuse to start the war. It was all about image. Unfortunately for them, my brother and Adam were two of the best pilots I'd ever known. Even if they saw us, they'd never catch us long enough to interrogate us.

It would be some time before we actually arrived at Eurkxo, and that was because we entered on Eurkxo's side of the sector. It wasn't considered one of the border planets, but it was close enough, which was a good thing for us. There were three main border planets: D'thaya, Láuran, and MioTamir. Eurkxo shared the same border as Láuran. To our knowledge, the MioTamir Union shouldn't be watching our side of the border, but with all the tension building, it was impossible to know for certain.

Rain finally gave us permission to leave our seats and relax for a bit. I didn't really want to go to my quarters right now. Instead, I figured it would be entertaining to explore the ship. When we had time to relax traveling through the Forbidden regions from planet to planet and back to the Realms, I'd mostly spent it with Adam, and Rain. Unfortunately, they had to remain on the bridge now to watch out for any ships that might threaten us.

I wandered aimlessly for some time without direction, but then a thought struck me. I hadn't talked to the three brothers from Láuran in a while. Perhaps I could try to find them?

I walked in the direction I thought was the way to the engineer room where I was sure the three brothers would be. They seemed friendly enough towards me, and it was better than just simply going back to my own room which was more like a closet with a bed. Plus, I wasn't tired.

I ended up wondering down the hall and past the cafeteria but wasn't sure where to go from there. As I stood in the middle of a three-way corridor debating where to go next, I heard footsteps coming from behind me and turned to see Rihaya walking towards me looking down at a tablet in her hands. Sensing my eyes staring at her no doubt, she looked up and smiled at me.

"Keeper," she said, bowing her head slightly. I smiled and bowed my head as well before lifting my hand up slightly to greet her.

"Please, just Clove." I said, giving her permission to use my nickname. She was my brother's friend, calling me Keeper felt way too formal.

She nodded, "Clove, then." She looked at me knowingly. "Are you in need of directions? I know my first few times aboard the Rectifier, I got lost all the time."

"Your services would be... greatly appreciated. Thank you." I answered while breathing out in relief. I was saved. "I'm looking for the engine room."

She raised her chin in understanding. "Ah, yes. It is rather confusing getting there." She motioned with one hand while the other held the tablet. "Take the right corridor, and then the first hallway on your left will lead to a ladder heading down to the engine room."

I smiled and tilted my head at her, "Are you also heading that way?" I asked, curious about where she was headed before she stopped to help me.

"Ah, no." She held up the tablet. "I'm going left, towards the storage chamber. I'm taking this with me to help me know which vault to open."

"Oh. Well then I wish you good luck." I answered, still smiling.

"And to you." She bowed her head. She walked past me towards the left corridor, and I go the opposite direction, down the right one.

Walk down the right hallway till reaching the first hallway on the left...

I thought as I walked down the hall until I finally saw the hallway. It was short, my eyes already saw the door at the end of the hall as I stepped into it.

I opened the door and saw the metal ladder heading down and grimaced. I disliked the thought of descending somewhere I hadn't been before, but I knew the brothers would be there, so it wasn't all bad.

Sucking in a breath, I gripped the ladder and started climbing down, the door closing behind me. It was dark, only being lit by small lights behind the ladder. I reached the bottom and sighed at the gloominess surrounding me. It was messy, with exposed wires and huge pipes running throughout it. The walkway was narrow, and I had to pick up my dress to keep it from hitting the sides of the dirty, rusted walls.

"Gross..." I mumbled to myself as I stepped over a rusted metal bar on the ground.

To think Rain would take better care of the engine room of his ship...

I thought to myself. But then this was the first time I had ever been in an engineer room. Maybe they all looked like this?

"Cloverlyne? Is that you?" I heard Tehayo's voice say from somewhere around the side. I stood on the tips of my toes, looking over the pipes. I finally saw him stretching his long neck to find me.

"Hello, sorry if I am intruding." I apologized, hesitating where I stood as I shifted from side to side. There was a chance the man might not appreciate a woman invading his private space. I'm sure the brother's thought of this as their room. "I got a bit bored on the bridge." I admitted, hoping to ease the awkwardness.

He shook his head quickly, throwing a rag over his shoulder. "No need to apologize, Cloverlyne! Your presence is very welcome!" He said enthusiastically as he waved his hand, dismissing my apology. "Come this way. There's an opening to come back here where my brothers are."

I kept walking forward, following him from the other side. I finally saw the opening but had to duck under some thick wires going across the roof of the room.

Tehayo grinned, motioning for me to follow him. "Excuse the mess, we are not used to having company and you know how engine rooms are." He shrugged.

I didn't know but made no mention of that. I just nodded, not wanting to seem ignorant. We made our way into a clearing in the room where I saw Morak sitting on a hedge, throwing a small ball into the air as if he were bored as well. The minute he saw me, he stood.

"Cloverlyne! What brings you down here to our little world?" He asked, looking thrilled that I was there.

"Just wanted some company rather than being bored on the bridge." I answered honestly. My eyes roamed around the room, searching for their other brother, Vis.

"He's on the other side checking the thrusters to make sure they're good for the rest of the trip." Morak explained when he saw I was looking for him.

"Oh."

Morak stepped to the side, indicating to the seat he'd stood from. "Please, sit."

"I am fine to stand, Morak. I wouldn't want to steal your seat." I said, declining his offer, but still wanting to be polite to the sweet young man.

He frowned slightly, as if it hurt him that I denied his request. "Please, I insist." He said again.

Not wanting to refuse him a second time, I reluctantly walked over to the hedge and hoisted myself up and shifted around till I was comfortable. There was a rather awkward silence. The boys glanced at each other as if they had no idea what to do or say. I guessed neither of them were good at socializing. Not wanting it to become any more awkward between us, I tried to start a random conversation to break the ice.

"Do you also live on Eurkxo?" I asked, setting a pleasant smile on my face. I knew the boys were born on Láuran. I remembered the complication about their beliefs that made it impossible for them to remain living there.

"Yes, the three of us share an apartment there."

"In Haphlen?" I asked, and both of them nodded.

"In the city of Cynhard." Tehayo specified as he leaned up against a metal bar above the room. My eyes perked up at the name of the city I knew as home.

"Oh? Do you live close to the Serenity Tower then?"

"Sort of, though it is still some ways away. We live closer to the wall, on the south-west side."

The Great Wall of Eurkxo which passed through the Sea of Glass. It was not a wall for keeping people in or out, but a wall built for the only purpose of being beautiful. It was painted with hundreds of different colors and decorated with fresh flowers daily. I remembered my first time seeing it. It looked like something out of another world.

"It must be quite the view."

I was impressed that they were able to live there. I didn't know much about them, but the fact that they could afford an apartment overlooking the Wall meant they must have been well-off at least. I guess my brother paid his engineers well. That was good.

"It certainly is!" Morak said with a dazed look as if looking back at a fond memory. He shook his head slightly and tilted his head at me. "And you? Do you live at the Serenity Tower with the other council members?"

I leaned my head back and laughed a little. "No, I only stay in that place when they need me. I prefer my own home."

"Understandable." Tehayo replied, shrugging his shoulders.

"Will you return to your apartment? Or will you remain on board the Rectifier when we return?" I asked curiously as I wiped a layer of sweat from my forehead. It was very hot in the engine room, but thankfully they seemed to have coolers. Without them I might not have been able to stand it.

"We will stay aboard the Rectifier until its maintenance is complete, then return to our apartment until called back by our commander, your brother." Tehayo explained. He took the towel off his shoulder and threw it into a corner.

We created small talk for some time. Mostly about what we would do after we returned home. Vis finally came into the clearing we were in and greeted me. I noticed that he wasn't much of a talker, keeping more to himself. I also noticed he kept himself away from his brothers. It made me think they maybe had some kind of confrontation before I arrived, and if that was the reason for his absence. Maybe I was just imagining things?

After some time, I stood up, knowing it was getting late. I excused myself from their presence. I needed to rest. This time, Morak walked with me back to the ladder and after we said goodnight to each other, I climbed out of the engine room. It took me nearly thirty minutes to finally find my way back to my room and by that time, all the ships lights except the ones lighting the ground had turned off for the night cycle. I was thankful the ship was set to Eurkxo's sun rotation so our bodies wouldn't experience any shock in our sleep schedules.

In my room, I found myself wanting to relax a bit before sleep and figured a shower would do the trick. After removing my clothes, and pinning my hair up with a clip, I took a quick rinse in the closet sized bathroom. It felt nice to let the water just run down my back even for only a few minutes.

I got out rather quickly knowing we had to conserve water. This ship wasn't made for pleasure, but rather for quick travel between worlds. I was glad my brother had at least invested in water with sanitation chemicals, so I didn't need to worry about washing my body. I could tell from the floral scent it gave off, much like most showers back on Eurkxo. Knowing my brother, he was likely to forget something simple like that. After all the traveling we had just done, I'm sure Rain would need to refill on a lot of things, which was probably why I'd seen Rihaya checking the storage earlier today.

I stepped out of the shower, wrapped a towel around my body, and dried myself off. Then, I slip into a fresh, white, underdress to sleep in. I switched the lights off and slipped into the small bed eager to get some rest. I relaxed easily into the bed, and before I knew it, I was already asleep.

11

—·—

Chapter 10

We arrived on Eurkxo with no issues just a few days after entering the Realms. As soon as we landed on the planet, we were immediately escorted to Cynhard, the city of the Serenity Tower in the Province of Haphlen. It was sad to leave the Rectifier crew with only a simple goodbye, I hoped I'd see them again someday. They were good people. I was glad to be back though, I missed the mythical beauty of Eurkxo.

Trying to describe it was like trying to describe a wild garden. You couldn't name all its flowers, but they were there. I never really took the time to appreciate the planet for its beauty, it was something that simply always was. Being away for so long though... It made me appreciate it more. I heard stories that Eurkxo was made to resemble a place known as the Hanging Gardens. A place created by the ancients of the first planet. I didn't know if it was true, but it would describe Eurkxo perfectly.

The Serenity Tower was one of seven towers on the planet. Each one was made from white crystals from the sea of glass which reflected light from the sun. It was breathtakingly beautiful in the light of day, and mythical looking in the light of the moon. Walking up the steps to the tower was said to feel like entering another world by off-worlders, but for me, it just felt like walking into any other building.

When we entered the Serenity Tower the Elders of Serenity called for a meeting to discuss our trip. This was the meeting where we would also mention the possible alliance. I hoped it went well. Me and Erayame were given one hour before the meeting began to rest. I wasn't really tired, so I spent the time preparing myself by cleaning myself up and gathering my thoughts. I had an attendant redo my hair into a braid that covered the top of my head like a crown and continued down the side. She then tied three flowers on the side of the braid, letting them hang. After my hair was finished, she helped me change into a flowing white gown which represented my position as a council member. White symbolized purity, and that my words would be pure against my own lips and to other's ears.

When I was finally ready, I joined Erayame outside the meeting chamber, waiting to go in. Eventually the door clicked open, allowing us to enter.

"Tha'ra zo, camo s'haki dianta zava'vio, Cloverlyne, Erayame." High Elder Tallimos spoke a greeting in Lechan, the tongue of his mother. She was from the planet Láuran, which made him only half Soaran from his father side.

"Tha'ra zo, Elder." I answered back in his tounge. Both Erayame and I bowed our heads respectfully.

"We read from the summary Erayame sent that there have been discussions of alliance?" He narrowed his gaze on us both.

"You are correct. We have discussed the possibilities of alliance with the race known as the Fehichen. They are from the planet Vaymos not so far from the planet of the little people." I responded carefully. We'd have to tread carefully talking about this. I wasn't completely sure how they'd react to the news.

"How did these mere trading discussions turn into talks of alliance?" He eyed between us suspiciously.

I sighed as I tried to come up with the best response. This wasn't going to be easy. My people were not as trusting as those from the Forbidden Region.

"They first questioned whether we knew about invaders terrorizing weaker planets in their galaxy. It seems our enemies have breached their worlds and the Fehichen claim they have been threatened. They wish to help us take a stance against these invaders. It is possible they are the MioTamir Union, or Elnorsefall themselves." I answered as honestly as I could and hoped he would understand the position we were put in.

"This is a grave situation indeed." He shook his head. "We could dismiss this alliance, but it is clear that with a threat from inside the Realms, they are not likely to keep silent."

"Indeed. If we do not form this alliance, they will fight them on their own. Without the knowledge we can provide, they will be killed." Erayame said matter-of-factly.

My jaw clenched. I knew he was right, but it was still hard to hear. High Elder Tallimos nodded knowingly.

"It is worse than that, Erayame. The MioTamir Union would not stop their interrogation until they have enough proof we crossed the border, and if they find out that they asked us for alliance..."

The room was silent as we thought of his unspoken words.

The War of the Realms would begin...

It wouldn't matter that MioTamir was also crossing into the Forbidden Realms. So long as they had proof we were, they had an excuse to attack us by the laws of war.

"It seems they have put us in a decision with only two answers." Erayame paused. "Fight together or fight alone." He shook his head again. There was only one answer for me, and it was for alliance.

"What do you think of them, Cloverlyne?" High Elder Tallimos asked me. I stayed quiet for a moment before answering.

"They are honest, brave, and people worthy of respect. Their hearts are pure and innocent. Despite them being inferior in technology, they have the willpower to do anything they put their minds to, and they have chosen to turn to the willpower they have to help us."

It was nothing but the truth. The other Elders around nodded their heads in approval.

"We will await their arrival from the ship Commander Rain has sent to them." High Elder Tallimos rose from his seat. Seeing him rise, the other Elders rose with him. Me and Erayame bowed our heads low to the ground as he walked towards us slowly.

"Rise." He said while lifting his hand. We both rose from our bow. "Cloverlyne, I take it you will wish to return to your own home?" He asked while placing a hand on my shoulder and gently turning me to walk towards the door.

I smiled, "It would please me very much, High Elder."

"Then my permission is given, you have done a good thing. We will continue this discussion upon their arrival." He said as the doors were opened by attendants.

"Will you need me present for the discussion?" I tried not to let any excitement seep through my voice. It was unlikely I would be needed anyways.

"This is a decision by the Elders, if we have need of you, we will summon you."

"Of course. Thank you, High Elder." I said with a short bow of my head.

I supposed it would be nice to not have to deal with any more difficult decisions for a while. He bowed his head towards me politely, and I felt him gently push my shoulder towards the door. We were being dismissed. I assumed he wanted us out quickly so the elders could discuss some things on their own.

It was a relief that he allowed me to return home, even though I was a little disappointed I wouldn't be here to witness the possibility of alliance. It seemed I'd become too attached to some of the Fehichen than I originally thought. Even so, it was a nice thought to return home.

As I walked down the hall away from the meeting chamber I caught sight of my oldest friend, Lucia Azhure. I smiled as I walked towards her. We were not able to speak often lately, but we shared the darkest of our days together. We both lost so much long ago which connected us in a way very dear to my heart.

"Oh, Clove! I'd heard a rumor you'd arrived. I'd come to know if it was true!" Lucia returned a bright smile back at me as she reached out her hands to grab mine.

"Lucia, I am glad you are here." I said, accepting the clasp of friendship, squeezing her hands lightly.

"Walk with me." She said as she wrapped her arm around mine.

"Of course."

We walk silently for a few minutes until we are completely alone in the hallways.

"So...?" She asked, drawing out the 'o' dramatically. Her pretty gray eyes gleamed with excitement as she stroked her silvery blonde hair with her other hand. I knew exactly what her question was.

"It was... incredible!" I exclaimed breathlessly, my voice turning high pitched when I spoke so excitedly.

"Oh! You must tell me everything, every detail!" She lets my hand go, clasping both of hers together.

I let out a laugh before becoming more serious.

"The Elders would not want me to speak of it." I said, giving her a sad look.

"Oh, but please! What must I do? Beg on my knees?" She rolled her eyes childishly, her youth shining though.

We were close in age, but she was fifteen, making her two years younger than me. Almost three now, since I would be eighteen soon. Our lives were similar in that we were both taken from our birth planet, V'rasór, as children due to circumstances out of our control. Eurkxo was our home now. She had yet to travel to other sectors and had only heard rumors of the Forbidden galaxy.

"Meet me at my house after the commotion calms, I will tell you everything about what happened." I promised quietly. Her eyes widened even more.

"Oh Clove! Thank you so much, I don't know how I shall repay this debt!"

"You owe me no debt. Now act with some dignity before someone sees us." I scolded, but I knew my eyes were laughing. She does her best to put on a serious expression, but her mouth continued to twitch in giggles.

"I must go. I hope to see you soon, Lucia." I bowed my head, and she did the same.

"I look forward to our next meeting!" She said, smiling before hurrying away without looking back. I assumed she hurried to her own room to laugh into her pillows. I smiled just thinking about it.

I made my way out of the building hoping to catch a flight to the outskirts of the city. When I was younger and had first arrived on Eurkxo with my brother and Lucia, we all lived together in the Towers with the other Elders and council members. We were taught the ways of this planet and ways of order. It was safer to have us closer to the Elders than to be hidden from them. As we grew up surrounded by their knowledge and wisdom, they promoted us to council members.

My brother was against the idea, instead deciding to join the military rather than council as he had chosen back on our home planet. He had always longed to be a fighter, even when we were little. Because he denied the Elders request, he was given a ship to travel aboard as a commander as a gift.

I stayed behind, accepting their request, but I didn't want to live in the Towers. I would've had Lucia live with me, but one of the council members who treated her as her own daughter asked her first, and I couldn't deny her a chance at having a mother again after losing her entire family back on V'rasór.

It didn't take too long to finally reach my home. I'd thankfully managed to reach it before dark. Standing outside it, I smiled at the deep gray walls and canopy trees which cover the small mansion. Fountains shot out from the ground giving it a mythical feeling. The Elders were kind when they gave it to me in exchange for my service to them. They were always generous to us.

I hurried to the door and even before reaching it, my attendant, Laloni, opened the door to greet me.

"My lady! You've returned!" She said with a pretty smile, curtsying to me. I smiled back and I quickly bowed my head to greet her.

"It's good to be home, Laloni." I answered, placing my hand on her shoulder affectionately.

"I will warm something up for you to eat right away!" She said quickly, hurrying away before I could respond. I let out a small giggle as I followed her towards my dining hall.

The Elders had been too kind in their gift of this house to me. It was grand, far grander than I deserved. I didn't request anything of the sort, but it seemed they enjoyed the thought of giving away goods. It was far too big for just me and Laloni, but Lucia and Rain did visit often which made the house livelier.

My eyes drooped as I walked into the dining hall. I was more tired than I was hungry, but I didn't want to tell Laloni otherwise. However, as she came back out and took a good look at me, she shook her head to herself.

"No, no food right now. You go up to your room and sleep, my lady. It has been a long day for you, I will bring food to your chambers after a few hours of rest."

I smiled, "Thank you, Laloni. You know me well." I walked away, retreating up the stairs to my room.

I immediately threw myself on my bed not even bothering to change clothes. My thoughts were filled with memories of the For- bidden galaxy, but I tried to push them aside. I was home now and needed to put that galaxy behind me. It had been almost a month since I'd been back, and I planned to enjoy every minute of it.

12

CHAPTER 11

I sat in a chair in my room staring up at the ceiling. It was made of glass so I could gaze at the stars at night. I always loved stars and their shimmering; it was calming. Today was the day they would arrive. According to Laloni, they'd arrived without any trouble at all. I should've been relieved, but I was not. It was unusual for our ships not to have even the slightest attention. They were making this easy, which meant they either no longer needed proof or had complications that needed to be dealt with elsewhere. The question is, what? It worried me, and I couldn't do anything about it.

I stood and opened the door to my patio, revealing my garden. It was one of my most favored places to be during the day. Knealing down, I gazed into a small pool at my reflection. I suppose I was considered pretty, for a Soaran girl. Many said I inherited my mother's soft features and her shade of blue eyes. They called her an angel born from the heavens.

I reached up to touch my hair, letting my fingers run through it. Long, straight, and black in color. The total opposite of my mother's angelic golden hair. I wish I'd inherited that feature at least, but me and both my brothers all inherited our father's hair color. I hated it.

I suppose I could've dyed it, but it was a reminder of where I came from, of who I came from. I wouldn't forget that.

I sighed, turning my gaze away from the pool. If only I could enjoy my own home without worrying about anything else.

"My Lady."

I heard the voice of Leilani, my attendant, and turned to greet her with a nod.

"Leilani, what is it?" I tilted my head back to look at her, still kneeling by the pool. She walked closer and gave a curtsy.

"Two guests have just arrived, and have asked for your presence, my Lady." She said gently. "I informed them to wait in the parlor."

"Thank you, Leilani. Do you know who they are?" I wanted to be prepared for their presence. It could be someone important. I wondered if Lucia had become unable to wait and came for answers already? The thought brought a smile to my lips. She was such a curious girl, even more than me.

"Believe me when I say, my Lady, I am not quite sure. Though, I must say they certainly are not from our worlds." She lightly shrugged her shoulders, and her expression turned quizzical as she placed her hands on her hips thoughtfully.

I stood as a wave of confusion came over me. Not from our worlds? Then where could they be from that she wouldn't recognize-

It couldn't be...

I hurried to the stairs leading down below. Before descending I searched for the quests, wanting to see if it could possibly be him. Finally, I saw him. Staring up at me, grinning like the happiest man in the universe, was Xorion. I met his stare. I felt my cheeks redden in response before quickly correcting my posture to look like a dignified person instead of a silly seventeen-year-old teenager. Shoulders back, and head held high, I walked down the staircase in my usual, practiced poise.

"I wasn't expecting guests. How did you learn where I reside?" I asked, trying to make my voice sound pleasant with only a hint of curiosity. I could hardly believe he'd dared to seek permission to travel here. Had he sought permission from the High Elder himself? Perhaps there were tower guardians accompanying him, but with a quick scan around, it was evident that wasn't the case.

"Oh? Did you think I wouldn't find out? Erayame was all too pleased to answer my question when I asked him why you weren't at the Tower." Xorion shrugged while smirking at me. "We decided to pay a visit."

"We?" Just as I asked, another Fehichen male walked around the corner.

Like Xorion, he also looked very physically strong. His shirt hung low, revealing dark gray, almost black flakes of patterns around his neck. His eyes were identical with only a few more copper flakes within them. His hair was long, and straight, hanging down his back and sides of his face, a dark bluish color. I'd never seen anyone with dark bluish hair. I wondered if it was natural. Then again, he was from the Forbidden Region, who knew what kinds of genetic mutations they had.

"My Friend, Cedric." He introduced. I gave him a slight nod of my head in acknowledgement.

"Cloverlyne." I introduced myself. He smiled brightly and bowed low. As he rose, he gave Xorion a quick glance, even going as far as crossing his arms smugly.

"Now I know why Xorion was all too eager to journey here." He said in a husky voice, his eyes looking me up and down. I raised an eyebrow at Xorion who happened to have a fit of coughs at that exact moment. He sent a frown towards his friend.

"I hope your journey here was a pleasant one." I commented dully, changing the subject. Xorion opened his mouth to reply, but Cedric beat him to it.

"We certainly did!" He flashed his bright, sharp, white teeth, causing me to crack a small smile. Xorion pressed his lips together before giving me an awkward smile. "It was rather exciting really, evading the guards, sneaking past the Towers gate..." Cedric continued on with a sly smile. I took a step back, shocked that he would openly admit they did such a thing. At my bewildered expression, he laughed. "One of the guards actually tried to halt us, which was an unfortunate thing to do on his part..."

I narrowed my eyes at his words and prayed to God above that he was joking.

"Xorion, is this the truth?" I demanded, not being amused in the slightest. I didn't expect him to be so foolish, it had to be a joke.

"Well...." He stammered out as if unsure about what to say. "It isn't entirely untrue..."

"What?" I groaned out.

How was I supposed to explain this to the Elders? Who knew what rumors already spread because they'd simply asked about me. Realmers were not very trusting. They feared the worst when it came to outsiders. My position as a council member meant that they could use me for ransom if they wanted to. What in Natarah were they thinking of sneaking out to come here without an escort?

"You seem surprised, I will explain. It's traditional, on our planet, to pay unannounced visits to the ones we pursue. In our culture it shows our commitment to them." Cedric said while grinning at Xorion, who reached over to punch his friend's arm... hard.

"Ow... What?" Cedric grabbed his arm dramatically, playfully looking heartbroken by his friend's actions. Xorion's face flushed, his worried eyes darting everywhere but mine. Cedric glanced at me and his face fell when he saw the look on my face. He shifted nervously. I could hardly wonder why. I'm sure my anger was written all over my face.

The idiotic fools! How could they even think of risking anything at such a crucial time!

As if it couldn't possibly get any worse than the situation already was, Leilani joined us, needing to tell me some untimely news.

"My Lady, you are receiving a call from the Towers... oh..." She cut herself off, surprised with the tension in the room. "It... can wait?" She questioned nervously, and her voice squeaked, knowing it was a bad time. I glared daggers at the two Fehichen males who kept their gazes lowered as if being apprehended by a parent.

"It most certainly will not." I whipped my head furiously around and walked out of the room. Leilani hesitantly trailed behind. Xorion and Cedric stayed next to the doorway, probably worried about making matters worse.

"I will take the call in the library office." I told Leilani, already halfway inside my office.

"Of course, my Lady." She stammered, hurrying to close the door behind me for privacy, but I figured it was mostly because she wanted to relieve herself from this situation altogether.

The green light flashed on my computer screen, signifying a call. My stomach churned with unease. I knew it was going to be about Xorion and Cedric coming here. I tried to relax my shoulders. It wasn't as if it were my fault, I couldn't control their actions. I just needed to come up with a convincing excuse for them. I clicked the green light, taking the call.

"Cloverlyne." The Elder's voice sounded distressed. I immediately started trying to explain before he could panic any more.

"Elder, I apologize in advance, they had no..." I stammered out an apology, but The High Elder cut me off abruptly, his voice full of fear.

"Child, they've come for us! They have their proof; a traitor is among us. They come to end us... all of us!"

A pain built up in my throat, unable to process his words. I started breathing heavily...

No... no, no, no... It wasn't possible. It could not be possible!

I began shaking, everything around me blurring.

"The war has begun."

I couldn't speak. The pain was building where my voice came from. A cold feeling overcame me, almost choking me. It was as if the entire galaxy had been turned upside down.

"I... I cannot fathom this." I hoarsely managed to whisper out at last. My fingers shook as I hit the button to end the call. The Union was coming here. To my home... to end us. I shouldn't be so affected by this; everyone knew it was going to happen eventually... but I still couldn't stop shaking. My throat dried completely. It was finally happening... the war we delayed for so many years. It had come, it was here. My knees suddenly became limp, and I slammed into the ground. I didn't even cry out. I couldn't even breathe properly. I just stared into emptiness as the room spun around me.

"Cloverlyne!" Someone shouted my name, but I couldn't process who it was. The figure seemed to have placed their arms around my shoulders, shaking me and fumbling out words that I couldn't understand. They lifted my chin to look into their worried, golden eyes.

"Xorion..." I managed to whisper out. Was it only a few minutes ago I was furious with him over such a trivial matter?

"Yes, I am here. I am here." He said quickly, his voice panicked. The room stopped spinning, letting me become aware of my surroundings once more, although I was still in a daze. I tried to calm myself down. I was in my library office, Xorion was here, rubbing my shoulder-

Wait, rubbing my shoulders?

I awkwardly tried to stand up. He reluctantly helped me, his eyes skeptical about letting me up.

"Are you sure you should rise? Perhaps you should drink something." I shook my head no, but he doesn't listen. Still holding my arm, he called out something in what I assumed was his native tongue.

Cedric, who I just noticed was standing at the door, gave a sharp nod, hurrying away.

"Here."

He pulled me over to a chair, gently urging me to sit. My thoughts drifted back to everything the Elder had told me. Free of my initial shock, I was able to process the information given. The Union was coming, someone gave them evidence of what we'd done, traveling to the Forbidden Regions and such. The question now was, who? There was clearly a traitor among us. My body went rigid. As much as I wanted to trust the Fehichen, I couldn't help but be wary of them now. I doubted they would do this, but I had to see their reactions.

Cedric returned with a glass of sweetened water, Leilani walking beside him worriedly as he handed me the glass. I took the cup from his hands and drank. After a few sips, I gave it back to him without a word.

They are coming, someone exposed us, they are coming... I could not let my people die.

"Cloverlyne?" Xorion asked in a weary voice. I took notice of my hands, clenched rather tightly in fists.

"I am fine, Xorion, thank you." I stood. "Leilani, I am being called back to the Towers, I will be leaving immediately. I want you to go stay with your family." I command leaving no room for question. Her face twisted in confusion, but she gave a curtsy to my order.

"Of course, my Lady. I will prepare for your departure promptly." At that, she left the room, leaving me alone with Cedric, and Xorion.

"Cloverlyne, should you be taking your leave so suddenly?" Xorion asked, not seeming to like the idea. I narrowed my eyes on him. It wasn't his place to question me. I needed to find a way to clear them from my suspicion before leaving.

"I must." I answered, eyeing him up and down suspiciously. How he reacted to the knowledge of the war would tell me if he was innocent or not or at least relieve some suspicion. He looked at me with a question in his eyes. Cedric tilted his head slightly in question as well. Both are no doubt curious about what could possibly have caused such a reaction out of me.

I sighed and decided to just get it over with. "Someone has given the Union the evidence they sought. They're coming for us, to end us."

Cedric paled at my words. "H-how is that... possible? How could someone-" He cut himself off, a dark expression coming over him. "Let them be damned, whoever would do such a deed." His fist clenched.

Xorion wasn't looking at me. He kept his eyes on the floor. My stomach clenched in worry. Had he known?

"Xorion?"

He tilted his head up. His eyes were burning in rage.

"Someone who knew about the trades with us exposed information to this Union group?" He stated, his voice shaking in his anger. I nodded slowly, carefully speaking my thoughts out loud.

"You are angry." I commented, somewhat relieved. I didn't expect an answer, but I got one anyway.

"Angry? I am beyond angry, Cloverlyne. I am furious." He paced back and forth before me. "The only ones who could possibly have evidence would've been someone who was trusted with that information. Someone is a traitor. Someone would allow their own damned self to give evidence to a group your people have clearly stated wants death, and for what? Power? Satisfaction?" His face twisted in disgust. "The very idea sickens me."

I cleared any suspicion about him from his words. His eyes... I could tell he was being truthful. Both of them were. He was right though, the very idea that someone who knew, someone who knew what they were and what they would do, and still handed them the only thing they needed, was sickening.

"Curse them to the place of eternal silence, A'kiro!" He practically yelled out. I was unsure what the last word meant, but from his tone, and with how Cedric raised a brow at him, it couldn't have been something pleasant.

"That's why I have to go. They will need everyone they can get to discuss our next move." I responded. They both nodded in agreement. "We will return with you; our people will need us as well."

Cedric turned and walked out of the room, but Xorion hesitated by my side.

"Are you sure you're okay, Cloverlyne?"

"Yes, Xorion. We must hurry to the Tower." I answered curtly. It was sweet of him to keep asking, but we had bigger things to worry about then my health.

"Then." He said while holding out his hand for me to take. "Let us hurry."

13

CHAPTER 12

Walking back into the Serenity Tower was painful. Xorion and Cedric didn't understand just how bad the situation was now. They knew, of course, that it was terrible that the war had officially begun, but they had no idea how little time we had. We were met at the door by an official who informed the three of us that the High Elder had called a meeting. Though I already knew the way to the meeting floor, the official still led us. It irritated me, but I supposed things were different now. No one could be trusted.

An uneasy feeling coiled in my stomach. No, they really had no idea how bad this was. It was interesting that both Xorion and Cedric were being called to the meeting as well. For the first time, I wondered who Xorion and his friend really were. I knew they had to, at the very least, be related to someone important to be invited.

The uneasy feeling continued despite me trying to distract myself, so I distracted myself by making conversation.

"It seems all of us will be attending this meeting." I said.

It wasn't a question, but I hoped they understood why I said it. I was only aware of them being warriors. Of course, as warriors, they should be made aware of the plans we would make, but I wanted more information than that. Both of them turned to each other hesitantly before answering me, confirming my theory.

"Normally, we wouldn't be needed for such things, but Aeis will want us to attend this meeting." Xorion answered vaguely. I notice his expression slightly darken and stood still for a moment, contemplating why he had that look before simply nodding. It wasn't my place to question their speakers' orders, and clearly, he didn't want to tell me.

I will have to look into it later...

Arriving in the meeting hall, we all sat around a half circular table. Aeis, Xorion, and Cydric sat representing the Fehichen on one side, five Elders sat in the middle, and me, Rain and Lucia sat on the other side. Aeis tapped his fingers on the table thoughtfully as the meeting began.

"We have only recently arrived. What information does our enemy know exactly? Will the warriors we brought with us be specifically targeted?" Aeis asked, learning back in his chair.

"I am afraid so, but we will do our best to divert their attention away from your warriors before they are ready." Elder Tallimos said, trying to comfort them.

"Divert their attention? You will only keep our warriors from proving ourselves against them." Xorion rose from his seat at the table. Aeis gave him a look, but Xorion was too busy locking eyes with the Elder. "Must we remind you that many worlds have been terrorized that we have sworn to defend! They take... children as slaves, they take resources and leave the poor to starve." Xoron shook his head, somehow looking much older than he was when speaking about those he cared about. "We're no longer fighting ghosts; we know our enemy now. Use us."

"What exactly is the current situation of your planet?" Aeis asked thoughtfully, motioning for Xorion to sit once more.

"Myan ships have closed around the border of our sector. They are waiting for the right time to strike." One of the other Elders answered for the High Elder, his voice hard.

"Our warriors are ready-" Cedric began but was cut off by the High Elder with a raise of his hand.

"That may be so. Unfortunately, even with your warriors, I fear the situation has become much worse." Xorion snorted at the Elder's words, dramatically waving his hand as if unbothered.

"Your enemies are surrounding you; how could it possibly get any worse?"

The Elder gave him a cold look.

"We have recently been informed the MioTamir Union has made a contract alliance with... Elnorsefall."

"What!" Me, Rain, and Lucia gasped out at the same time, earning raised brows from both Xorion and Cedric.

"This... It can't be." Rain said, slowly rising from his chair in disbelief. Elder Tallimos gave him a sad look, close to that of pity.

"But I'm afraid it is, Rain."

"Elnorsefall?" Xorion said slowly, as if testing the word on his tongue. "Another evil?"

"For now, both Elnorsefall and the Union attacking us together is only a possibility." Another Elder tried to explain, but Aeis' brows still wrinkled in confusion.

"What do you mean by possibility? I think it can safely be assumed they will attack your planet. Have they not allied for this very reason?"

"Alliances don't work like that in the Realms." I answered his question while fidgeting with my fingers, not bothering to look at him.

"Allow me to explain." Elder Tallimos said through a sigh. "Elnorsefall and the MioTamir Union are two different organizations. However, Elnorsefall is not in union with their entire planet, but the MioTamir Union is."

"And this means...?" Xorion asked, his tone almost sounding irritated which earned a glare from Aeis. The Elder leaned forward, folding his hands under his chin.

"It means that as allies, Elnorsefall can only assist the Union through providing currency, food, and weapons, but can't engage with them in war... Unless they give a reason affiliated with their personal organization. Just as the Union has reason for attacking us by law of the Realms, Elnorsefall can use their alliance and claim they are assisting the Union for their own personal reason." Elder Tallimos paused, letting his words sink in. Aeis looked down thoughtfully before speaking.

"And do they have a reason?"

He looked around the room, his only answer being the lowering of our eyes. He crossed his arms, irritated by our lack of answer. "Do they have a reason to attack your planet?"

The High Elder placed his hands flat on the table and straightens his posture.

"Long ago we gave refuge to three children of V'rasór, the birthplace of Elnorsefall. They will use this as a reason to attack us."

"But only if the children are still on the planet during the attack." Another Elder added.

"Why would this Elnorsefall want these children?" Cedric asked curiously, leaning closer.

"Because these children were royalty. In order to claim planetary rule, the royal families had to be killed off, and in order for the Emperor of Elnorsefall to establish a right to the throne, he needed his own heirs and heiresses dead." Elder Tallimos words made me feel so much smaller than I was. I wondered what they would think of such a crisis. I glance up to see Xorion's face twist into disgust for the second time today.

He seethed in anger. "A father killing his own children for the throne?" All three of them looked very disturbed by the idea.

"If you send these children away, Elnorsefall will go after them. They will seek to kill them once and for all, and V'rasór will have no means of a future." Rain said quietly. Although he kept his emotions out of his words, he still stared into the Elders eyes almost painfully.

"We have done all we can for them. If they remain here, we won't stand a chance. Not against Elnorsefall." The Elder crossed his arms without an ounce of compassion. A sharp pain shot through my heart. His words hurt, even if they were true.

Xorion scowled at him. "There must be another way. You can't be thinking of casting children from the home they've built on your planet, it's not-"

"The children will leave this world. It is the only way to ensure Eurkxo's safety against Elnorsefall." I said, cutting him off. Xorion stares at me, disbelief stretching across his face. He looked down and clenched his fists. Even Aeis frowned deeply at my words.

"We will not accept handing off your people to this Elnorsefall for your own protection." Aeis said finally. He glared around the room, leaving no room for argument. One of the Elders glared back at him, not appreciating his tone.

"They are not our people. They are V'rasórian royalty. Their place is to rule on their home planet."

Rain's eyes flashed in anger and the Fehichen started to stand in protest. Elder Tallimos raised a hand to silence the Elder that spoke such cruel words but made no move to deny it.

"I hate to have to explain this bluntly, but I am afraid they are not our problem anymore. We must protect our planet first."

"The children will understand." I responded before anyone else could. Rain and Lucia gave me a defeated look, but didn't contradict my words. There was nothing we could do anyway. The Elders had already decided.

The Fehichen stared at me, shock evident in their faces. My eyes fell on Xorion as he stared daggers into my soul. It was the first time I felt his anger being directed at me. I didn't enjoy the feeling at all.

He pushed his char back, standing fully. "Understand? You chose to protect them! Now you choose to cast them from your world just because it isn't convenient for you?"

"The Elders are making the right call, Xorion." I said, trying to de-escalate the situation, but it seemed I only made it worse as Xorion slammed his fists on the table. Cedric raised an eyebrow at his friend, but Xorion didn't seem to care as he kept his eyes locked on mine.

Aeis rose from his seat as well, although more calmly than Xorion had. "If we can't change your minds, then we ask this. Allow us to offer our protection to these children. We three offer ourselves to protect the three children you will send away." He declared.

"You would do this?" Lucia asked softly, speaking for the first time since the meeting started. Aeis looked at her and gave a tight nod. Rain shrugged his shoulders, leaning back lazily into his chair.

"I suppose we should go pack our things then."

Aeis tilted his head at Rain, surprised.

"Why would you-"

Elder Tallimos smiled tightly, choosing to rise from his seat as well.

"I suppose since you so boldly offered yourselves to protect the children, we must introduce you to them officially. Cloverlyne, Rain, Lucia, perhaps you would like to personally reintroduce yourselves to your new guards?" Silence fell over the room as the information sunk in. Aeis was the first to find his voice.

"You three... you are the refugees?" We nodded at his question. Xorion gaze morphed from anger to astonishment as he looked over me as if seeing me for the first time.

"Your... royalty?" He asked no one in particular. One of the Elders chose to answer him anyway.

"Both Lucia and Cloverlyne are crowned royals themselves."

Aeis frowned, "Crowned royals?"

"It means they inherit the throne by V'rasórion law." The same Elder answered again. Aeis glanced at us, his frown deepening as if to ask us if it was true. Rain nodded stiffly in response.

"Rain and Cloverlyne are of blood-born relation to the self-appointed Emperor of Elnorsefall himself." The High Elder said carefully, dipping his head our way.

I looked away, not wanting to show my anger towards the High Elder for revealing that. More silence followed at the revelation of our birth. I glanced up and see Xorion's eyes narrow further at the Elder. He turned his head to me sharply.

"The creator of Elnorsefall is your... father?" He exclaimed as he shook his head in disbelief, "Your royalty," he whispered quietly to himself once more. I bristled at his words, even if they were true.

I narrowed my eyes "He is no father of mine."

"He is of your same blood. Who is he to you then?" Cedric asked stupidly. Even Xorion and Aeis gave him a look at his question.

"Being of the same blood does not earn him the title, father." I stood so fast that the chair I was sitting in slid back with the force. The anger burning through me was surprising, but then again, there weren't many who said such things to my face.

The Elder braced his hands at his sides "This matter is no longer the concern of Eurkxo." He gave a slight wave of his hand, and I sat back down slowly at the silent command.

Rain shook his head through a sigh "The Custodian Emperor would want us to return to V'rasór. It may not be a current issue to Eurkxo, but it is the concern of our origin planet, and you know that means it will concern the entire Realms soon enough."

"He may want that, but he will not be able to deal with both his enemies and royals. You should evade his attempts to bring you in if he sends any. I will acknowledge your statement as well, Rain. If you die, it will certainly concern us. We hope you will remain safe." The High Elder words would've seemed more caring if he hadn't just ordered us off our home world.

Like you didn't just send us away so eagerly...

I thought bitterly. Another Elder threw in a comment on the subject.

"V'rasór is the center planet which holds the Realms together. If it goes..." He trailed off, but we all knew the unspoken words.

We all go.

Aeis sighed as well and took a deep breath in and out.

"I believe we have other matters to address." He nodded to himself.

"Yes, there is the issue about a traitor being among us." Cedric said, voicing Aeis thoughts. He tried to sound calm, but it was noticeable that he was greatly disturbed. They all were.

"The only ones who would have that information would be the Rectifier crew and the Elders." Lucia said, speaking softly. She hesitantly looked at Aeis. "...and your own people." Aeis tensed at the accusation.

"Believe me when I say, my people would never give that information away. Nor would we allow the information to be stolen in the first place!" Aeis accused back, anger filling his eyes. All the Realmers around the room glared at his own accusation but ignored his comment.

"How can you possibly be that confident?" Rain asked instead. He leaned back in his chair and crossed his arms suspiciously. I asked the same question to myself. Even if Aeis didn't believe his people would do such a thing, there was always a possibility. Yet he spoke with such confidence that it was not them.

Aeis hesitated, conflicted whether or not he should tell us. "We..." He sighed. "Some of us possess the ability to... influence our people."

We narrowed our eyes at the three of them. I specifically tilted my head at Xorion, who just shrugged calmly as if he figured this information would be exposed eventually.

"What do you mean by influence...?" Lucia asked curiously.

"Some can influence our people for the common good of all. Keeping them from stating that which is not to be said or that which is not to be done." All of us glanced at each other, disturbed by the idea.

How controlling...

"It is very rare for those to be born with the gift. Those who have it are trained to use this only for the good of all." Aeis was so confident in his words I almost believed him fully. "A dangerous gift, but we trust them dearly. They would die before they used it for something other than good." He was proud, proud that he could trust his people.

I tried to imagine the power that that being would have to influence people's decisions, and didn't think I could ever fully trust them.

Xorion was looking at me with a curious expression, and I was tempted to tilt my head at him and question why he looked at me like that.

The High Elder frowned, "We must assume anyone can relay information to our enemies."

"I trust my crew." Rain said, crossing his arms at the Elder.

"But I can no longer." The High Elder retorted back. "Any information given in this room is considered confidential. Punishment of immediate death."

We all went still. It was one of the highest forms of punishment, on Eurkxo anyway.

Elder Tallimos eyed the three Fehichen. "You should separate with the Royals now and leave immediately before anyone can find out. Travel separately and tell no one where you will go." Aeis swallowd, suddenly looking nervous.

"This galaxy is unknown to us. We wouldn't know where to go. It might be better for us to stay together." He said worridly.

"Out of the question. The moment it's known who was in this meeting room is the moment they will be after you. You will each travel with one of the royals. They will be your guide through the Realms." He bowed his head towards us.

"Aeis will go with me." Rain said immediately. I raised a brow at my brother's claim over Aeis. I wondered if the two got along better than I had thought. Perhaps they would become friends.

Me and Lucia looked at each other and then at the two remaining Fehichen.

Xorion calmly stood and smiled at me. "Would you care to join me, Cloverlyne?"

My mouth twitched into a smile, and I nodded. This would prove to be quite interesting.

"I suppose that leaves me with the beautiful Lucia." Cedric said with a grin, walking over to her. Lucia smiled shyly and bowed her head in greeting. Much to my surprise, he offered her his arm, and in an even bigger surprise, she took it.

I turned to Xorion. "We should arrange routes as soon as possible." I told him, mostly to distract me from teasing Lucia.

"Too bad we can't travel to my home world." He sighed, "There's always places to hide there."

"Travel well, Royals, Fehichens." The Elders nodded to us. Rain walked over to Xorion with a blank expression only to turn into a sigh upon his approach.

"Take care of her." He said, lifting his arm to Xorion's chest, a symbol of trust and goodbye. Xorion hesitates as he lifts his arm. He had never done such a gesture before, but only after some hesitation he placed his arm on my brother's chest, pressing into him.

"It is my honor as a warrior to protect your sister." He said proudly, and I suddenly felt safer with him by my side. Rain nodded, putting his trust in the warrior. "No harm will befall her while I continue to have breath in my lungs."

14

—·—

CHAPTER 13

I would get sick if I kept sitting at this desk any longer. In fact, I already felt queasy. I'd spent over four hours planning routes, but there were just too many variables to consider. Being forced to leave Eurkxo was devastating. If Eurkxo weren't about to be attacked, it would have been the perfect place to hide.

My first idea was to travel to the planet, Láuran, but within minutes of researching its cities, I quickly dismissed the planet. With so many islands, it would've been a nice place to lay low. Each island only had a small population, so we'd avoid attention. Unfortunately, Láuran had no defenses and would end up in great danger if the Union thought they were hiding us on their planet. Also, the planet was not known for its space travel. We'd end up being stranded on the sandy beaches forever. It would also be a poor choice to drag them into our problems. They hated conflict and be more likely to hand us over to Elnorsefall themselves to avoid any.

I shook my head at the thought. No, Láuran was not the place we would hide. My second thought was D'thaya. A planet with jungles so thick you couldn't see the sun. It would've been the perfect place to hide... If the locals were even half civilized.

Ovidōians were devious beings. They were incredibly manipulative, always getting what they wanted. The Echloi weren't much better either. They were untrustworthy, and secretive. We'd have to watch out for both Elnorsefall and the locals. As for the planet Ardiamus... Well, the minute the war was announced the Knights of Kingsemcore would definitely refuse to give us refuge, and if we were discovered it would only make things more complicated. It wasn't like my people were on bad terms with them. Actually, we had quite a decent relationship, but they were smart. If they found us on their planet, they would use us as leverage against Elnorsefall, or worse, hand us over to the custody of the Custodian Emperor.

I let out a deep sigh, holding my head in my hands. This was becoming increasingly more difficult by the second. A throbbing headache nagged my thoughts, and I bit back a muffled scream of frustration. The feel of hands on my back rubbing up and down caused me to gasp out in surprise.

"Shhh..." The voice said. "You work yourself too hard. Relax." My mouth twitched into a smile when I realized who it was.

"Xorion." I sighed, "I-" He cut me off abruptly.

"No, I won't allow you to work yourself to exhaustion this way. I promised your brother I would take care of you." He scolded.

I sighed again. He was really taking his new job of watching over me very seriously. I wasn't sure if I liked it or not, but I didn't want it to stop either. I guess I liked the attention, even if it was annoying.

"I can't rest now, Xorion. I can't find a suitable place for us to lay low... I'm worried." I rubbed my head with my hand, continuing to sigh softly. He paused rubbing my back as he thought.

"It should be a place where many ways of escape are possible." He tilted his head thoughtfully. "...and it should have many different species so we can blend in with the diversity. A place... where they will be unable to directly attack."

My eyes widened with a sudden idea.

"Wait a minute!" I exclaimed. "The Cleopa is in flight! I had only thought of it now when you mentioned a place they would be unable to directly attack!" I was surprised I didn't think of it before.

"What is Cleopa?" His brows furrowed at the unfamiliar word.

"A space traveling cruise ship known as The Cleopa." I explained excitedly. "It travels around the Realms, sometimes even entering your galaxy, but only on the edge for sightseeing. Many go there for... pleasure. It's the most popular resting point for enjoyment and vacation."

"Vacation aboard a spaceship? Seems like our type." He joked, and I saw the ghost of a smirk on his face. I smiled thoughtfully.

"It's definitely a sight to behold."

Memories of the bright lights and exotic music fill my mind. I'd only been there when I was very young, but just those few days had been embedded into my memories. My smiled tightened knowing we could not stay there forever, but at least we could stay there long enough to stay off Elnorsefall's radar until we found a better place to go.

Xorion placed his hand on my shoulder and gave it a reassuring squeeze. "We will be fine, Clove. You don't need to worry so much. I won't allow anything to happen to us no matter what happens."

I felt comforted by his words, and I reached up to touch his hand that was on my shoulder. A fluttering feeling in my stomach came over me. I enjoyed the warmth he gave off.

I frowned. Was I developing feelings for Xorion? I searched my emotions. I felt warmth, but that was it... nothing more. It would be nice to enjoy his warmth and the way he looked at me. I suppose it could be just a bit of fun, and why would I refuse such a nice feeling? If he wanted to give his warmth to me, I was okay with that. There was no harm in it.

I turned my head to meet his eyes, and we stared at each other for a few minutes. His other hand brushed the side of my face moving some loose hair with his thumb as he tilted my chin up. He leaned in slightly and I let him, wanting him closer.

"Clove..." He whispered. "I-"

"Entrance engaged, clearing computer information."

We both abruptly turned towards the doorway only to be surprised by Adam standing there, staring at Xorion with a menacing scowl on his face.

"What'er be going on 'ere? Am I'er interrupting somthin'?" Adam grunted out, looking back and forth between us.

"Yes, we were going over our arrangements together." He stressed the word 'together' as he smiled in the most suggestive way ever as Adams' face tightened.

I frowned at Xorion, but he didn't seem to take notice.

"Is that a problem?" Xorion asked, his grip on my shoulder tightening. Adam seemed to catch the gesture, narrowing his eyes at where his hand laid on my shoulder. I shifted uncomfortably and opened my mouth to ask Adam what he was doing here but stopped when he spoke first.

"Nah, not'r in the least. What'er be yer discussing ay?" He casually shrugged as he looked Xorion up and down with his signature smirk.

"I don't believe it's any of your business what we do while we are together." Xorion stepped closer to me. Adam's expression darkened, and his muscles stiffened as he took a threatening step forward.

"Enough, both of you!" I said suddenly, having seen enough of this ridiculous scene. Both males turned towards me surprised. I shifted away from Xorion. He frowned when I moved away, and I noticed Adam smile smugly.

"Adam..." I addressed him through a sigh. "The information we were discussing is confidential, you know this." I tipped my head at him. It wasn't a question. He should know not to question about such things. I turned apologetically towards Xorion.

"Would you mind stepping out for a moment? I believe Adam needs to speak to me."

Xorion's face tightened, but he nodded, leaving the room. I wait till the door closed behind him before turning my attention back to Adam.

"I don't understand why you dislike him so much." I shook my head. They were going to give me a worse headache than I already had. I would've thought the two would get along quite well... I supposed not now.

"I'er don't understand why yer don't! I'er don't trust 'em." Adam said darkly, his eyes lingering on where Xorion exited.

"Why? He's a good man... kind, thoughtful, and-"

"Hiding somethin'." Adam spat out, finishing my sentence with his own words. I shook my head dismissively.

"And what would he have to hide?"

"The exposure of 'er alliance or our travelin' into the Realms." He said matter-of-factly.

I narrowed my eyes on him. "His people would gain nothing from exposing us, and the notion has already been mused out." I shot back, letting him hear the irritation in my tone. I trusted them and couldn't see why Adam didn't.

He stepped closer to me, and I looked up at him with a tilt to my head. His eyes lingered on my shoulder, and he sighed with a blank expression I didn't understand.

What were his thoughts?

He placed his hands on my arms and looks down at me, his gaze softening.

"Be'a careful with him, Clove. He's hiding somthin', I'er knows the stance he is givin'. It is one whose motives 'er hidden... motives never to be known." Adam's expression was unreadable as he said the words.

"Don't worry about me, Adam. I'll be fine." I said, giving a reassuring smile.

"I'er knows the stance he is givin'"

I heard his words repeat in my mind.

What could he mean by that?

"Dont'er do 'dis Clove, please." Adam begged in a desperate voice. Sighing, I tried to explain to him without sounding above him.

"I've been ordered by the Elders, something not even I can deny. Adam, it is for my own, and Eurkxo's safety that we leave."

"At least'a tell me where I'er find yer... to protect yer-" I gently placed a hand on his chest, stopping his words.

"It's against protocol. You know that, Adam." I answered in a warning tone. Adam wasn't the type to always follow the laws and although I knew he could easily keep it a secret if I did tell him, I couldn't.

"Not'a even for me, ay?" He said bitterly as if knowing my thoughts. His hand reached out to hold mine where I had placed them against his chest.

"Adam..." I let out a short breath. "Why can't you trust me to take care of myself?"

"I'er don't want ye to feel as though you're being... pushed away-like you're the only one who can care for ye. You and Rain lived 'ere so long. This is y'er home, ye'er shouldn't be made to leave."

I forced my hand out of his grasp at his words, lifting them to hug myself. My eyes studied the floor, fixing on all its patterns. He lifted my chin with a finger to face him once more.

"Im'er here, Clove. Always will be." He dropped his hands and opened his arms to me. My eyes moistened, but I forced the tears not to fall. Instead, I threw myself into his arms, hugging him.

Yes, Adam was always there for me. He would never push me away. Adam is and will always be my brother. He is everything I wished Cronos could have been, for me.

After a few minutes, we separated. He gave me a soft smile and turned to leave, and I found myself smiling too.

I heard the noise of the door opening and turned to see Adam bumping past Xorion with a smirk. Xorion narrowed his gaze on him, his expression dark. He hurried over to me and searches my eyes.

"What did he want?" He frowned slightly at the word 'he'.

"He was simply being like any older brother, Xorion." I shrugged while giving him an exaggerated eye roll. "We have known each other for many years. He worries about me... especially with the war starting, and him being on the hunt for me and the other royals." I wrapped my arms around myself again.

Xorion nodded at my explanation before coming up to me and shockingly embracing me in a hug. I hesitated before returning his embrace.

"I will not let him hurt you." He leaned down and whispered into my ear. "I will always protect you. Trust my promise."

"I do trust you." I whispered quietly back to him. It wasn't the complete truth though. I trusted him, sure. But did I trust his promises? No. Not until he proved his promises could be trusted.

We embraced for a few more minutes until he finally stepped back, smiling down at me.

"We best be on our way, yes?" He said, offering me his arm. I smile and take it.

"Yes, let us take our leave immediately."

We made our way to the ship docking bay carefully not wanting to be seen. I chose a small ship that would take us the short distance to the Cleopa. From my research, it was currently in flight the sun, Gladis, which was the name of the star the three planets Eurkxo, Láuran, and Ardiamus orbited. It would only take a few hours to get there if we set the ship to full speed, which was good. The longer we were out in the open, the more dangerous it would be.

Even though I knew I was clearly the better pilot, Xorion insisted on flying. I got the impression he was trying to impress me, but some hours into the trip it seemed the ship and him didn't get along very well.

I glanced over at Xorion who sat in the pilot seat next to me. His face was wrinkled in displeasure and frustration as he glared at the controls. He had never flown one of our ships before and he was learning while we went. I stiffened a laugh as he fumbled around with the controls. He was actually doing pretty well for his first time flying our ships. They were known to be quite complex, especially when compared to ones flown in the Forbidden region.

The ship suddenly dipped, throwing us both forward. With a low growl, he quickly tried to steady it, but it seemed the computer had no idea what he wanted it to do. I placed my hand over my mouth to hide my laughter.

"You're confusing it." I teased, leaning over to look at the controls. He let out a huff of annoyance.

"I'm confusing it?" He shook his head. "It's making our lives miserable on purpose... stupid machines." He mumbled the last part, and I let out my laugh, not bothering to hide it anymore.

"Dear Natarah!" I continued to laugh softly. "Here, let me take co-pilot controls." I pressed the button which sends the co-contrals to my computer.

"You fly?" He asked, somewhat surprised.

"Adam taught me a little. I don't practice often though." I remembered Adam laughing hysterically as I'd fumbled around with the controls as Xorion was. He patiently taught me how to use my reflexes and my mind to pilot the ship, removing all other thoughts so I could focus on the task. It brought a smile to my face from the memories of that day.

"Ah." Xorion crossed his arms with a sigh. "Adam." I glanced over at him and smile sadly.

"He is one of our best pilots, you could learn alot from him. He's a good person and a good teacher." I suggested with a shrug, steading the ship as I speak.

"Nothing against him, he does seem like a good person it's just-" His voice trailed off with another sigh. He turned away, focusing on what's in front of him.

"It's just?" I urged him, wanting him to continue. I hated it when people just cut off what they were going to say. If it was important enough for them to mention it in the first place, then I wished they'd say it outright.

"Nothing." He said, waving it off.

"I can hardly believe it's nothing now." I raised an eyebrow at him. Why was he hiding his thoughts? He seemed to hate it when I did that.

He frowned, glancing at me before turning away again.

"I realize the two of you don't get along well right now, but in the future, I hope you'll perhaps become-" I paused, searching for the right words. Obviously, they wouldn't become good friends, but I just wished..."a bit more friendly?" I said finally, deciding on something close to the truth.

"Can't say it will happen soon, but... perhaps." He shrugged. I wanted to ask why they simply couldn't just get along, but I knew it wasn't my place to talk about it, so I remained silent. I really did want them to get along though. I enjoyed being with Xorion, but Adam was as close as a brother, and I didn't want to be in the middle of their scuffles.

"Entering Cleopa Sector"

The computer's voice said loudly, and we both turned to each other nervously. I had only been on The Cleopa once. That one time had been when Cleopa was used as a meeting point for all the planets in the Realms. From each sector people would come to congregate for the common good of the Realms, but that time was over and had been gone for over a decade. Now, it was more like an oasis in the desert. A place people could go to get away.

"How do you open the display screen?" Xorion asked excitedly. It would be his first time seeing a space city.

"There." I said while pointing to one of the buttons on his control panels. He gently reached over to press it. The display screen opens to reveal the incredible sight. The Cleopa had two huge engines in the front and back and a city in the center covered by a protective bubble shield. It was as magnificent as always.

"By eternity!" Xorion gasped, his eyes wide.

"Not what you expected?" I laughed at his expression.

"I knew the Realms was more advanced than us, but I could never imagine-" His mouth remained slightly parted as he gazed in awe at the sight. Traffic lines of ships came at every corner of the Cleopa, and lights shone around every angle gleaming like a beacon of hope in a dark galaxy.

"Take the ship down to the entering line over that way." I nodded towards one of the less crowded gateways.

"Right." He said, narrowing his eyes in concentration. He guided the ship down and eased into the line.

I leaned back in my chair and relaxed, closing my eyes. We had gotten here without any issues. It seemed The Cleopa was left unbothered by the Union. We were safe for the moment.

"Clove?" I heard him ask in a worried voice. He took in a sharp breath.

"What?" I opened my eyes suddenly, looking around to see what was wrong. I saw his arms raised questionable from the controls.

"I believe we are being scanned." He glanced nervously at me.

I sat up and took a look at the controls. Information flew through the screen, and a transmitting symbol appeared on the upper corner. I shuffled in my seat nervously but tried to remain calm.

It is only their protocol, Clove. Nothing to be alarmed about...

I thought, letting out a deep breath.

Besides, what would they even find that could be used against us? We had nothing that was of value... Besides myself, and Xorion...

I shook my head at my nervous thoughts. They would not find out who we were.

"They're probing us, finding out information. Making sure we are not a threat." I said calmly before giving him a sly smile. "Much like you did to me."

He rolled his eyes.

"Except I knew you wouldn't be a threat." He turned his body to face me and smiled. "And I enjoyed getting close to you." He said more quietly.

I nudged his shoulder with my hand, rolling my eyes back at him. He laughed lightly, continuing to give me quick glances.

Why did I do that? Completely out of character...

I turned my eyes away from him for some time, before giving him a quick glance after he went silent. His mouth tipped into a firm line.

By Natarah, what was it now?

I let out a sigh, a bit annoyed. Rather than asking what was troubling him, I looked away.

"Are we?" He asked suddenly after a few silent minutes. I turned and tilted my head to the side, confused.

"Are we what?"

"A threat?" He sighed at my confused expression. "To them." He jerked his chin towards the gate which we were about to hopefully enter.

I let out a soft huff, choosing not to answer right away. Leave it to him to ask the one thing that was tormenting me on the inside, but what else were we supposed to do? We were not safe anywhere. No one was, and the sooner everyone realized that the better.

But would it really be for the better?

"Right now, everyone is a threat." I said simply. I gave him a sad look. "We can't keep them from this war. People die, it is the way of life."

"But you want to." He pointed out. It wasn't a question. I looked away, trying to rid myself of any emotional attachment to the question.

"I try not to wish for the impossible, and neither should you. You'll only end up disappointed. It's not like our lives belong to us anyways..." As soon as the words slipped from my lips, I regretted them. I didn't believe them, not really. It was easier though, to pretend I didn't care.

He frowned at me. "I try not to let others rule my life as you do."

"What exactly are you trying to imply?" I asked, narrowing my eyes warningly.

He shrugged, not caring for my warning. "I'm implying that you have a voice that was destined to be heard, and you don't use it. It's pathetic the way you let them rule your life. Your royalty, aren't you? Why don't you stand up for yourself, for the other royals? Take a risk... say no? Force them to hear you." He shook his head as if he were disappointed in me. "You'd rather allow them to send you away from your home, letting yourself be driven by fear of your own father, your own flesh and blood."

My nostrils flared at his little speech.

"You-"

"What are you so afraid of? Is he not just one man? You are so much more than you make of yourself. You act like you're being held up with strings." He spat out with a humph of frustration, obviously saying what he thought to say all along.

I glared at him before turning to look straight ahead.

He has... no idea who he is and what he has done. Pathetic.

I clenched my fists.

Pathetic.

"What are you so afraid of?"

A tear escaped my eye.

He has no idea what fear is. Fear that was planted into you as a child. Fear that would never go away even though you always pushed it away, never feeling it, never thinking of it because it was always too painful to bear... Always running because I am too afraid to stop and see that he's all around me. Afraid of myself to become the very thing I was born of. No.

I thought wiping the tears away. I couldn't let his words get to me. Never.

We ended up being allowed to enter the Cleopa but were sent straight to our room without being given a chance to look around. Being a loud partying ship, the halls echoed in music and rapid chatter. As it turned out, Cleopa had a curfew for all new arrivals which was set into motion as soon as Eurkxo was threatened. They wanted to keep all their members accounted for. Unfortunately, we were only given one room with one washroom.

We stood awkwardly near the front of the room. At least it had two beds on each side and a table set with two chairs in between and a receiver set for entertainment.

"Clove..."

I heard Xorion say softly, but I chose to ignore him, moving away to one side of the room. I was still angry at him. Not because of what he said as much, but because when I really thought about it... he was right. I did allow the Elders to rule me, never fighting back from what they wanted. He had asked what I was so afraid of. I was afraid of becoming like my parents. Power hungry as my father was and vulnerable and naive as my mother.

"Clove."

I heard him say my name again, harsher this time. Before I could tell him to leave me alone, he grabbed my upper arm and spun me around to face him. I fought to release myself from his grip, but he was too strong for me without willing my phantasm.

"Will you at least hear me out?" He asked desperately.

I looked up at him, still glaring.

"Please?" He said softly. The desperation in his eyes got to me and I finally nodded and stopped fighting him. "Look, I'm sorry about what I said earlier. I was... afraid, about coming here and about having to leave my people. I took it out on you."

I looked away, not knowing what I could say to that.

"I don't want to lie to you and say that everything I said was just out of fear though. Some of what I said was true. I hated watching you let them send you away. Things like that are unheard of on my planet. You have a voice, let yourself be heard. Like right now. Speak to me, share your thoughts with me." He said, holding my shoulders firmly, forcing me to face him.

"I... can't." I answered softly.

"You can and you will." He demanded. His words surprised me. No one had ever been so demanding with me before. "Don't hide yourself away. Do not think that will protect you."

"Nothing can protect me!" I shouted angrily at him finally letting my boiled-up emotions take over. "I live my life submitting to others, acting as though I have power because that is how they want me to act. A leader others will think is strong, but not strong enough to overtake...No, not as my father did!" I looked at the ground, tears filled my eyes once more. I lifted my hand to wipe them away, but he stopped me.

"No, don't dry your tears. They make you stronger. Do not let anyone tell you that it is wrong to feel for yourself, that it is wrong to live for yourself."

"You have no idea-"

"No, I don't, so tell me." He urged, shaking me gently.

More tears spilled from my eyes, but for some reason there was a part of me that wanted to tell him. Tell him a short sad story. My story.

15

CHAPTER 14

I was often told how my mother was younger than most when she was crowned Empress. She was naive and childish. My grandfather was one of the Emperors of V'rasór at the time. I was told he was very protective over her. She was his only daughter, his heir to the throne, and he wanted only the best for her.

He allowed no men to see her and only allowed attendants to speak to her. Even when she was betrothed to Lucia's uncle, he only allowed him to visit her once. Even then she was not allowed to be alone with him. She was intelligent, but only in political matters. She was raised with little to no social skills. I remembered how she told the story to me as a child.

She would tell me, "A young dreamer, a genius of the empire, but a lowly common man. He lived near the palace, and while everyone feared my father's wrath, he bravely climbed the walls of my garden. I enjoyed playing in my garden which surrounded the palace gifted to me by my father and he dared to approach me when no one else had before. He watched me play for some time before finally speaking to me, and I was in love."

My mothers' advisors told me a different story though. The real one. My father, Zaphon Salvek Rehyemph, was a very ambitious young man. He was respected in his work, but his ambition led to his darker traits. My mother had never talked to a boy like my father before. He was charming, ambitious... bold, very different from herself. However, he was manipulative, and he wooed my mother easily. My mother was valuable to him, but not because he loved her. She loved him, I was told, but he only loved the status she gave him. She was the daughter of the Emperor, and she would become an important piece in his plot... A plot to proclaim his desires in front of the council.

My mother immediately asked my grandfather to let her marry him. Of course, the Emperor refused the marriage, but my father didn't take no for an answer. He convinced my mother to go against her father and run off with him for a little while. My mother knew nothing about what this meant for them, but my father knew that the scandal would force her father to accept them. He would have to agree to marriage in fear of embarrassment to the royal family. Once married, no one could deny them. Her father was forced to acknowledge the marriage, especially after my mother became pregnant. The only condition was that the children she would have with him, if any, would not rule in their own right. The only exception being if there were no other living heirs of the bloodline. Soon after, my mother became Empress after my grandfather died, and her first-born son, my eldest brother, was betrothed to the heir of Northern V'rasór, since he couldn't rule.

My parents had three children, Me, Cronos, and Rain. We lived in delusional happiness for many years, but every good thing comes to an end. Then again, was it ever a good thing? My father, with the permission of my mother, was able to have his first meeting with the council after years of waiting. He proposed outrageous ideas. It's said that in that room he proposed a one ruler over all V'rasór, a dictator. He claimed the council should be disbanded. He gave ideas of a hierarchy in which those who weren't pure Soaran's should be lower than those who were pure. He claimed that the powers of phantasm should not be for just anyone, but only for those who, by his standard, deserved it. His final words were that anyone who refused the hierarchy should be silenced.

When his ideas were rejected, it's said that he became like a furious dragon, yelling and screaming uncontrollably at the royals, and especially at the council. The council was furious with his ideas, and even my own mother, who attended this meeting, was shocked by his intentions. They banned him from further meetings forever. Outraged, my father threatened that he would force them to agree if he had too. The court didn't allow his words to go unchecked, and my father was imprisoned.

My mother couldn't live with his sentence. Blinded by her love for him, she begged them to release him, to have him banished instead. Because they didn't wish to deny the Empress's wishes, it was done.

Life continued and my eldest brother Cronos was destined to rule alongside the Empress of the North V'rasór as tradition. At age twelve, Rain renounced his claim to the throne desiring to become High Commander of the military. At nine years of age, I was too young to make a choice, and the council saw no reason to have me betrothed to another royal. I was still content to play with my dolls then.

It was during that time of peace my father returned despite his banishment. Cronos wasn't at our home when it happened, he was visiting the North, but me and Rain saw everything. He walked into our home as though he had never left. My mother had tears in her eyes as she ran to him, as if desperate for his touch. Me and Rain hid and watched them, wanting to give them some time alone before we ran to the man, we knew was our father.

We had no way of knowing who he really was, mother had only spoken of him as her love. Rain had to place his hand over my mouth to keep me from screaming when I saw him pierce my mother's flesh with a knife. I remember the blood seeping from her as he kissed her, keeping her from screaming as well. I watched her fall to the ground in a poodle of her own blood and I remember his words as he let her fall from his arms. ElnorseFall.

Xorion held me in his arms, shaking in anger as I finished my story. I looked up at him, tears streaming down my face.

"He named it after my mother." I choked out, closing my eyes as I let more tears fall. "After her fall. Every day I hear the words, and it rips me apart knowing the words are about her."

He tightened his grip, pulling me into a deeper embrace without saying a word.

"His soldiers came into our house after he killed her. He wanted us dead, his own children, because he feared we would threaten his claim to the throne."

The memory of his eyes turning our way after he viciously stabbed my mother and walked out our door, leaving her in a pool of her own blood filled my mind. He knew we watched the entire thing; he'd felt us in that room, and he'd smiled at us as if he were happy that his children witnessed his evil.

"Why would they allow him to be Emperor after this?" He spat out bitterly.

"They didn't allow him, it was law. When an Emperor or Empress marries, their spouse only has equal claim to the throne if their partner dies and if they have no children together." I whispered out as I tried to swallow the pain in my throat. "They didn't want to let such a man rule, but they had no way of fighting him. It was the law. He had gathered supporters who acknowledged him as Emperor. My mother was not the only royal targeted that day. Both Lucia's parents, and the Emperor of the Western Empire were assassinated at the same time. Anyone on the council was killed on sight." I let my head rest on his chest and held my hand to my heart. There was a pain throbbing there that wouldn't go away.

It hurt... it hurt so much...

"V'rasór was thrown into chaos, and he took advantage of that chaos to become an Emperor over my home world. The only one standing in his way of ruling the entire planet was my brother, the Custodian Emperor. He's the only royal on V'rasór known to still be alive." I couldn't help but let out a laugh despite the pain I felt. "And he isn't even from the North! It is why he is called the 'Custodian' Emperor, because he is standing in as Emperor after his betrothed, the true Empress of the North, was killed by my father's followers... like the rest."

"He is only one step away from being the one ruler of your planet." Xorion said, pulling away slightly. He looked me up and down as if wanting confirmation. Even though it wasn't a question, I nodded.

He tilted his head thoughtfully. "What about you and your brother, Rain? If he wants you dead, doesn't that mean that you can take his claim away? From what you said, he has no right to the throne since his children live."

I sighed at his question. He wasn't wrong. My mother being an Empress made me the first inline to the East now that there were no other heirs to the Eastern throne. However, proclaiming my claim would spite Zaphon. He would stop at nothing to kill me even if it meant turning V'rasór into a warzone. Rain, of course, denied his claim to the throne many years ago, before my father even returned, which made him incapable of inheriting the throne. We also had Lucia, and if either of us royals had a child, they would be the heir to the fourth throne of V'rasór, the West. I could do it, remove Zaphon from ruling due to him being of no royal blood, but he would descend hell upon all the Realms for it.

"Rain cannot rule because he has denied the throne..." I explain, "...And- Well, I was sent away for the very reason that Zaphon would do everything to make sure I don't take his place. I am that planet's last weapon against him." My voice went quiet. "Even if it means the massacre of everything that I love... and all to break me from even trying. Truthfully? I am already terrified to go against him. I have seen what happens to those that do."

"We can't allow him to win, Clove. He will be stopped, I promise you."

"You should not promise things that are impossible to achieve by me and you." I said with a scoff. He wasn't the first man to promise me that. It meant nothing.

He placed his finger over my lips. "It is not impossible, nothing is."

I remained silent, processing his words again. No matter how sweet the words were to hear, I didn't believe them, but before I could say so, he spoke again.

"I can't get over the strangeness of your people's ways... what kind of people slaughter their own blood and send their own away to protect themselves?" He asked, his eyes staring off past me.

I knew he wasn't just speaking about how I was sent away from Eurkxo, but how all the royals were also sent away from V'rasór to protect them from Elnorsefall as well. He seemed genuinely surprised by it and looked almost... disgusted that my people would do such a thing. I wondered what the reason behind his disgust was. What had he been taught that made him believe so differently?

"The royals are a liability. Elnorsefall doesn't care who dies in the process-" I tried to explain, but he cut me off angrily.

"To hell with this Elnorsefall! To kill one's own flesh and blood. It's... worse than monstrous! It's like something out of a nightmare!" His voice shook with anger.

I tried to calm him down by rubbing my hand up and down his back soothingly.

"Not such a common thing on your planet then?" I asked, wanting to know why it was bothering him so much. Sure, my father was a monster, and possibly something out of a nightmare, but there were plenty of people from the Realms who had family disputes that lead to their death. Mine just happened to be affecting the entire Realms because I was born into royalty.

Xorion looked at me with such a look of horror that I almost wanted to drop the subject entirely.

"Blood... against blood? Never! Never in all my life..." He cursed to himself. "Never even in my father's, father's lifetime has there been such a case. May the Great Soul strike down anyone who would even think to do such a thing!"

My eyes widened in surprise. How could it be such a disturbing thought to him? How could families have gone without such disputes? It was unnatural.

"Not even from the planet's your people protect?" I wondered out loud with a hint of envy. Surely not everyone in his galaxy was that peaceful?

I almost laughed at myself. Here I was trying to find the cruelty in his galaxy so I would feel better about my own. As if it was wrong that their world was so peaceful. Maybe I was just jealous?

Xorion looked at me with eyes full of pity and I shifted uncomfortably. I didn't want him to pity me, but how could he not if all I knew was war and chaos, and all he knew was peace?

He sighed, "Most of the planets in my galaxy are too busy trying to survive harsh winters rather than anger their gods with bloodshed. But... I've heard of such in stories, but that's all they ever were, stories. Never real, with someone..." He grabbed my hand and squeezed it tightly. "Never with someone I care deeply for."

I started to understand why he reacted the way he did even through my envy. It was like a nightmare coming to life for him. Things like this never happened in his world. He couldn't believe a world could be so cruel and it made him angry. I supposed I did like that. I liked that it made him angry, because it made me angry too.

Sucked into my own thoughts, I almost missed his next words, which surprised me even more than I already was.

"You know I love you... right?" He tipped his head downwards to look at me. My eyes widened in surprise.

He loves... me?

"You love me?" I asked out loud, not sure if he was being truthful. We hadn't even known each other very long, yet he claimed love? It was ridiculous.

"I've loved you since the moment my eyes first saw you. You walked into that room so graceful, curious... and alive. Yet you were in pain, and I wanted to... be there for you." He brought his hand to my cheek and gently stroked it. "You were the most beautiful being

I have ever seen." I knew my face was scrunched with confusion. He loved me. Love.

What was it really? This feeling that I have within me, it wasn't love. Perhaps I do care for him though...

I tried to push away from him, but he still held me with his other hand. We barely knew each other. I didn't even know how I felt about falling in love. After all, my mother fell in love. Everyone knew where that got her. Dead.

"I can't, Xorion. You have to understand..."

"Having feelings for me does not make you like your mother. I am not your father." He eyed me knowingly. "Hey..." He tilted my face towards him. "Look at me, you know what I am telling you is true."

"You were just probing me..." I murmured, my eyes darting away. He reached up and held my face with both his hands.

He once again tilted my face up, closer this time. "I meant everything I said in that room." His breath was warm against my forehead. I closed my eyes. "I have not once regretted saying yes to Aeis when he asked me to go to you." He dropped his voice to whisper. "Because I would never have been brave enough to walk up to someone as beautiful as you." He leaned closer. "Afraid I would lose the one thing I wanted..." I opened my eyes, and he stared longingly into mine, full of desire, and of... his declared love for me.

"You."

With those words still on his lips, he kissed me... and I kissed him back. His hands slipped from my face to hold the small of my back, and I moved my arms to wrap around his shoulders. He tilted my face, deepening the kiss. He kissed and kissed me, not letting me break away for air.

No one had ever kissed me like that before, so passionately. It was as if he was afraid I'd disappear. I'd kissed boys before, but most were more... innocent like. There were a few who were rougher with me when I let them be, but this was different, this was wild. Strangely, I found myself liking it. There was this need, a need to continue.

He sighed into me, pushing me back against the bed as he switched from kissing my lips viciously, to gently along my jaw. His other hand fell lower, squeezing around my waist, holding me close to him.

"I've wanted to do that since the moment I met you." He whispered in my ear, breathing heavily.

I didn't answer, not knowing what to say. Honestly, I hadn't thought of him in that way. I was attracted to him for good reason. He was handsome, and had an alluring personality, but that was all. However, within me, I felt a want, a need for his closeness like an insect attracted to a precious light.

He leaned back in to continue his attack, and I found myself leaning into him as well as my markings began to glow dimly in blue light. We started kissing again and he groaned and moved until he was fully on top of me, supporting his weight with his arms on either side of my head, and I held myself up by squeezing my grip around his neck. He started leaning down more, bending his elbows... closer and closer. My hands suddenly let go of his neck and moved down to the middle of his chest, stopping him from his descent. He lifted himself back up while both of us panted breathlessly.

He quickly sat up and looked away, his cheeks flushed. "I'm sorry, I shouldn't have-"

I smiled at his self-conscious expression while sitting up as well. My hand slid to his cheek and tilted his face to look at me before leaning in and kissing him gently on the lips again. A more romantic kiss than before.

He closed his eyes. "That was..."

"I want this, Xorion..." I sighed against his lips before pulling away. "But you must remember that I'm V'rasórian royalty, not just anyone. I want to go about this the right way, not diving headfirst into something we can't come back from."

He was silent for a minute, before nodding. "I understand." He chuckled. "Got a bit carried away, didn't we?"

I laughed along with him. "Only a little."

I felt torn inside. I liked him a lot, but what he'd almost done... him, a mere citizen from a forbidden galaxy of all places, and I, a royal. I was going to have to be careful with this relationship. I cared for him enough to know I didn't want to hurt him. He needed to know that, and I'd rather voice the worries to him now rather than later.

"I just- I want to be honest with you, about my feelings..." I whispered, my other hand reaching out to grasp his.

"You do not love me... do you?" He asked, his hand clenching in mine. His face held a sad smile.

"I do... find you attractive and perhaps one day I could come to love you, but this is happening really fast and I-" I stammered out, but he quickly placed a finger over my lips to silence me.

"I am not upset, Clove. I expected as much. I will be honest too though; I will not let you go so easily. I will fight for you in the hope that you will one day return my love."

His words made my heart warm inside. Perhaps being with him wouldn't be such a bad idea. Was this, okay? Using him, without loving him? Xorion was kind, faithful, and passionate. For a moment, I knew that there was a strong possibility that I really could love him in a romantic way, but it was only for a moment. I nodded at his answer. I hoped he could see that I would be open to receiving his love at least.

Xorion continued sitting on the bed and I moved to lay on his thigh as he gently stroked my hair. After a few minutes of resting in each other's presence, I quickly sat up and he murmured a protest, but instead of acknowledging it, I tugged on his arm for us to rise.

"What are you doing?" He wondered out loud. I sent him a knowing smile, cocking my head to the side.

"Aren't you curious about The Cleopa?"

He immediately jumped up so fast that the release of weight on his side caused me to tumble over. I burst out laughing, and he bent down to hold me up, looking at me sheepishly. Giggling, I stood and took the arm which he offered me. Together we made our way out of the room.

The Cleopa's hallways were huge, filled with decorative metallic walls, and lights all around. Afraid of getting lost, we followed a few other couples who seemed to know where they were going. Not far along, the hall opened into a huge dome-like room. Many beings hurried around playing gambling games and drinking at the bar near the front.

Someone coughed near us, and we turned to see a seemingly elderly being that looked to be a cross between an Anari and some other species. With a jerk of his chin, he called us over. Xorion placed an arm around my shoulder protectively and looked at the being expectantly.

"Greetings to you." The man said. "I am called Solomon, at y'er service." he gave an elaborate bow. His eyes rested on me and his face relaxed into a smug smile. Xorion narrowed his eyes on him and gave him a bored look. Solomon chuckled loudly.

"Welcome to Cleopa!" He said, throwing his arms into the air. "Home to the biggest parties, best drinks from here to the next galaxy, and the prettiest of ladies!" he winked at me. "But it looks like you've got that covered, don't you son?"

Xorion grinned at him and rubbed my arm affectionately. "Most definitely." He looked around for a moment before questioning further. "Where would you suggest I take my woman?"

I felt my cheeks heat up and leaned into Xorion. Solomon smirked at us while resting his chin in his hands.

"My best opinion, young man, is over that way." He tilted his head to the far side of the room which was dimly lit and had brilliant lights of all colors. It also seemed to be where the main music source was coming from. Solomon shrugged, "That's where most of the couples are heading tonight." Xorion glanced over at me before nodding to him.

"Thanks for the advice."

Solomon rolled his eyes. "No worries young man, go out and enjoy your young selves." He made a shooing motion with his hands, and we obediently scurried off.

We watched as other beings around us danced and moved to the beat of the music while others played table games around the dancers and pumped their fists into the air when they won a bet. Many kept to themselves in groups, talking and laughing on the large couches. Above us was a walkway that was used to go from floor to floor. It was a truly incredible sight, even if I felt a bit out of place.

We finally made it to the far side of the room. The dimly lit section had a huge beam of light which was cast down from the top ceiling, but it was more than a beam of light. I was unsure of the scientific reasoning behind it, but the light was like a field that changed the gravity levels, but only within the light. It was beautiful. The swaying of colors shone in a violet tint, and it felt as if the music ran throughout your entire body. Couples of different species danced as they floated around in the misty purple, gray, and blue beams. They swayed and sang in all different languages to the music blasting.

"Now this, I am looking forward to!" Xorion grinned beside me, before taking my hand in his. "May I have this dance?" He asked, his eyes twinkled playfully in both amusement and hope. I batted my eyelashes at him childishly.

"You won't step on my toes, will you? I'm afraid you might not be able to keep up with me... I am quite the expert when it comes to dancing." I said sweetly, holding my hand just out of reach. He laughed at my joke.

"It's you who will not be able to keep up with me, but I accept the challenge." He grabbed my hand gently, tugging me over into the light. The minute he entered the beam, his legs began to float. He smiled and reached for my other hand.

"Come on, let us dance." He insisted, tugging me along.

I laughed and let myself move into the beams. Once in the beams, we floated higher. He moved his hand, placing it against my waist while placing the other held my hand softly. I place my other hand over his shoulder, and together we glided across the light, swaying to the beat of the music. His eyes were glued to mine as if they were daring me to look away. Not that he had to dare me, I didn't want to look away. He spun me around, again and again. After some time, he slipped his hand from mine, resting it on the small of my back. I moved my arms up and wrapped them around his neck. In this position, I had to look up just to see his face. He tilted his head down at me, smiling contently. We continued swaying together to the beat, enjoying each other's presence.

"By eternity..." He said softly.

I tilted my head at him, and he just smiled even brighter at me.

"I simply can't get over how beautiful you are."

I rolled my eyes but felt myself blush at his compliment.

"Truly." He insisted. I remained silent, still dancing, but content to just sway back and forth. Some kind of current began pulling us, along with other couples, down to the ground after some time. Before we reached the bottom, Xorion swooped me up. I gasped. He was carrying me bridal style. I raised an eyebrow at him.

"What are you doing?"

He tilted his head at me, grinning.

"What does it seem that I'm doing? I am carrying you."

"I can walk..." I mumbled, but didn't struggle against him.

He nodded, "I'm well aware of that, Clove, but I rather like carrying you."

I groaned in response but couldn't hide my smile. He chuckled, well aware that no matter how much I denied it, I did in fact enjoy it. He carried me all the way back to our room and laid me down on one of the beds before walking backwards before his legs hit the other bed.

"We should get some rest." Xorion said, staring at me intensely. I nodded in agreement. I knew I was still wearing my dress, but I was too tired to change, and it probably wouldn't be a good idea to undress in front of him with that look in his eyes. I closed my eyes.

A short rest would do me good, even if it wasn't the night cycle yet. Within minutes, I was asleep, but I was sure I heard him say goodnight, which made me smile. Darkness surrounded me, and suddenly I was back in the palace of V'rasór.

"Cloverlyne! Where are you?" I heard my mother call out.

"I'm here, I'm here!" I yelled out, running through the halls trying to find her. I turned a corner, and on the ground was my mother, blood pouring out from a wound on her stomach. Blood dripped from her open mouth as she spoke.

"You can't save me, Cloverlyne. You can't save anyone."

I awoke with a start, our only warning being the sound of sirens. Had it only been a few hours? What could've happened in such a short amount of time? Voices rose and the sound of feet shuffling in the halls caused panic to slowly come over me. We both sat up in our beds, seeming to have the same idea. It sounded like someone was attacking The Cleopa, but who? Xorion stood and hurried over to my side, grabbing my hand.

"Come on!" He said sharply before hurrying us out the door and into the hall which was overrun by people running everywhere.

Was it the Union? If it was, we might have a chance at escaping without any likely issues. As far as we were informed, they weren't searching for us. However, the more I thought about it, the more I knew the coincidence of the situation didn't add up. What were the chances the Cleopa would get attacked only a few hours after our arrival... as if they knew we would be here? The more I thought about it, the more I was certain it was true. We were the targets of this invasion.

We were pushed left and right, and someone shoved me trying to get past. I let out a painful yelp from the force of the shove. Xorion turned and mumbled a curse before pulling me forward to tuck me under his arm protectively. I moved a bit closer to him and hurried my pace. I was glad Xorion was shielding me. I didn't want to have to use my phantasm here. It would give us away too easily. Suddenly, we heard shouting from the other side of the hall. One voice rang out louder than the others.

"The 7th gate! They come from the 7th gate!" The being shouted, and panicked screaming could be heard everywhere at the new information. Moving faster, we shoved past terrified beings, all heading to their ships. I was becoming more worried with every scream around us.

Our ship was near the 7th gate...

"We'll make it." Xorion said as if he could hear my thoughts. I nodded even though he couldn't see me. We had to make it; it wasn't a question.

We hurried down the halls taking the back routes, but it was still very crowded with terrified beings. Turning a corner, I saw two heavily armored figures walking our way with guns. I tried to make out their affiliation but was unable to because of the crowd.

"A'kiro!" Xorion spat out. "Wilting Mother of E'arka! Can't we have had better luck?" He whispered angrily. I could only wonder what his words mean.

"We need to leave this area. Now." I urged desperately as I tugged against his arm. "More will come."

He nodded, but before moving he glanced around as if looking for something.

"What-" I was going to ask what he was looking for when he moved to step in front of two unknown beings who wore dark hooded cloaks. The beings stopped, fearing his piercing gaze.

"Give me your cloaks." He demanded with a fierce look.

"But..." They started to protest, but Xorion didn't let them.

"Now!" He shouted, and they quickly removed their cloaks and handed them to him. He turned back to me, allowing the terrified beings to be on their way.

Normally, I wouldn't approve of that kind of behavior, but this wasn't really the time for pleasant requests. Now wearing the cloaks, we hurried more comfortably towards our ship.

"Dear Natarah." I mumbled out as we quickly moved swiftly through the crowd. "Let us make it."

Our luck seemed to hold as we finally made it to our destination.

"We won't not ask for permission. We leave the moment we board our ship." Xorion said as he typed the sequence to open the door to where our ship was parked. I couldn't agree more.

"We'll travel to D'thaya, it's the best option right now." I stammered out, and he nodded quickly. We walked into the docking bay only to stop suddenly at the scene before us.

"Leaving so soon? How unfortunate. The Emperor was looking forward to such a lovely family reunion, Cloverlyne."

We froze. Before us were four guards all pointing their weapons at us. Seeing them this close I finally realized who dared to attack The Cleopa. Who could it only ever be?

ElnorseFall.

16

CHAPTER 15

How they knew we were on the Cleopa was a mystery. We'd told no one of our plans. Aside from ourselves, no one should've been aware of our presence aboard the space city... and to find us in such a short amount of time? It was as if they'd followed us from Eurkxo.

We were forced to board the Elnorsefall ship and placed into separate isolation cells. On the bright side, we were near each other and could still speak to one another. They'd only separated us by individual cells. The guard that brought us here forced a neutralizer around my neck which kept my phantasm from flowing through me as quickly as I was used to. I felt drained and had to focus on breathing normally. My body wasn't used to the heaviness of having lower levels of phantasm.

Xorion paced back and forth inside his isolation cell while I sat and watched him. I knew he was attempting to come up with some plan to escape, but it wouldn't be possible. I knew these ships. They were of V'rasórian warship design, specifically Elnorsefall warship design. According to usual protocol, our ship was likely already destroyed which meant we'd have to escape by taking over this ship, and in order to do that we'd have to capture and somehow bribe the pilot.

Pilots of warships were implanted with chips directly into their brains which allowed them to activate the control systems of their ships. Most were loyal to the bitter end, and even if they were disloyal and by some miracle wanted to help us, the commander of the ship could have the chip explode, instantly killing them.

I relaxed into the transparent wall of my cell. It was obvious we weren't going anywhere anytime soon.

"What will they do to us?" Xorion asked suddenly, stopping his pacing. I sighed at his question. It wasn't exactly something I wanted to think about.

"You won't like it, and it doesn't really matter if you know or not." I said in hopes he got the hint not to ask about it further. Unfortunately, he didn't get the hint.

"Perhaps not, but I'd rather know." His eyes burned into me. I groaned, wanting to ignore him. I guess he did have a right to know. If I were in his position, I'd probably ask the same.

"He will most likely order them to torture us for any information we carry. Then he will probably use you as an example to the other Fehichen who are still in the Realms fighting with Eurkxo." That wasn't even the bare minimum of what he was capable of doing, but there wasn't a need to tell Xorion that.

"I'm going to guess it's not something quick then." He placed his hands on his hips with a quick huff. I shook my head. He sighed in defeat.

"And you?"

Now that was a question I really didn't want to answer, let alone think about. However, I knew the imagination could often be worse than reality, so I forced myself to think about it and give him an answer.

"I- I don't know for certain. I've heard rumors about the experiments he does. He's been attempting to pull phantasm directly from our cores. It won't surprise me if he tries to do that on me, it's never been tested on a royal after all." I said as bravely as I could even though it was torture just to think about.

"Pull phantasm directly from your core?" He asked both bewildered and horrified. "Is that even possible?"

"Unfortunately, yes. There's only been records of it being done a few times for scientific and medical reasons, and all of them ended in the death of the subjects. It was banned from practice, but he's brought it back. I'm not sure why other than for pure entertainment." I shuddered at the thought. I remembered when the Elders first made us aware of his disgusting practices. It took everything in me to not become sick at the images of the battered bodies of those his scientists tortured and thrown out.

"As far as I'm aware none of his subjects have survived yet. I'll just be another one of his failed attempts. I read it's like ripping your heart out of your chest. Possible to be done, but..." I didn't even bother finishing the statement as my throat clenched. His expression darkened noticeably.

"How can you be so calm about this!?" He shouted at me, but his tone didn't even phase me.

"I'm trying not to panic, Xorion." I said calmly, my voice a mere whisper. The truth was, I was too scared to even imagine what it would be like having my phantasm drained from me. To die while having part of me ripped away? It terrified me. Like being cut to pieces bit by bit, but still alive. I knew he wouldn't waste the opportunity to attempt it on me, not when I was a young, powerful individual of royal descent.

"We're going to get out of here." Xorion seethed out, his voice trembling in anger. "I don't know how or when, but I will not allow him to hurt you. I will not!" He bangged his hands against the isolation shield.

I remained silent. What was there to be said? Give him false hope and say we would escape? Take his hope away and say we wouldn't? When it came down to it, this was always going to be my fate. I just wished it wouldn't have been Xorion's as well.

We heard the screeching sound of the door to the room opening, and an armored Soaran guard walked in, smirking at us.

"Does his Lordship wish to see us?" Xorion said mockingly as he spat on the ground.

"Nah, The Emperor has more diplomatic issues to handle then escorting you scum to his planet, V'rasór." The guard took out a knife from his belt and fiddled with it in his hands. He was probably attempting to intimidate us. Like we could be intimidated anymore then we were? We already knew we were going to die.

"V'rasór is not his." I hissed out angrily.

"All will be his." He sneered. "Even you, Keeper."

"What did he do to The Cleopa?" I dreaded the answer, but I had to find out. I only hoped for their sakes that Elnorsefall rushed out from their excitement at capturing a Forbidden one and royal. The guard laughed loudly and then looked at me pitifully,

"We left our signature, Keeper."

The thought sent a sickening gag up my throat. Their signature was death. Always, death.

"Didn't think we'd leave there without giving a proper hello now did you-"

The ship suddenly quivered, lurching us forward with the force. A loud alarm sounded above us so loud that I had to place my hands over my ears.

"What the-!" The guard said as he was thrown forward once again, falling flat on his face.

When I looked up, I noticed the isolation shield was flickering as if it was about to shut off. Xorion quickly took advantage of the flickering, and with one strong slam into it, it dissipated. He stumbled for a bit, surprised it actually worked. The guard looked up from the ground, his eyes widening. He lit his markings as he readied to use his phantasm to subdue us, but before he could even fully stand up, Xorion sent a powerful punch to his face. The guard stumbled back to the ground in a daze.

The ship quivered again, and both of them were thrown up against the wall.

"You will not escape!" The guard shouted angrily, spitting out blood from his mouth. "He will never let you go!"

"Save your breath soulless creature!" Xorion pounced on the guard, grabbing his neck to choke him. "You're going to need it."

I stood, about to scream at Xorion that he was making a mistake by pouncing on the guard, but before I could say anything, he was thrown across the room by the guards' phantasm.

"Xorion!" I shouted, but he didn't move from the ground.

"Worthless!" The guard spat out more blood dripping from his face. He used his phantasm to help lift himself off the ground. Raising his hands, he got ready to send a finishing blow of phantasm down on Xorion's limp body.

"No!" I shouted while releasing a blinding amount of phantasm from my body. Whatever was happening on the upper levels of the ship seemed to be affecting the cell's protocol systems down here as well. I bent my phantasm to my will, twisting it like the point of a sword, and struck him. The guard, unaware that the neutralizer had been disabled, screamed in agony as he fell to the ground. My phantasm continued to wrap around him, constricting him until he stopped twitching.

I swallowed hard as I looked at the guard laid on the floor. Had I killed him? My throat tightened at the thought. I stepped closer and noticed the soft rise and fall of his chest. It was faint, but he was alive. I thought I wouldn't care if I had to kill someone to protect myself, but I guess I did. I ran over to Xorion, who was laid out awkwardly on the ground.

Please let him be alive...

I thought as I gently shook him.

"Xorion, awaken!" I held his face in my hands, praying he would be okay. He let out a groan, and slowly opened his eyes. When he saw me, his eyes softened.

"I feel like I was hit with lightning." He moaned, closing his eyes again.

"Yes, it would feel like that. That was foolish! What were you thinking pouncing on him like that? With a Soaran of all species? Without any weapon that counteracts phantasm?" I scolded.

You never jumped in front of a Soaran without proper weapons or armor after they activated their energy. It was common sense. Jumping in front of them would allow our phantasm to make a direct hit to your brain, or worse, your heart. The best way to win was at a distance, where it had longer to travel and direct hits were rare.

"Yeah, I forgot about that rule which was explained in such great detail." He said sarcastically, forcing himself to stand.

It seemed he'd dodged just enough for the blow to only graze his side. At such close range, I was grateful he had such fast reflexes. If he didn't, he could've been killed. He placed a kiss on my forehead.

"I'm alright, Clove. It takes more than that to take me down. Wasn't ready for it, that's all."

"You could have died. Please be careful... please." I begged, keeping hold of his arm.

"Hey," he said, tilting my head upwards. "I'll be more careful, don't worry about me." I nodded, grateful for his reassurance.

Worry still ate at me though. That guard hadn't even hesitated to try and kill him, which meant they didn't need him alive, or rather, they may have already been given orders to have him killed. It was obvious the guard hadn't wanted to kill me, but Xorion?

I shook my head. This was going to get really dangerous for him. He walked over to the guard and took his gun from him.

"Let's find out what in eternity is happening on the upper levels." he said while grabbing my hand, his other hand holding the gun comfortably.

I nodded eagerly, "Agreed."

We hurriedly made our way out of the containment cell, and moved carefully through the ship halls, trying to avoid roaming soldiers. Something was clearly happening, it defiantly felt like the ship was being attacked. The ship continued quivering every so often as if it was being shot at, and the soldiers ran around in small squads.

At the end of the hall, we spotted a lift. We both glanced at each other, having the same thought. We might be able to get a hold of some kind of communication device somewhere on the upper levels, but before we could even touch the door to the lift, it opened to reveal three surprised soldiers. They wasted no time willing their phantasm to strike at us. I used my own phantasm to act as a shield, and without any hesitation, Xorion started firing the gun at them. He managed to get one, but the other two protect themselves. They threw powerful waves of phantasm meant to constrict our bodies, but Xorion managed to leap on top of me, throwing us to the ground to dodge it.

I threw my hands out from under him striking one of the soldiers in his right arm. Immediately, Xorion used the soldier's distraction to stand and run at him, sending a kick to his stomach. The soldier stumbled back but still managed to balance himself with his phantasm. His arms lifted high, ready to constrict phantasm around him. I stood to help Xorion, but the other soldier I'd struck down earlier threw his energy around me. I scarcely had time to process what was happening as I was thrown backwards, slamming into the wall.

I crossed my arms over my chest to protect myself from the hit. The way he conducted his phantasm was known as a power trial, and the only way out from the exchange of energy was to win. Fo the first time, I was sincerely grateful for all the training I'd been given at the Elder's request. It would probably save my life.

I yelped out as the soldier moved closer to me, his hands placed against each other, willing his energy forcefully over me. If I let him get too close, I would have no chance. I needed to get out of this defensive pose and go on offense. I focused all my energy to my heart, letting it protect me, and in a swift movement, I moved my arms away from my chest, spreading them out to my side allowing his energy to take its direct hit. The room blazed in light.

I had no way of knowing what happened to Xorion, but I knew I had to finish this soldier off. Grimacing in pain, I moved my hands together, gradually kneeling to the ground. As expected, the soldier came closer. I opened my arms with a jolt and create a shock wave, blasting the soldier to the other side of the hall. He hit his head hard and slid onto the ground. Whether he was unconscious or dead I didn't know, and I really didn't want to find out. I breathed in and out tiredly, needing a rest for a moment.

Strong arms grabbed my shoulders, and I jerk forward, fighting against the powerful grip thinking it was another one of the soldiers trying to restrain me.

"Clove, it's just me, calm down." I heard Xorion say, and I relaxed.

I turned my head to glance behind him curiously. The soldier he fought laid in a bloody pool on the ground. My eyes widened at the sight. It wasn't often you saw a Soaran crumbled on the floor, bruised and bloodied. It seemed Xorion found a way to fight around our phantasm, or more likely, the soldier had underestimated him.

"Are you okay?" he asked as he gently lifted me up by my arms.

"Yes." I nodded towards the lift. "We have to continue."

We quickly got inside and moved to the upper levels. Once at the top, we exited and continued down a new hallway. Halfway through the hall, I noticed a figure up ahead. I quickly motioned for Xorion to halt.

"Someone's coming." I whispered. He nodded, taking out his weapon. The figure was hooded, and stopped some ways from us, their arms crossed in front of them.

The figure lifted an arm to point towards me. "I believe I should thank you, for taking care of what's mine." The figure said in a robotic voice.

Xorion moved to stand in front of me. "You're mistaken, she's mine." he hissed out. I looked up at him, surprised. What in all Natarah's power did he mean by his? The figure tilted their head,

"Oh? And what's the meaning of this?"

"The holder of my heart. Mine to defend, and mine to protect." Xorion said as he aimed his weapon at the figure.

I gave a small smile. So, I was the holder of his heart? He loved me and would protect me, even if I didn't love him back. The figure took a step back as if surprised.

"Try and take her, and I'll hunt you down here and in the next life." Xorion growled out as he took a threatening step towards them.

"Does she feel the same?" The figure asked softly. I stared between the two of them for a moment, not sure what to make of the scene before me.

"You're not from ElnorseFall." I concluded out loud. If they were, they would've attacked by now, and certainly wouldn't have the patience to ask such a strange question.

"Answer the question and I will answer yours." The figure retorted back stubbornly. Xorion's body tensed in front of me, even though he knew my feelings.

Wonderful.

I sighed, deciding to choose my words carefully.

"I'm the holder of his heart, and I trust him with mine." Not necessarily a dismissal of the question, but not an 'I love him' either.

The figure stared at me for a long time behind their mask as if searching my soul for the truth. I stared back. Something was familiar about their stance. Suddenly, the silent spell was broken by an explosion down the hall. All three of us turned to see seven

Elnorsefall soldiers hurrying at us, markings blazing, and weapons in hand.

The figure spared no time creating a shield which was instantly fired upon by phantasm strikes. The moment they released their phantasm, I felt a presence that was intensely familiar to me, but it couldn't be...

"I fight alongside you!" The figure said, leaping back to stand with us. They took out a small shock gun from under their cloak, and threw it to Xorion, who caught it with ease.

"Clove, take the front, I can't shield both of you!" The figure said while throwing off his cloak and mask revealing who they were. I gasped out in astonishment.

"Rain!" How could he be here? How did he even know?

"I'll explain later, we have to survive this!"

Phantasm waves attacked from every angle. I released small, but sharp thrusts of phantasm, acting on mostly defense, while Xorion used the gun to fire shock beams at them. With the number of lights flashing around from phantasm, it was quickly becoming difficult to process what was happening.

"Smite on your left!"

I heard Rain's voice shout out. I did as he said, trusting his judgment. Turning, I saw a soldier who apparently found a way around my shield when I was distracted. He was forming a spin attack of phantasm.

My hand shot forward, my middle and pointer fingers facing up, thumb to the side allowing my phantasm to shoot out from my fingers sharply. I kept my other hand close to my chest to protect my heart. Seeing my now offensive stance, the soldier sent his spin attack forward. Acting fast, I pulled my hand in and will my phantasm to constrict around his spinning phantasm. With my other hand, I pulled any extra phantasm from around me and threw it at his neck. The soldier screamed out, but I held fast, my phantasm strangling him. Out of the corner of my eye I noticed Xorion becoming over-whelmed by four of the soldiers who were targeting him.

He needs help!

I thought desperately.

They're targeting him, he can't take them all alone!

I tried to find Rain, hoping he could help. The two of them should be able to take down the soldiers.

Suddenly, piercing phantasm waves threw me into the ground. I groaned, my vision blurry. More light flashed around me as the phantasm took hold around my lungs.

I can't breathe!

In a panicked yelp I counterattacked it with a sudden surge of sharp phantasm, like a knife cutting through a surface, forcing it off of me. It seemed my phantasm was by far more powerful than theirs. The soldier noticed, and angrily pounced on me, trying to tackle me into the floor. He took out a knife and aimed to pierce my neck.

I used my phantasm to protect myself by sending an opposite force against his knife, but he countered it with his own phantasm. Exhaustion was overtaking me; I didn't think I could continue much longer. My vision started to fade as I lost focus.

I don't want to die... I don't want to die...

My eyes opened wide as the soldier was suddenly thrown off me. Rain was there, blood seeping from a wound on his shoulder, drip-ping onto the floor. He looked down at me, his face full of concern. He leaned down and lifted me up with one arm, his wounded one staying stiffly by his side.

"Good?" He asked, not looking at me, but rather at the dead soldiers around.

"I-" I stopped when I saw Xorion's body lying on the ground next to four dead soldiers. "Xorion!" I yelled, hurrying to his side. "Xorion! Dear Natarah! What happened?' I asked Rain desperately as I held Xorion's hand trying to find a pulse, but it was quiet.

"They keep targeting him because he is from the Forbidden Region. Elnorsefall wants them all dead." He said a little too calmly for my liking. I put my ear to his chest, but to my dismay, I heard nothing.

"His heart doesn't beat! Rain I can't feel his heart beating!" I cried out, tears falling from my eyes.

Rain immediately pushed me to the side, holding his uninjured hand over Xorion's chest. He forced his phantasm to surround Xorion's heart, circling around it and forcing it to beat. It was a gift he managed to master where I could never. Sweat quickly started to drip from his forehead as his body trembled from the strain of phantasm.

"I can't keep this up for long." He gritted out painfully. "We need to get him to a med bay."

"We'll never make it in this state with all the soldiers." I said, shaking my head in despair.

"We will, I believe these soldiers were the last wave that tried to escape them." Rain said as he tried to lift Xorion up while keeping his heart beating. He failed miserably. I froze at his words.

"Them?" I asked, confused.

Who was it that attacked an Elnorsefall transport ship?

"Us."

I whipped my head around to see more soldiers standing at the end of the hall, but not the ones from before. These soldiers' armor had different symbols, not the symbols of Elnorsefall, but of-

It couldn't be...

"The Custodian Emperor sent them." Rain whispered stiffly. I paled.

What did you want with us Cronos? What did you benefit from this?

It seemed our time to return to V'rasór had finally come.

17

— • —

CHAPTER 16

It had been a few days since we were forced onto the V'rasórian mothership under the orders of the Custodian Emperor. Rain's shoulder was completely healed now, thanks to the medics aboard the ship who quickened the healing process through a precise phantasm manipulation.

It was a manipulation of phantasm that could only be learned on the planet, Láuran, and was very difficult for outsiders to master. Much to my irritation, the medics were reluctant to help Xorion in the same way. Rain managed to convince them by telling the commander of the ship a more elaborate tale of our relationship, and I regretted saying anything to him at all. I would be lucky if they even let him look at me after Rain's speech about how much he disapproved of our relationship, which the Custodian's Emperor's most trusted advisor was very interested to hear about. Not that the advisor believed Rain's tale of our love story. He assumed I'd obligated Xorion to be at my side. I was sure they knew I had no real love for him, and further thought I would never.

For some reason, that assumption made me angry. Just because I didn't love him now didn't mean I wouldn't love him later, and even if I didn't, it wasn't any of their business. I'm sure they thought they could convince me to have a relationship with some elite Soaran, but I doubted they knew how stubborn I could be. Actually, when I thought about it, it's probably better this way. If they knew he was someone I cared about even in the slightest, he could end up in more danger than he already was.

Me, the advisor, Rain, and Aeis sat together in a lounge room on board the ship. All three of them were attempting to convince me my relationship with Xorion was a terrible idea.

"No, absolutely no." The advisor said calmly. I held back many choice words of defiance I wanted to say. He was Cronos's advisor, not mine. He couldn't tell me what to do.

Rain pointed at me with a relieved look. "No? See!" He pointed back at the advisor with his thumb. "I like him."

"And what in Natarah is your problem with him?" I threw my hands in exasperation. First Adam, now Rain, and this advisor who would relay everything to the Custodian Emperor? Things were not adding up to my favor, I really needed to fix that somehow.

"My problem?!" Rain slouched in his chair and looked up at me like I'd lost my mind. Perhaps I had, but I kind of enjoyed how riled up my mere supposed relationship with Xorion made them. Xorion was my choice, and no one could tell me we didn't belong together, because they didn't know otherwise.

"He stole the heart of my ne'la, stole my guardianship over you, and threatened me? All without my permission?!" He rolled his eyes and turned his attention to the advisor. "Oh, and talk about one's heart having stopped over a girl." He threw his hand out in the direction Xorion was resting in the medical bay. "Literally!"

"I-" I wanted to explain that we hadn't known it was him, but he cut me off in his frustration. It annoyed me, but I let him continue. Besides, he would need to vent eventually, why not now?

"And to think I let you talk me into saving his shabby hide... your welcome for that by the way... Oh yes!" He snapped his fingers. "I haven't even received a 'thank you' from you." he shook his head and spun around in the chair. "What a nice family we have." He added sarcastically.

"I agree that Xorion acted too rashly." Aeis shook his head as well, showing his disapproval.

"Yes, thank you. Maybe you can talk some sense into your brother once he stops dying." Rain shook his hands dramatically in the air.

Bother...?

I looked at Aeis skeptically. Xorion hadn't mentioned anything about having a brother, and Aeis looked nothing like him. I wonder what Rain meant by that. I shake my head, setting the question aside for later. There were more pressing matters present.

"Me and Xorion's affairs together are not a concern right now, nor will they be of great effect in the future."

"I doubt the Custodian Emperor will see it that way." The advisor said as he narrowed his eyes on me. I didn't even bother asking for his name since I hoped I'd never see him again.

"Look ne'la, I understand you might find him pretty looking-"

"He loves me, Rain." I said, cutting him off. Suddenly, I really did want to be in love with him. I wanted my brother to know I'd chosen this man, and that I could love him. I lifted my chin, glaring at my brother. He looked at me blankly for a moment, and I wondered if he actually believed it.

He sighed, "Right..."

"And if it is an issue with the Custodian Emperor, then the matter is for me and him alone. Is that understood?" I said, daring them to argue with me. No one did.

"Now, I want to know how you found us..." I indicated to the advisor with a jerk of my chin, "...and how they did." I continued, speaking about the Elnorsefall soldiers.

Rain tensed, "The Fehichen were right when they said the traitor should be our top priority." He said darkly.

"You think the traitor relayed our information to Elnorsefall?" I asked, shocked at the implication. That was impossible. The computer deleted that information before we even left the room.

Rain scratched his chin in thought. "Yes and no, someone relayed our information to Elnorsefall at first, but not yours. If they gave yours at the same time, they gave ours, we wouldn't have been able to rescue you. They also didn't reveal Lucia's information to them it seems."

"I don't understand, they couldn't have had that information at all. Even if they did, why would they reveal yours and wait to reveal mine? That seems illogical if they wanted to capture us, and why wouldn't they reveal Lucia? She's a bloodborne royal on both sides of her family." I wondered out loud, confused. It made no sense.

"I don't know, Clove. I'm as confused as you are." Rain held the nape of his neck, breathing out deeply in frustration.

"Whoever they were, they backed out of their little plan. Shortly after the information was sent to Elnorsefall, they gave Rain's cords to us as well. Along with the message that Elnorsefall had found the royals." The advisor crossed his arms. "That's how we were able to rescue your brother and Aeis. Because they wanted us to."

"We found this when we had searched our ship." Rain said as he took out a small rectangular device and handed it to me. Upon closer inspection, it appeared to be a transmitter. I blinked, wondering if what I was seeing was correct.

I eye Rain for confirmation. He looked at me angrily and voiced my own thoughts out loud.

"Whoever it was, knew me, Clove. They knew which ship I would choose and were ready with a tracker in place." He said through gritted teeth.

I nodded, trying to stay calm, but it was difficult. The traitor was someone who knew Rain, knew him well enough to know what ship he would take.

"That doesn't explain how they knew where me and Xorion were, and how did you find us? Did they give you our location later?" I chose to ask instead. Whoever they were would need to be inside the towers. They would need both knowledge about the way we thought, and knowledge about the protocols given. There were very few people who knew that, and none of them would betray us... would they?

"Actually." The advisor voiced thoughtfully. "We weren't given information on you or Lucia at all, only Rain's team." The advisor sat himself down in a nearby chair. He tapped his fingers against a table, a worried look coming over him.

"Then how?" I asked, more confused than ever.

Why tell Elnorsefall Rain's location, only to allow them to be rescued, then hesitate to give my location but inevitably sell me out completely? Did they change their mind? Did they want to confuse us? If so, it was working.

"They appeared not to be as interested in Rain's group. They were far more interested in yours. We found out your location only after you were captured. The transport ship that was sent for Rain's team had been receiving information with the other carrier. We figured they would have tried to target you as well, since they had sent one for Rain's team." The advisor said. He stopped his tapping and glanced up at me expectantly.

"You mean you didn't know if we'd be on that ship?" I raised an eyebrow at him.

"Correct. We were lucky."

"I don't believe in luck; this entire situation makes no sense... their logic... it doesn't add up." I held my head in my hands. They wanted me, my team. Not Rain, not Lucia. No, they wanted Rain, but the traitor didn't want them to capture him, only us. Why?

"If they were able to find the information about us, then it must be assumed information about Lucia and Cedric has also been compromised. They must be found and protected." I wasn't going to let the woman I considered my own sister suffer a fate we'd almost fallen too.

"We cannot..." Aeis started to say slowly but trailed off when I stared at him through narrowed eyes.

"I wasn't making a request."

"Clove, they're off grid completely. We think Cedric took her into the Forbidden Region." Rain's voice tightened at his own words.

"What? Why would he do that?" I turned to face Aeis. "You were specifically informed not to enter the Forbidden Region." My voice was shaky as I spoke.

I was more than angry; I was also really scared for my friend. I knew she could take care of herself, but she's rarely left Eurkxo, let alone entering an entire new galaxy. I knew Cedric was Xorion's friend, but that didn't mean I trusted him with my friend's life.

"I trust Cedric. If he had to enter our galaxy, then there must be a reason for it." Aeis said, confidently dismissing my worries.

"And that reason could be that they were forced into it by the Elnorsefall!" I hissed out. They could be stranded, lost, or worse, captured with no hope of rescue.

Rain stood up and walked towards me cautiously.

"Look, Clove. If there was something we could do, believe me I would be fighting about this right alongside you. There's nothing we can do right now." Rain said as he placed his hands on my shoulders.

I shoved him away. A hurt expression came over him as I did so, but I only glared at him in response.

"I will be informed about all information concerning them." I demanded from the advisor. He nodded, thankfully not arguing with me about it.

I was furious at the thought of Lucia's disappearance, and not being able to do anything about it. As much as I hated to admit it, they were right. There was nothing I could do about it right now. It was probably a good idea to try and clear my head until I heard any news that could be used to find them.

"Now..." The advisor said, drawing the word out as if he was about to say something he didn't want to. "We'll be reaching V'rasór shortly, and there will be a meeting with the Custodian Emperor."

I looked up at Rain with a knowing expression. I didn't want to see the young Emperor. I hadn't seen him in so many years... He was forgotten to me, just as I was forgotten to him.

"His Highness isn't too busy?" Rain crossed his arms, giving the advisor a dull look.

"Eurkxo has started a war, Rain. Now isn't the time for you to complain about family scuffles."

Both me and Rain narrowed our eyes on the advisor.

I pointed at the advisor accusingly. "If his majesty didn't encourage the exclusion of our planet in trade, we wouldn't have had to enter the Forbidden Regions and start this mess in the first place!"

"V'rasór is your planet, my Empress, not Eurkxo." The advisor said as if talking to a bratty child. I was about to give him an earful before I actually processed what he'd said. I blinked at his words, dropping my hand from pointing at him.

"She's not your Empress, and Eurkxo is our planet." Rain said, raising a brow at him.

"Here with us, and on V'rasór, she is our Empress. As for Eurkxo, it's no longer your concern. To kill a plant, you have to start at the root. V'rasór, your home world, is the root. If we don't take it now, then the Realms will be lost forever." The advisor matched our glares at his rather insensitive words.

The way he spoke about Eurkxo made me angry. He talked about it like the planet we were raised on wasn't in the middle of a war with the Union where people were dying left and right. Unfortunately, the logical side of me knew he spoke the truth, as hard as it was to hear. V'rasór was the root. It needed to be dealt with, but I didn't know why he insisted on calling me an Empress. V'rasór only had two Empires now, why would I be considered an Empress? Unless...

"What is the Custodian Emperor planning?" I tilted my head, narrowing my eyes on the advisor once more. He looked at me with the same annoying, calm expression.

"You will know soon, Empress."

18

CHAPTER 17

I moved a lock of hair from Xorion's face. He looked so peaceful lying down, asleep. He was mostly healed now. The medic said he would wake up soon, so I decided to wait at his side.

I laid my head on his chest, listening to his heartbeat and let out a sigh of content, thankful I could hear it again. To think if the Custodian Emperor hadn't sent a ship to get us, he'd be dead. We'd both be dead. I didn't think I could handle him being taken from me. Watching someone get taken from me after I'd come to care for them... It would kill me.

I felt him let out a deep breath as he groaned in pain. I raise my head to look at his face just as his eyes flutter open. When he saw me, he smiled.

"Hey, Clove" he whispered while moving his arms to wrap around me. I smiled, letting myself relax in his embrace.

"Hello." I said quietly. He moved to sit himself up, and his face contorted in pain. I willed phantasm into my pointer finger and pushed him back down. I wasn't about to let him strain himself when he'd only just woken up.

He rolled his eyes at me. "Love, I'm fine. It doesn't hurt-"

"No, you will lay down and rest until we arrive." I said, cutting him off firmly. I kept my finger on his chest to hold him down.

He held his hands out to the side in surrender. "Of course, Meirv." He grinned while saying the last word.

I tilted my head. "What does Meirv mean?" I asked, pronouncing it slowly.

Instead of answering, he just smiled and relaxes into the bed while closing his eyes. I frowned at him. He really wasn't going to tell me. Suddenly, his eyes flew open, and he tried to sit up again. I gave him a mock glare and hold up my finger again, warning him to stop what he was attempting.

He stopped with a wary glance at my finger before furrowing his brows "Clove, you said arrive, where are we? What was your brother doing on that ship?"

I smiled softly at his expression; it was rather cute.

"Oh, now he questions, hm?" I teased while turning my head away, pretending to dismiss his question as he had done to me.

"Clove." He stressed, his frown deepening.

I sighed, "We were rescued by order of the Custodian Emperor of V'rasór."

He opened his mouth as if to ask another question, but I quickly placed my finger over his lips.

"Before you ask. No, it's not really a good thing... but it isn't a bad thing either. As for why they helped us..." I let out an even bigger sigh than before. "It's complicated."

"Isn't it always?" He said while raising an eyebrow at me. My finger slipped from his lips, but he reached out to catch it with his hand. His mouth morphed into the ghost of a smile as he slid his hands further up my arm. Once he reached my upper arm, he gripped it and pulled me down until my head laid on his chest.

"So... V'rasór, huh? That's the world with..." He searched for the right word. "...issues?" I responded with a huff of annoyance.

"V'rasór holds people who view themselves in a much higher superiority." I said slowly, not particularly proud of it. He lifted my chin off his chest to look at him with a finger.

"Isn't that all of the Realms?"

"Well... yes, to the Forbidden Region." I looked at him sheepishly. "But even in the Realms there are those who still consider themselves on top, and others they assume are on bottom." I said, thinking of Eurkxo. It was always considered on the bottom, even if they were just as advanced, if not more, then some of the other planets in our galaxy. "It hasn't always been this way, believe it or not. Before I was born, the Realms used to be united, but..."

"It didn't last." He finished knowingly.

We stayed silent for some time, letting the words sink in. Finally, I tilted my head at him curiously. Now that he was awake, I could ask him a few questions I wanted to know, particularly about him and Aeis.

"I overheard Rain say that Aeis was your brother, is that true?" His mouth twitched into a smile.

"It's..." He paused to search for the right word. "Complicated."

I frowned at him. "It can't be half as complicated as my family, Xorion."

He nodded his head, agreeing with me.

"We have no siblings on my planet-"

"What?" I said, cutting him off. How could there be no siblings?

"If you allow me to finish?" He tilted his head to the side while raising a brow again, but his eyes danced with amusement.

"Right, of course." My cheeks turned red in embarrassment. I nodded my head a bit, indicating for him to continue.

"We only have one child for each family. When we become a certain age, we choose our brothers and sisters from other families and are raised together."

"Only one child for each family?" I asked in wonder. "Has it always been this way, or did your planet suffer from overpopulation?"

"It's always been this way. When a family is gifted a child, they are the one and only, and their existence is honored. The Great Soul grants them a gift, a destiny of sorts... for them to follow, for the good of all." He rushed out the last part, his eyes betraying that he wasn't quite sure how to explain it. I was grateful for his attempted explanation though. Now I understood why Aeis wanted Xorion to attend the late meeting with the Elders. It was because they considered themselves brothers. But what happened if a mother had twins? They were siblings, weren't they? Were there laws that removed the second child? Perhaps their people simply couldn't have twins.

"I can sense a question on your lips, Clove." Xorion said with a twinkle in his eyes.

Was it that obvious?

"I was only curious what would happen if a mother were to have twins." I let my question awkwardly slip free. He smiled.

"Twins? I assume that means two children born from one womb?" He tipped his head down thoughtfully. "It's rare, but not unheard of. The children are thought to be born from one soul, making them two halves of one individual. They are not considered siblings."

"Oh."

I fiddled with my fingers, another question lingering on my lips. Before he could tease me, I decided to just ask him outright.

"You mentioned this... Great Soul, not the Mother. You don't worship the same deity as the E'arkan beings?" I knew they didn't from what he said, but I asked anyway, curious for more information.

"No, they worship nature as the Mother. Their Mother is the nature that surrounds them granting them life as she grants all things life. Traditionally, my people believe in a higher power we call the Great Soul and..." He hesitated. "Bestower of our destiny," he said at last.

"I have to admit, I wasn't sure your people believed in a higher power at all," I said, still fiddling with my fingers.

He let out a light chuckle. "We're not very religious, but everyone believes in something, right? Whether they believe their gods are themselves, an object, or a higher being who created everything," he said with a shrug. "If you were to ask me for my personal opinion, I think the Great Soul shows himself differently to different people."

"That is almost the belief of Eurkxo due to the variety of species that live there, but every planet in the Realms has their own beliefs. Personally, I'd say I believe in one God, our great creator. Some might say that has to do with my upbringing though. Those born on V'rasór are known to be especially religious and there are many cathedrals on the planet dedicated to the prayer and worship of our God," I explained, folding my hands together awkwardly. I remembered my mother often taking me and my brothers to the palace cathedral. She used to have us light small candles and hold them up as we sang for blessings. I enjoyed those days.

"Back to the main point," I muttered, feeling my cheeks heat up, embarrassed for rambling.

He chuckled softly at my heated face, and although I was still embarrassed, it was a nice sound to hear.

"So, you chose Aeis as your brother?"

"Yes, we were childhood friends and when we chose each other as brothers, no one was really surprised. We've lived almost our whole lives together." He smiled, but it didn't quite reach his eyes. "We have grown our own way now." He whispered, his saddened smile more apparent.

"I'm sorry." I knew what it felt like to grow apart from a brother. To have been so close, only to be pushed away.

"Don't be. We are still close, just on our own path now." He said, rubbing his hand up and down my arm. He smiled again, a real one. He took a deep breath in and releases it with a huff of air. "Anyways..." He started, dropping his hand from my arm. "The Custodian Emperor, eh? What does he want with us?" I figured he was just trying to change the subject.

"I'm not sure." I answered honestly. I knew the Emperor was planning to use us for his own plans. As for what his plans were. I had no idea.

"He's your brother, right? What's he like?" Xorion asked while stretching his arms out to the side. I stiffened at his question, something he seemed to notice. He tilted his head, stopping mid-stretch. Before he could ask about it, I answered the first question as best I could.

"He's a young ruler. Very smart... he knows how to get his way." I said, looking away. I knew my answer wasn't what he was really asking about, but it was the best I could do. I really didn't know my oldest brother. I only knew what I'd been told and what I could remember from childhood.

"You're not close with him... are you?" He raised his hand to turn my face back towards him. I shake my head slowly.

"No, we're not close. We only had a few years together and were not raised in the same household. He was sent to the north to be close with his betrothed." I tried to keep emotion out of my words, but as he stroked my cheek, I couldn't keep my voice from cracking while speaking my next words. "I- I don't really consider him a brother." I whispered, trying to look anywhere but his eyes. He slid his hand to my lower back and gently rubbed it up and down.

Xorion didn't seem to mind when I showed emotions. He seemed to like seeing me like this, vulnerable. If he liked it, I supposed I could keep showing him this side of me, since I couldn't give him anything else right now. Besides, no one else would want to see it.

He tried to sit up, flinching at his own movement. I narrowed my eyes in warning. He let out a muffled laugh at me.

"I must rise sometime, Clove." He said, smiling painfully.

"You shouldn't." I mumbled, but didn't stop him this time. He sat up all the way, flexing his muscles. He slid his hands to my waist and pulled me forward to sit fully in his lap. I gave him a quizzical look, wondering what he's doing. I opened my mouth to ask, but before I could let the words out, he took advantage of my open mouth by leaning in and kissing me.

"Glad you're okay." He said against my lips. He pulled away only to rest his warm breath against my cheek.

"Your heart was constricted by phantasm, and you're glad I'm, okay?" I rolled my eyes, gently pushing his chest away from me. One of his hands rose to my face and he tilted my chin upwards to gaze into my eyes. I stared back into the golden orbs, feeling the seriousness of his next words.

"Clove." He whispered. "You will always be my first priority."

"And I wish you could be my first priority, but-"

"I can't be, I know." He finished with another sad smile.

I dropped my eyes, slightly ashamed. "I don't want you becoming an even bigger target then you already are as a foreigner in the Realms."

The more people knew I cared about him, the more they'd try to use him against me. I may not love him, but he was innocent, and I would do my best to protect him. Afterall, any threat against him was a threat to me if they believed I loved him.

"I understand, Clove, but remember what I said. I'll always stand beside you, even without your love." He paused for a moment before his mouth twitched into a smirk. "But don't think I've given up on seducing you into loving me."

I let out a breath, thankful he understood. To think I'd find a partner willing to stay at my side without demanding anything in return. Well, besides hope. I almost felt bad, but it wasn't like I was forcing him to stay at my side. He was willing, hoping I would love him one day. He held me in his arms for some time, and we enjoyed each other's warmth. Once we're down on the planet, it would be difficult to be together. I wouldn't be able to accept his public affection or give it, without consequence. Besides, I was sure Cronos would find a way to try and separate us. He wouldn't approve of me finding a partner for myself.

Thinking about Cronos and what he wanted from us had my thoughts falling to what he wanted from me specifically, and an ache in my heart told me he wanted to use my royal blood to hold some kind of power that would combat Elnorsefall.

How would he do that...?

My eyes fell.

Would I ever have peace?

I heard footsteps approaching the door, and I quickly angled myself away from Xorion, slipping out of his lap. Seeming to understand, he pushed himself back against the bed, as far from me as he could get. The door opened and Cronos's advisor walked in. His hands were clasped behind his back as he stepped towards us.

"We have entered V'rasór's sector."

Xorion's face wrinkled. "I didn't feel a thing." He mumbled.

My mouth twitched in amusement. "He meant we have entered the space territory of the planet V'rasór, not that we've entered the planet itself. This ship was not made to even land on a planet." I explained, trying not to smile when his face twists into even more confusion.

"If it doesn't land..." he started, but the advisor coughed to get his attention. He gave Xorion a bored look.

"I hope you are well enough to walk, forbidden one. We have some traveling to do." The advisor looked down at Xorion with his chin lifted. I knew this look all too well. It was the look V'rasórians gave those they found inferior. It's how we were taught to look at others on V'rasór, even me, when I lived there. I was young, so the teachings hadn't stuck as much, but Cronos, and even Rain were quenched with the ideology. Something you could easily see when they interacted with other planets. V'rasór may be the center planet, but they certainly weren't the most liked by any of our neighbors.

"Come, Empress." He said while turning to leave. Xorion slid his legs off the bed, pushing himself to stand. He arched a brow at the word Empress. I gave him a look I hope read, 'I'll explain later.' Without saying a word, he nodded. We both walked out of the Medbay together, side by side. Xorion limped as he walked. I knew he was trying to put on a strong front, but I saw him flinch in pain every few steps. He glanced at me with a look that was a sorry attempt to convince me he was okay. I reached over and took his hand in mine, giving it an affectionate squeeze. Taking in a deep breath, I closed my eyes as I willed my phantasm through my fingers. I let out that same breath and pushed a small amount into his body. He let out a silent gasp at the feel of my phantasm entering him, and I opened my eyes to look at him.

Would he accept it?

He breathed in deeply and I maneuvered the small amount of phantasm around his wounds and his heart. When he exhaled in relief, I couldn't help but smile. My phantasm had filled him and left no room for the pain he had before. I was surprised it worked so well. I'd attempted this trick a few times before, but never on someone who had no phantasm in them at all. I could already feel the small strain of circulating my phantasm through him, but thankfully, it wasn't bad.

He leaned close to me and whispered. "I don't know what you just did but thank you. Thank you, Meirv."

I didn't answer back. Instead, I gave his hand another squeeze before letting it go. We both needed strength for what was to come. I wasn't a fool to think the Emperor would treat this like a happy family reunion. I could almost see his cruel blue eyes piercing through me, but I wouldn't let him hurt me this time. Never again.

We were taken down to the planet in a much smaller ship. V'rasór was just like I remembered. Planet of the blue sun and silver seas. Technology beyond all. The planet no one trifled with... yet was being torn apart from the inside.

V'rasór was engulfed by phantasm, its location tends to pull it towards the planet. It was known for its spiral skyscrapers and translucent bridges connecting the buildings together. The land was covered with enormous canopy, silvery trees with white and copper flowers that hang like trumpets. Neon beams of light cast from the palace walls, lighting the sky in brilliant green lights.

We were immediately transported to the palace, which rested on a rather large peninsula, surrounded by the great silver sea. The palace, like the city, rested above the ground, held up by great pillars and a massive platform. It was built from metallic silver, with soft green lights adoring the sides. Its walls separated at the top, twisting around to hold a beautiful round structure, like an eye, the symbol of the North.

The giant creatures known as the Avarnee soared high above us, symbols of raw strength and power as they glided through the powerful winds currents of the planet. They were creatures born of the sky and sea, bound to the people with mutual respect in a symbiotic relationship. The silver waters absorbed most of the heat from the burning blue sun, keeping it from scorching the planet, and the Avarnee bodies absorbed heat from the waters as they swim. The beasts breathed hydrogen, and when the hydrogen is heated in the bellies of the beasts, they float from the waters to take to the skies, until reaching a height where the powerful winds never cease.

Watching the beasts, I noticed the riders on their backs, soaring through the skies with the creatures. I figured the riders were keeping us under surveillance.

Wonderful...

I thought with no small amount of bitterness.

If Cronos decides we were an asset, we would never be leaving this place, and if he decides we were a liability, we will never see the light of day again.

I hadn't been on my birth planet since I was child, but looking around, it really hadn't changed much. I stole a glance at Xorion, who stared at everything with wide, impressed eyes. Despite the circumstances, I smiled. I took the beauty of my birth planet for granted. It truly was beautiful. His admiration stirred something in me. We had so much more than Xorion's people could ever dream of, and we had the ability to protect those around us. If one good thing came of the war, it was that it would force change.

Our group followed the guardians down the fine, modern halls of the palace, decorated in rich greens. The advisor hurried ahead of us, saying something about needing to update the Emperor. When I turned back to steal another glance at Xorion, I noticed both him and Aeis walking rather stiffly. They looked almost scared as they glanced at the ground. Giving the ground a quick look, I immediately understood their fear. The building floors were made of transparent metal. I hoped for their sakes, they didn't fear heights. Anyone born on this planet learned not to fear falling. Our gravity was much less dense than most planets, and along with the high wind currents, dying from a fall was nearly impossible. Besides, we had our phantasm that protected our bodies, but it wasn't like Soarans jumped off cliffs or purposefully made unsafe buildings.

The guards in front of us suddenly halt and turned sharply towards us. One of them reached up and touched a small black device around his ear, a communication device I assumed.

"The forbidden ones will separate from you." One of the guards' commanded.

I narrowed my eyes at their expressionless stare, and even Rain tensed up. Aeis yielded to their command, stepping away from us, but Xorion hesitated at my side, something the guards seemed to notice as their expressions twisted in displeasure. I quickly gave Xorion a look that told him everything would be okay. He responded with a slight darkening of his eyes, as if to ask whether I was sure or not. I nodded my head, and he finally stepped away from me. One of the guards' motioned for us to continue, the other guard deciding to stay with Xorion and Aeis. I turned back, my eyes betraying my unease. Seeing me, Xorion gave a reassuring smile.

I turned away from him, following the guard. I wished we could've stayed together, but I was glad I at least had Rain at my side. He wasn't a very comforting presence, but he was my brother. I knew him the most out of anyone.

Me and Rain were taken to a room at the far end of the hall and told to enter. The guards stood at either side of the door, clearly wanting us to enter first. I gave Rain a look that let him know how much I didn't want to enter. Cronos was probably there, and even as children, we never really got along. How in all Natarah was I supposed to be civil to him now? Rain rolled his eyes at my look and opened the door, holding it open for me as we both entered. The guards came in after us, and let the door shut firmly behind them.

I recognized him immediately, even with his back turned away from us. He stared out the window of the room. His straight, jet-black hair flowed down to his knees, and a golden band was placed on top of his head. Our older brother, Cronos. The advisor was already at his side, whispering something to him as we stopped in the middle of the room.

Probably updating him upon the situation...

I think while fighting the shuffle my feet. Cronos finally turns to face us. His face structure was a copy of my own, with high cheekbones and slightly darker blue eyes which were, at the moment, narrowed down on me.

"So," his voice was deeper than I remembered. "What is the forbidden one to you?" he asked, his tone curious. Rain shifts his weight awkwardly.

Really? That was his first question after all these years...?

"He is but the object of the Empress's affection. Really child, you could do so much better. He will be nothing but a liability to the Empire." The advisor remarked while shaking his head in disapproval. My nostrils flared at his words. How dare he treat me like some child he could undermine.

"He is not an object as you say, and if I ever hear of him spoken about in such a way again, you'll be dealing with a very angry woman." I threatened while mocking a humorous tone. My hands clenched in fists at my sides. I should've expected them to insult our relationship. After all, what else could be expected from a born and raised Soaran? All others would be looked down upon.

"Only thing worse than a woman who gets her way?" Cronos started the old Soaran saying almost playfully. He tilted his head at me expectantly.

"Is a woman who doesn't." I finished, my mouth twisting into an unimpressed smirk as I cross my arms tightly over my chest. I wanted him to know that I could play this same game if he wanted to. The tension around the room was almost suffocating, and both the advisor and Rain grew to look more and more uncomfortable, but they remained silent. Me and Cronos stared each other down, both our eyes dark and untrusting.

"Never thought that would be you, royal." He said the last word almost mockingly, and I let out a dark laugh, giving him the best unimpressed look I could muster.

"You don't know me, Emperor." I threw the title at his face like a knife.

"No." He admitted. His voice dropped to a strained whisper. "But I would like to."

I took a step back, my eyes widening in surprise before anger took over. His words were not what I'd expected.

Was he really going there with me now of all times?

He turned to his advisor.

"Leave us." The advisor hurried to obey, eager to leave the scene before him. The guards followed him out, and the door shut behind them, trapping us inside. He turned back to face me, his mouth settling into a firm line.

"Let's drop these formalities, sister."

My mouth twitched into a dark smile. My hand slid to my hip as I gave an exaggerated curtsy.

"Oh Emperor, it wasn't me who insisted on those formalities first."

Who did he think he was? Did he really have the nerve to start this now? After so many years?

I watched him visibly flinch at my words.

Apparently, he did.

"Ne'la... please," his words only snapped whatever composure I'd managed up until now, which wasn't much. A cold chill ran down my spine, and I threw my hands up in the air widely, no longer restraining my words.

"I'm not your ne'la! You forgot me! Or is your memory a game of pick and choose while the rest of us suffer? What makes you think that I would ever turn to you again?" I snarled at him, saying the word you with disgust.

Hurt flooded his eyes as his chin falls, and I enjoyed watching it. I really enjoyed it. Through the corner of my vision, I noticed Rain move to stand slightly between us with his hands raised. He bit his lower lip, his eyes glancing between us warily. Sighing, I turned away, not wanting to upset Rain with my anger any further. "I'm tired from the trip, I'm going to retire for the night." There was no reason for me to stay and make the situation worse. Rain could finish this meeting by himself easier without me.

"I'm sorry..." I barely heard the words slip from Cronos's lips, but they froze me in place all the same. I never thought I'd hear those words from him. For a moment, I hesitated, but then he continued.

"I couldn't-"

"Save it." I hissed out. I didn't want to hear his excuses. I made my way to the door, reaching out to open it.

"I didn't say you were allowed to leave." His tone changed, cold authority returning to his voice.

My eyes moistened with angry tears. "On V'rasór, according to you, I am an Empress by law. I don't answer to you."

I left the room without turning back around. I wouldn't give him the satisfaction of seeing my tears.

I couldn't.

19

CHAPTER 18

I walked down the halls with my head held high. Those who walked past me, paused to stare as if they weren't sure how to react before they bow their heads in respect, but I gave them little mind. I was searching. If my eldest brother wanted me to be an Empress, I would play the part of an Empress. It couldn't be different from being on the council back on Eurkxo. That council was established based on V'rasór's.

To secure one's position, one needs to get people to follow you. It was the same concept as being Empress, except I needed a lot more people to follow me. I needed more than a title, I needed devotion and trust. I did have an advantage, unlike my brother, I wouldn't be a stand-in, and I was new. Those who disliked certain things about my brother would look to me in the hope I would be different. I spotted a lone guard standing by the wall of the hallway.

My first prey...

The guard immediately stood tall when he saw me approach him, and he gave a low bow of his head.

"Empress, how may I serve you?" The guard asked as he lifted his head. His eyes gave away his excitement. He was happy I approached him.

"Escort me to the chambers the Emperor has prepared for me." I ordered, keeping my tone level as I tried to appear confident. The guard immediately bowed his head once more and stepped forward to lead the way.

I remembered the palace vaguely from when I was young and would visit my brother, but it was so long ago that it was difficult to recall the layout to its full extent. It was better to ask for an escort then to be seen wandering around until I finally found my way. Besides, this would give me a chance to introduce myself to Cronos's Watchers.

"Of course, Empress. Right this way." The guard said, indicating for me to follow him. He led me down a staircase and down another hallway until we reach a room that has two pillars of water flowing at the sides of its door. When the door sensed our arrival, it opened.

"Greetings."

The female robotic voice said as I entered. It was way bigger than my bedroom back home. I tried not to gasp in awe as I turned around to dismiss the guard.

"Thank you for your assistance."

The guard bowed his head at my thanks, and I flicked my wrist to dismiss him. As soon as the door closed, I made my way over to the washroom to take a shower. I was too tired to enjoy a long wash, so instead I just took a quick rinse. Though the water scented sweet hinting it was sanitizing water, I decided to still smear a bit of the soapy substance over my body, letting it sink into my skin, cleaning my pores. I ran the substance through my hair, cleaning out the excess oil it produced. Unlike Eurkxo, this planet's sun was bigger, and brighter, and though it didn't feel as hot because of the water on the planet absorbing the heat, our skin was still delicate. I knew most body applied substances had ingredients for protection against it, something I'd need if I was going to be staying on this planet for a while.

I shut off the water, and the surrounding walls shot out warm air, drying my body. As soon I was dry, I threw on a clean underdress and take advantage of the bed, throwing myself on top of it while swinging a blanket over me. I was so... tired.

I wanted...

My thoughts drifted away as my eyes fluttered shut. It had been a long day. What I wanted was to sleep.

My dreams were filled with memories of my brothers, of us all playing together as children. Me and Cronos always fought. Rain was always the one to stop our quarrels. I didn't like thinking about the memories. It felt like my dreams were mocking me.

Slowly, I came out of sleep. I hadn't fallen into a deep sleep it seemed, but it was long enough that the sun was already lowering in the sky, soft blue rays seeping through the grand window of my room. It seemed I'd slept the day away. My body was still adjusting to the time difference on V'rasór.

I felt a presence at my door, and quickly sat up from the bed.

"Guest requesting access."

The robotic voice called out. My body tensed up.

"Enter." I said, and Rain stepped inside, looking at me warily.

I breathed out in relief and threw myself on the bed again.

"It's only you." I mumbled. I felt his weight shift the bed as he sits next to me. A loud sigh expressed his mood.

"He has done things that he stands by, but regrets, Clove..."

"Do not defend him!" I snapped at him, knowing exactly who he was talking about. He looked over at me, surprised, but not at my words.

His eyes softened, "Merely explaining..." but I refused to listen to his words. I sat up and lifted my chin haughtily while turning away from him. I didn't care if I was acting like a temperamental child.

"Sometimes the easiest way to do what's best for the people we love, is to pretend we do not. Otherwise, they would never let us go, even when they should. You will understand that one day." He placed his hand on my shoulder. I glanced at him, focusing on his eyes. He was being sincere. There was a part of me that wanted to believe him, but the other part refused.

"It doesn't matter. I don't know why you buy into his words. You know better than... anyone, that he only has us here because he plans on using us for his plans. And when he does use us, it won't be a request." I shifted away from his hold.

"I might argue that he really does need us here with him. We have been through a lot, Clove. Even he has to be wary of those he can trust."

"So, he needs us to comfort him?" He turned away, annoyed at my tone. "The way he so lovingly comforted us when we needed him the most?" I held my hand over my heart in a mocking gesture, pitching my voice up in case he didn't understand my clear sarcasm.

"Clove." He said in a warning tone. I looked up at him with innocent eyes.

"You stayed with him, didn't you? What did he want?" I crossed my arms, eyeing him dully. A part of me was curious though. He gave me a sideways glance, which I shrugged to.

"We were correct in our assumption the minute they called you Empress."

Of course we were.

I thought, pursing my lips. He continued, rubbing his forehead as if thinking about it was giving him a headache. "He wants to reestablish the four empires again, starting with you."

I massaged the back of my neck, "That's going to make Elnorsefall furious." I said through a sigh.

"I fear it may be worse than that." He crossed his arms and rubs his fingers together. A nervous habit he's had for many years. I gave him an exasperated look.

"How can it possibly get any worse?"

"He doesn't want to crush the Eastern Empire's ruling and place you in as Empress after Elnorsefall is removed from the planet."

"Then wha-"

Rain grabbed my shoulders and turns me sharply towards him to lock eyes with me. My breathing stopped as I stared into his eyes, full of a fear I couldn't understand yet.

"He wants you to remove our father as Emperor by announcing yourself Empress of the East now, completely legal and by law, and under Cronos's command."

I stared at him in complete shock before I really processed it. My emotions shifted to horror. He wanted me to take the place of the Emperor of Elnorsefall! I swallowed hard. He was going to use me as a puppet, all titles and no power over the largest Empire on V'rasór. Cronos would use me to rule the subjects of Elnorsefall, without taking responsibility for ruling them himself. I would have all the hatred, but I would have no power without Cronos's authority. He would be the true ruler. Not that they would actually follow us with loyalty, but then they would have no choice. Not if we managed to kill Zaphon.

But... to rule the empire built by my father, named after the fall of my mother...

My fists clenched at the thought. "You are the only person in the universe that is able to." He whispered, his eyes drifting away from me. His head fell, defeated. "If I could only take your place..."

I knew he couldn't. He abdicated any claim to the throne when he was twelve. He desired to become a military high commander. I was the last of our father's bloodline still eligible. I was the only one who could take his throne. It was the reason he wanted me dead, to secure his position. Once Cronos announced me as Empress, our father would stop at nothing to kill me. Dear Natarah, he would send his entire fleet on a suicide mission to Cronos's Empire if it meant killing me. They would put the entire Realms into flames. Worse, I would be under Cronos's ruling, unable to make decisions except for his decisions. If Cronos was the one who announced my claim to the throne, without me having any followers, I would have no choice then to sit aside while Zaphon reigned death on the Realms. I couldn't let that happen.

I needed to speak to Cronos.

I glanced around till I saw a remote device lying by my bedside. I quickly reached over to pick it up. Rain stared back at me with a curious expression, wondering what I was up to. I clicked the button on it and spoke into it.

"Have the nearest guard report to my chambers immediately." I commanded.

"Guard being sent now."

The voice said.

"What are you doing?" Rain asked. He sounded worried. I threw him a look that told him not to question me. He held up both hands in surrender. I stood, heading towards the door.

"Dear Natarah." I heard him groan miserably. "You're not actually going to go talk to him, are you?"

I just hummed in response, letting the door open before me.

"And here I thought you despised him."

"I do." I said with a forced smile, not caring much for his sarcastic statement. A light brown-haired guard with light violet eyes stood in front of me. He bowed his head low before looking up at me almost warily, no doubt wondering why he'd been called. I smiled at him, letting him know there's no trouble. He relaxed, but the second I made my request to him, I saw his jaw tighten.

"Escort me to the Emperor's chambers. Now."

He blinked twice at me, before obeying my command.

"Right away, Empress."

I followed him to the upper level of the palace. After some time, we stopped in front of a beautiful doorway full of colorful patterns engraved into the wall around it. Before the guard could inform the Emperor about my presence, the door flew open. Cronos stood with his hand resting on the side of the doorframe in loosely fitted blue and black robes.

"Clove...?" Cronos asked almost drowsily. It looked like I'd woken him up. His eyes widened more than usual. He was surprised I came to see him.

"We need to talk." I let him feel my icy stare. His jaw clenched at my tone, and his wide eyes narrowed.

"Let us talk then. Come in." He said, his usual cold tone returning. He moved to let me enter his room. He turned to the guard.

"You may take your leave."

The guard bowed to Cronos, "Yes, Emperor," he turned to me "Empress," he turned to leave while Cronos closed the door behind us. He looked at me intently, opening his mouth to speak, but I beat him to it.

"Do they know? Of your plan?" I asked while circling around him like a predator. Even though he was taller than me, I still found a way to look down on him. His eyes were curious, but guarded, following me as I moved around him.

"You mean Elnorsefall?" he tilted his head to the side thoughtfully. "I would believe they'd easily figure it out, since I brought you here. Though it hasn't been officially stated, if that's your concern."

I raised my voice angrily. "This is exactly what we were trying to avoid! Now you stand here willingly antagonizing them, using me?" All these years of averting the war, only to push them so suddenly. I couldn't even imagine how many would suffer for his choice. Eurkxo mainly.

"What you were trying to avoid. The war was always going to come. We are prepared for this." He shrugged his shoulders, his arms falling lazily to his sides.

Is that all you care about? The war?

"Fool! You think you're the only one who has prepared for this? You are playing into exactly what ElnorseFall wants." I spat out, glaring at him. It's not the war I was trying to avoid, it was the deaths from the other worlds that would come from carless planning, something Cronos wouldn't even care to glance at. Not if it meant forcing our father off V'rasór and keeping himself in power by keeping me below him.

"It isn't your choice. We must go by law for this. You are the only blood relation that can challenge him." He said calmly, which only added to my frustration. How could he not see that Elnorsefall never played by the rules? They knew they couldn't rival Cronos directly, so they would look for alternatives, forcing us to play their game by manipulating the situation. They would look for a weakness elsewhere, they would kill and destroy everything until they got their way. I would not be the subject to the deaths that would follow if I played by Cronos's rules.

"I won't allow the innocent to be slain for your impulsive and arrogant plans!"

He and I needed to come to some kind of understanding. If he thought for one minute that I would blindly follow his plan, he had another thing coming.

"We can't protect everyone, Cloverlyne." He said emotionlessly, breaking from my stare. Anger filled me. I thought I could believe those words in the past, but I couldn't. Who were we? If we could not protect those who were innocent in all this. Who were we? If we let others plan our lives for us without a fight.

Cronos looked back at me almost smugly at my silence. He thought he won the argument. He was wrong. I would not let him use me.

"I will become the Empress of the East. Know this though, Cronos. I will not answer to you. You won't command me, and I won't come to you for your armies. They will come to me. You may question my decisions, but you won't stop me if I choose to follow through. The East will not be under the North." I smiled darkly as his eyes widened with surprise.

"You are much too young to make decisions that affect the entire Realms, my guidance is necessary. Besides, you have no influence, you have no followers. I've granted you the right to claim-"

"My becoming Empress is by me alone, and by law." I gave a short laugh, looking at him pitifully. "You will not hold this over my head, Cronos. I will have followers, and I will command them. If you choose to go against me, then I will have no choice but to retaliate." I smirked as his jaw clenched so tight I wouldn't be surprised if it snapped. "And I don't think you want me as an enemy, Emperor." I let my markings light up in shimmering light and willed my phantasm to rise above my shoulders to show just how serious I was. Hands clasped behind my back; I made my way past him. Both his hands were clenched at his sides in angry fists.

I'm not a little girl anymore, Cronos.

I sneered at the thought.

Stop imagining me being such.

"I will be in my chambers. We may discuss the securing of my position soon." I said sweetly, throwing him a performed smile. He gave me a tight smile in return, his eyes blazing in flames as he simply nodded as I left his room.

I was happier than I thought I'd be. I just spoke up to the Emperor, my older brother, and openly defied him. I was almost giddy at the thought. Before I could celebrate the feeling though, an overwhelming feeling of loneliness replaced it. It wasn't going to be easy to find followers on this planet.

I wished I could see Xorion, but I doubted he'd be allowed in my presence. I wondered when I would see him again. His presence was nice.

I looked around and watched a group of guards walk past me, all gave me respective bows of their heads, but a set of violet eyes held my gaze longer than the others. I recognized him immediately, and an idea came to mind.

I stopped walking, "You there."

They all turned to look at me, and I made eye contact with the guard from earlier. He pointed to himself,

"Me, Empress?" The guard asked.

"Yes, you are the guard who escorted me earlier are you not?" I asked, and he quickly nodded.

"Yes, Empress."

"Walk with me."

"Yes... Empress, of course." The guard turned away from his comrades and walked beside me.

"Your name?" I asked, keeping my chin raised. I didn't want to seem too mysterious and unapproachable, but I did want him to be at least a little intimidated by my presence.

"X207, Sovren, Empress." He said a little hesitantly. I tiltted my head towards him and smile.

"Sovren, I have a request for you."

He glanced at me, his eyes wide and excited. He was quite young, to be a palace guard anyways. He only looked a few years older than me, perhaps a year or two older than Rain.

"Yes, Empress?"

I could hear the excitement in his voice.

"Inform my brother, Rain, to report to my chambers tomorrow morning. Understood?"

He nodded, "Understood, Empress."

"Good, and..." I stopped and faced him. He gave me a curious look.

"Know that things change, and that change brings progress and success. Change is coming very soon, and it is important we do our duties, but it is also important to believe in our passions. Some choose to act on old laws and regulations. I choose to act on instinct, determination, and honor. Think about this." I continued to walk without a second glance back at him. He trailed behind me in thought, before answering.

"Yes... I agree with you, Empress. Thank you." I smiled at his response.

"You may return to your comrades, Sovren."

"Thank you, Empress." He bowed low, before hurrying off. I continued to smile after him.

And the shift of leadership begins.

I thought to myself, continuing to make my way towards my chambers.

Everything was going according to plan. As soon as I arrived in my chambers I sat down in the nearest chair. I held my head in my hands, sighing to myself. I was still so... tired. I wished I didn't have to argue with Cronos, but I wasn't going to let him think I was soft either.

A warm hand was suddenly placed on my shoulder. I jerked my head up, my markings lighting defensively. Soft, warm lips pressed against my neck, and I relaxed, knowing who it was. Standing above me, was Xorion.

I gasped out in surprise, "Xorion!"

He chuckled as he leaned down to place a soft kiss on my forehead. I stared up at him, dazed from surprise as he continues to kiss my forehead.

"Do I even want to know how you got into my chambers?" I raised a brow at him. He leaned back and reached his hand up to scratch his chin thoughtfully, before shrugging with a knowing smirk.

"Probably not, I wouldn't want to give away my secrets... but-" I don't let him finish. I stood up and threw my arms around his neck, giving him a passionate kiss on his lips. There was no harm in enjoying his affection. Besides, he started it. His arms curled around my waist, pulling me in closely.

"It doesn't matter." I murmured against his cheek. "I'm just glad you're here."

I rested my head against his chest, overcome by tiredness again. The short nap I took earlier wasn't nearly enough sleep. He smiled and surprised me by scooping me into his arms. I gasped softly, but didn't make any move to discourage him.

"You've worked yourself too hard." He mumbled into my hair. I really hadn't done anything except argue with my brother today, but instead of telling him that, I stay silent. He took me over to the bed and laid me down. Then, he simply sat on the edge next to me. I sat up slightly, letting my back relax against the pillows.

"Thank you." I whispered, giving him a sincere smile. Words couldn't describe the feeling I had seeing him again. I didn't want him to get stuffed away by Cronos. I wanted him at my side. A mesmerizing smile lit up his face as he looks down at me. I loved the way he smiled, so pure.

I tilted my head at him seeing his eyes holding a lingering question, and a bit of a sparkle as well as he continues to pursue me. He wanted to ask me something.

"What is it?" I asked when he continued to say nothing despite the look he gave me.

He let out a breath and moved closer to me until he was sitting right in front of me in the middle of the bed with me pressed back into the headboard of the bed. He was behaving strangely, and it was only making me even more curious. My stomach clenched in slight unease, warning me that I was alone in my room with a male who was now looking at me with desire in his eyes. I pushed the unease away. I was reacting towards the situation and not the individual. I trusted Xorion. He was honorable and pure.

He stared deep into my eyes, as if searching me for something. I met his stare, daring him to ask me the question. I only realized he was carrying a bag with him when he reached into it and pulled out two small cups. He handed one to me and placed the other one next to him before reaching in the bag to take out another item. This time, he pulled out a small bottle full of a bluish liquid.

I furrowed my brow at the bottle, but he doesn't seem to notice me as he poured half the bottle in his cup, and the other half in mine. It was only then that he finally spoke.

"No one has to know about the love I have for you, or how much you care for me, because I know you do." He kept his eyes glued on mine.

"I do care for you." I agreed. I glanced down at the cups and nod my chin at them.

"What does it mean?"

He smiled warmly at my question.

"It's made from an ancient flower that's only grown on a field of the highest mountain on my planet. It's considered sacred by my people, a place to call upon our God. When a man wishes to court a woman, he gathers two petals from the flower and makes a tea from them. The tea is only drunk by him..." His eyes looked deep into my soul as I hold my breath. "And the one he chooses to live the rest of his life with."

It amazed me that such a warrior like race could have such a... romantic tradition. I was a bit curious about the gender roles of his planet. I figured his people were much more traditional than mine, but it never occurred to me that it might be a problem. I wondered if the power dynamic of my royal status would bother him later. It didn't seem to be a problem with Xorion right now. Maybe he was open minded to other cultures?

"So, me drinking this would indicate?" I questioned with another quick glance down at the cup.

"That we'd be courting each other." He said as he continued to search my eyes for hesitance.

Courting him would be good for me. Cronos wouldn't be able to have me marry another Soaran, and Xorion, as a foreigner, wouldn't be able to secure influence or power. I would have his love, his support, and all the ruling power to myself. It was a good match, a match I chose for myself when I could have cut him off, and yet...

Everything that happened today crashes down on me as reality sinks in. I knew the sadness must have shown on my face because he lifted his empty hand to stroke my cheek.

"Tell me." He demanded, and I did.

"I threatened Cronos today and... I'm being placed in a position against the Emperor of Elnorsefall-" I trailed off when he looked at me bewildered. "By claiming my right as Empress by law." I finished while trying to turn my face away.

He doesn't let me. His eyes darkened as he lifts my face upwards. "Remember what I said before? I will always stand beside you."

"But you will become an even greater target then before, and I can't-"

He cut me off, "No one comes between my love for you."

"It is my heart that wants to protect you from this fate... my fate..."

"Clove, when are you going to realize that I don't need you to protect me this way? I am stronger with you, and you are stronger with me by your side." he stressed.

"Stronger because I can trust you, trust that you will be at my side through it all." I whispered to myself. It was selfish of me to choose to be with him. I was using him. I wouldn't claim love for him, but my heart did need him in some twisted way. If I was going to marry anyone, I wanted it to be someone I could trust not to abuse the power of my title, and I knew he wouldn't. I swallow hard, my decision made. I lifted the cup he gave me to my lips, and he lifted his.

"Together."

Both of us whispered to each other before drinking from our cups. I sipped every last drop. The taste was perfect. Perfect amount of sweetness that soothed its way down the throat with a tinge of honey and citrus flavor.

I handed my cup back to him, and he placed it into his bag. He turned back and gazed down at me with an almost lazy smile, his golden eyes pursuing me with a new possessive attraction. It was official. He was my fiancé.

We leaned into each other's embrace. I buried my head into his shoulder while he rested his head against the top of mine as his hands gently stroked the ends of my hair. We stayed like that for some time before finally pulling away from each other.

Xorion scratched the back of his neck, "I should return to my room before anyone notices." He said sheepishly. I rolled my eyes playfully at him.

"Yes, go, go!" I shooed him away with my hands.

"May you rise, my love." He got up and ran a finger down my cheek. "My Meirv." He walked backwards towards the door.

"Goodnight, Xorion." I said softly. He gave me one last smile, before leaving my room. I stared at the door for about a minute before finally changing into a new underdress for sleep, deciding to just leave the dress I'd worn on a chair rather than hanging it up. My eyes fluttered shut as I threw myself back onto the bed.

So many things happened today, and one thing was for sure. My life was about to change. I only hoped I could handle everything that would be thrown at me. Without even being really conscious of it, I fell asleep with a small frown on my face.

20

CHAPTER 19

I woke up early, just as the sun began to rise. I felt surprisingly relaxed and ready for anything. Throwing the covers off, I walked straight to the wash basin to clear my face from noticeable implications of tiredness. I chose a long light blue dress from my wardrobe and slipped it over my white underdress. For shoes, I slipped on traditional black V'rasórian boots which were slim, and knee-high. Before I attempted to do anything else, I used the device by my bedside to call for an attendant. It doesn't take long for my door to open and a much older woman to walk in.

"Greetings, Empress." She gave me a low curtsy.

"Greetings..." I paused and looked at her expectantly.

"Magida," she said, already at work tightening my dress behind me. After my dress was well fitted, I sat down so she could help me with my hair. I knew how to do simple styles myself, but since my hair was so long, and because I wanted to look professional, I preferred having attendants do it.

"Any particular style you want, Empress?" she asked, brushing my hair and looking at me through the mirror.

"Just a traditional braid," I said simply. "The kind with the twist on the front left."

She nodded, a smile twitching on her face as she began her work. I was used to braids and enjoyed wearing them because it kept my hair out of my way, but the lifted twist was a V'rasórian style that most royals did. If I was an Empress, I may as well look the part. Once I was pleased with my hair, I placed two gold bracelets on my upper right, and left arm.

"Thank you, Magida. You may take your leave," I said while looking over myself one more time.

"Thank you, Empress," she paused for a minute. "You look perfect, Empress." She said with a smile, curtsying once again. I smiled at her.

"I hope so, Magida. Thank you."

She smiled even brighter, before leaving my chambers. I relaxed in my seat, waiting for Rain. Not even a few minutes later, I felt Rain's presence at my door.

"Guest requesting access."

"Enter." I stood as the door opened. Rain walked in slowly wearing a Watcher uniform, his eyes pursuing me. He finally found my eyes and smiled.

"I heard a rumor that the Empress who rises may end all Emperors."

"Is that so?" I asked, smiling back at him.

"They say she demanded the attention of Cronos with a voice of fire, and that she has threatened a change in power. If refused, she will release her fiery fury," he laughed. "And that was just the vague one. Some, I even heard, claimed they saw Cronos digging his own grave in the gardens."

"Oh, not rumors, dear brother. It would be the wisest thing Cronos could do right now," I let out a short laugh. He nodded, stifling his own laughter. He tilted his head as if a thought struck him.

"What?" I asked, wondering why he was looking at me like that. He pointed at me with his chin.

"Style looks right, but you're missing something." He reached into a bag that was hidden under his uniform. From it, he took out a beautiful, golden, circlet crown. He walked over to me and placed it on my head.

"The final touch, Empress," he said, bowing low. His voice was light, but it had a hint of sadness to it. "I wish this was not your fate..."

"Do not wish away who I am." I gave him a sideways glance as I turned to look in the mirror. The crown was the perfect touch. He walked up behind me, gazing tenderly at my reflection in the mirror.

"Beautiful."

"Thank you, Rain." I gave him a soft smile.

"Cronos is making the official announcement today to his small council, although he really doesn't need to tell them anything. I think most already know... Perhaps you may be able to convince Cronos to speak to them about-" We both froze, suddenly cut off by the robotic voice of the door.

"Guest requesting access."

"Enter." I said suspiciously. Me and Rain mirrored each other tensely, both of us narrowing our eyes at the door. The door opened to reveal the guard I knew as Sovren, and two other guards I didn't know who wore helmets. Sovren glanced at Rain, but then made eye contact with me, holding it.

"Yesterday," He started, stepping forward. "You spoke of change that would come. We want change. We want Elnosefall to fall into oblivion. We will follow you if that is your desire." All three of them dropped to the ground, kneeling before me. Rain looked over at me with raised eyebrows and leaned into my ear.

"What in Natarah did you say to Cronos's Watchers?" he whispered furiously. I shrugged, whispering back,

"They are tired of Cronos's incompetence in taking a stand against Elnorsefall. I won't do that." I leaned away and walked forward to stand before the three guards.

"Rise," I commanded, and they immediately followed my order, standing tall before me.

"We were part of the Custodian Emperor's observation force. We were ordered not to act against Elnorsefall, no matter what they did," Sovren's eyes went dark. "The things we have seen of Elnosefall..."

"They are monsters." The one on Sovren's right said with a shake of his head.

"They must be stopped. We have to show them we will not ignore the blood they've split. We must protect not just our own planet, but those who stand no chance against them. Elnorsefall will force their rule over everyone, and death will be the punishment if they don't submit." I stared at them with daring eyes.

Would they finish what I start?

"By your command, we will not allow them to shed the blood of innocence." They each bowed their heads, a fire in their eyes.

"Then spread this word my warriors and give me an army that will not stand idly aside while those around them suffer." My markings lit, a show of my promise to them. They would look to me as their leader.

"We will gather those we command my Empress. They will follow." The one on Sovren's left said.

"Your names?" I asked, glancing between the two guards at Sovren's left and right. They removed their helmets, still bowing their heads, before lifting their eyes to meet mine.

"X303, Kaycion," The one on the right said. His eyes were a dark green, with matted dark brown hair and dark skin. A permanent scar ran down the left side of his top lip.

"X299, Garettano," The other said. He was a soft blonde with a round face and had light yellow eyes, one of which seemed to be smaller than the other.

"I want you three as my personal elites. You will be high commanders over all others. You no longer serve the Custodian Emperor, Cronos, you now answer only to me and Rain." Their eyes lit up at my announcement. They bowed low, their right hands resting over their hearts in fists.

"Empress Cloverlyne, we will serve you to our last breath," They vowed.

They would follow me. I can see it and can feel it. But...

"Prove your honor through your actions. Prove that you can be trusted by me," I narrowed my eyes as they looked up at me. "Prove your loyalty."

"We will prove ourselves. Our phantasm is yours to command," Sovren said confidently, speaking for himself and for the others who make no objection. I nodded back, firmly.

"You may take your leave then, my elites," I smiled softly at them. They bowed their heads once more in respect, before they turned and left my room. Only until the door was firmly shut did I turn to face Rain. My smile brightened when I saw the look on Rain's face. His eyes were wide in astonishment. It seemed my plan was going better than I'd had hoped.

"How intriguing," He mumbled, crossing his arms over his chest. "Cronos will be furious with you for splitting his military."

"Oh, I'm counting on it. People who act on their anger are surely not to be followed. Besides, there's nothing Cronos can really do about it. He's the Custodian Emperor only, after all," I stepped towards the table in my room, running my fingers over it gently. I looked up at him innocently. "Unless he wants me as an enemy." I sat down in a chair by the table, motioning for him to sit as well. He sat down more slowly, letting out a loud sigh.

"I wish you wouldn't willingly put yourself in these situations."

"Do you know them? My new elites I mean," I asked, purposely changing the subject. He shrugged,

"I have heard of Kaycion; he's a skilled strategist. And Garettano is a fine leader, I have witnessed his skills in training sessions. Although, I have yet to know either of them personally. However, I do know Sovren. He's famous for his skills in phantasm, he's very powerful," he tilted his head thoughtfully. "We've spoken quite a bit. He's a good man, a good friend to me."

I smiled at his answer. I was glad my elites were good people by my brother's standards. Good people were often hard to find. I looked down, folding my hands on my lap. I could feel Rain's eyes on me. I knew he wanted to say more, so I waited in silence. I didn't have to wait long. "I feel like you're being too vicious, with our brother. He is not the enemy, Clove," he said at last. I raised my head and scoffed at his words.

"We are in the middle of a war, Rain. Spare me any lecture on peaceful negotiations."

"I know, but he is still our brother-"

"This is not about our brother. It is about proving to the Emperor of another Empire that I keep my word. I will not be controlled. If I can't stand up to him, then how can I stand up to anyone else?" I explained. I knew I didn't have the best relationship with Cronos, but maybe it was better that way. It gave me the strength and confidence to rise up against those who thought they could belittle me, even if they weren't even trying. Cronos couldn't keep seeing me as his little sister.

Rain stiffly nodded, understanding my reasons. From his tight expression, I knew he wasn't happy about it, but he didn't say anything more about it.

"Once word of your new army reaches Cronos, he will be forced to work with us." Rain said, sitting up straighter. I agreed with a nod.

"Rain?"

"Yes?"

"I want you to be my elite's overseer and advisor. I meant it when I said they will answer only to me and you." I hoped he would support me. I knew it wasn't really fair, asking him to choose between me and our older brother, but besides Xorion, Adam, and Lucia, he was the only other person I trusted.

"Of course, ne'la," he stood and reached out to hold my hands. I stood and reached out to accept his hold. "It would be an honor" He squeezed my hands once more before dropping them. He then moved toward the door, and I followed him more slowly, knowing he would be leaving my chambers.

"It is such a beautiful day outside," he said pointedly, throwing me a look over his shoulder. I raised a brow at his words. He wasn't the type that commented on weather unless he was being sarcastic. He turned back towards my door while shrugging. "Perhaps you should show a certain Fehichen around..."

A ghost smile twitched on my lips and an excited flutter ran through my stomach. I was a bit surprised he suggested it first, since he objected so strongly against our relationship. I let out a chuckle. I suppose he figured he could use Xorion to get my mind off my current situation. Ever the strategist. His next words confirmed my assumption.

"Besides, you've been cooped in here for far too long, even leaders must rest. Enjoy being back on our birth planet. Relax," he opened the door, but before leaving he threw something at me. I fumbled forward to catch it. It was a flute. I looked up just as he walked out, not waiting for my response.

I stepped out of my room, watching him leave. He walked away, waving his hand above his head in goodbye. I paused for a few minutes, watching as he disappeared behind a corridor, but then my face bloomed into a brilliant smile. A perfect idea filled my mind.

Why was I hesitating?

I needed to find Xorion and get out of this room. I carefully set the crown Rain gave me on the table and switched out of the blue dress I was wearing for loose tan pants that tightened around my waist and ankles and found a wrap-around top that buttoned at the back of my neck. I grabbed a handbag and threw the flute in. Without even bothering to hook the dress up in the closet, I hurried out my door and ran down the halls, hoping to find Xorion somewhere in the palace.

It took me a while, but after asking a guard about his whereabouts, I managed to find Xorion, alone, slouched down in a lounging room. I shifted near the doorway. He hadn't seen me yet. I placed one hand on my hip, and the other on the doorway as I called to him.

"You seem so relaxed, should I leave you?" I asked jokingly. I knew he wouldn't dare ask me to leave. He immediately stood, turning towards me at the sound of my voice.

"No," his voice was low and husky. I stood silent, watching him closely as he pursued me. He stepped closer to me until he was only a foot away, taking in my attire, and loose hair. I watched his eyes travel down and then back up towards my face. I raised a brow at him with a smile. He closed the gap between us, making me have to tilt my head up to look at him. He reached out both his hands and clasped them around my upper arms. A flutter ran down my spine.

How could he take my thoughts away from everything else in only a few seconds of looking at me?

"What's the occasion?" his eyes lingered on my lips while his mouth twitched into a smile. I couldn't help but smile.

"I'm taking you on a date," I lifted myself to be even closer to him, letting my breath fall against his mouth.

"Now..." he grinned playfully, maneuvering his hands to the small of my back, holding me. I reached out to wrap my arms around his neck. He tilted his head at me. "I believe I'm the one meant to take my girl out."

I rolled my eyes at him playfully while letting go of his neck to grab his hand.

"You're taking too long," I grumbled, gently pulling at him to follow me. He let out a laugh, making me more irritated. I knew it was because, despite my pulling, he knew I wouldn't be able to pull him along without him letting me drag him. He was physically so much stronger than me without the use of my phantasm.

Together, we made our way out of the palace, gaining a few strange looks from attendants around, but none of them dared to question us. After asking a kind, elderly attendant for specific directions, we managed to find our way to an outdoor lot for palace vehicles. I led him to a two-seater hover-ship. I typed the overall location I wanted. Despite being gone from the planet so long, years of drilling in geography lessons rose to the surface.

Xorion watched me type in the location, but I wasn't worried about him spoiling it for himself, it wasn't like he would know the place even if he saw it. He crossed his arms, giving me an exasperated look.

"Can I get a clue?" he huffed out childishly.

I crossed my arms and popped my hip out playfully.

"Nope!" I smiled sweetly.

He frowned at my bluntness before changing his expression to a begging look. His hand came up to my face and he tilted my chin up at him. He stepped closer until he was only a breath away and then proceeded to lean down and kiss my lips. Warmth spread throughout my body as I leaned into the kiss. It only lasted a few seconds before he pulled away and I was able to see his face. He wore the smuggest look ever.

"I'm sure I can convince you."

I gently tried to push him away, but he moved his hand over mine to stop me.

"My Meirv wounds me!" he dropped his shoulders dramatically. I quickly tore my hand away, turning my attention away from him and towards the controls. We had about five minutes before we reached our destination.

It was time for Xorion to rid himself of his fear of heights.

A sly smile covered my face.

I heard him sigh behind me. "You're really killing me here, Clove."

I threw him a grin over my shoulder. "Oh, what a pity," I lowered my eyes and pursed my lips out. "We haven't even started yet," I said, stifling a laugh. His eyes brightened curiously.

"Really?" he tilted his head, contemplating. "Well darling, we do seem to be alone..."

"We're here!" I said loudly, cutting him off. I took out a small flute from my handbag and opened the door of the hover-ship.

"Are you going to play something?" He asked while following me out.

I laughed, "Something like that."

"Wow!"

I heard him say as we walked away from the hover-ship.

The location we traveled to was a secluded cliff edge that over-looked the silver sea below, property of the palace. At this altitude the wind currents blew with such a high force that we had to fight the winds to keep ourselves steady.

"It's beautiful!" He yelled out, trying to be heard over the loud wind. I gave him a quick glance and he easily caught my gaze, his eyes softening. "Even more so with you here."

I barely heard the words but blushed anyway. I lifted the flute and stepped closer to the edge of the cliff. The wind blew the loose hairs of my braid wildly. I closed my eyes, allowing myself to completely relax in its embrace.

"Don't you just feel so much more... alive?" I took a deep breath, "Here?" I spoke mostly to myself, but he answered anyway.

"Yes, but should you stand so close to the edge?" His tone sounded worried. I turned back, noticing that he refused to step any closer to the cliff then from where he exited the hover-ship. I ignored his question and turned back towards the sea. I played the song taught to me as a child, the short tune carrying through the wind. Pleased, I turned back around to smirk at him.

"There's a reason why I'm wearing riding pants today, Xorion," I watched as his eyes went from curious to pure horror in mere seconds. Just as I thought he would run back into the safety of the hover; a loud howl was heard from below. I laughed as a massive Avarnee soared up from below. It soared above our heads for a few seconds before landing on its belly near us. The beast took one look at us and threw its head up to the sky making a loud hooting sound mixed with a series of clicks. I mimicked the clicking sound, walking towards it, and gently reached my hand out, placing it on the beast's head. The Avarnee closed its eyes in submission, flattening out its body as if it knew my request.

"Come on!" I yelled over to Xorion, who just stood staring at the beast, speechless. "Xorion?" I tilted my head while indicating to him to move forward. He visibly gulped but finally walked forward. I smiled, glad he didn't refuse. I used the creature's giant blue scales as footholds to climb onto its back. Once I managed to settle on the already fitted saddle, I reached my hand out to Xorion.

"He won't drop you; I promise."

He sighed at my promise but stepped forward to accept my outstretched hand. I helped him climb up behind me, and was thankful the saddle was made for more than one person. From what I remembered from my childhood lessons, most Avarnee could carry up to four people.

"I don't know about this, Clove... Are you sure this is safe?" he murmured while fidgeting in different positions.

"Guess you'll find out." I leaned forward with a grin. He wrapped his arms tightly around my waist. I hadn't ridden an Avarnee since I was a child, but it was actually safer than driving a hovership or any ship in general.

The Avarnee navigated themselves, sensing which wind currents to ride through. You only had to say short commands for general direction, all which I remembered. Even if you fell, you were safe. The only reason they wouldn't catch a fallen rider was if they were deathly injured.

"Clove, I-"

Before he could say another word, I made two more clicking sounds. The beast hooted again and used its massive wings to push itself off the cliff's edge. As we fell, the beast's wings folded against its side, making it shoot straight down like an arrow. Xorion's arms tightened so tight around my waist that I struggled to breath.

"I-" I tried to tell him so calmly, but Xorion cut me off from speaking.

"Clove, this is madness!" he yelled so loudly that I heard him clearly over the power of the wind. I tried to spread my weight out so we would be more comfortable as I was taught to do years ago, but it was difficult with Xorion clinging to me.

"Stay calm, Xorion. He might feel your fear and decide he no longer wants you on his back!" I yelled out to him jokingly. Unfortunately, he seemed to take it too seriously. I felt his breath on the back of my neck become fierce huffs, and I felt his heart pounding against his chest.

"Xorion, you are the opposite of calm. Relax!"

"Are you seriously telling me to relax- A'kiro!" he yelled out, seeing that we were nearing the bottom of the cliff where the silver sea was. "We're going to crash!" Seconds before colliding with the silver waves, the Avarnee's wings shot out to the sides as we flew across the waters. The beast absorbed the heat from the sea, and the wind currents began pulling us towards the sky.

I stole a quick glance back at Xorion as our pace settled now riding a calmer wind current. His eyes were closed.

Dear Natarah! He had the spirit of a child when it came to flying!

"You can open your eyes now." I told him gently, watching as he slowly opened his eyes. They widened as he looked around, gasping at the view before us. High above the clouds, the blue sunlight rays reflected off the water.

We rode the current that was leveled with the puffy white clouds. I leaned into the beast's ears and commanded it to take us higher, hoping it would understand. To my delight, it caught a different current, rising above the clouds. The rays of the sun shone through my hair, warming my face. I felt Xorion relax from his tight embrace.

"There are no words to describe this." He said in awe.

I agreed. It had been far too long since I'd flown outside the protective shell of a ship. I forgot how incredible the feeling was to be at peace among the clouds. I sat up straighter, leaning my head back as I held my hands out to my side. It felt nice to completely feel the wind pressing against my chest. I leaned back until my head rested against Xorion's chest. He looked down at me, much calmer now. I smiled up at him and he leaned down to place a kiss on my forehead.

"Thank you for this." He smiled as he glanced around in awe of the magnificent view. I loved this, but something in me desired a bit more excitement. I jerked forward and began making a series of clicking sounds to the beast. In response, the beast began hooting, its head jerking upwards to each of my clicks.

"What are you doing?" Xorion asked, tightening his arms around me once more.

I laughed, "Giving you a better view." Before he could say anything, I yelled out a command.

"Ha□eroh... Ha□eroh!" I said again and again. Each time I said it, the beast jerked up a bit higher until it finally created a pattern of twisting from side to side, traveling straight upwards by catching each of the wind's currents.

"Clove!" Xorion said in warning, worry creeping back into his voice. I twisted back to face him.

"Trust me." I motioned for him to lean forward with me to stay balanced. The beast twisted with each current until we reached the highest point. The height made it a bit difficult to breathe, and I knew we wouldn't be able to be up here very long. Xorion was already starting to pale. I glanced back at him again.

"Trust me and hang on. I'm going for a ride," I yelled out to him above the winds, and without saying anything more, I let myself slip off the beast. I thought I heard him scream my name, but the wind was so loud I couldn't really hear clearly.

I needed this right now, the feeling of the wind screeching around me, falling through the clouds. The beautiful rays of sunlight reflected from the clouds onto me. Around me I could hear the howling of other Avarnee, which flew around me concerned. A brave one caught my eye and dived for me. I reached out my hand and grabbed one of the massive spikes on the back of its head and sat myself down on its saddle. The new beast twisted, catching a different wind current. I caught sight of Xorion, who looked at me in shock.

I grinned at him and yelled over to him, "Dive!"

He looked confused for a second, but the beast he rode understood the word, and so did mine. Both brought their powerful wings in and plunged straight down. My beast, seeing another rider, began to twist, and circle around Xorion's beast while he mimicked mine. We danced around each other the entire way down.

"This is amazing!" I heard Xorion yell out to me, his voice carrying along the wind. He was smiling now. Seeing him smiling made me happy. I was glad he was finally enjoying the flight.

Once we neared the ground, both beasts leveled out their wings to break our dive, slowing our speed. I made more clicking sounds to both beasts, and they understood that it was time for our ride to end. We reached the same spot we left from, and the Avarnee landed on their bellies. We both hurriedly slipped off the beasts, who wasted no time in diving back into the silver seas.

"Too bad we couldn't stay out longer..." I heard him mumble, and I looked back at him surprised.

"You liked it?"

"Well, even though I believe I nearly had a heart attack when you went and jumped off, it was the most thrilling experience I have ever had." He laughed while fixing his hair which was messy and windblown due to the wind. I could only wonder what my own looked like. As if he could hear my thoughts, he walked over to me and pushed a lock of hair out of my face.

"I like you this way," he said softly.

I wrinkled my eyebrows together. "What do you mean?"

He indicated my clothes, and loose hair. "You look more free, more confident in yourself."

I sighed but was grateful for his kind words. "Thank you, Lord knows I needed this," I murmured the last bit, but he caught it.

"Something happened earlier?"

"Alot is happening right now," I answered honestly. "Sometimes, it feels difficult to control my own life."

"Don't worry, if you ever need me, I am here. Sometimes it's good to get an outsider's opinion," he said as we walked back into the hover. I typed in the coordinates back to the palace.

"I agree," I answered.

He was right, it was good to get outside opinions. Everyone knew Cronos would push his ruling over me no matter how much I threatened him not too. I had to find a way to keep some amount of power. As we neared the palace, an uneasy feeling came over just from looking at it. Xorion put a hand on my shoulder and began massaging out the knots. I tried to relax, but my instinct told me something was going to happen soon. I could only wonder what it was.

21

CHAPTER 20

"Can't this wait?" I glared at the guard who shifted uncomfortably beside me. It had been mere minutes since Xorion and I landed that Cronos had demanded my presence. I hoped he had a good reason and hoped it wasn't anything serious. I was having such a good day so far. It would be a shame if an argument with my brother ruined the day.

"No, Empress. He called for you directly." The guard said firmly. He was clearly loyal to his Emperor. That was unfortunate for me.

I sighed, "Of course." I turned to Xorion, wishing I didn't have to leave so hastily. He waved his hand as if telling me I didn't need to explain anything. He leaned into my ear and whispered.

"I will see you in the morning." He leaned away and winked playfully at me. I smiled at him before giving my attention back to the guard who eyed Xorion curiously. I coughed to gain his attention.

"Lead the way." I motioned for him to escort me.

He nodded, "Of course, Empress."

He led me through the palace, taking me up top until we reached a beautiful double doorway. He opened it for me and I took a peek inside. It looked like a conference room. I stepped inside and dismissed the guard, who closed the door behind me.

"Ah, Empress. I'm glad you could make it." I noticed Cronos standing on the opposite end of the room, holding a tablet from behind a circular table.

It's not like you left me a choice...

I grumbled to myself. I was annoyed, but tried to push the feelings aside. I'm sure Cronos had a reason for demanding my presence, he wasn't the type to waste people's time. "Hope I did not..." He looked me up and down, taking in my wind-blown attire. He smiled suggestively. "Interrupt something?" I frowned at him.

"Of course not, why have you demanded my presence?" I wanted to get straight to the point. He nodded as if understanding my desire. The smile he wore changed to a blank look, and I knew whatever it was he wanted to talk about, wasn't good.

"It seems our neighbors are finally making their first move. Which is unfortunate for the border planets." He clicked a button on his tablet which projected a map of the Realms above the table before placing it down.

"Elnorsefall?" I clarified while eyeing the projection. He nodded again and pointed to one of the planets being projected. The planet I knew as D'thaya.

"D'thaya is their first target. They've lowered their fleet to harvest their resources. It's not really surprising, they've been isolating them for some time. We've been informed of hundreds of labor camps being set up. It's all rather unfortunate, D'thaya will become a plentiful harvest planet for them which will only strengthen them more." His voice was devoid of any emotion even while he spoke about the labor camps, but I couldn't hide the sickened feeling that came over me. How could he speak about such horror with so little emotion? I took a deep breath to calm myself.

"I'm sure they will expect us when we give them our aid. We should play into this. Perhaps we will find some way to use their knowledge of our plans against them." I attempted to advise, but Cronos was already shaking his head sharply at me.

"Help them? You misunderstand me. I was merely relaying important information about the status of the war to you. We have no reason to offer aid to D'thaya. It's far too dangerous. I have other plans for you in order to counter this annoying situation."

I blinked at him, shocked at his words.

"Too dangerous for who?" I narrowed my eyes on him. He gave me a look reserved for a parent lecturing a child.

"The second we show interest, we will enter their little game. Believe me, Empress. It's a game that's best left un-played." His tone was light, as if he was talking about something as simple as the weather. He picked up a tablet on the table and started typing something on it. I slammed my fists on the table to regain his attention. He looked up from the tablet with his eyebrows raised up, his fingers frozen in place.

"This isn't a game, Cronos! Those people are innocent civilians subject to a horror that was born from our planet! He will butcher them!" I raised my voice at him, not yelling yet, despite my desire to. I hated the look in his eyes. He acted like I was overreacting.

"Might I remind you, Cloverlyne, D'thaya may be a promising agricultural planet, but its location is not in our favor. Láuran is far more promising. And unlike D'thaya, Láuran has not been breached by Elnoresfall, or the Union for that matter. We will send our forces to Ardiamus and strengthen our alliance with them. The Anari are very protective over Láuran, and if we create a stronghold there, then we will be assured resources from both Ardiamus and Láuran.

Together we will become a much stronger force that will be capable of protecting the Realms from these unruly forces, which is why I'm planning on sending you there personally." He turned his attention back to his typing. I took a step back, not believing what I was hearing. He wanted to ignore everyone on that planet who would die because of Elnorsefall, just like he abandoned us.

"Ardiamus... send our fleet to Ardiamus?" I whispered quietly in disbelief. I eyed his body language to be sure I understood him correctly. He appeared completely indifferent. I couldn't contain myself anymore.

I lashed out in fury. "Those people are dying, Cronos! Ignoring Elnorsefall's takeover will only make them stronger, and a bigger problem in the future. You're delaying stopping Elnorsefall's treachery and innocent people will pay the price for your incompetence! The longer we avert our eyes to what they're doing the more people will die!" I flung my hands in the air dramatically as I spoke, wanting some sort of reaction from him. My sudden yelling caused us both to freeze. He finally gave me his full attention, which was merely an expression of annoyance rather than concern.

"Yes, and more will die if we play their game, falling into exactly what they want! Do you think they care about any of those people? No. They are merely luring any sentimental idiots foolish enough to run straight towards them so that they can dispose of their armies and gain even more power. If D'thaya was more use to us, I might relent. But it is not, Cloverlyne. This discussion is over." He retorted back harshly. His eyes dared me to argue. He believed he'd won, but he didn't know me. I would fight for this, and I would never stop fighting.

"What about the discussion of morality? It's our responsibility as leaders to protect our Realms! We are the center planet, if we cannot protect those around us then what are we? We abandon the very thing that unites our Realms. The only thing that can keep the Realms together... are us! To abandon one, is to abandon all, and everything we believe in! You may have given up on that dream, but I never will!" I yelled furiously at him, ignoring how my body shook from rage.

Cronos sighed. I almost believed my words had finally reached him. That maybe... maybe I could get him to see how wrong he was to abandon those innocent lives. For a second, I saw pain flicker in his eyes, but the hope shattered as I saw his expression harden once more. With that one look, I knew he would never change. He raised his chin and looked down on me.

"You are an Empress of V'rasór now, Cloverlyne. Not all decisions will be easy for you. No matter how cruel I may seem, know that the decisions I make are based on the value they will contribute to my people. Everything I do, every decision I make, is for the betterment of V'rasór. We are not responsible for all the Realms, and it's ignorant to imagine we have that kind of power."

I opened my mouth to say some choice words to him, but he cut me off, continuing his little speech.

"Think." He raised his finger, shushing me. "If we were to send our forces to D'thaya, which I'll remind you is on the other side of the Realms, our military will be cut off from any planetary power which Elnorsefall will already have. Our soldiers will have no resources, no reinforcements, no planet backing them up! If you think the Ovidō or even the Echloi who reside on that planet will help us, you are mistaken. They will be broken, scared, and abandon us to fight their battles for them. Who's to say Elnorsefall would not just return after we push them away? Do you plan on keeping our soldiers there permanently? Please! We don't have the strength to stretch our forces that thin! We'd be leaving our own planet open for an attack. You know as well as I do that Elnorsefall would drop everything just to conquer us, and we'd practically be inviting them to do it!"

He paused and took a deep breath, before continuing. "Now, if we strengthen our allegiance with the Anari, Láuran will share its resources with us. We'd have a flood of resources and the strength to stretch our forces across the entire Realms if we wish. Not to mention the Knights of Kingsemcore will be on our side, the largest military strength in the Realms! The Union seems only interested in Eurkxo right now, but that could change at any time. Once we gather enough power, perhaps we can protect D'thaya permanently from Elnorsefall."

"Protect who? You mean after everyone is already dead?" I spat out bitterly. Nothing he's said so far changed my mind. We could not allow Elnorsefall to grow any bigger than it already has. We had to stop them now, or at least show others that we wouldn't let them get away with everything. Cronos seemed to realize that he didn't change my mind because he placed the tablet down and crossed his arms.

"You have a pure heart, Cloverlyne. I'll admit that I envy that." He whispered softly, his eyes dropping down for the first time. "But you cannot let others take advantage of that, especially not our father. One day, you will learn just as I did. Just because something feels like the right choice, does not mean it is, even if your heart begs you to follow it. It's not pretty, but you have to learn to live with your own choices or no one will follow you. It's our responsibility to make the impossible decisions that no one else can. You have to understand this, Cloverlyne."

I felt like a student receiving a lecture from my teachers back on Eurkxo. It only made me angrier. I wasn't a child; I understood the impact my choices could have. But someone had to try. I would listen to his advice, but that didn't mean I had to act on it. If I did, it wasn't because he convinced me, but because I convinced myself. There had to be another way. There had to be another choice rather than to simply abandon them.

"I will show you just how much I understand, Cronos. This is your choice, not mine." I turned on my heels, taking a step towards the exit.

"Heed my words, Empress." His voice was as cold as ever. I gave him a sideways glance.

"I never said I wouldn't, Emperor." I threw the title back at him just as coldly. I opened only one of the doors and headed out. Me, Rain, and my new elites had a lot to discuss, and the sooner, the better. With a wave of my hand, I signaled a guard standing by to come over to me.

"Have Rain sent to the closest office near my chambers in one hour. Inform him to bring my elites with him." The guard nodded before giving me a curious look.

"Elite's, Empress?" The guard hesitantly asked, clearly wondering who the Empress's Elites were. Maybe he was envious. I was a bit shocked he was brave enough to dare question me, but unlike some royals perhaps, I didn't mind questions.

"Yes, he will know my meaning. Go." I said vaguely. I didn't want the information on who they were spreading just yet. I'd rather keep Cronos's guard up. The guard left quickly without saying anything more. I hurried to my chambers and requested Magida, the attendant from before, to come to me. When she entered, she curtsied low. I smiled at her while changing my shoes to new black, non-heeled, knee high boots with laces that were crimson red.

"What style of dress would you like, Empress?" Magida asked, her eyes following me as I stared in the mirror in the walk-in closet. I turned my head to the formal section of dresses, but quickly dismissed them. I head to the back of the closet, choosing to look in a more secluded part of the closet. Magida hesitated beside me. All the clothing in this section was worn for specific meanings, which was why I decided to look there for a dress. I needed something that would make a statement. Then, I saw it. It was one of the only ones, but it would be perfect.

"Are you certain, Empress?" Magida asked, carefully pulling the dress out. I nodded.

With Magida's help, I finished getting ready, my hair being pulled back in a double set of braids on both sides of my head and hung down in two braids along my back. The crown Rain gave was placed on my head. Magida then proceeded to help me into the dress. I stared at my reflection in the mirror once the dress was fitted on.

"It will give you what you wish for, Empress." Magida said, stepping away from me.

I grinned darkly. The black and red evening gown flowed like flames rolling off of me. Its long sleeves fit tightly, and my boots are showing off because the dress is short in the front but long in the back, like a cape. I chose to wear my signature two golden bands on my upper arms, they were my favorite pieces of jewelry. Gold seemed to suit me more than silver, or perhaps I just preferred it because gold was popular on Eurkxo.

"Yes, Magida. It will be more than enough." I smiled at my reflection confidently. Dark red, the symbol of bravery, and of war. If I needed to play this part to prove I was not someone to say no to, then so be it. Cronos wasn't the only one who inherited our father's stubbornness. I did as well. I wouldn't lose myself though, or my beliefs. No. Losing myself wasn't an option.

I was ready.

Dismissing Magida, I made my way over to the small conference room that was closest to my chambers. When I reached it, I waited outside the door for a minute to gather myself. I wanted to make a lasting impression. I would officially be defying Cronos with this. The doors flew open as I strode confidently into the room.

Rain, and my three elites bowed respectfully to me as I entered. As they raised their heads back up, Rain found my eyes and stared a bit longer than the others. He gave me a subtle nod that told me he was prepared for whatever I had to say. It was his confidence in me that gave me the strength I needed.

"Thank you for attending this meeting." I started while motioning them to sit at the table. They sat, and looked at me expectantly, waiting for what I had to say.

"I've just been informed by the Custodian Emperor of a most serious situation." I started off slowly, carefully eyeing each of them. They all leaned forward expectantly.

"I was told that Elnorsefall forces have come down upon D'thaya. They plan to use their resources to gather strength, no doubt to gather the means to attack our planet directly. They've set up labor camps on the planet's surface. It's obvious they want a reaction out of us." I watched as they visibly cringed when I mentioned labor camps. It seemed Cronos's guards had more soul than he did.

"The Custodian Emperor has refused to send aid to them. Instead, he plans to send me to Ardiamus as a political figurehead to secure our alliance." I folded my hands and looked to the ground as I spoke, then raised my head. "I disagree with him. Tell me, how much are you willing to risk for them? And for me?"

Rain's face tightened. I know he knew exactly what I was planning to do. I hoped he wouldn't try to stop me. The others looked at each other, but then nodded towards me. Sovren spoke up for the others as usual.

"If you may permit me to speak freely, Empress." He bowed his head towards me.

"Permission granted."

"Not long ago, a ship was forced into the Elnorsefall sector against their will. The Custodian Emperor refused our request to enter their sector to rescue them, even as we begged before him."

All three of them frowned bitterly. A dark shadow came over Sovren's face as he continued. "We found the ship many days later outside of their sector. Most aboard that ship could no longer speak due to the trauma. Ten people were stripped of their clothing, and strung up by their feet, in the cockpit of the ship, dead. You've thought it was the positioning of their bodies that killed them... but no." He opened his mouth to continue speaking but no words came out. It seemed he couldn't bring himself to say any more. The one named Kaycion continued for him.

"They cut out one word of Elnosefall into their backs, Empress. From what it looked like, he made the entire crew watch." Kaycion shook his head angrily. "One of the dead was an Ovidō female. They sliced her wings off and shredded them on the ground. She was the only one where they burned the letter on her back instead of cutting it. She was also the youngest, not more than fourteen years of age."

The worst thing about the story was not what they had done, or who they'd done it to. It was that no one in the room was surprised by the horror. These were the things they were doing to the civilians on D'thaya... perhaps worse. They needed to be stopped.

"This is why we follow you, Empress. We will not question your orders. Tell us what we must do, and we will obey. We only ask that we won't be made to hold back." Garettano promised. The others agreed, nodding their heads at him.

"Then hear me well. Gather those who follow you. Let them become my army. We will travel to D'thaya as soon as possible. We will find a way to aid them. I don't need the Custodian's Emperor's permission to act."

Everyone nodded in agreement. I dismissed them, knowing they were eager to gather their followers. It was only after they left that I turned to Rain. He gave me a curious look.

"Are we really doing this?" He rubbed his fingers together.

"Yes, I am afraid we must." I slouched in the chair I sat in. He sighed, following my lead as he slouched down in his own chair.

"Cronos will not be happy about this..."

"It's not his choice, it's mine." I snapped my head up sharply. He didn't answer. Instead, he changed the subject.

"Nice outfit by the way." He blurted out randomly. I glared at him, knowing he changed the subject on purpose. We both had our own opinions about Cronos, but even he knew our older brother was being unreasonable, which was why he was here, helping me instead of him. Even irritated, I couldn't help but smile at his comment.

"So..." He drawled out the word. "Is your boyfriend coming?" He asked. At first, I thought he was making fun of me, but then I realized he was being serious. I rolled my eyes. I forgot he didn't know he was my finance now. Actually, no one really knew yet. It was probably better that way for now.

"Perhaps." I wondered how it would play out if I didn't tell Xorion about this trip. I knew he could be of some help at least. He came from a warrior race, but he didn't know our ways. He could end up being a liability, especially since it was Elnorsefall we would be dealing with. Rain seemed to read my thoughts.

"It wouldn't be safe for him to remain here either." He gestured to the surrounding area with his hands. "Alone."

"I agree, but-" I stopped short, unsure what to say. I took a breath and continued. "He should be allowed to come on the journey, but I do not want him involved in any mission that is directly dealing with Elnorsefall soldiers." Rain nodded slowly, agreeing with me.

"It will be a fast-paced journey, are you prepared for this?" He raised a brow and stared into my eyes as if searching my soul for the answer. He would find nothing but dedication there.

"Yes, Rain. I am more than prepared for this."

22

CHAPTER 21

"**K**eep the ship steady, once our cloaked shuttle breaches the planet we will send you a signal," I told the captain of the ship we were in.

"Understood, Empress." The captain said, keeping his focus on the controls.

Nearly twenty hours ago, I fought with Cronos again. He suspected what I'd planned and tried to stop me. I didn't let him. Cronos was firmly against the mission, but there was little he could do to stop me. Thanks to my elites, a decent number of Cronos's Watchers now stood with me, preparing to help D'thaya. After all, Watchers pledged themselves to serve the Emperors and Empresses, and Cronos was only a stand-in for the Northern Empress that should have been. My authority overtook any vow they may have given Cronos, but even I was surprised by the number my elites managed to convince to join me. I felt a tad bit sorry for Cronos, I'm sure he didn't think his soldiers would ever choose to follow someone else. I advised Cronos that he should send a messenger to Ardiamus anyways, tell them to prepare if our mission went wrong. It could create the diversion we needed if Elnorsefall thought we were at Ardiamus. They would be more relaxed. Our argument actually ended with him agreeing with me, much to my sunprise. I supposed he figured he wasn't going to change my mind anyways.

We left immediately, flying directly to D'thaya. We'd reached the planet in record time and rested our ship in the planet's gravitational pull. The plan was simple really. Secretly head down to the planet, offer our aid to the civilians, and possibly cripple the arrangements Elnorsefall had for their planet. Hopefully we would just have to start off, and those below would finish what we started. We might find critical information as well, something we could use against them.

"We are just out of range from their scanners." One of the pilots informed me, looking down at something. He raised his head and switched to another screen. "It'll be about a minute until I finish calculating the cords you'll breach the planet with."

"Excellent, I want those sent straight to Rain the moment you have them." I commanded. I turned and left the bridge, knowing I wouldn't be much help there. I needed to be in the shuttle bay. I was going on the mission down on the planet, mainly for diplomatic reasons. I called this mission, and it was my responsibility to earn the Ovidōian's trust.

Down the hall, I saw one of my elites hurrying towards me. When he reached me, I recognized him as Sovren.

"Sovren." I greeted him with a nod.

He nodded back, "Empress, I am here to escort you to the ship. We will be leaving as soon as we arrive." He straightened his shoulders and turned to walk with me.

"Thank you. Let's hurry, shall we?"

We hurried down the halls as soldiers ran past us to their posts. This was all a new experience for me, and I hoped I would be ready for it.

"Empress!" I heard being called from behind. I turned to see a soldier I don't know running to us in full armor. He abruptly stopped before me, taking a breath, and bowing his head low.

"We have received word that Emperor Cronos's message to Ardiamus has been received. We believe Elnorsefall received the same information. We found a ship orbiting the other side of the planet in long range sensors; they've begun to move away from the planet." The soldier said quickly. I glanced at Sovren, who gave me a knowing look clearly thinking the same. Things were moving much faster than we'd anticipated. The soldier raised his hand to his ear, listening to a command sent to him through his earpiece. He bowed his head again before leaving my presence, yelling something to another team running by.

"We must hurry, Empress." Sovren shifted his feet anxiously. Without another word we turned the corner and got into transport. It only took about a minute to finally reach the shuttle bay, where we were greeted by Rain, and many other soldiers. To my surprise, Xorion stood with them, vested in armor slightly too small for him and carrying a weapons belt.

"What are you doing here? You were not called-" I started to say, frustrated that I was wasting time having to explain why he wasn't coming. He knew he was not supposed to be on this mission. If I'd wanted him here, I would have sent word to him, but I had my reasons for purposely keeping him out of this.

"I am going with you, you can't talk me out of this, Clove." He said casually, which earned silent gasps from the soldiers around. His eyes met mine while he slipped a shock blaster into his belt.

"No, absolutely not. I forbid it!" I spat out, walking past him while ignoring the whispers around us. Xorion grabbed my arm and spun me around to face him.

"I'm not waiting up here while you are down on some Soul-forsaken planet! You do not command me, Clove," He warned quietly. My nostrils flared in anger, and I jerked out of his hold.

"You-"

"We're wasting time, let him come, ne'la. We need all the help we can get. Besides, it's better that we keep an eye on him for both your sakes." Rain said, cutting me off. He pointed two fingers above his head towards the shuttle entrance.

"Everyone inside!"

I huffed in annoyance, but didn't push the matter any further. Rain was right, we needed to move out. We entered the small shuttle, it was crowded, but it held the capacity we needed.

"Empress, by me!" The pilot of the shuttle shouted over the sound of the engines starting up. I made my way to the front, the soldiers parting to let me through. I eyed him questionably.

"Sit there please, Empress." He pointed to a metal seat in the middle of the cockpit that had thick wires plugged into the ship's mainframe. I held my breath for a minute. It would be my first time doing this on an actual ship. I let out the breath I'd held and sat down in the seat. The pilot motioned for one of the soldiers to strap me in. My arms, legs, and chest were secured, and I felt restricted as I breathed heavily. Once I was secured, the soldier who strapped me in pressed a button on the side of the chair, and it lit up in green light, making a buzzing sound. He reached up and grabbed a device from the ceiling, pulling it down. It split to cover the front of my chest, and my back where my heart was. He apologized and gently tugged the back of my dress, undoing two of the buttons to let the cold metal device rest on my bare skin. Thankfully, the front metal was able to rest over the soft material of my dress, especially with a ship full of mostly men, although there were some female soldiers too. He took out two smaller devices and clamped them on each of my wrists, particularly over my veins. I felt my heart start to beat faster with every move he made.

"What are you doing?" I heard Xorion ask. Hearing the concern in his voice, I momentarily forgot I was annoyed at him.

"The mechanism takes her energy and focuses it throughout the ship so we can enter the planet at a speed that they won't be able to track. The Empress is the most able female on board for this task." The pilot explained to him, but Xorion still wasn't satisfied. He shook his head.

"Why can't you just use one of the male soldiers?" I could almost see him narrowing his eyes down on the pilot. The man didn't seem to care much, his only expression of annoyance being a release of a deep breath.

"Females channel faster than males do within their bodies. It's rare to find a male who can channel phantasm at a fast rate, and it also means that the male's overall force wouldn't be as powerful as usual for males of our kind." He threw Xorion a smirk. Xorion frowned at his words. The man pinched the bridge of his nose. "Quite worrying, she's an Empress, a born royal. Her channeling and force are much higher than any normal Soaran." Xorion simply mumbled something under his breath in response. Once everything was set up, the device on my chest started buzzing softly. I felt a small amount of phantasm being pulled from me. Without me even trying, my markings lit up in shimmering flashes, not nearly to their full capacity yet though. The man went back to his own seat and strapped himself in.

"Everyone double check your restraints!" He yelled. I heard shuffling around the ship as the soldiers checked their restraints, making sure they were tight and fitted. I was a bit annoyed at being strapped in so well that I couldn't even turn to look around me. I tried to focus on relaxing and leaned back while closing my eyes. The ship began to shake violently.

"Departure on 5..." The pilot of the shuttle said over the intercom system. The smaller size meant that every vibration could be felt. If we weren't strapped in so well, it could've been very dangerous. "...3, 2, 1....!" The vibrations got quieter as our shuttle left the mothership docking bay. It took a few minutes to get a safe distance from the ship, before the man who had helped strap me in called out to me.

"Empress, on my count, give a level four pulse." I swallowed nervously. A level four wasn't the most powerful I could do, but it would be draining either way.

"Pulse on 3, 2, 1...Now!" I emptied my mind of all doubt, and pulsed, feeling the amount of phantasm I needed to channel throughout my body. My phantasm surged through the mechanisms of the chair as my markings glowed in a blinding blue light. My eyes shot open at the feeling of phantasm being channeled throughout the ship, and I was blinded by light. Just for a second, it felt like all my blood had gone cold. I could feel the ship being lurched forward into the atmosphere of the planet at impossible speeds, as if our ship had become one with Natarah for a fraction of a second. Perhaps it had. I wasn't too sure how the whole process worked. Just as I began to feel like I couldn't take it anymore, it was over. My whole body jerked forward as the ship stilled, and an agonizing headache pierced my skull. My ears rang painfully as my senses returned to normal. I saw the pilot before me, his lips moving, but I had no idea what he was saying. He tilted my chin up to be leveled with his face so I could read his lips,

"Cloak is on, landing soon." Where the words I picked up. I nodded in response, tugging at my restraints. I knew I wouldn't need them for the landing because of the type of ship it was. I surprisingly managed to squeeze my hand out of one of the restraints myself, and thankfully my hearing gradually came back to normal.

"We'll be landing in the center of Yusami Trakan." The pilot said calmly, moving to each of the computers easily. He skillfully typed on each with one hand. I felt someone tug on the other side of the restraints, helping me take them off. When I looked over, I saw that it was Xorion helping me. I narrowed my eyes at him, but he kept his eyes on the pilot.

"Yusami Trakan? Like 'Trekin' which means fall? " He asked curiously, but the pilot ignored him, preoccupied with his own work.

"It means 'fallin' trees,' and yes, it would be similar." I answered as he helped me slip out of the last of the restraints. I sat up and rubbed my shoulder blades. "The language of the planet E'arka we think was derived from Kêva, the language of D'thaya, the planet we're currently on"

"Really?" His eyes widened.

"It's just a suspicion, but it's the way we were able to translate the language on E'arka so quickly." I answered. He rubbed my arms gently.

"I remember when your ships arrived to take us to Eurkxo, the crew implanted us with translators." He said in a questioning tone. I nodded.

"Yes, that's why you understand the universal language of the Realms." I averted my eyes from his intense stare. I wasn't really angry at him for coming, but I still wish he hadn't come. I wasn't being fair, I knew. If I were in his place, I would've done the same. My body jerked forward slightly, but it was nothing compared to what I felt earlier. I figured we must have landed. "Rain!" I called out. He appeared before me, his eyes flickering over me once, making sure I was okay before straightening and waiting for any command. It felt odd, giving my older brother commands, but Rain was used to acting on commands rather than leading, other than his own Rectifier crew of course.

"Separate the soldiers into groups, the elites as leaders. I want you to select a few soldiers to help you secure the surrounding area."

He bowed his head at my command.

"It will be done immediately, Empress." He turned to move away from me, gathering soldiers. I glanced at Xorion who hesitated around me, looking off where Rain disappeared to.

He wants to know if he should go with them...

I thought knowingly. He wasn't officially part of the V'rasóian military, he probably never would be until I securely took the throne. But...

"Tell Rain it's my request for you to be on his team." I watched as his eyes lit up at my words.

"Really? I mean, thank you!" The pilot glanced up at him with his eyebrows raised. Xorion looked at him confused, but then realization dawned on his face.

"Oh right. Thank you, Empress." He bowed his head sheepishly. He winked at me and hurried off to where Rain disappeared. I smiled at his awkwardness. The pilot looked where Xorion had left, and then back at me before just shaking his head in disapproval. I narrowed my eyes on the back of the pilot's head.

"Send a signal up to the mothership. Tell them we've safely landed." I ordered. He immediately took out a smaller tablet and typed in something before looking back at me.

"Done, Empress."

"Good."

He turned back to focus on his computer screen, typing furiously and frowning as he corrected commands and signals. I knew he was more than just a pilot. Rain had mentioned something about him being a high ranked technician. He also mentioned something along the lines of him being married to his work. It was just the two of us still inside the shuttle, the others had already left to set up camp outside. I frowned, realizing I hadn't even asked for his name.

"Might I ask...?" I started while placing a hand on his chair. He jumped at my question, startled.

"Apologies, Empress." He looked up at me, fixing his spectacles. "What was your question?"

"Your name?" I smiled at him softly. He blinked at me.

"Oh..." He breathed out in relief. "My name is Jamieson, Empress." He turned back to his work.

Jamieson...

I mentally noted. I could remember that.

"You are good at your work, Jamieson." He didn't answer me, but I saw his face turn red. I silently laughed, hiding it behind my hand. I headed to the back of the shuttle and sat near the exit. The seats were more comfortable there, and I could breathe in the fresh air outside. It was bright, and the sweet scents of the jungle filled my nose. It would be about an hour at least before Rain would return from securing the area. Until then I should probably stay out of the way. I didn't want anyone having to worry about me when we had so much planning to do. Wandering around an unfamiliar area would be foolish, even if I was curious. I tried to sit still, but I quickly became bored watching the soldiers move stuff around outside. I shifted in my seat to watch Jaimeson. He was so immersed in his work that he didn't even notice me watching him. I wonder what he was working on? Perhaps he'd discovered something in the signals we were monitoring? The curiosity was making me fidget in my seat until I couldn't stand it anymore. I stood up and walked back over to him, looking down at what he was doing. I watched him glance at me out of the corner of his eye and flinch.

"What are you working on?" I looked down at his screen, trying to make sense of it. I failed miserably. He frowned as if he didn't really want to have to explain it to me but did so anyway.

"There's some strong signals being sent up from the planet. By calculating the exact distance of where it's being sent, and anticipating the moment it's being sent there, it may be possible to redirect the signal to run through this shuttle's very own main computer. I could have a direct link to Elnorsefall's plans. However, the process is slower than I'd thought it would be." He stumbled out. He frowned again. "Probably because of how small this shuttle is, they don't care to put in decent computers that actually get the job done." He smacked the top of the tablet harshly while letting out an angry puff of air. I give him a blank look. He spoke so fast my brain couldn't keep up with him. He continued, not noticing my confused face, "You see, in order to receive the signal, I would have to stop the signal from being sent to them completely by channeling it to this computer because I don't know where the signals being sent to yet... which would ultimately give away our position, but then I figured I could simply-"

"Jamieson." I said, stopping him mid sentence. I simply wasn't able to follow what he was saying. "Please, as interesting as this is, I would like a simple explanation that I would be able to understand about the task you're attempting to complete and why it benefits us." He sighed as if it wasn't the first time he'd been told to do so. But thankfully, I could see him thinking of how to explain it in a simpler way.

He nodded, "I am attempting to tap into Elnorsefall's signal that they're sending off-world without giving away our position." I let out a breath I didn't know I was holding.

"Have you made any progress on this?" I asked, praying for a yes or no answer. When his face lit up excitedly, I prepared for yet another long explanation.

"As a matter of fact, I have!" He pulled up his tablet's information onto the main computer screen. Pointing to the mappings of a signal being sent to and from the planet with calculations by it that I don't understand, he began.

"The location of where the signals being sent is hovering just above the planet, on its dark side. I believe it's safe to assume it's another ship, Elnorsefall to be exact. It's guarding the planet, as we'd expected them to do. When it sends the signals back, there is a...

flicker, just as it breaches the planet. The why's not really importa nt... I'm currently working on the calculations to gain its exact point, and hopefully with that I can manipulate the signal to run through this computer so we can read everything being sent. Unfortunately, I don't think I'll be able to send it back to the mothership. It's too massive, they'll take notice." He stopped for a brief second, taking in some air. "There's a good chunk of information they won't send through a signal like this though. If they do, it'll be in code, but where the signal is being sent from..." He lifted his finger and pointed to the end point of the signal and zoomed in. The place where the signal was being sent was just a random point in the jungle, in a much higher elevated zone.

Probably surrounded by soldiers as well.

I thought with a sigh.

"This information could be vital to our cause, Empress. They don't know we are here, if they did, they would have stopped sending the signal when we arrived. Also, we would be able to send information to our own ship without their own ship knowing." He stared at his screen. I stared at it as well. He was right. That information was vital to our cause, but if Elnosefall found out we intercepted their signals... even finding out we had gained one of their secrets was enough to send them on a rampage. It seemed too easy though, all that information just there for us to find. It wasn't like Elnorsefall to be so careless, even if they thought we were going to Ardiamus instead. Maybe they were though? Maybe they got relaxed here in the jungle?

"Empress! The high commander has returned!" I heard someone shout from outside the shuttle.

So soon?

I was surprised.

"Keep working." I told Jamieson. He enthusiastically returned to his work.

"With pleasure, Empress!" He smiled at his tablet screen lovingly.

Talk about being married to your work...

I shook my head. I hurried out of the shuttle to meet Rain and Xorion. The musty, thick humidity hit me as soon as I stepped outside. Around the clearing were tall, twisting trees with vines hanging from the tops and enormous flowers as big as my whole body laid in random locations. A heavy fog was beginning to set in, covering the tops of the trees. It got slightly darker, but the sun was still able to shine through the fog. I wiped my brow. I'd been out here less than two minutes and I already felt myself becoming fatigued with the heat. Trying to ignore it, I made my way over to the soldier who called me out. He bowed his head to me and took me over to Rain. As we approached, I couldn't help but gasp in shock. They'd returned with company. Both Xorion, and another soldier each held onto an Ovidō being, one female, and the other male. Both looked equally terrified but were doing very well hiding it. I stared at them, placing my hands on my hips as I thought to myself.

Well...This just got more interesting.

23

— ❦ —

CHAPTER 22

The two beings were forced onto their knees. I stared them down, observing them. They didn't look good. Their clothes were nothing more than rags, and the female had nasty-looking bruises over her arms and legs. The male didn't look much better with fading cuts and bruises along his stomach. I looked up at Rain with a raised eyebrow. He walked over to be face-to-face with me.

"Report," I said, glancing back at the two beings shivering on the ground. Whether they were shivering from fear or pain wasn't clear.

"We found them spying on us near the camp. When we tried to question them, they didn't cooperate. They resisted." He relayed the information without any emotion in his voice. I narrowed my eyes on the two beings and stepped away from Rain to address them.

"Who are you, what do you want, and why are you here?" I asked all three questions in the same sentence trying to avoid having to ask later. The two stole a glance at each other. The female opened her mouth to speak, but then stopped. She lowered her head once more. The male lifted his eyes to stare into mine. His eyes were huge, the color of amber, but with a light silver ring around the outside of his pupil. His face was round and he had short, curly, bright red hair just like the female. They looked similar to each other, I guessed they were related somehow. It made the most sense since the two didn't seem to be romantically acquainted. I didn't want to assume anything though.

"I'm named Ravaphalor." His voice was raspy and his words slurred together oddly. I knew that their species had difficulties with our language, even universal as well because their tongues were split in the center making two halves. They couldn't pronounce certain letters. A 'b' sounded like a 'v' or a 'k' sounded like an 's'. I'd heard them speak in their own tongue before, it just sounded like a series of high pitched sounds, and hisses that our tongue made impossible to mimic. The being- Ravaphalor- glanced at his companion, and then back at me. He jerked the side of his head at her, and continued speaking.

"She 've Vi'vesshia."

"Continue." I said a bit harsher than I'd meant to. He gave me a narrowed look. I bit the bottom of my lip. The Ovidōians could be so unpredictable at times, and I really didn't want to aggravate him and cause us trouble.

"S'we spying on you, yes. Thought'a more Elnorsefall." He shrugged his shoulders casually.

"What makes you think we're not?" I raised my brows questioningly. It wasn't like I wanted them to think we were, but I was curious how he could tell. I wanted to hear our differences. He threw his head back, giving a wary laugh.

"If you were Elnorsefall, you would'a sliced off our wings already ...yes? Or worse." He grimaced. I cringed at the thought. Their wings were as part of them as their arms or legs. It was also their strongest connection to phantasm. Like us, without that connection, they would go mad.

"Now that you know we're here, we can't release you. You will be kept here, under guard. I apologize for this, but we need your full cooperation in relaying information on the planet's situation. I give you my word that you will be treated well, if you cooperate."

"Lovely' for us, hm?" He rolled his eyes sarcastically. The female- Vi'vesshia- shuddered at my words. She hadn't said anything this entire time.

"Your friend doesn't speak much, does she?" I narrowed my eyes on him and watched as his face morphed into anger.

"No, she wouldn't, would she? She's got no tongue no more." He spat on the ground. "My cousin was taken to one of their camps. One of the guards decided they didnt like her voice, so they cut out her tongue. She'd be dead if I hadn't got her out." As soon as he said the word 'camp' none of us were surprised. I stole a glance at Xorion, who looked down at the male in horror.

"You both escaped from a camp?" He nodded in response. "Near here?" I asked. Nodding once more, he pointed with his chin in the southern direction.

"Few miles that way."

My fingers reached up to gently stroke my chin. So it was close enough for us to reach. If these two managed to escape, there must have been others. I'm sure they would still be around trying to help their friends and family. The only issue was, if we attacked a camp, they would know we were here instantly. We would need our ship to cause a distraction, or perhaps we could manipulate a rebellion within the camp without actually attacking it. I frowned. Maybe I was getting too ahead of myself. Afterall, I wanted more than to free just one camp. I needed to stay patient. I glanced at the two beings still held by Xorion and the other soldier. With a flick of my wrist they released them.

"You." I told the soldier who had just released the female. "Continue to watch them." He bowed his head, accepting my command. "They will be given a proper meal, and a place to sleep. We will discuss more later."

"Thank you...?" Ravaphalor tilted his head as he stood. He stressed the last letter as if waiting for me to fill in with my name.

"I am Cloverlyne, Empress of V'rasór." His mouth fell open, eyes widening even more than I thought possible.

"V'rasór send help to us, Empress?" He seemed bewildered at the thought.

"Through me, yes. If you choose to accept this help is another matter." I answered bluntly. He nodded, aware of what he'd become involved in.

"We will help you in any way we can, Empress. Just please, please help us save others from their death. Or in the least, save them from the pain of a prolonged one." He begged with his eyes.

"To you, I make this promise, As long as I am Empress, I will do everything in my power to keep your people from this suffering." I lifted my chin high to show them I was both proud and serious about that promise. Vi'vesshia stared at me curiously, then made signs and gestures with her four fingered hands that I didn't understand. Ravaphalor watched the symbols closely.

"She asked if something has happened to the Custodian Emperor, and if you are the new Empress." He translated and tilted his head to the side. "I admit, I'm also curious about that, Empress."

"The Emperor lives, I am my own Empress of V'rasór." I answered simply, and their faces wrinkled in confusion.

"There are three royals who rule now?" He asked with a puzzled look. I nodded amusingly.

"Soon, there will be four." At this revelation, gasps were heard around me from uninformed soldiers. From their gasps I guessed Cronos had told his people very little about his plans. I didn't think there was much of an issue announcing it. It wasn't like it could make the situation any worse, and our people could use a little hope.

"V'rasór will be whole once again, and so the Realms will heal! Let Elnorsefall taste their own blood when they learn this!" Ravaphalor's wings fluttered excitedly. He then flew into the air and gave a spin while laughing hysterically, clutching his stomach.

"By eternity, they actually fly!" I heard Xorion cry out near me. Ravaphalor flew in his direction, smirking.

"Never seen an Ovidō, have you Forbidden one?" Xorion blinked, then nodded cautiously. He laughed at Xorion, then flew behind him. Before Xorion could react, he climbed onto his back. My guess was that Ravaphalor was in his early adulthood, though compared to most creatures, he was the size of a six-year-old child. He leaned into Xorion's ear and began to whisper.

"I am certain you'll enjoy yourself here, Forbidden one. We wee things can be... pleasant when we want to be... or not." He suddenly bared his teeth at him, making a hissing sound. Xorion jerked forward, knocking him off his back. Ravaphalor in return, just laughed again.

"Oh! What a sight, a great giant! What are you called?" Xorion stared at him blankly. "Name, number, any identification?" The little being said impatiently, tapping his foot on the air he hovered.

"Xorion, my name is Xorion."

Ravaphalor made a painful expression in response.

"Ew! What a name, it's not even pronounceable!"

"Oh please, you're the only one incapable of pronouncing it." I placed one hand on my hip, smirking at the little being. He made a humming sound and winked at me.

"Easy for you to say darling, your name is downright lovely' and perfectly pronounceable, see? Cloverlyyyynnnneee." He drawed out the last three letters. He turned back to Xorion, crossing his arms and concentrating. "Tell you what big guy, from now on, you shall be known as S'orion." A few of the soldiers snickered at the name he called him, and in return, Ravaphalor grinned playfully at them. If my knowledge was correct, the word closely sounded like the name of a giant beast on their planet whose meat was frequently traded throughout the Realms. It was known to be massive, but submissive, often running from its own shadow. Not that Xorion would know the implications, but I didn't like that this little creature was poking fun at my fiance in front of me. I opened my mouth to put the little being in his place, but closed my mouth abruptly. If I spoke up for Xorion now, it wouldn't look good for either of our's image in front of the soldiers. Xorion was a strong warrior. He could fight his own battles, he didn't need me stepping in.

"Xorion is my name. I'll keep it, thank you." Xorion rolled his eyes at Ravaphalor, who put his hand over his heart, looking offended.

"But great giant! I call you S'orion, it's your name now!" He insisted with a grin from ear to ear. Xorion pinched the bridge of his nose, as if he was dealing with a child. The soldiers looked at Ravaphalor with amusement, and even I smiled. Xorion was keeping his cool, now the little being just looked annoying rather than clever.

"No, it isn't."

"Yes, it is."

"Alright enough!" I called out to them both, but my eyes stayed on Ravaphalor. The little being turned to me with a startled expression. "Everyone back to your post. You two Ovidōians, your guard will show you where the food and resting tent is." I nodded over to the guard who had just stood there watching the entire situation quietly.

"Thank you kindly, darling!" Ravaphalor said, tipping his head forward. He then said something in his own language to the female, and they both fluttered off after the guard.

"Thank eternity!" Xorion exclaimed loudly. Other soldiers lingering around breathed out in relief that they were gone as well. I burst out laughing. It probably wasn't appropriate for me to laugh at the situation, but I couldn't help it.

"Poor you." I teased. "I found him quite charming."

"Did you?" He asked warily. He shook his head with a sigh. "Are they always like that?"

"Unfortunately, yes. These two are actually more calm compared to some." I answered honestly. The last Ovidōian's I met was on Eurkxo. I remember him flying around in circles, bumping into things, and then laughing about it as if he were drunk... which in a way he was. Because of the way phantasm affected their biology, they were constantly active, and overly hyper. Their thoughts never paused, and they never stopped having things to say.

"My three elites, and Rain, join me." I raised my voice loudly, hoping everyone could hear. We needed to have a meeting on what we were going to do next. If those two Ovidōians were able to get out of the camps, then it meant Elnorsefall wasn't as secure as usual. That would be very helpful to us. Xorion's eyes lingered on me in a sad way. I knew he wanted to be a part of this, be at my side as both a protector and as an equal. I almost wished it could be that way. I met his lingering eyes and gently shook my head. For the sake of both our lives, I needed him at arm's length. If I pulled him any closer, he would only be in more danger. I watched as he visibly tensed, but still managed a sharp nod of his head.

"I'll see you around?" He asked, still a bit tense, but a small smile tipped his lips.

I smiled back, "Of course. For now, stay with the other soldiers."

He nodded more enthusiastically this time, and turned to follow the other soldiers who were heading toward the other side of the camp. I used the back of my hand to wipe a sheen layer of sweat from my forehead, and made my way near the back of the ship. My elites and Rain followed behind me. Finally reaching a more private spot, I turned to face them.

"I suppose it's time to settle on a plan for moving forward." Sovren commented with a bow of his head.

"Agreed, we need options." I responded, and their heads nodded at my words. "If we infiltrate the camps first, we would gain those that are imprisoned. If two Ovidōians managed to escape the camps, I see no reason why we would not be able to release the rest, but we would also be revealing ourselves sooner than we expected."

"We could distract them by sending in the mothership." Rain suggested. "It was always our plan to reveal ourselves eventually." I nodded, because that was my original plan, but with Jamison's new information about the Elnorsefall ship being signaled too, it may not be a good idea to reveal ourselves already.

"The pilot, Jamieson, has given me a different thought from my original idea. There is a ground station sending signals up to an

Elnorsefall mothership." My eyes darted around to each of them. All of them leaned in at my words.

"A signal? Does he know what's being sent up?" Kaycion asked. Elnorsefall was stubbornly careful. Their Emperor was more than just smart, he knew his enemies well. He knew us. They kept their secrets by keeping their own in the dark, which made it difficult to gather any kind of intelligence from them, and it was impossible to infiltrate them since those required connections. And those who followed Elnorsefall, died for them proudly. That was why any scrap of intelligence we could get was vital to this war.

"He is currently attempting to tap into the signal. That information could be very useful to us, but I fear it will distract us from our original goal... The facility sending the information out is quite near us." I tipped my head downwards. Rain's face wrinkled in confusion.

"Why would they send a signal out? Wouldn't they assume we'd come here? At least as a precaution?" He asked almost to himself, crossing his arms nervously. I frowned in thought. He was right, they were being careless.

"I agree, it's suspicious, but also remember that they are used to dealing with Emperor Cronos, who would never risk sending soldiers here to aid the prisoners he's taken. He knows we sent protection to Láuran, perhaps we have fooled them. I suppose they felt safe, and perhaps the information is too large to send any other way, even if it is a risk for them."

"That's true, perhaps they have become arrogant." Garettano said, finally speaking up. I noticed him and Kaycion seemed much quieter than Sovren.

"Arrogant, yes. But they are not fools. There must be more to this." Sovren shook his head and leaned up against the ship while looking up at Rain, who eyed him back knowingly,

"I don't like it either, but you're right. If they are being forced to relay information using this planet as a signal base, then it must be too large to send otherwise. It could be intel on a weakness!"

"I doubt it. Doing this basically says 'look at us, were giving away vital information on our own weakness, come and get it!'" Sovren said sarcastically, making quotations with his fingers. Kaycion nudged him, giving him a look that said 'not the time'. Sovren waved him off.

"I'll see if Jamieson has gathered any more information on this. Rain, find out as much information you can get from our two guests. The rest of you, prepare yourselves and those you command. We may be taking a little road trip soon." I flicked my hand to dismiss them. They bowed and left to attend to their duties. I hurried to the shuttle's entrance and took a breath to prepare my questions before entering. Jamieson was still inside, typing furiously on his tablet. He didn't even seem to notice someone entering. I didn't want to frighten him, but I had to gain his attention somehow.

"Jamieson..." I said slowly, but frightening him couldn't be helped. He jumped and twisted around to see who it was. Unfortunately, his movement made him drop his tablet.

"Dear Natarah..." He mumbled angrily. I glanced at him sheepishly.

"Apologies." I started, but he quickly shook his head, dismissing my apology.

"Oh no, no, no, Empress. It was not your fault. I just wasn't expecting anyone at this time... that is time which I do not know what time it is. Ah... Oh right!" He bowed his head worriedly. "Empress, how can I be of help?" I released the breath I hadn't known I was holding.

"How is the progress on your... discovery?" I asked gently, holding my hands behind my back as I stepped forward. He sighed, "Slower than I had hoped I'm afraid. The codes are incredibly complex, and it seems the information is encrypted, but I am getting closer with every minute!" He said excitedly. "It's so much that I can only get a fraction of it, as I said before, but I believe something big is happening. If I could get inside the facility..." He shook his head and reached down to pick up his tablet.

"Damn." He muttered. When I leaned in to see what had upset him, I saw a small crack was now on the screen of the tablet. The crack was so small that it shouldn't have upset anyone, but Jamieson looked at it as though his whole world had been destroyed, which didn't surprise me. It probably was.

"I'm certain it can be fixed." I tried to soothe. He sniffled which made me freeze. Was that a tear I saw? He jerked away nodding at my statement.

"Yes, yes, I'm sure... anyways." He murmured, setting the tablet aside. I coughed, raising an eyebrow at him, he shifted uncomfortably as I asked him for more detail about his work.

"So you've managed to tap into their signal?" He rubbed his fingers together nervously, which made me dread the answer. Then, his eyes brightened as he held up his pointer finger.

"I have identified the main stream of the signal and isolated it on my system here." He said, indicating the tablet. His eyes lingered on it for a second and he frowned, but quickly smiled brightly once more when he looked up at me proudly. I smiled in relief, curious why he had not mentioned that before he mentioned that going to the facility would be our best hope of finding the information.

"Excellent! When can we look through it?"

"Look through it, Empress?" He asked, giving me a puzzled look. I blinked at him.

"Did you not just say that you identified and isolated the main stream of the signal?"

"Yes?" He said questionably, still looking confused. I blinked twice at him.

"So what is the issue in looking through the information?"

"You can't." He said as if it were obvious. I blinked again at him. He had just stated that he isolated the signal, why couldn't we start gathering information from it?

"And why not?" I asked impatiently.

"I have isolated the signal, but in no way can I transcribe it on this mere shuttle, or send it to our mothership without them noticing. The codes it contains are too complex, and I am still trying to crack the encryption." He said with a shrug. I collapsed into the nearest chair, my jaw tightening as I tried to remain calm. I spoke threateningly quiet, which he seemed to notice as he stilled.

"And why did you not..." I breathed out, still trying to remain calm, though I was feeling quite the opposite at the moment.. "....mention that in the first place!" I raised my voice sweetly through clenched teeth, trying to cover up the fact that I was so frustrated with him. He shuttered.

"Apologies, Empress." He said, bowing his head. I waved my hand letting him know it was fine. He raised his head a little. Seeing that I wasn't going to say anything more, he fully raised his head. Fumbling with his spectacles, he picked up the tablet once more.

I sighed again, "Just... keep working." I told him.

He smiled happily, "Yes, Empress!"

I gave an exasperated smile while retreating from the inside of the shuttle. I needed some fresh air.

"Empress?" I heard someone near me say. Whipping around I saw Sovren, and Rain walking towards me rather quickly.

"Sovren, Rain." I greeted them with a weary smile.

"You look exhausted." Rain frowned as he looked me over. I dropped my forced smile, sighing.

"I'm hoping for some good news."

"Good news indeed!" Rain nodded his head, and looked at Sovren, who looked back at him tilting his head as if to ask for permission. Rain gave him a curt nod, and he turned to face me, straightening his posture. I gave them both curious glances. Sovren grinned widely at me,

"We have a plan."

24

CHAPTER 23

"I'm listening." I crossed my arms while looking between the two of them, waiting for whoever was going to speak first. The second my eyes fell on Sovren, he spoke up.

"We don't have the power to face them head-on, not with a mothership hovering above us." He smirked, "So we don't."

"Explain." I tilted my head curiously. This time, it was Rain who spoke up, making exaggerated gestures with his hands as he continued for Sovren.

"We were talking to Ravaphalor. That facility you told us about? It's new. It's their only current command center on this planet. It's their only communication with the mothership. Without that command center, their authority will fall apart."

"It will send the soldiers in command of the camps into chaos." I thought out loud. Rain and Sovren nodded their heads enthusiastically.

"Those soldiers will be called back to protect that facility." Sovren explained. "And the prisoners will have an opening to rebel against them. We just need a way to let them know without exposing our plans."

"That intel Elnorsefall's sending up is vital, Empress. If we go for it, then we'll not only give the prisoners a chance, but we could make a real difference in this war." There was a hope in Rain's eyes, a hope I wanted to believe in. It could work, it was risky, but this entire mission was. I couldn't back out now.

"And how would we let the prisoners know when to rebel? We would need them all to attack at once in order for it to be effective." I asked skeptically. I wanted to believe this would be easy, but nothing with Elnorsefall was ever easy. "We don't even know the location of all the camps, and we would need to get in contact with them without alerting Elnosefall of our presence. An encrypted message perhaps?"

"Yes, in the tongue of the locals." Rain suggested. "They know their home best; they will know the camp locations."

"If they choose to do nothing..." I murmured, but Sovren was already shaking his head.

"They will act, Empress."

"But if they don't." I insisted on an answer. I couldn't put our trust in them. I would not put our survival in their hands.

He sighed, "They have been imprisoned, tortured, and thrown to the side on their own planet. I don't believe they'll care about the consequences of fighting back. The Ovidō are clever beings, when the opportunity arises, they will not hesitate."

"So you believe." I accused, narrowing my eyes. I sighed again. It had so many ifs, but what choice did we have? "For our sake and theirs, I hope you are right."

"Empress, it will work." Sovren said desperately, locking eyes with me. I stared back, daring him to doubt himself. To my relief, he didn't. I trusted his confidence. Nodding, I turned my attention back to Rain, who waited patiently for me to address him.

"Then we should prepare to travel, shouldn't we?" I asked.

Rain nodded again, "This is the best option we have, but..."

"What?" I demanded, and he shifted his weight from left to right.

"If there's another option... You informed us earlier that there's a possibility that the intel could be gained without having to take the risk." He searched my eyes for signs of hope.

"It's not possible. Even if we did, there's no way to keep the intel without sending it to our mothership. And that would expose us." I replied with a huff. I wished I could've given them more reassuring answers. Rain and Sovren gave each other a knowing look.

"It's well guarded isn't it?" Sovren murmured to himself, giving off a short laugh. I glanced at him, confused about what he was talking about.

"The facility?"

"It was my suggestion, Empress..." Rain bowed his head as if asking for permission to continue. I gestured with a nod for him to keep going. "We should only take a small team to infiltrate this facility. If that information is as valuable as we think it is, it's worth the risk. Either way they'll flood the facility, but we may have time to escape quicker if we have smaller numbers..." He paused for a moment, looking at me sheepishly. "That is if..."

"We will proceed with your plan." Both men's eyes gleamed with approval. Clearly they were proud of themselves for coming up with the idea. "And Rain?" I said his name to get his attention with a small smile. He looked up at me, tilting his head.

"Me, Jamieson, and Xorion will be on that team traveling to the facility."

"What!?" Both Rain and Sovren said in shock. I raised a brow at their sudden outburst.

"Apologies, Empress. You surprise us. We worry about your safety." Sovren said worriedly, then shut his mouth awkwardly before just simply nodding and accepting my terms. However, Rain being my brother, didn't share in Sovren's formalities and didn't apologize. Rather, he continued to express his overwhelming concern.

"Empress." He smiled tightly through his teeth."If I may, it's best if you stay where the shuttle is."

"No, I'm going." I responded stubbornly. "That is final." Rain opened his mouth to fight about it, but one stoney glare from me and he abruptly closed his mouth, although his eyes still fummed angrily. Sovren stood nervously, casting a sideways glance from Rain to me.

"I admit, Empress, I don't like it. However, I agree with your decision." Sovren bowed his head to me before murmuring an apology to Rain, who just glared at him for agreeing with me. I smiled sweetly.

"Prepare yourselves, and inform the others of the plan." Without another word, I turned and walked away in no particular direction. I looked around the camp. When soldiers heard the word 'prepare' I'm sure only one thought came to mind. Weapons. Even though my phantasm was significantly stronger than most due to my lineage, I could still easily tire. A knife, or even a gun would be a wise thing for me to bring. I wasn't as familiar with weapons as my brother was, but I could manage. Both Rain and Adam took me to a training center with them a few times back on Eurkxo. Adam had said I was pretty good with my aim. Although, I'm sure it's different in a real situation, but it shouldn't be that different.

I glanced around for a supply tent before spotting it near the center of camp. It was more of a giant camouflage sheet held up by four poles. I made my way over to it, ignoring the soldiers that bowed their heads respectfully towards me. I inwardly smiled at their respect. I liked it... I craved it. It made me feel powerful. It made me feel like I could really make a difference. Reaching the tent, my gaze fell over each of the crates carrying supplies and weaponry. I hesitantly opened one. Inside was a bunch of rather large guns that were laid tightly together. I frowned. Not exactly what I was looking for. I slid the crate away. Sitting down on my knees, I chose another crate to open. Inside the new crate, I found smaller handheld guns. Perfect. I picked up the one closest to me and double checked the safety before standing and aiming it at the nearest tree-trunk. I shuffled with it until I felt comfortable with my form. I was far from being considered a soldier, but it would have to do. I wished I could just rely on my phantasm, but it wasn't a good idea for me to rely on it fully. Long fights could lead to exhaustion. Overusing phantasm and pushing yourself too far often led to painful side effects. I wasn't well versed in the nature of said side effects though, I only knew what I was taught. Basically, it would hurt. It would hurt really, really bad. It was part of the reason why Eurkxo was willing to trade cores for that gas the Fehichen offered. We could've used some right about now. Guns were preferable in an army, and not just for those reasons. They also gave a clearer shot in battle of who was hit. Our phantasm could be... unpredictable. Sometimes, it could just knock someone off their feet, while other times, it could kill in an instant. It could go wild when it wasn't controlled properly, something that came with age and maturity.

There were those that claimed it had a mind of its own. A cult, the Rizen... They believed it was its own separate being, a thoughtful creature of desire. A truly bizarre and mad belief for a rather insane group of people. The whole concept was laughable. Our phantasm was a part of us. We were born with it just as we were born with hands and feet. Our hands did not have minds of their own did they? The very notion would be ridiculous. It always just... was. It was us.

I sighed while setting the gun back on the table, staring at it for a few moments and contemplating the thought of being in battle. I fought before, but it was always in self-defense. Would this be different? I didn't know the answer.

I felt someone move behind me, and before I knew who it was, they placed their hands on my shoulders, massaging them. I took in a deep breath, easily knowing who it was. It was Xorion. I glanced around, noticing that some of the soldiers were eyeing us before completely avoiding looking our way. This wasn't a good look for either of us, especially since I just insisted that both of us were going on the team heading to the facility. I shifted my weight. Still, I didn't want to refuse him. The way his warm hands worked through the knots in my shoulders felt good. I didn't want him to stop. His lips pressed against my ear.

"Want to take a walk?" he whispered, letting his hand drop to mine. Clever man. If we could get out of the vision of soldiers, we might just have some alone time. His other hand slid down my back just right so that I felt a warm jolt of excitement spread throughout my entire body.

"Yes." I murmured, still in a daze from it. He chuckled and grabbed hold of my hand, leading me out of the tent and into the jungle.

We were silent for some time until we reached a small clearing. He cleared his throat, and I looked up at him expectantly.

"Rain told me about the plan." He stared off past the trees. I looked down, fixating my eyes on a leaf that appeared to be moving.

Perhaps there was a small critter taking shelter there?

I sighed before replying.

"Did he?" I said a little too darkly to escape his notice. He looked at me with concern. Did it bother me that Rain told him before me? Yes. Did it matter? Not really, but it did to me. Rain really needed to stay out of my personal business. Xorion was my responsibility. If I had wanted Rain to tell him, I would have told him to. Unfortunately, what was done was done. I hoped Xorion wouldn't try to argue with me about it.

"I take it there's no way to talk you out of this?" He scratched his chin thoughtfully. I lifted my head, narrowing my eyes on him.

"Nope."

He sighed again, releasing a deep breath.

"Then I won't." He reached out to lift my chin, so we were eye to eye. He dropped his hands to rest on forearms, before curling his hands around them and sliding his hands down.

"I missed you." he whispered.

"I missed you too." I said, looking up at him with a sad smile. His hands shifted to my waist as he pulled me to him and walked backwards until his back hit a nearby tree. As his back hit the tree, he gently slid down, gently tugging me down and turning me so that I was sitting comfortably in his lap. He curled one arm around me, steading me. His other hand lifted to my head, and he ran his fingers through my hair. I closed my eyes and leaned back until the side of my cheek rested against his chest. It felt nice to be held by another. He wasn't the most calming presence, but he did make me feel special. Before I knew it, all my worries left my mind as I listened to the rhythmic pattern of his heartbeat.

"I want you." I murmured. "I want you by my side... always." In response, his hand that had gently been running through my hair, slid to my neck, gently stroking my skin with his warm fingers.

"I know." he said quietly. He tilted my chin upwards while he smiled down at me. He leaned in and kissed my lips. "I won't get in your way so long as you don't jump into some kind of fire. I can't just ignore my protective instincts." He chuckled at the last part, and I nestled back under his chin.

"Do you miss your home world?" I asked, changing the subject. He sighed pulling me closer to him.

"Every day," he whispered back longingly. "I wish I could take you there. I wish we could be there, together."

"I sometimes wish to be elsewhere too. The Realms... it's so broken."

The Realms was my home. Home was a place you were supposed to feel safe in. How could anyone feel safe here though? My mother died by a madman, the rest of my family slaughtered by him, and now my friends were being hunted. Lucia was still missing, possibly already dead. It was all Elnorsefall's fault. She was so innocent. She was younger, and far from the scene when her parents were killed, unlike I was. She didn't deserve to die out there, alone. A small tear fell from my eyes. I reached up to wipe it away, but Xorion grabbed my hand, stopping me from doing so. I looked up at him, a bit confused.

"What did I say before about your tears?" I looked away sadly, letting the tear roll down my face. "Why do you cry?" he asked.

Somehow, I knew he wanted me to answer for myself, rather than for him. I really didn't want to talk about it, but I knew he would only keep asking until I did.

"I was thinking about Lucia. I miss her, worry about her... If she is hurt, or worse... I think my heart will fall into a million pieces." I choked out, more tears falling from my eyes. She was considered family to me, just as Rain, Adam, and now Xorion were. I trusted her, and there were very few people I trusted. All I wanted was to know she was safe, but we had no word from her. I feared we never would.

"I trust Cedric, he would give his life in her protection. I'm certain they're both safe." He tried to soothe. I knew that of course. Him and Cedric were friends and trusted each other, but Cedric had given me no reason to trust him, so I didn't. I couldn't tell that to Xorion though, I wouldn't be cruel in making him doubt his friend.

"I just don't want to lose anyone else." I murmured, burrowing my face deep into his chest. He gently rubbed the back of my head with his hand. "Promise me you will never leave me. Promise that you will not give your life for mine, I couldn't bear to live with the knowledge you did that. I'd rather die." I begged him.

He tensed at my words, "Clove, I cannot promise that I wouldn't-"

"We leave this life together." I cut him off. My tone was final. "Do not make me choose to live with your death on my conscience. Do not torture me in that way." He stayed quiet for a moment. To my relief, he finally nodded.

"If there is a choice, we leave this life together."

We stayed there together for quite a while before I mentioned we should return. Someone would become curious about our whereabouts.

"They'll be wondering where we are." I stood up and stretched my arms and legs. He smiled knowingly.

"They'll be wondering where you are Empress, I can go wherever I want, and they wouldn't care." He chuckled.

"Well you have a gift for getting out of trouble, something I'll admit I envy." I mumbled to myself. He got up, and pulled me up with him while squeezing my hand gently.

"Only the best kind of trouble." He smirked suggestively as he stood over me. I hit him playfully on his shoulder. He laughed, and placed a gentle kiss on the back of my neck.

We slowly made our way back to the camp. This jungle of trees all looked the same, it would be like a maze when we started our journey. I froze, my eyes lighting up with the thought. How would we be able to navigate through the jungle without any knowledge of it? What if we got turned around or lost... or attacked by some animal?

"Clove? You alright?" Xorion gently shook my shoulder, unfreezing my daze.

"Yes, I just had a thought. How will we navigate through this jungle?" I asked, continuing to move forward. Xorion thought about it for a moment.

"You're right, we need someone who knows these forests." He agreed while crossing his arms over his chest. I watched his brows come together as he concentrated on finding a way to fix the new issue. An issue I'd already solved.

"What we need..." I started confidently, "Is a guide."

"A guide?" Xorion asked as if he hadn' even considered it. I smiled widely at him.

"Yes, and I know just who it will be."

25

—— ◆ ——

CHAPTER 24

I found Rain and Sovren together near one of the tents along with Garettano, talking to a group of soldiers. I hurried over to them and they bowed their heads when they noticed me coming their way.

"Rain, Sovren." I turned towards Garettano and nodded my head. "Garettano, I take it you've been informed?"

"Yes, Empress."

He turned towards the soldiers and motioned for them to disperse. The group hurried off to do whatever tasks they'd been assigned, and Garettano turned back to me, giving me a look that said they were ready for whatever I had to tell them.

"We lack a way to navigate, we don't know these jungles. We don't have the time to get lost or scout out a safe path." I said, getting straight to the point. Sovren nodded as if he'd been thinking the same.

"You're correct, Empress. We risk losing our way."

"We could have Jamieson arrange a map to the facility, but it may not be accurate." Garettano chimed in thoughtfully.

I shook my head in response. "It would take too much time." Before any of them could respond, I continued. "I had a different idea."

"What's the idea?" Rain asked, crossing his arms in interest.

"I thought perhaps we should arrange a guide."

"A guide?" Both Rain and Sovren said at the same time with a glance at each other. A soft smile appeared on Garettano's lips.

"Ah, I get what you plan to do."

"Yes, the young Ovidō male we have here with us. He seemed to know these woods well enough. I am almost certain he knows where this facility was built." Understanding dawned on Rain and Sovren's faces.

"I do believe Ravaphalor knows it well, I've asked him many questions about the layouts in these woods, and his answers add up." Sovren commented proudly.

"Empress, if I may. We don't know if he can be trusted." Rain said through a frown.

I nodded, "I understand that, and as much as I don't like the idea of putting our trust in an Ovidōian, he's our best chance at getting there as quickly as possible."

"The Ovidō may be greedy creatures, but they are not fools. He knows he has a better chance of survival with us than helping Elnorsefall." Garettano said, supporting my decision. Sovren turned to Rain and shrugged.

"I see no real harm in it other than him driving us crazy."

Rain frowned deeper as if the thought hadn't occurred to him till now.

I smile, "Excellent, inform him that he will be accompanying us." I noticed Rain shifting and I tilted my head at him.

"Empress, what of the other? His cousin?" He stroked his chin thoughtfully. "She would be here, left alone. He will not agree to her being a prisoner here."

"Of course not, from this point forward, neither of them are considered prisoners." Another idea forms in my mind. "Let both of them know of our plans. She could be an asset in spreading the word to the camps. She will be our contact. As for us, we leave tonight."

"Understood, Empress. If I may, I suggest you change into something more appropriate for... rougher terrain." Sovren's cheeks turned slightly red as he looked over at me. I raised a brow at him, but knew he was right. I needed something comfortable, but also something that would blend in with the rest of the soldiers.

"Acknowledged, Sovren." I nodded my head in goodbye and walked away. With a quick request to a soldier to point me in the right direction, I found the tent that kept extra uniforms. This tent was different than the others in the sense it was an actual covered one on all sides, which I was glad for because I needed to change. I just hoped there was one my size. Most of the female soldiers were considerably bigger than me from building up their muscle mass, whereas I hadn't. Most civilians and royals had no need to build muscle. Our military only did so in case their phantasm was compromised. Greater physical strength could easily become an advantage if the enemy was sloppy with their control. I made my way over to where a stack of female uniforms laid out in crates. I checked to see if anyone was on their way in before quickly slipping out of my dress into the more comfortable fitted pants and long-sleeved vest that surprisingly kept me cool rather than hot. It also came with a weapons belt. The material was fascinating. I'd never worn something like it before, but I'd felt it from Rain's past uniforms. It was specifically made to work with our agility and phantasm makeup. It hardened upon impact but remained soft until then.

I tied my hair back with a quick, messy braid, and twisted it up into a bun to keep it out of my face. I looked down at myself and smirked. I bet I looked like a proper young soldier rather than a headstrong Empress.

I hurried out of the tent and headed to the weapons tent where I'd previously been. Giving a quick glance around, I found the crate filled with the gun I'd selected. I picked one up and clip it to the belt of the pants. As I walked outside, I noticed the color of the uniform was changing colors. I hadn't given much thought to the other soldiers' uniforms and how they matched our surroundings, but I suppose it made sense to have some kind of camouflage. It wasn't a perfect mimic, but it was better than nothing. I glanced out from under the tent and saw dark clouds filling the sky as night fell. It was time.

I made my way over to the edge of the camp where other soldiers, Sovren, Rain, Xorion, Jamieson, and Ravahalor were gathered. Neither Garettano nor Kacion were present. I supposed that was a good thing, someone had to watch the camp and make sure those encrypted messages got through. I gave a curt nod to each of them, and then looked off into the distance. I turned back towards the Ovidōian.

"It's good of you to join us, Ravaphalor."

"As if I had a choice..." He mumbled to himself, tossing a glare at Sovren.

Sovren smirked, "Oh, I assure you it was your choice. If you don't wish to join us, I'm sure we can arrange for you to be elsewhere." He said as he lightly slapped his shoulder. Ravaphalor grunted in response, before shrugging.

"Have to say Empress, I never thought I'd be escorting V'rasóians, and a Forbidden one to an Elnorsefall facility... What a strange time we're living in. Also, my Lady can call me Rava, if you wish." He said, winking at me with a toothy smile. Xorion sighed loudly, and I couldn't help but let out a laugh.

"Thank you, Rava." I said through a smile.

"Very kind of you." Rain said sarcastically. He swung his hands towards the jungle.

"Let's go."

We stepped into the jungle, beginning our long journey. We walked in silence for only about an hour, climbing over roots, and ducking under low twisting tree-limbs. It was definitely not my favorite planet to be on.

"And I thought the clearing back at our camp was hot." Sovren said, speaking for the first time since starting the trip. He miserably brushed the sweat off his neck.

Rava grunted, "It's not even the peak of the heating season yet." He looked around as if searching for something. "But now that you mention it, I do think there's a river village around here. It's abandoned now, but it was built along the river over that way." He jerked his head in no particular direction. Xorions eyes perked up at the word 'river.'

"Perhaps we can take shelter there, how far is it from where we are?"

"A good four hours I think." Rava said, shrugging.

"Do you know if Elnorsefall searches the villages?" Sovren asked curiously.

"Nah mate, they already cleared this one. I met some of the villagers at my old death camp."

"And there's plenty of fresh water from the sounds of it." Xorion said, eyeing me as if hoping I'll agree with him. It seemed to be a valid idea, and we would have to take shelter eventually anyways. Fresh water was always good to have, but I suspected it was something more to Xorion's people based on the way his eyes always lit up when he either saw or drank it. Perhaps it was considered sacred in their world? I wasn't sure. Perhaps I could ask him later about it. I guess it didn't matter, I'd forget about it by the time this trip ended. I was about to agree with Xorion's idea when another soldier I didn't know spoke up.

"Why don't we just take the river then?"

"To the facility?" Xorion asked, wanting to clarify his question, and the soldier nodded enthusiastically. I didn't want to say anything, but I believed if there was a way to take the river, Rava would have taken us that way in the first place. As expected, I saw Rava laughing hysterically in front of us. The soldier, seeing this, turned bright red in anger at being laughed at.

"Funny giant!" Rava said, still laughing. "The river doesn't go that way, stupid giant. Also, it runs downhill, hence the facility being on high ground, we couldn't take the river even if it did go that way... It's not even necessary to mention the river's treacherous ways." He rolled his eyes. "Didn't think Elnorsefall was as dumb as that, did you? They never would have come to be if they'd had your brain!" The soldier bit his lip until blood seeped out, and Rava chuckled in amusement at the sight. The soldier seemed to be at his limit of self-control, but Rava didn't seem to mind as he continued his insults. I felt bad for the soldier. He was the object of Rava's boredom. "Come to think of it, I can't really say that now, can I? I mean, you came to be so there's that... I guess you've just inherited it from your family bloodline... You'd think your people would have fixed that problem already, being the perfectionist they are." The soldiers' markings flared at Rava's words.

"Watch your tongue insect! Or you might lose it!" Then the soldier smirked. "Or does that run in the family too?"

"Enough, soldier!" Rain yelled at him, but the damage was already done. Rava literally had some kind of smoke coming from his mouth. I shuddered, remembering that some of their species had the ability to release a fire-like substance from their lungs.

"If you dare say anything about my cousin again, I will fry you in your sleep, human." Rava sneered out the last word, and the soldier took two steps forward, clearly wanting a fight, but Rain stepped in front of him.

"You take one more step in revenge, and I'll throw you out of my ranks." Rain warned, and the soldier sank his head in shame.

"Apologies, High Commander."

I wasn't surprised the soldier reacted the way he did. Although, it wasn't like calling someone 'human' was offensive, it wasn't. But most used the word as a way to mock each other by stating that we all share the same genetic makeup. Early wars started for the same reason. We wanted to separate from each other, from the first planet. The fact that we were still 'human' at our core, connected us. Most used it in an offensive way though, like saying 'Whatever you say to me is of your blood as well.' V'rasóians especially would be offended by that since we're closest to the human form, and I'm sure Ovidōians just loved to annoy us in such ways.

I should've been paying attention to my footing rather than thinking. Before I knew it, my foot caught on a root, knocking me off balance. Thankfully, Xorion was behind me, catching hold of me before I fell. I blushed as his hands wrapped tightly around my waist.

"Thank you." I said quietly, still blushing deeply. He flashed me a toothy smile and helped me regain my balance. Before he released me, he tightened his hands and murmured something in his language that I didn't understand. Based on his tone, I gathered it was something I would have liked. I smiled at him, but then frowned when I realized those around us were watching. I hoped no one was watching too closely. The last thing I wanted was for Rava to start yapping about it. Dear Natarah! Ovidōians were such blabber mouths. They couldn't keep their little mouths shut even if it saved their lives. I noticed Rain's eyes lingering on us, but then he simply turned away and coincidentally started to cough loudly. Realization dawned on me as I noticed most of the attention was taken off of me and Xorion to ask if Rain was okay. My heart beamed. Rain was protecting our relationship.

We continued walking for what felt like hours. Rava continuously chatted about some game that was popular among D'thayans, but I was too zoned out to pay him any mind. I stared at the ground, watching my own feet, careful where I placed them. I didn't even know how long I was doing that for, but it seemed to be long enough for my neck muscles to become tight. I lifted my head and rolled the muscles out, making a few popping sounds. I glanced around to take a good look at our surroundings. The forest was thick with greenery. Thick moss clung to the trunks of trees, and flowers hung out of holes in the trunks as well while pretty vines full of red fruit hung from their branches. The smell is mouthwatering, but Rava warned us not to touch, let alone eat them. According to him, the vines lured prey to eat their fruit, and when touched, the fruit seeped out a kind of acid onto its victims, paralyzing them while the vines constricted its victims. Not a pleasant death in the least. We kept our distance after hearing that.

Looking off into the distance I noticed some flickering orange lights. Curious, I asked about them while pointing a finger in their direction.

"Is that the village?" Others turned their attention to the lights after I pointed them out.

"Yes, Empress." Rava answered, nodding to me. "Half an hour's walk till arrival."

"Oh! Thank God above!" Rain groaned out while giving an elaborate stretch. "We've been walking forever!"

"Y'all just slow. If it were only me, I would've been there already." Rava grumbled, clearly annoyed he couldn't just fly off wherever he wanted.

"And if you would turn off your constant yapper about ridiculously unnecessary conversations such as your mother's soup, we would not be half out of our minds, unable to walk in peace!" Xorion blurted out from behind me. Rava gave him a look of utter shock at the implication his conversations were unnecessary.

"Why you good for nothing simpleton! For your information, my mother's soup is the most magnificent! Famous in all this half the galaxy!"

"Yeah, go figure that." Sovren chimed in, rolling his eyes at Rava. "You're the only ones in this half of the galaxy!" I groaned, placing my hand on my forehead. One would think they'd run out of things to argue about by now.

"Gentlemen, please." I begged, feeling a headache overtake me. Xorion, and Rain looked at me with concern, but Sovren and Rava continued their little debate.

"You wouldn't understand unless you've tasted the magnificentness of it!" Rava threw his hands in the air, quickly dismissing me.

"I'm sure Elnorsefall flew all the way over here just to try it!" Sovren said, sarcastically snapping his fingers. "And that's hardly even a word!"

"Sure, it is!" Rava insisted, ignoring his earlier comment. "All other soup is invalid!"

Soven scoffed, "Oh joy, I can imagine!"

"I don't know what's harder to believe..." Xorion grabbed my shoulder and whispered into my ear. "The fact that they haven't run out of remarks to say, or that they're arguing... about soup!" He shook his head in amazement. "Soup!?"

I sighed, feeling myself zone out once again, but it wasn't for as long as last time. The half-hour went by quickly, and Rava announced we had entered the village.

The village looked like it had been abandoned for a long time. Most of the giant lanterns lay broken on the ground, while some were still on their post and were burning with an artificial flame. Weeds grew through the path so tall that it was hardly recognizable, and thin vines not so unlike the previous ones clung to the doors of the houses. However, most of the houses still possessed a sturdy stone fence and gate. Unlike most houses I'd known, these had roofs that were larger and taller than the house itself, and at the top, overgrown gardens were kept. I frowned at the gardens at the tops of the roofs, wondering how they got up there when there were no stairs to climb up. I stared for a second longer before letting out a laugh. They had wings! Of course they didn't need stairs, or ladders unless their wings were injured. The houses also had enormous open windows bordered with pretty, yet rather wild looking vines, and every house was made of the same rustic wood and looked considerably cozy considering the condition of the unkempt houses. The river flowed through the center of the village and continued downhill. I followed the others across a low bridge that crossed the river. Most of the soldiers used their hands to quench their thirst, while others like me chose to simply refill our water containers and drank from there. One of the soldiers brought out a supply bag which was filled with supplements to give us energy, but Rava had other ideas. We watched in interest as he grabbed two bags and flew up to the roof gardens. When he returned, the bags were filled with deliciously smelling fruit.

"Take your fill." Rava insisted, following his own advice by biting into a red and yellow fruit. Juice poured out the sides of the fruit as his teeth sank deeply into it, and the fragrance was unbearable to just sit and watch. Following Rava's example, I reached into the bag and pulled out a soft green colored fruit. I turned the fruit in my hands, inspecting it. I found that the soft green part was actually not part of the fruit, just the outer skin. I happily peeled off the outer cover. The fruit underneath was soft, and pretty blue. I bit into it slowly, letting myself smile as the aroma filled my nose. It was the most delicious fruit I'd ever tasted in my life. It had the perfect mixture of sweetness that was balanced by a sour flavor. I continued to eat, enjoying every bite while I watched the others more hesitantly choose theirs.

"What happened to this village? Why did your people abandon it?" Sovren asked curiously as he chewed a deep yellow fruit. Rava shrugged.

"I heard they'd got a warning that Elnorsefall was coming this way to interrogate the village folk, so they either left for another village, or vanished into the jungle."

"I figured that they'd want to take them to the camps, not interrogate them. What would they want to interrogate a bunch of village folk for?" Rain asked, just as curious as Sovren was about the ordeal.

"They wanted to find the Echloi river passage." He said simply. All of our heads snapped up at the mention of the Echloi.

"The fish people? Why'd they want them?" Sovren asked in shock. I frown a little at Sovren's remark. Even though their name literally translated to 'fish people' it wasn't very respectful seeing that we were on their home planet. They were like the Ōvidoians I heard, but with some differences in their wings, size, and environmental needs. I'd never met one before. They were an oddly silent people I'd been told, and never traveled off planet. Rava gave Sovren an exasperated look.

"Elnorsefall wants to rule everyone. Why would they not want them?" Sovren shrugged his shoulders, not caring for Rava's explanation.

"True enough, but still, unless Elnorsefall wants to get their uniforms all wet diving into the waters of their river kingdoms, I would think they're safe from all this."

"Safer than my people will ever be. We would give up their location in a heartbeat for our own safely, and any Echloi knows that. It's why they keep to themselves." Rava pointed out with a sad smile. I tuned out the conversation, not caring to hear more about the evil plaguing the Realms. I supposed that no matter what planet you were on, no one could escape the clutches of division. Although, it was curious how easily Rava made a point to bring that up to us. As if he wanted us to know just how divided his planet was. I shook my head. I thought way too into things sometimes.

Once everyone finished the fruits, Rain stood to address everyone.

"Tomorrow, we have a long journey ahead of us. Everyone get as much rest as you can." He glanced around. "D371." One of the soldiers' heads popped up.

"Yes, High Commander?"

"You and I are going to take the first watch. The rest of you be prepared to switch on the hour." He announced, speaking directly to the soldiers who bowed their heads in understanding. I looked around and noticed a pile of blankets that must have come from inside the houses. I grabbed one and found a comfortable spot near the side of the river, at least it would be cool there. I let myself relax, closing my eyes while feeling a cool breeze run through my hair. It was nice to sit down by the water after walking for so long. The hairs on my arm began to tingle, and I felt the stare of someone watching me. Opening my eyes, I turned to see Sovren staring at me. When he saw me glance his way his eyes widened slightly and he looked away, but I noticed his eyes still glancing my way. I raised an eyebrow at him curiously and called out to him.

"What is it?"

He turned to look at me, opening his mouth slightly before closing it again.

"Sovren?" I said his name hoping it would prompt him to say whatever was on his mind. He hesitated, but finally walked over to me.

"Sorry if I made you feel uncomfortable, Empress." He said while bowing his head. I waved his apology off with my hand, wanting him to speak to me freely.

"I- it's just." He sighed, "Sitting there, staring off. It reminded me of my little sister." My eyes widened in shock. I had no idea Sovren had a sister. Of course, I'd never asked, but I thought he might have mentioned something like that sooner considering he was friends with my brother.

"You have a sister?" I asked, motioning him to sit down. Instead, he just knelt on one knee beside me, looking off into the distance.

"Had."

"Parden?" He gave me a sideways glance before looking off once more.

"Had a sister." My eyes fell. Of course he wouldn't have mentioned a sister, she was no longer around.

"What happened to her?" I whispered carefully, not wanting to impose on something personal to him.

He sucked in a deep breath, "I don't know."

I opened my mouth to try and comfort him, but he continued before I had the chance to try.

"She was much younger than me when our mother abandoned us, we didn't even know who our father was. He was just some random fellow I guess- It's why I joined the military to become a soldier so young... so I could take care of her. They offered us a place. I trained and she took care of the apartment, and all that stuff. It was good, for a while, but-" he let out a sigh. "She never was that together upstairs." He tapped his right temple with a sad smile. "It only got worse after our mother left. I didn't know what to do for her, we were both so little at the time. I was just trying to focus on my training, but she really needed me then. Her phantasm was strange... it was taking over her mind. She couldn't control it, never could." He paused for a minute, taking in a short breath before continuing. "It was around the time when things were getting really bad on V'rasór. We were stuck in the East before they transported all training soldiers to the North. They told me she'd be evacuated with the refugees. They promised..." He sucked in another breath, "But the borders closed, and she was stuck on that side and- I never saw her again..." he trailed off.

"I'm so sorry Sovren, that must have been horrible." I said, not really knowing what else could be said. To think our stories were so similar. A family torn apart by him. It made sense why he was so willing to follow me.

"I tried looking for her, after things calmed down some. After Elnorsefall relaxed." He shook his head. "But I found nothing, not even a death certificate. She just... disappeared."

"Maybe she is alive and escaped to another planet." I wondered out loud.

He swallowed, "If she is alive, somehow, someway, she's not in this galaxy." He pointed to his heart. "I would feel it. I would feel it here." I looked down. He sucked in another breath and wiped a hand over his eyes.

"Sorry for keeping you, Empress. Thank you for listening. I better go... let you get some rest." He stood, getting ready to leave.

"May God grant you peace of heart, Sovren. And know that wherever your sister is, she is in his arms."

He nodded, "Thank you."

He walked off then, disappearing into the shadows of the village. I layed back down, closing my eyes while thinking about everything Sovren just confided in me. He was so much stronger than he knew. We were so much stronger than anyone knew. What would we become? We would be weapons pointed right back at those who dared to create us. They tore our families apart, and they would pay with their lives.

26

CHAPTER 25

I was floating, my body unresponsive as I floated in space. How was I not dead? I felt myself being thrust forward. An inky mist cleared around me, and I saw Eurkxo, my home. It was as beautiful as always, just as peaceful as I remembered. I smiled, happy to see my planet again. The happy moment lasted only a few seconds as a flash of light shot across the space above my planet. I watched in horror as the impact struck the surface, my planet turning alight.

"No!" I felt my lips form the words, but the sound was gone as fire swam around me like snakes. I shrieked as my body was once again thrown through space, but this time it was away from Eurkxo. Everywhere I looked there was burning. I felt my back hit something hard, and I watched pieces of glass break around me. Falling through the glass I realized it was my mother's crown. Its center crystal was broken into pieces from my impact. I saw many planets burning inside the broken pieces of glass, along with Eurkxo. I watched completely useless, I couldn't even cry. Fiery arms were placed on my shoulder and spun me around. I bit back a scream as I realized it wasn't fire, it was a hand. The hands of my father as he held me in place as I watched ships being destroyed around me.

"When are you going to realize, Cloverlyne?" I heard his voice whisper darkly. His red markings burned so brightly that they seared my skin as I struggled against his firm grip. "You will never be able to end me. I live within you, daughter. I live within all of you,"

My eyes shot open as I bit back a scream. A nightmare, I realized while struggling to breathe. It was only a nightmare. Rain was above me, shaking my shoulder gently as he looked down at me. Concern written on his face as he observed my clearly irregular breathing.

"You okay, ne'la?" He asked, tilting his head. He placed his hand on my forehead. I swatted his hand away while giving him my best annoyed look.

"Of course I'm okay, why wouldn't I be?" I snapped, trying to keep him from questioning further, but one glance at him and I knew he didn't buy it. Still, he simply nodded, not asking anything more about my distress.

"It's time to pack up." He said instead, offering his hand to help me up. I tried to open my mouth to ask when we were going to leave, but no words came out. I panicked, wondering if I was still in my nightmare, but sighed in relief when I realized my throat was simply dry. That relief was overtaken by fear when I remembered the fiery death that plagued the planets in my nightmare. I knelt down next to the river, and used my hands to cup the water, bringing it to my mouth. Once my throat no longer felt dry, I folded the blanket that I slept on and hurried over to one of the houses to put it back. It was not ours to take.

"Are we ready yet?"

I cringed when I heard Rava yell across the camp, fluttering around as if he were in charge. It was much too early for such noise, especially after last night. I let out a yawn, covering it with my hand.

"Not a morning bird, Meirv?" I spun around hearing Xorion's voice. My cheeks heated up with embarrassment.

"No, I'm afraid not." I sighed as my thoughts drifted off to the darkness I'd seen. Flames were around me once again, and planets burned. A shiver ran down my spine.

"What's wrong?" Xorion said, suddenly standing right in front of me. His eyes looked me up and down as if he were searching for the answer on me. I tensed up. The last thing I wanted was everybody thinking I couldn't handle a simple nightmare, even if it was anything but simple.

"Nothing is wrong, Xorion. What could've given you that idea?" I walked past him, glancing back with my best quizzical expression. He blinked at me, confused.

"Something happened." He said, stepping in front of me once more. I frowned at him, and willed phantasm into my pointer finger as I pushed him aside. His eyes widened, his mouth agape. I didn't know why I was so angry, I just didn't want to speak about it. Not even with Xorion.

"Clove-" He tried to say, but I purposely cut him off.

"Come on, I believe the others are already waiting near the edge of the village already." I indicated for him to follow. I felt his eyes continue to stare at me for a minute longer before he stepped forward to walk with me.

"There they are!" Rain said when he saw us. He crossed his arms as if annoyed. "Now we just have to wait for Jamieson."

"Where is he? I have yet to see him this morning." I asked curiously. Rain looked sheepishly towards Sovren, who just smirked back at him. Xorion seemed to know what they were signaling each other about, as his mouth twitched into a smile before letting out a small laugh. I stared at all three men, confused.

"What's going on?" I demanded. Sovren shrugged, and started fidgeting with his backpack. Rain scratched the back of his head keeping his eyes averted from me, and Xorion started coughing, obviously trying to hide his laughter. I glared at Rain, and he sighed.

"He, uh..." He stopped, trying to find the right words to tell me.

"Oh please, you Soaran's are so proper." Rava said with a roll of his huge eyeballs. He stared at me with a mocking, serious look. "He had to go fertilize some soil." I froze at his words.

Had he really just-?

Rain, along with some of the other soldiers, started coughing and shaking their heads in disapproval, while a few, along with Rava, laughed.

"Right, he's here. Let's go!" Sovren said in an unusually high pitched voice as Jamieson strode over completely oblivious to the... previous conversation.

"Took your lovely time, didn't you?" Rava said through laughs as he fluttered around him. Jamieson's face turned red, not answering. Rain gave him an apologetic look before motioning for us to start our journey once again.

We maneuvered under flowers as big as houses, and trees with roots that extended several feet into the air like doorways. There were many sweet smelling plants around us, but Rava continued to warn us that the prettier they appeared to be, the more dangerous they were. At one point, he had us take a detour due to our path being overrun by beautiful giant, yet extremely poisonous trumpet flowers. According to Rava, breathing in the fumes was enough to cause hallucinations, and during that time, the flower stalk would shoot out tiny darts. These darts not only killed their prey, but caused the body to deteriorate faster, so the dirt around the flowers could be fertilized. He also added that some people used the petals of the flowers as a cream to keep themselves cool. Xorion playfully asked if we could get some, but Rava, thinking he was serious, only said that it would take too long. He also pointedly said that because we were 'dumb alien tourists' it would probably kill us within minutes of wearing it, let alone breathing it in.

"How long till we reach the facility?" Sovren asked suddenly. Rava shrugged mid flight.

"Not long." He answered simply.

"That's not a number." Jamieson grumbled.

"Okay, three." Rava spat back with an annoyed flutter of his wings.

"Three what?" Sovren said, letting out an exasperated sigh.

"Three nothing! You said you wanted a number!" Rava shouted, spinning around to face him. Sovren glared at him and knitted his brows together.

Here we go again...

I thought to myself.

"Jamieson was the one who said that, I just wanted a direct answer to how far we had left to go!"

"I gave you a direct answer." Rava glared right back at him, his nostrils flaring. "Not long."

"That's not direct." Sovren put his hands on his hips, flicking his wrist to dismiss any argument.

"Yeah, emphasis on the not." Xorion said pointally, casting Rava a wary look, and Sovren nodded in agreement.

"Do you have any idea what it looks like?" I asked, mostly just to change the subject. Rava tilted his head, thinking.

"Big, gray, enclosed... the typical terrifying Elnorsefall style."

"So we're basically trying to break into a prison?" Xorion waved his arms sarcastically.

"Always thought I was the type to break out, not in..." Sovren let out a sigh.

Xorion nodded. "I suppose there's a first for everything, my friend."

"You're really breaking in there, you giants?" Rava fumbled with his fingers nervously. Sovren gave him a sideways glance.

"Why do you ask questions you already know the answer to?"

"I just have a bad feeling about it. Don't you think coming here was a mistake?" He rubbed his back against a tree-trunk.

"Don't we all?" Xorion said sarcastically, a line appearing between his brows.

"Oh I don't know about that, I find that I'm rather enjoying the trip." Rain said lightly, baring his teeth. Sovren raised a brow at him.

"Of course you would." He pointed at Rain accusingly. "It was your idea!" Rain rolled his eyes.

"Well, what can I say? It's a good plan-"

"Quiet!" Rava said suddenly, stopping mid-flight. Rain blinked, giving Rava a dull look.

"Did you just shush us you little-"

Rava bared his teeth giving a silencing hiss. "We just got shushed by an Ovidō yapper, who would have thought?" Although Rain's tone was full of mischief, he lowered his voice to a whisper. I watched as his hand casually slipped his gun out of his belt.

"What is it?" Xorion asked as Rava usured the rest of us into a crouching position.

"Exac Sirakak." Rava said in a hushed voice, slipping out a knife and gracefully balancing it between his fingers. We all stared at him with the same looks of confusion.

"Exac- what?" Rain blurted out only to earn a glare from Rava.

"Big." He said as if we were supposed to understand. We continued staring at him blankly. He made a gesture for something very large with his hands,

"Big'a Sirakak." He waved his hands worriedly, not knowing how else to describe it in our tongue. The soldier's eyes darted around nervously,

"What in all eternity is a Sirakak-"

"That!" Rava yelled just as a massive beast roared, falling from the treetops. The creature was huge! Long ugly brown hair covered its entire body, and it easily maneuvered around with six long legs. It looked like a mixture of some kind of wooly bear and a worm at the same time, and the noise it made... It was ear piercing! Rain lifted his gun to shoot the beast, but Rava stopped him.

"You either kill it on the first try, which is impossible, or don't use the gun!" He warned. His wings began to glow as his movements became faster with the help of phantasm. "It will call other creatures of the forest, they are attracted to noise, and most have learned a gun's sound means dinner is close by. We can't afford that." Rain grunted while slipping his gun back into his belt. He lit up his markings, sending a brilliant light through the forest, a light the beast does not seem to appreciate. It roared again, its mouth wide open revealing jagged teeth that are shaped like a spiral, ready to tear apart its victims. It charges at Rain, leaping off the ground with each step. He twisted into a perfect backflip, aiming a blast of phantasm on the ground in front of the beast. Blue flames of phantasm danced along the ground at his will, crackling like lightning. The beast hesitated its charge.

"Go!" Rain yelled as he formed his phantasm into a shield, the beast made a shrieking sound, and rammed into the shield. Rain held himself steady, keeping his legs apart and his arms held firmly forward, controlling his shield. "I mean it, go! We can hold it back, we don't have time for this!" Rain grunted out, irritated that we didn't obey the first time. Despite his command, I couldn't move. I didn't want him to fight the beast alone, he could be injured. I took a nervous step forward ready to open my core, but a firm hand gripped mine.

"Empress, don't! Rain can hold his own, if we stay we'll only distract him." Sovren said as he physically pulled me back, ushering me to run. Xorion sent a fierce look towards the creature.

"What if he needs us?" Xorion argued, hurrying to my side. Sovren gave an annoyed grunt of disapproval.

"Try and help him and he'll knock you down for getting in his way, now let's move!" At that, we ran. I strained my senses to hear the noise from the fight, but with all the running, heavy breathing, and crackling of sticks and leaves, I couldn't hear anything.

"All clear!" A voice yelled, and we slowed down our run before completely stopping. I leaned up against a tree, and placed my hands on my knees, trying to catch my breath.

"That was the ugliest creature I've ever seen!" I said more loudly than I thought I did. The other turned towards me and I felt my cheeks heat up in embarrassment as they chuckled at my words. Xorion tilted his head at me as he also tried to catch his breath,

"T-that was your first time seeing that... things?" He huffed out, pointing to where we'd run from. Both me and Sovren raised an eyebrow at him, confused. He stared at us, and then shifted uneasily.

"I just thought- I mean, you spoke about this planet like you'd been here before."

"I have." Sovren raised a finger, still keeping his brow raised. "Just a trading post though. I mean, they don't exactly keep those things as pets now do they?"

"I should hope not." Jamiseson mumbled from behind us. We turned to him and saw him rubbing his arms with his hands, his whole body shaking from all the excitement.

"You okay there, Jamie?" One of the soldiers plopped himself comfortably on the ground next to him with a smirk.

"Just wonderful." He grumbled miserably while taking some ointment out from his pack. He began to rub it into a few cuts he got from the plants we had run through.

"Careful buddy, you heard what the Ovidōian said." Another soldier says with a wink. He gestured to the cuts with a jerk of his chin. "I believe you may have run through some of the 'bad uns'." He made quotations with his fingers. Jamieson's eyes turned wide with worry as he looked over the cuts.

"What?" He squeaked out.

"Yeah, didn't you hear? I believe one of the symptoms was tingles or something... and chills." The soldier sitting on the ground beside him casually said with a shrug. Jamieson started shivering even more. As if noticing he was shivering for the first time, he began rubbing himself more fiercely.

"You get any weird symptoms like fungus growing out of those cuts, Jamie, you just let us know 'aight?"

"Dear Natarah! Fungus?!" Jamieson shrieked, his eyes widening even more with horror.

"Silence." I told the soldiers. I didn't want them toying with his fragile nature. "Busy yourselves, soldiers." They immediately jumped up at my command, finding something to occupy themselves. I turned to Jamieson. "Don't worry, you'll be fine. The cuts are minor." I said calmly. Jamieson noded, but gulped as he continued to dress his cuts with the ointment. We waited another fifteen or so minutes before finally seeing Rain and Rava walking into the clearing. Rava had blood dripping from a nasty cut on his arm.

"Well." Rain said, shaking his head tiredly. "That was fun exercise."

"Yeah, the best." Rava muttered, scowling at his wound.

"You two okay?" I asked, hurrying over to them. I put my hand over Rain's arm. He nodded, giving my hand a squeeze with his other hand. We both glanced at Rava, concerned over the amount of blood he was losing. Jamieson offered some of the ointment he had been using, but Rava shook his head. He landed on the ground near some bright green leaves. He picked some up, threw them into his mouth, chewed them, and then tore off a piece of cloth from his shirt.

"Yeah." He answered the previous question between chews. Then he spat the chewed up leaves into the piece of cloth he had torn off, placing it tightly around his wound.

"That's disgusting." Sovren said, dramatically gagging at the scene while he jabbed a finger at Rava. Rava shrugged his shoulders.

"It works."

"We have medicines." Jamieson said pointally, indicating the ointment once again. Rava sent him an annoyed glare at him. Jamieson held his hands up in surrender.

"Natural heals faster." Rava explained, dropping his glare with a sigh.

Now that everyone was calm, or noticeably calmer, I brought up our current situation.

"How much longer do we have to go?" I asked, keeping my eyes fixed on Rava. He tilted his head upwards, thinking for a moment before answering my question.

"Only in a few hours I'm thinking." He said finally, stretching out his wings. Sovren glared at Rava, obviously annoyed that he wasn't giving a direct answer again.

"How many is a few? We have to get there while our mothership is still within range of the signal." Rava grimaced at his tone, but nodded as he tried to match Sovren's seriousness.

"Perhaps two hours, maybe less if we hurry."

"Can we get there before the moon's rise to its peak?" I asked, glancing upwards. The clouds had already turned a lighter gray color. "It's best if we infiltrate the facility in the cover of darkness, and we're running out of time."

"If we hurry." Rava repeated, flying to the front of the group.

"Agreed." Rain said, gripping his belt. "Let's move."

We continue walking, entertaining ourselves with idle talk, until we finally return to complete silence. Well, complete silence if it weren't for Rava's consistent streams of chatter. Sometime during our journey, Rava stopped us. Rain pulled his gun out seeing that Rava had tensed up, but Rava shook his head, telling Rain not to. I followed Rava's gaze, and sucked in a breath. Another being stood not too far from where we were, perched on a branch. They wore a green and brown cloak, making it almost impossible for us to notice them without a warning. Rava stepped forward with his hands held up in a universal surrender. The being jumped down, their hood coming off as they did so. This was no Ovidōian, I realized as I stared at their much taller appearance and fin-like wings and ears. No, this was an Echloi. The second sentient species that shared this planet with them. All of us remained silent, wondering what would happen. The Echloi faced Rava, their eyes flashing in anger as they glanced at us.

They probably think we are Elnorsefall...

I thought to myself. With that in mind, I motioned us all to take a step back, showing that we weren't hostile. Rava spoke in his own language, but I noticed that he was using more high pitched sounds that I didn't recognize. The Echloi shifted uncomfortably, making quick glances at us, and then back at Rava. Rava spoke up again, and this time I detected a question in his tone. The Echloi shrugged, and pointed a little off from where we were headed. Rava made another sound, and the Echloi hurried off back into the jungle. Rava came back to join us.

"What did it want?" Rain asked, his eyes still following the creature's trail. Rava stayed silent for a moment, which was surprising.

"She was a scout, I think. She wanted to know why I was traveling with you."

"She asked you that? But she didn't speak a word." I wondered out loud. Rava gave me a curious look.

"No one knows the voice of the Echloi, Empress. You don't need to concern yourself over this encounter." He said through narrowed eyes. He looked almost... threatening. The message was clear. Don't ask any more questions about it. Rava turned back to the others. "She says it's only a few miles in that direction. We must go now." Rava said, pointing off in the same direction the creature pointed too. We all nodded, eager to continue our journey. No one spoke. Most likely everyone was thinking about everything that had happened on our journey so far. I knew I was. I didn't even know how long it had been, only that it became tenser with every few steps.

"Empress." Rava said suddenly, stopping in the front of the group. Rain, and Sovren stopped alongside him, staring off into the distance. I walked forward, wondering why he had called me, but then I saw it, and what I saw sent a shiver down my spine.

"We have arrived."

27

CHAPTER 26

The facility was much bigger than we expected, though its design was familiar. Dark gray walls covered the outside embedded with red swirls. A large sparking fence surrounded its outer layer, and guards paced along it with an apparent schedule. Though we couldn't see them, we knew heat sensors were placed along the fence.

Impossible.

Was my first thought, but we had no choice but to keep going.

"Alright, how y'all doing this?" Rava asked, stepping back. He smirked at the looks on our faces after seeing the facility for the first time. Rain was the first to compose himself and sent a smirk right back at him.

"You mean to say how are we doing this?"

Rava's mouth dropped open at the implication. He then laughed awkwardly.

"Ha! No, I'm not stepping one foot within that prison!" He turned and flew in the opposite direction. "I did my part bringing you all here, you're on your own now!" Before he could fly too far away, Rain reached up and grabbed the top of his wing, keeping him in place.

"There's been a change in plans, you know too much." Rain said, smiling down at Rava's pale face.

He threw his hands up in the air angrily, "Do you people have a death wish?!" he pointed to himself. "Do I look like the kind of guy that wants my wings ripped from my own skin? Or be burned alive in our own boiling chambers?" he snarled and jerked out of Rain's grip, but didn't fly away this time.

"Now here me out, my sad little friend." Rain said with a look of pity. "Know that whatever will be planned for you, will be mercy." Rain's face went dark as he chose his next words. "What they will do to us will be much, much worse."

"What makes you think we'd ever let them take us alive?" Sovren asked, raising an eyebrow at Rava while pulling out a small box from his pocket. Rain and Sovren shared a nod, and Rain called out to everyone.

"Gather!" He shouted, and we crowd around him. He held up a small pill that Sovren handed him from inside the box. I recognized it immediately.

"This, as many of you already know, is a flare pill." Silence fell over the crowd as Rain demonstrated slipping the pill into a secret compartment at the top of his uniform.

"You only get one, use it wisely. When you swallow it you have about twenty seconds to prepare yourself." He looked around the crowd. "Is that understood?" The soldiers nodded solemnly.

"After twenty seconds it will release a chemical into your body which will blow you up. So, anyone that doesn't care to die needs to get the hell away before that happens." His eyes softened as they found mine, before I watched them flicker to Xorion. "...Unless you prefer to choose to die together."

A hand fell over mine and squeezed it. Without even looking, I knew it was Xorion trying to comfort me.

"Now." Rain said, his voice turning dangerously serious. "If you see me, Sovren, Jamieson, or the Empress being taken alive without any hope of rescue or any sign we are unable to take the pill, you shoot on sight. Is that understood?" Rain asked, raising his voice loudly.

Nervous nods went through the crowd as they glanced warily at one another. None of them wanted to be the one responsible for our deaths, even if it was necessary. Rain frowned when he saw their hesitation.

"Is that understood!?"

"Yes sir!" The soldiers responded more confidently this time. Rain nodded, satisfied with their response.

"Good, now..." He set a tablet on the ground, and we watched as it burst into light, a hologram of the facility appearing above it.

"Here's the plan."

28

CHAPTER 27

My back pressed into the facility wall. Beside me, Rain held his gun near his head, his back also pressed against the wall while he peaked around it at the tall fence before us. Rava only had about thirty seconds to start phase one.

I smiled at the thought. Phase one was my idea. The plan was simple really, Rava would cause a distraction by lighting a makeshift bomb near the fence on the far side of the facility, and while they were distracted with a supposed Ovidōian conflict, we would use our phantasm to protect ourselves while we scaled the fence. I hated to think what would happen if we touched it without protection. Based on the sparks coming off of it, I was sure we'd be fried in a second.

Come on Rava, we have to get inside before the guards cross to our side of the fence...

My eyes darted to the far side of the building, waiting.

"There!" Xorion shouted while pointing to smoke rising from where I was looking. I let out a breath of relief. The explosion would happen any moment now.

"Prepare to shield!" Rain said furiously, his marking glowing in blue light. I turned to face Xoron and raised my hands to touch his arms.

"This is going to feel-"

"Amazing?" He said with a smug look. I glared at him, but I couldn't help my lips twitching into a smile.

"I was going to say, unusual." I closed my eyes, focusing on my phantasm. I found where it settled in my heart, being pumped through my body along with my blood. I willed it to the surface and opened my eyes. With a pulse, I pushed my energy onto Xorion, settling it like a shield covering his body. He gasped, and his body tried to jerk out of my grasp at the feeling, but I held tight.

"Breathe, my phantasm is just settling, that is why it feels like this." I explained, rubbing his arms soothingly. He didn't respond, but he seemed to calm some. Finally, it stopped fluttering within him.

"There, I think it's done." I removed my arms from him with an exhausted breath. He blinked and stared off past me.

"Xorion?" I wondered if I pushed too much phantasm onto him. He snapped of whatever daze he was in at the sound of his name,

"Oh, yeah I'm good." He shook his head, "You were right, that was... unusual. Not unusual in a bad way, but not good either. It's unsettling, a power I cannot control."

"No one can truly control it, only as much as we can control ourselves. It has no conscience, nor is it alive. It is tied to your mind, but it's mine, so you don't need to worry about it. It just is as it is, a part of us." I tried to explain.

A loud booming sound suddenly rattled the surrounding area. I tensed up and covered my ears, but Rain forced us to move towards the fence.

"Go!" He shouted, gesturing for us to start climbing.

Xorion immediately started climbing the fence, but I hesitated. I'd never done anything like this before, I didn't like admitting I feared being unable to do it. His hand reached down.

"Here, let me help you." He said, giving me a soft smile.

I eagerly took his hand and let him pull me up alongside him. "Just remember, one hand, one foot. Just keep with that pattern and you'll be fine." He said calmly as he settled one hand on my back. I nodded, sweat already pouring down my face.

Willing energy onto others' bodies as well as mine was tiring me so much, I didn't know if I would be able to make it over the fence. Only me, Sovren, and Rain's energy was strong enough to cross the fence.

It wasn't the most complicated task I've used my phantasm for but commanding it in another's body as well as our own was exceedingly painful. Especially since Xorion didn't have any phantasm to compensate me with. My breath became short gasps, my eyes strained, and my shimmering's flickered, losing their light.

"Hold on, Clove, we're almost there."

He kept one hand gripped tightly to the fence while his other handheld my waist, keeping me steady. I let out a groan of pain in response and pushed forward. Just a little way and we'd be over the top.

A constricting pain shot through my heart, and an ache pierced the back of my skull. I tilted my head to rest on the fence for a second. Rain was higher than me, a soldier shielded with his energy at his side. He seemed to be struggling almost as badly as I was, maybe more. His face looked red, and his markings were lighter than they ought to have been.

"Clove, we must move." Xorion gently pressed into me, pushing me upwards.

One hand, one foot, one hand, one foot...

Higher and higher we climbed till we finally reached the top. My whole body shook in pain. "Look at me." Xorion tilted my head to look at him as we paused at the top of the fence. Was it just me or was the world spinning? Xorion's face blurred as if someone had moved us underwater.

"I'm... help you... switch... side, okay?" I tilted my head, wondering what he was trying to say, I could barely understand him. I wished he would speak more clearly; it was as if time around him had slowed... Everything was moving so slow. I felt my body being guided to the other side.

"Clove... with me..." I felt a hand wrap around me, guiding me down the other side.

It was hot, so hot. I just wanted to let go. My grip on the fence relaxed, my feet slipping more easily. I felt myself being moved more quickly, but my grip on the fence was slipping, and so was my grip on my phantasm. I heard voices whispering furiously around me.

"Keep... steady!"

"Can't... her... let go!"

"Clove... NO!"

I couldn't take it anymore, my hands completely let go of the fence. I felt myself falling, yet I was still pressed against warmth. My vision went dark before even hitting the ground.

I wasn't sure how long I was unconscious before opening my eyes with a gasp. I glanced around, desperate to know what happened. The last thing I remembered was blanking out... and falling.

Oh, dear Natarah, falling! Xorion, was he alright? Did my energy give out before we let go?

It was then that I registered that someone was holding my arm. I turned to face them, and Xorion grinned down at me warily.

"Enjoy your ten-minute nap? Because it's all you're going to get." He chuckled softly.

I opened my mouth to ask about what happened, but he placed a finger on my lips, silencing me. "Before you ask, I am fine, we fell before your phantasm gave out. Thankfully, your power remained over me when we made contact with the ground, so neither of us were injured." His voice lowered into a mumble. "But then you wouldn't have felt anything anyways since you landed on top of me." I shook my head, only one question remaining.

"Rain?" I asked, glancing around.

Before I blanked out, I remembered seeing him looking as unwell as I was. Xorion jerked his head to the side. I looked in the direction he pointed to. Rain was seated up against two backpacks, holding some cloth to his mouth, part of the cloth was stained red.

"Dear Natarah! Is he okay?" I asked worriedly, trying to sit up to go to him. Xrion held me down.

"He's fine, you won't help him by tiring yourself. All three of you need rest. Jamieson says that you need time for..." He glanced around, as if unsure of what he was saying.

No doubt Jamieson had tried to explain it, and he wasn't exactly a person who gave simple responses.

He shook his head, looking back at me sheepishly. "Phantasm to settle from all the excitement?" He said in a more questioning tone rather than a statement. I just nodded, grateful to rest a moment, knowing that everyone was okay.

"Has Jamieson begun working on phase two?" I asked, closing my eyes at the tingling sensation in my heart. I'd strained myself far too much.

"Yes, he is almost finished disabling this part of the fence to let the rest of the soldiers through. We'll begin our infiltration soon."

"Good." I forced myself to sit up. He looked at me warily, but I raised a hand, telling him not to stop me. I was fine, more than fine. I was ready to fight. I glanced back at Rain. He looked better, but not by much. I wondered what had happened.

"Go. Join the soldiers, I'll be with you shortly." I told Xorion, still keeping my gaze fixed on Rain.

"Alright." He said simply, and I heard him jogging away from me. I walked over to my brother, wishing he wouldn't make me worry so much. I sat on my knees as he shifted positions, acknowledging me coming over to him, but doing so only caused him to let out a groan of pain.

"Sorry." He mouthed, and then started a series of coughs. A small stream of blood dripped from his mouth. He frowned and lifted the cloth to wipe it away.

"Still yourself." I ordered him.

I knew full well he wouldn't listen to me otherwise. He grunted stubbornly in response but obeyed my order. I took the cloth from him and wiped the blood away for him.

Physically he appeared fine, but he had stressed his phantasm to a point that his mind and heart were unable to keep up. Much like what had happened to me. Essentially, when a person overused their phantasm, it took over our bodies, but our physical bodies were not able to handle that kind of power, causing us to wither away. It was sort of like a fail-safe, our bodies would shut down before phantasm took over our minds.

Since me and Rain were royals, the point of our bodies shutting down was longer, but made it more dangerous. Phantasm was not an energy that was to be taken lightly, by anyone. I sighed when he coughed again.

"What happened?" I both wanted to know and didn't at the same time. He let out a half-hearted laugh.

"I was fine half-way up, but Sovren wasn't. He was losing his grip on Jamieson."

I set my mouth in a firm line. It was incredible that Sovren was able to push his energy over another in the first place, let alone able to control it in both him and another. It didn't surprise me that he wasn't able to handle it, even if Jamieson already had phantasm and was helping keep control, it was still incredible.

I fought the urge to slap some sense into Rain, though I knew it was the only reason Jamieson and Sovren were alive.

"You split your phantasm to shield both you, your soldier, and Jamieson."

"I-" He chuckled, then coughed up more blood. "I thought I could handle it for a few minutes at least."

"Clearly you were mistaken." I scolded.

He was either insanely brave, or insanely stupid. I was barely able to handle just Xorion, who possessed no phantasm at all, but still. Rain rolled his eyes at me.

"Yeah." He gestured to himself, blood and all. "Clearly."

"Empress."

I heard Jamison's voice say, as his footsteps moved closer to me. I quickly stood to face him. His tablet was held protectively in his left hand, like a parent holding a baby. I nodded to him respectfully. Rain remained leaned up against the backpack, listening with alert eyes.

"I have successfully disabled this section of the fence, and the soldiers have already begun their climb over to this side of the fence."

"Have the Elnorsefall guards started searching the perimeter?" I asked, a hint of fear in my voice. We were moving slower than I would have liked, considering we were on enemy territory now.

"No, Rava must have found some other way of distracting them. This could go more smoothly than we anticipated." He was obviously trying to ease my mind, and it was surprisingly working.

"Maybe he used the animal parade I advised." Rain joked. I smiled, remembering his idea. The thought of Elnorsefall guards getting infiltrated by wild animals, ignoring our calm entrance, would've been priceless.

"Perhaps, Rain. It's a shame we won't be witness to such an enjoyable scene."

"Shame indeed." He agreed in a mockingly heartbroken voice. Jamieson remained serious, despite our joking.

"Either way, we must finish phase two." We both nodded.

Rain grunted, forcing himself to stand up. I narrowed my eyes on him, but didn't try to stop him from moving this time. The soldiers were arriving on this side of the fence, and the last thing they needed to see was their commander lying helplessly on the ground in pain. I knew Rain would never stop me from rising had I been in his position, no matter how much it hurt.

He limped as I walked with him over to the soldiers who had already crossed the fence, but I still didn't offer him help. He straightened, addressing the soldiers.

"We've delayed longer than the Empress would've liked. Move quietly, but cautiously." He said firmly, leading the way towards our entrance to the building.

I found Xorion in the crowd of soldiers, and we nodded to each other in acknowledgement, but I refrained from walking over to him. I hoped he understood. Instead, I fell in step beside Rain, who was right in front of Sovren, who looked mentally beaten.

I glanced behind me, seeing Xorion hurry his step till he was behind Sovren. I watched as he gently tapped him on the shoulder.

"You alright, friend?" He asked with a raised brow.

Sovren glanced up at me, but it was too quick for me to read his expression before he answered Xorion. I tiled my head to the side in wonder. Did he not feel well and didn't want to reveal pain in front of me or the soldiers?

"I'm well, all things considered."

He was strangely formal, keeping his eyes dead ahead. I narrowed my eyes on him before turning my head to look forward once more. I suddenly realized the reason for his strange behavior now. He was ashamed, yet he had no reason to be.

"All things considered?" I asked in a tone that forced him to answer me. I glanced back once more and watched as his head dropped. I paused in front of him, waiting for his answer.

"I was unable to keep hold of Jamieson, Empress. Forgive me." I sighed, fully turning around to place my hand on his shoulder.

"There is nothing to forgive, Sovren. Your energy is more powerful than the greatest of soldiers. Believe me when I say it's not an easy task to will phantasm in such ways, nor will it ever become easier. The fact that you were able to keep hold for as long as you did is incredible. Know that even I lost hold of my phantasm in the end." He didn't speak for some time before finally nodding and placing his hand over mine.

"Thank you, Empress. Your words give me peace." He said at last, his tone more relaxed now.

"I'm honored my words do so, Sovren." I smiled at him, and he smiled back. Xorion flashed a grin at his friend.

"Come, Rain will not wait for us."

Sovren smirked, "No, he certainly will not."

He turned and winked at Xorion, quickening his pace to not walk with us. I raised an eyebrow at Xorion, who shrugged it off as if nothing happened.

Perhaps they'd become closer than I was aware of? I supposed it would be fine to walk with him, no one seemed to pay us any mind.

We walked for a bit longer together before Rain raised a hand, and the group stopped moving. We'd finally reached where we would enter the facility. Rain turned and eyed all of us.

"You know our groups; you know your jobs. All I can say now is this..." He looked to the sky, exhaling as he spoke. "May our God be with all of us."

"And the Great Soul," Xorion murmured.

My group consisted of me, Xorion, Sovren, Jamieson, and three other soldiers I didn't know. Rain's group was the rest of the soldiers and would meet up with Rava. We had to blow the door to enter. A surprisingly simple task, but if Elnorsefall wasn't aware we were there before, they would know we were now. We entered the building together, but the hallway split. It was time to go our separate ways.

"Hey." Rain said, holding onto both of my hands. "We're going to finish this and go home. All of us." I smiled at his reassurance.

"I'll see you in the morning." I joked, since it was still very late into the night.

We'd both been raised with very consistent bedtime schedules by our mother when we were younger, and then by the Elders on Eurkxo, and they'd stuck with us. All those small rules seemed so pointless now. He laughed, but then turned serious as his eyes fell on Xorion and Sovren.

"Take care of her."

I rolled my eyes at his words. I could take care of myself, but all three men were startlingly serious.

"On our life, Rain." Sovren said, and both of them placed a hand on my shoulder. He smiled, walking backwards down his side of the hallway.

"See you soon." He nodded his head in farewell. "And goodluck!"

"To you as well." I responded, watching as he ran off with his soldiers. Sovren took out his gun, holding it with both hands.

"Right, let's get this over with." He said, making his way to the front of the group. "Time to run and stay alert!"

We ran down the halls, occasionally stopping when there was another hallway, we needed to be sure was safe. The halls were empty, something we didn't expect. An uneasy feeling swirled in my stomach. Xorion shook his head beside me.

"This is too easy; we haven't seen any guards for a facility of this size."

"Maybe they're in a meeting." A female soldier said sarcastically. I rested my back against the wall.

Sovren sighed, "As much as I like easy, Xorion is right, everyone be ready." He said, and we continued forward more slowly this time. Sovren suddenly stopped moving before stepping into a four-way hall. He ushered us back with his arm, pointing to the right hall with two of his fingers.

"Looks like eight little rats." Another soldier said, peeking around the corner. "They are coming fast; I think they're scouting the area." The other two soldiers pulled out their guns, readying themselves for a fight.

"Any chance we can evade them?" Sovren said, his markings glinting. The soldier shook his head.

"Their standing between us and the only entrance to the control center." He peaked around the corner again and glanced back at us with an exasperated look. "And they're coming straight this way."

"Looks like being easy is over with." Xorion said, pulling out his gun. Instead of pulling out mine as well, I willed my phantasm to the surface, allowing my markings to shimmer.

"It's even worse, look at their tattoos!" One of the soldiers' remarks. "They've been upgraded by the Rizen." I groaned out.

The Rizen were evil experimenters when it came to phantasm. They would push themselves to a deathly limit, yet they always found a way to survive, breaking the inner barrier. Once this barrier was broken, it's said phantasm enters the soul, making you more powerful, but tainting your spirit.

"Nothing we can do about that; we have a job to do. We need to get to that control room." Sovren said as he jumped out of hiding, surprising them.

He sent the place alight with beams of light shooting from his gun. The soldiers followed him into action, firing their guns on the guards. Two of them go down, but the other six put up shields, readying a counterattack. Sovren stood in the front, dropping his gun to force his energy onto them.

"Sovren!"

He didn't turn back, but I knew he heard me because he paused for a split second. I threw my hands forward, shooting him with a power surge. He grinned at the amount of power and ran forward to start fighting hand to hand combat with two of the guards.

I positioned myself in the center back of the group, using my hands to force my phantasm at the soldiers standing. Jamieson was somewhere behind me, ready to shield any attacks thrown at me while I was distracted. Xorion hesitated by my side, shooting the guards, but all it was doing was annoying them now that their shields were up. He eyed Sovren who seemed to be struggling with the two guards combating him.

"Go!" I told him, blasting another guard so Xorion could go to Sovren. He nodded and ran to the front to help Sovren in hand-to-hand combat, throwing a punch to the guard's neck. Out of the corner of my eye, I saw one of the guards we thought was dead, moving, but before I could blast him, he pressed something on his arm.

"Xorion!" I yelled, and he kicked the guard he was fighting away for just enough time to look at me. I pointed to the guard on the ground, "He pushed something!" Xorion glanced at the guard and nodded.

"Clove, watch it!" I turned just in time to see Jamiseon block a shock wave of phantasm directed at my head.

"Thank you, Jamieson." He nodded, keeping his eyes fixed on where it came from.

Sparks from the blast dissipated, and I saw that one of the standing guards had decided to turn his attention to me. I turned my focus on him, but the female soldier leapt in front of me.

"Continue what you were doing, Empress, we got this." She said, and used her phantasm to pick up speed, as she ran at the guard.

"No!" I heard Xorion say, and beside me, Jamieson was thrown backwards. Both guards that were on the ground before got up and were targeting me as well.

I guessed they had found out who I was by now. I raised my hands to block them, but they moved fast, surrounding me.

"The Emperor will want you alive." One of the guards taunted, phantasm sparking all around him.

I shot my phantasm forward, but he just barely dodged it. It wasn't as powerful as it should have been, and I felt weaker. The one that moved around me must be using his phantasm to weaken my attack.

The guards were confident in their upgraded power, their phantasm thrown around wildly, and they knew we were outnumbered. I stared past the guards and saw three more guards arrive, one aiming their gun to the ceiling above me. I watched in horror as the guard fired at the ceiling and it fell on top of us.

I used my phantasm to shield myself and Jamieson, but doing so distracted me from the guards that were surrounding me. The one in front of me pushed his hands forwards, blasting me with an explosion of phantasm. My body rammed into Jamieson who was standing behind me, and we both crumbled against the wall.

I coughed, blood dripping onto the floor from my mouth. Jamieson groaned beside me, blood dripping over his face from a head wound.

We were losing this, there was no way we would make it to the control room at this rate. We needed to retreat. I looked up, seeing the guard preparing to blast me a second time. I reached up a hand, but I knew I wouldn't be able to shield his blast. It couldn't be over, it couldn't be. I closed my eyes.

My eyes suddenly opened wide as a blinding purple light brightened the room, and Sovren jumped into the air, his movements slowed by his phantasm as he defied gravity. It sparked around his hands, as he lifted his fist into the air.

"Tell your master to eat this!" He yelled at the guards and shot himself at the ground so fast that I was barely able to catch his movement. Even though the phantasm was directed at their guards, it threw everyone, including me, backwards.

The last thing I heard from the guards was screaming, then all I heard was just a ringing in my ears. Time seemed to slow as my senses came back to me. The first thing I noticed was that Jamieson was no longer beside me. Instead, it was Xorion who was at my side, gently shaking my shoulder, and helping me up. He had a look on his face I couldn't describe.

"We have to go, Clove. That guard you pointed out, they called reinforcements." He sighed. "And if they've had the same upgrades as this last group, then we can't sit around and wait for them." I nodded, leaning into him as I stood.

"Where's Sovren?" I asked, looking around. Xorion's face turned away. My stomach churned uneasily. "Where is he?" I demanded.

He slowly lifted his finger to point to the middle of the hall where the dead guards laid. His voice cracked as he finally spoke.

"Over there." I followed his finger and stilled. There, with his head lying on Jamieson's thigh, struggling to breath, was Sovren.

29

CHAPTER 28

My body went rigid at the sight.

This can't be happening...

I rushed over to him, ignoring Xorion's reaching arm. Sovren, one of the strongest men I knew, lay on the ground, struggling to breathe.

It can't be...

I dropped to my knees and took hold of his hand while looking up at Jamieson, desperate for answers. Jamieson shook his head at me, telling me nothing could be done to help him. Xorion knelt beside me, tears streaming down his face.

"You're okay, you're going to be okay." I said soothingly, moving a lock of hair out of his face. He smiled painfully.

"You're lying... but thank you." He sighed, tightening his hand around mine. "They always said I was careless with my phantasm, but I wouldn't change it if it meant saving you, Empress."

"We can save him, I know we can save him." I told Jamieson, but he was already shaking his head before I even finished my sentence.

"Not here, Empress."

My eyes flashed with anger.

"Then we take him with us!"

"We can't, Clove." Xorion said, rubbing his hand up and down my back. I shifted away from him, my vision blurring with tears.

"We can't leave him here, they'll find him!" I yelled, trying to talk some sense into them. I wasn't going to leave him, I couldn't just leave him. Sovren squeezed my hand again.

"Yes," he said calmly. I looked at him confused while he continued to smile. "Yes, they'll find me, but I'll be ready for them." With his other hand he took out the pill Rain handed out to all of us.

"No! Sovren, no." I begged. "I-"

"Clove, go. They'll be here soon." Sovren said desperately. I shook my head, refusing to just leave him behind.

"I'm the reason you're here, I-"

He rolled his eyes at me.

"I made my own choice, Clove. Don't take that from me. Wouldn't have changed anything at all about my life. I get to die taking their scum down with me." he grinned, "I would have followed you to hell. It was my choice in the end, don't blame yourself."

He coughed, blood running down the side of his mouth. His voice dropped to a whisper so all three of us had to lean down to hear him.

"Do something for me, will you?" He closed his eyes. "Live. Finish the mission, and live." He opened his eyes and looked at me, then at Xorion. "You two deserve that much. Live on... for me."

I choked back a sob as Xorion grabbed his friend's face, putting his head to his.

"The gates of your eternal paradise will be opened wide for you, my friend." he whispered. Alarms started blaring around us, and the soldiers shifted worriedly, anxious to get out of there. Sovren gave Xorion a thankful smile as he pulled away, and whispered,

"Go. T-That's an order."

Xorion lifted me up to my feet by my waist. I didn't fight him, even though I wanted to, but I had to respect Sovren's last order. He pulled me away from Sovren, dragging me forward by my arm. I turned my head to give one last memorable look to Sovren as red lights flashed around us, and wished him a safe journey to the next life.

"We're going to bring down this facility, we're going to kill every last Elnorsefall being who dares target us. For you, Sovren." With that promise, we run.

"We must get to the control center!" Jamieson said through pants as we ran.

"This way!" One of the soldiers said, taking the lead. We turned down a corridor to follow the soldier. I squeezed Xorion's hand as we ran, and he glanced down, squeezing it back in acknowledgment. I wasn't okay, but I had to be for now. I could mourn later.

Voices were heard from behind us, then guns firing.

I closed my eyes, knowing it was Sovren. I almost stopped when I heard a loud scream followed by a distant explosion of phantasm, then silence as we got further and further away. Xorion had to forcefully drag me forward, not daring to look back as he muttered unintelligible curses.

We ran as fast as possible, not bothering to be careful. Elnorsefall already knew we were there. We'd set off the alarms, but at least the guards that were sent to find us were now dead, thanks to Sovren.

We ran until the soldier in the front, leading us, stopped. Her eyes examined a massive door on the side of the hall. She said something under her breath that I couldn't hear, and took out her gun, firing at the doors panel. She used her body to try and force it open, but it took Xorion and the two other soldiers helping her to finally get it to budge. It slowly slid open enough for us to go through.

"Go, go, go!" She gestured us to hurry through with her hand.

"Is this-" I was about to ask if this was our destination, but my question was answered by the lights coming on as we entered. It was the control room. Two soldiers kept watch at the door as it slid closed behind us. The new lead soldier addressed Jamieson.

"Do what you need to do, and fast!" She glanced around nervously, "We don't have much time left." Jamiseon nodded, fully aware of our time limit. He took out his tablet and began his work.

I breathed heavily, Xorion's hand still in mine.

Something was wrong, I didn't know what, but something was wrong. I looked up at Xorion, wondering if he felt the same, but he wasn't looking at me, he kept his gaze fixed on the door, as if waiting. Minutes passed, and no guards showed up, but that didn't mean they wouldn't. Rain's group may have been distracting them, but he wouldn't be able to get all of them.

"Jamieson..." I said warily. He glanced over his shoulder at me, then back at his tablet.

"Almost there now, Empress." He typed furiously. "Just one more ..." He pressed a few buttons on one of the panels. "There! I'm done, the signal has been sent to our mothership! Download is complete." He said proudly, slipping his tablet into his pack.

"Wonderful, let's get the hell out of-" The soldier never finished his sentence, the door of the control room exploded in light, and some kind of gas started to fill the room, choking us.

"We got company!" The female soldier yelled out, firing at some unknown force.

Xorion leapt in front of me, pushing me to the side with his arm. I willed my phantasm to the surface, but something felt wrong. It felt weaker.

I coughed, choking on the gas. I wasn't the only one affected by it I noticed. Jamieson, and the three soldiers were struggling as well. Xorion seemed to be the only one who was fine as he looked helplessly around.

"There's too many of them!" Someone called out, but I couldn't see who.

No, we wouldn't go down like this. I wouldn't let us be captured alive at the very least.

I forced my phantasm to the surface and cried out as I pushed against the walls of my limit. Pain shot through my veins, a warning that my body couldn't handle it. We'll, it would have too. My markings blazed and I shot rays of light so we could see and secured a shield around myself.

"Xorion!" He glanced back at me. "Catch!" I yelled while throwing him my gun. He caught it with ease and fired at the enemy guards blocking the exit.

I felt something seep from my mouth and reached up to touch it. It was warm and sticky. Blood, I realized. Shaking my head I forced myself towards the exit that was blocked.

"Clove, get back!" Xorion yelled at me, dodging a beam of phantasm from one of the guards.

I ignored him, running into a side flip and landing in a kneeling position in front of my soldiers. My right-hand planted firmly into the ground as I rebalanced myself. With a single thought, I shoot my arms out to the sides. Phantasm shot from my hands, and blue light danced around me like fire. The phantasm shield I held around myself dissipated as I moved it to appear in front of us.

I felt someone try to pull me back behind everyone, only to let out a shriek of pain. My phantasm was like lightning, anyone who thought to touch me would be burned. Figuring this out, I stood and stepped out of the doorway into the hall, using my body as a living shield.

This was dangerous, this was very dangerous. My own phantasm could kill me if I pushed myself any further. As it was, I'm sure I'd have side effects from doing this, but it felt so... good, so... right.

More, more, more... I want this... I want more.

Shaking my head, I focused on the threat in front of me. If I got distracted, my phantasm would take over any logic, and I really would die. I couldn't let that happen yet; I needed time for the others to get away.

Closing my eyes, I felt out where the guards were. My right arm shot forward, my hand spread out flat, aimed at my new targets. Phantasm flowed around the sides of my body, and with my thoughts, I willed it into a spiral form, shooting it forward at the enemy. I heard the guard's scream.

Guns were firing loudly around me, and someone was calling my name, but the only thing that my brain could focus on was my own phantasm hovering around me. I could barely register what was happening to the others.

I felt my body getting shot with massive amounts of phantasm from the remaining guards, but strangely, it only tickled. Changing tactics, I felt their phantasm connect to me, and this time, I held onto it, constricting it, and threw it back to its source. My phantasm slowly surrounded my heart and pushed against my chest to be released.

With a cry, I raised my fist high above me, and my phantasm crackled above me just like the thunder from a storm. I saw nothing but blue light and assumed my eyes were glowing. With another cry, I threw my fist into the ground, falling to my knees. One arm naturally stayed out to my side, keeping me balanced. My phantasm, which crackled above me, fell down over the guards, knocking many of them to the ground in screams of agony.

Like blades of fiery ice...

I thought with a grin.

I wanted them to feel my fire, breathe it, and be consumed with my fury...

I shook my head again. My thoughts were getting out of hand. I turned back to where my soldiers were.

"Go!" I screamed at them. They hesitated, looking at me with expressions mixed with both awe, and fear. "Go! I can't hold this much longer! Go back to the camp and tell them to leave. Now!" I screamed again. They still hesitated, not wanting to leave my side. "Please." I whispered, still holding the guards down with my phantasm, but they were beginning to stir again. This time, my soldiers nodded and moved to leave the control room.

"Jamieson!" I shouted out to gain his attention.

Thankfully, his eyes found mine.

"If I don't follow you in ten minutes, tell the mothership to blow this facility!" He looked at me horrified but bowed his head.

He said something to me, but I didn't bother trying to figure out what it was, my mind was too far gone. I flicked my wrist towards him telling him to go, and he did. The only one who remained was

Xorion. Instead of leaving with the soldiers, he ran to me. Holding both his gun and mine in his hands, he stayed at my side.

"We go together, remember?" he said, giving me a fierce look.

I wanted to scream at him. To tell him that he needed to go, but I didn't. I knew I would have done the same thing had it been him.

A tear fell from my eyes. I wanted to live, have a family, and rule my planet, but it seemed fate chose differently. I looked around the hall, which looked like an open field now. There were so many soldiers firing at us. Too many.

The only reason me and Xorion were alive right now was because my shield was protecting both of us. Out of the corner of my eye, I saw five of the guards start to run after my soldiers and Jamieson. Xorion immediately shot at them, and I blasted them with my phantasm. We made a good team, me and him.

We kept our backs together, blasting and firing while the rest tried to get past our shield. On my right, three guards fused their energy together, causing a blast so powerful that it knocked me to the ground, disrupting my shield.

Fortunately, Xorion had managed to maneuver us from being a direct target that would have been fatal. I grabbed at one of the beams with my own phantasm, twisting it, and constricting it with my own will. The guard it belonged to groaned out, trying to fight back. I jerked at a sudden sharp pain. He was targeting my heart. Before he could do any permanent damage, I let go, flinging him backwards.

Blood was dripping from my mouth, and probably my ears too by now. My skin was wet with sweat, and my breathing uneven. How long would it take them to contact the mothership to blow the facility? I didn't think I could hold on any longer. It was a miracle I wasn't already dead from the amount of phantasm I was using.

I used one arm to guard myself, and with the other, I took out the pill from the secret compartment in my uniform. I let myself smile softly at Xorion, who watched me with wary eyes, his focus now on the pill.

"Your choice, Clove. I will follow," he said with an encouraging, but saddened smile.

More tears fell from my eyes. I knew I needed to take it. It was now or never, but taking it meant no future. No tomorrow, no knowing if Lucy was alive, and Xorion... We would never know what would happen to us in our life together. One of the guards yelled something at us, but I ignored it.

I held the pill up to my lips, preparing for death. I was so focused on taking the pill, I failed to notice that the soldier who had yelled out earlier threw something at my feet. It was a small object that was blinking with red light. I froze, immediately knowing what it was. I quickly shoved the pill in my mouth, swallowing it without a second thought. Light flashed around us, and the device released an isolation cell that would freeze our bodies.

I mentally smiled. If they took us on board their ship, I would take it down with me.

For you, Sovren. For everyone.

30

— • —

CHAPTER 29

My eyes fluttered open, but white lights blinded me. I tried tilting my head to the side but couldn't.

This must be the afterlife, maybe I didn't have a body anymore? Maybe my spirit was surrounded by light.

Blurry faces appeared above me, looking down at me through some kind of mask. A million questions flew into my mind.

Was I dead? Was this the afterlife? Who were these blurry faces surrounding me? Family... Friends?

The faces moved away, replaced by another. Their figure was dark, making them look like a shadow in the light. The figure reached a hand forward, and I felt their cold touch against my cheek, tucking my stray hair behind my ear.

I guess I still have a body then, but why am I unable to move?

I tried to jerk my body to move away from the figure, an odd feeling of discomfort coming over me. The figure tilted their head at me, then started to laugh softly.

I froze, my muscles becoming stiff. My body physically feared the figure.

Who were they? How could they gain this involuntary reaction from me in one touch? They were so blurry, so dark. They... terrified me. As if knowing that, they leaned down to whisper in my ear.

I shuddered at the depth of their voice. A voice that was vaguely familiar. It couldn't be... I must be dreaming.

"Sleep child, sleep."

I didn't want to, but I couldn't keep myself from obeying the command in their voice. My eyes closed, and I surrendered to the darkness once more.

My dreams were filled with strange memories. I saw my mother, her beautiful face smiling down on me. Another flash and I saw Cronos wrestling with Rain. Flashes of faces surrounded me of people I'd met, but didn't personally know. They spoke loudly around me, but it was all gibberish. One clear voice sounded above the others as the world began to shake.

"Clove, wake up." The voice called, but I didn't want to answer it. The urge to keep my eyes closed overwhelmed me.

"Wake up, Clove." That voice... I knew that voice well. I forced my eyes open, and I found Rain looking down at me. I bolted straight up.

"Were dead... we died? Right?" I asked while glancing around the room. It was small and gray, with one bright light hanging from the ceiling. I was sitting on a bed, though it was more of a slab of metal sticking out of the wall. Rain sat next to me, shaking his head slowly.

"No, Clove. We're not dead." He sighed. I stared at him in horror.

"No... that's impossible, Rain." I shook my head in denial. "I took the pill. We were surrounded by guards, and I took the pill, I-" He put a finger over my lips, silencing me.

"I know, Clove." He dropped his finger and turned his head away from me. "I took the pill as well. Three of my soldiers did."

"We can't be alive right now. We can't be." I murmured in disbelief.

I hoped this was just a horrible nightmare and we would soon wake up surrounded by the beauty of the afterlife. Perhaps this was a test. I'd heard of trials some faced before journeying to paradise. This was it, wasn't it?

"We have to be dead, Rain... We have to be." I stressed, burying my face in my hands.

"We should be, we were supposed to be. But they-" He sucked in a breath and stood up angrily. "It was a trap, the entire thing. Just a set up. They knew we would come, they gave us the facility, drawing us in. By letting us save D'thaya, we fell right where they wanted us." He looked back at me, his hands clenched in angry fists. "Because that's what they've always wanted. Us. They must have found an antidote for the pills... Guessing the Rizen has something to do with that. Typical..." He growled out the last part.

"I wonder what they'll do with us." I whispered out loud. Of course, ultimately, we would die. But he could have just let us die down on the planet. Why keep us alive? To gloat in our faces?

Rain turned back towards me and snorted.

"Same old torture." He shrugged his shoulders and sat back down beside me. He stared at me intensely, and opened his mouth as if to say something, but stopped.

"Say it." I ordered. I didn't care if he thought I wouldn't like it, I didn't want him keeping anything from me.

He frowned, "Say what?" he said innocently, as if he hadn't been about to say anything. I glared at him.

"What you were going to say. I want you to say it."

He leaned down, resting his elbows on his knees. "It doesn't matter."

"Yes, it does."

He stayed silent.

"Rain." I stressed. His eyes found mine, and I held his stare, daring him not to tell me. He finally relented.

"Clove." He dropped his voice to a whisper. "He is here." I tilted my head, confused.

Who did he mean?

Rain sighed when I still didn't understand.

"He is here, he is aboard this ship."

I froze at his repeated words, giving it time to sink in. My body started to shake, suddenly realizing who he meant. He was here. He was on board with us. On this very ship!

"No..." I whispered, still shaking. Then, I let out a sudden scream.

I realized who it was that had touched my cheek with such cold hands. Who had stood over me while I had no power to get away from him. Someone my body knew to fear even when my eyes couldn't even register who they were.

"Clove, calm down!" Rain grabbed my shoulders, holding me still. I breathed heavily, my heart racing with a fight or flee instinct.

"He touched me, Rain. He touched me!" I trembled, clawing at my face as if to wipe his touch away. "A-And I could do nothing about it!" Tears poured down my face as Rain pulled me into a hug.

"Shhh, it's okay, I'm here... I'm here for you. He will not touch you again, I promise." He tried to soothe, rubbing his hand up and down my back. I held him tight, needing the comfort.

"Hey, look at me." He gently pulled me away from him and I gazed into his eyes.

I wanted nothing more than to be pulled into his arms again. It had been a long time since I'd hugged my brother. Too long.

"They will take us before him." He said carefully.

A knot formed in the back of my throat, and I gave a tight nod, unable to answer with words.

He studied me before continuing. "You cannot let him break you, Clove. You must promise me. Whatever happens, do not let him break you, try as he might." Rain gave my shoulders a gentle shake. His eyes begged for me to understand.

I nodded, but Rain still frowned.

"Say it."

He searched my eyes for recognition. I opened my mouth, but no words came out. "Clove, say it. I have to hear you say it." He said, his tone darkening.

"I-I promise." I promised through a cracked voice.

Saying it out loud seemed to make everything so much more real. He nodded, accepting my verbal answer.

My eyes swept over the room once more. I realized for the first time that we were the only two people in the room. My breathing quickened as I felt panic overtake me.

"Where are the others? Xorion-"

He placed his hand over my upper arm and squeezed. "I don't know. We were separated. Our only hope is that they didn't give them the antidote."

I stiffened at his words, but Rain was right. Our best hope was that they were dead. If they were alive, their lives could be used against us. My thoughts shifted to Xorion, and I felt tears spill down my cheeks.

It's better that he is dead, that he is gone. He is safe now, safe from you.

But even as I thought that another thought hit me. Xorion never took the pill, he thought the blast from me taking the pill would kill him too. I latched onto Rain's shoulders, shaking him.

"He didn't take it, Rain. He must have thought my taking it would be enough, but I'm alive which means he-"

"Don't worry about it. Xorion can take care of himself." Rain soothed, trying to keep me calm, but I watched his jaw clenched. He was just as worried as I was. I forced myself to breathe, blinking my eyes furiously to keep more tears from spilling down.

"God above, take care of them. Allow them to enter your arms peacefully." I whispered a prayer to the heavens, hoping those above could hear me in this dark place.

I held onto Rain's hand, taking comfort in his presence. All we could do now was wait, and I hated waiting.

Rain's head perked up, and his eyes darted around the room before settling. Following his eyes, I saw he was staring at the door. "What is it?" I asked, but he placed a finger over his lips.

"Listen." I stilled, straining my senses to hear what he was talking about. I gulped when I finally did.

"Footsteps." Rain spoke out loud what I'd heard.

We both stood up. Rain positioned himself in front of me, keeping me behind him with his arm. The door to the room we were in slid open, and cold air shot in, making us both shiver. Five guards stood outside the doorway, all wearing gray cloaks and helmets painted with the normal red swirls of Elnorsefall.

One of the guards had a black streak running down the front of his helmet, and it continued down the front of his uniform, circling around the back. The guard carefully removed his helmet, revealing a blonde-haired man whose hair was dyed with red and black streaks. He also had a tattooed flower around his right eye. I assumed he was in charge based on all the extra colors he had. The way he boldly stood in front of the others kind of gave it away too.

He smirked before giving us a mocking look of pity as if he felt sorry for us.

"His highness has called for you to meet him."

"No thanks." Rain said, crossing his arms. I remained frozen by his side, not daring to say anything.

"Oh, but he insists, and I don't believe you would wish to anger him." The guard smirked again. "Would you?"

"Quite the contrary, we take immense pleasure in angering him." Rain gave a smile that was more like a baring of teeth.

"Do you now? I'll be sure to tell your comrades that." The guard gave us a knowing look. Rain's jaw clenched, and I felt my fists shake with anger. I wanted nothing more than to punch the smug look off the guard, but I knew that's exactly what he wanted.

"Come on." He said, gesturing us to follow. "Don't make this difficult."

"We kind of like it here." Rain mumbled sarcastically, but still grabbed hold of my hand to pull me forward anyways.

"I'm sure you would." The guard's eyes sparkled in amusement as we passed by him.

The other guards moved to follow behind us.

"Compared to where he could have put you..." he continued, quickening his pace to fall in step beside us. "But his majesty was feeling rather generous today. Since, of course, he got double the prize." He glanced at me, and I gave him my best disgusted look. He smiled tenderly in return as he took the lead in front of us.

"Good for him." Rain's tone darkened considerably. The guard laughed.

"Yes, and good for the rest of us too. He was sure you would walk right into that trap we set up. I, for one, was prepared to have my head sliced off, but I guess he knows his children well."

"He knows nothing of us." I spat out angrily. The guard threw me a look.

"I'll admit, it was a brave thing to give the D'thayans a chance. Stupid, but brave either way. He didn't think you would come yourself. Actually, he didn't think his other son would let you leave his sight after his big announcement that you would be Empress by right."

"Glad to surprise him." I removed my hand from Rain and crossed my arms tightly across my chest.

"I believe you'll continue to surprise, little Empress." He turns to face me, forcing us to halt our step. "Including myself." His eyes rolled over me, trailing downwards, and then up to meet my eyes again. An uncomfortable feeling came over me at the intensity of his stare. I didn't like him looking over me like that.

"I thought the rumors of your beauty were exaggerated, but now I believe they have not done you justice."

I narrowed my eyes, my nostrils flaring in anger. I hated not being able to do anything about his stare, looking at me as an object of desire rather than a person. How I'd love to throw him against the wall with my phantasm.

Rain put his arms around me, glaring at him. The guard threw his head back as he laughed at us. "A shame really, I hope he decides to keep you around." The guard turned away and continued walking.

Rain's arm tightened around me while gently pushing me forward to keep walking. I clenched both my fists and my jaw but kept moving.

We'll see how much you dare to speak once I am free to do my will to you!

I thought as I felt a glint of my phantasm fluttering within me, angry and restless.

We walked for some time before we were finally made to stop in front of a door. The guard swiped his hand over the doors panel and held his hands behind his back as the door opened.

He smiled, gesturing us forward as he stepped to the side. Me and Rain stole a glance at each other, then stepped through the door.

The room inside was huge and formal, with bright lights hanging from the ceiling. Red and black swirls covered the light gray walls, and huge sofas were placed in a semicircle on the side of the room where two people slouched on them, both staring curiously at us. Their faces were painted, and the sleeves of their white jumpsuits had been cut off revealing a tattoo of a red upside-down winged creature with its talons tied together.

I shivered at the sight. Those two were Rizen members.

Just thinking of the Rizen had drilled in knowledge from childhood flying to the surface of my mind. They were psychotic killers. They took pleasure in the pain of others. They worshiped death. They claimed that what they did to their own was mercy compared to what they do to outsiders, and what they did to their own was unimaginable. My stomach churned at the thought of what experiments they would do to us if we were handed over to them.

I forced myself to look away from them, distracting myself by counting the guards that stood around the room like statues, frozen with their guns held in both arms. There were eight guards in the room with us, not including a man who stood with his back to us, staring out a huge window that covered half the room.

I recognized him easily. How could I forget his figure? It was the man that killed my mother. My father.

He wore all black with a black shoulder cape as well. His dark hair ran straight down his back, long and perfectly placed.

He snapped his fingers, and an Ovidō female servant stumbled over to him. She seemed to have a hard time balancing, and I had to bite my lip when I noticed her wings. They'd been torn from her flesh. Most likely, her tongue had also been taken from her.

It was disgusting, the things they did to them.

I watched as she held up a tray for him. He paused a minute before placing a glass on top of the tray, and then flicked his wrist to dismiss her. He slowly turned to face us. His light red eyes rolled over us, taking in everything about us. I felt Rain reach up to squeeze my bicep.

"Hello, children." He smiled at us.

He was older than I remembered, his face not as young looking as it did in my nightmares. Those same red eyes burned through us like a predator who drew in his prey. He wanted to intimidate us. His smile mocked our pain.

I dug my nails into my skin. I hated this. Both me and Rain refused to make a sound. We had nothing to say to him.

"Come now, is that any way to greet your father?" His lips lifted as if amused. Me and Rain immediately took a defensive stance and let our markings blaze. He was going to kill us anyways. Why not go out in a blaze of fury?

The guards around us aimed at us with their guns, but our father just laughed as if it was the funniest scene he'd ever seen.

"What do you want from us, why have you kept us alive?" Rain demanded while holding one hand in front of me and another one in front of himself, guarding us both from our father. He tilted his head at us, his mouth twitching into a smirk.

"To the point. I like that, Rain." He walked towards us, and we responded with a step back. His eyes flashed to mine. "You have inherited your mother's incomparable beauty, Cloverlyne. She truly was divine was she not?" I clenched my teeth together. He had no right to speak about her, how dare he! It took everything in me not to lash out at him. If it wasn't for Rain's hand in front of me, I might have.

"You did not answer my question." Rain said a little too calmly. I knew he was trying just as hard to restrain himself as I was. He nodded at Rain.

"I want your phantasm, but I assume you already knew that" he said matter-of-factly.

"Then what? You kill us?" I lifted my chin high into the air, trying to seem as if his words didn't affect me. He let out a mock gasp.

"Dear daughter, you offend me. Why would I kill you? I admit I have no use for Rain, but you..." he smiled, "I have a special use for you."

"And what might that be?" I narrowed my eyes on him. I almost prayed he wouldn't answer, but of course he did. Why wouldn't he? He took pleasure in torturing others.

"You will stand by my side, Cloverlyne. I need an heir, and you're still young. I believe you can still be tamed."

I laughed. I couldn't help it; his plan was ridiculous. So, he wanted to tame me like a dog? I'd rather take my own life.

"You're a bigger fool than I thought if you truly believe that."

"You know, I was fascinated by the ones in my cells." He said casually, ignoring my statement and taking another step forward. "Especially that young... What was he again? Fehichen?" His face twisted in disgust as he said the word, as if it were a bad taste.

I forced myself to keep my expression neutral.

"A lovely boy, I think, but certainly not for my daughter?" He smirked again, but this time more darkly. "Surely my daughter has better taste than to associate with forbidden scum?"

I shrugged my shoulders as if I didn't care.

"What is it to you who I associate with?" I responded suggestively as I tilted my head to the side. I crossed my arms trying to make it seem as if Xorion meant nothing to me, even though my heart dropped at the revelation.

If he knew I cared for him even slightly, he would use him against me. "Besides, I have my choice in men. I'm not as my mother was with you." I gave my father an unimpressed look. He snorted, jerking his chin up at my implication.

"Speaking of men, there was another young man aboard who wished to see you. He was quite persistent, and I didn't have the heart to tell him no." He said, easily changing the topic.

I gave him a curious look, hiding the fact that I was terrified of the thought that someone he knew wanted to see me. Rain stiffened beside me, clearly feeling the same.

Perhaps it was someone who despised the royals? Or a friend of my fathers who was curious about me? I really didn't care; I didn't want to meet anyone who was in leagues with my father.

"Call forward the one who's been working with us."

Two guards nodded and left the room.

Me and Rain looked at each other with the same look, both wondering the same thing. Who was it? And what did they have to do with us?

"Oh, I'm sure you will enjoy this boy's presence. He was quite the charmer." Our father said, chuckling softly.

Me and Rain turned, keeping our eyes fixed on the door as we waited for the guards to bring the individual before us. I felt my father's presence grow closer as he moved to stand right behind us. We both stiffened, but didn't dare move.

The door opened, and the two guards stepped through, bowed to my father, and moved to the side of the door. Everything seemed to stand still as the individual walked through the door, confident and completely at ease with his surroundings. He wore rich dark brown robes, and the Union symbol painted in black ink over his face.

Even with his newly painted face, I recognized him. I couldn't breathe, I couldn't even move. All I could do was stare. This was a nightmare; it had to be. A horribly realistic nightmare that couldn't be real.

Rain sucked in a breath beside me, his hand reaching forward to grip my arm tightly. I barely felt it, my thoughts blank with shock.

"No, it's not possible! I don't believe it!" Rain shouted.

I felt his tears fall down my arm. It had been years since I'd seen my brother cry, and yet I hardly noticed them. I was too numb with the scene before me. He strode forwards with his head held high, and stood right in front of us, his mouth twitching into a smile.

"Eller', good to see 'yer again."

My body suddenly felt weak, the only thing keeping me standing was Rain, who held onto me with a death grip. I'm sure he felt like it was just some horrible nightmare as well. But it wasn't, it was real.

"Adam."

31

●

CHAPTER 30

"**M**e, yah." Adam said with a laugh. Feeling returned to my body in hot rage. No longer feeling numb, I finally spoke. "But it's not possible... no."

I didn't want to believe it; I didn't want to feel this sickening rage swim through my body. "How long? How long have you been working for them?"

It was a question I dreaded the answer to but needed to hear. We needed to know just how long we'd been compromised even if it hurt as if someone was ripping my heart out of my chest.

"Since always. The Union was never interested in y'er folks, just conquering other worlds." He shrugged his shoulders as if it should've been obvious.

Breathe, you must breathe. This is what your father wants, to break you. You can't let him.

I lifted my chin and forced my muscles to relax. I could do this, I just had to take the hardest step forward of my life. Adam raised an eyebrow at me as I stepped forward, but I ignored the gesture, choosing to stand tall.

"We thought it was a Fehichen who betrayed our alliance and trades, but it never was, was it? You were working with the MioTamir Union from the beginning, feeding them information on us."

My fists clenched at the memory of how he'd acted when we chose to ally with the Fehichen. "Which would explain why you disagreed about going to Vaymos for a possible allegiance with them." I let out a short laugh. "Because even you knew that forming that alliance would be something the MioTamir Union wouldn't overcome so easily."

He jerked his chin up haughtily. From his reaction, I knew I was right.

"They're an unfortunate complication but being dealt with'er just fine." He insisted.

I gave him an obviously fake sweet smile. "Oh, I'm certain you're trying."

Since leaving Eurkxo, we had had very little contact about how their war was faring, but from his response, I took it Eurkxo was winning. He laughed darkly in response.

"Please, Clove. We'er be victorious in this battle. 'Specially after we'er have help from our new friends." I noticed his speech was more formal than I was used to. His accent was hardly noticeable anymore.

I guess that all had been a cover too...

My heart clenched at the thought.

"So, in return for helping Elnorsefall catch us royals, they have offered the MioTamir Union aid in their battle against Eurkxo? Pity that you're not strong enough to take them down yourself. I'm not surprised, after all, I'm the one who decided an alliance with them would be vital."

"An ingenious decision I must add, daughter." Zaphon, my father, said from behind me.

Hearing the pride in his voice made me sick to my stomach. I felt myself tense up as he stepped so close, he was nearly touching me. I prayed he wouldn't. I knew I wouldn't be able to keep myself from wanting to get away from him, and I didn't want him to see just how much this betrayal was affecting me. I looked Adam dead in the eyes when he stepped before me. There was only one last question I had left for him.

"What did you do to Lucia?"

He stiffened, a real expression coming over him for the first time that made him almost look... sorry. It quickly vanished before I could say anything.

"The MioTamir Union ambushed them, but they managed to disappear'n the Forbidden Region... for now." He grinned sinisterly at the last bit. Hope bloomed in me at the thought of Lucia being safe. It was the only good news I could have in this situation.

"As pleasant as this reunion's been, we have work that must be done."

Zaphon motioned for the guards that escorted us here to step forward once more. He turned to the sofas where the two Rizen members sat, and they immediately stood and walked over to him without a word. Their heads curiously tilted as they looked over us, but their eyes remained vacant.

"Prepare the experiment in the labs. I don't want there to be any issues." The two beings nodded at his orders, turned on their heels, and left the room.

I didn't dare to turn around; I couldn't look at him. Nevertheless, he walked around me to stand next to Adam and found my eyes anyways. He smiled and kept eye contact with me as he addressed Adam.

"Take them back to their cell. I will call them forth when it's ready."

"Of course, Emperor." Adam said, bowing low. His right hand covered his chest, a sign of respect in our culture. The gesture caused bile to rise up in my throat.

Zaphon tilted his head at me, before glancing at Rain who stared at the ground. I wished Rain would say something, or do something, anything. I wanted to yell at him that he needed to show that we weren't affected by Adam's betrayal, but I couldn't. Not just because I didn't want to give our father the reaction, he wanted from us, but also because I was barely hanging on myself. I knew that when I broke down later, Rain would be the only one able to put me back together again.

But this experiment my father spoke of-

I sighed to myself. It probably wasn't the best idea to think about that right now.

Forcing my feet to move I started to follow the guards, but stopped when I realized Rain hadn't moved. I quickly took hold of his hand to drag him along. His eyes flickered to mine, full of pain and sorrow. Adam had been his best friend, his brother. It didn't surprise me that he wasn't handling this well. He knew Adam a lot longer than I did. They'd been through so much together, we all had. Learning that everything was a lie... every laugh, every cry, every pain, every happiness... It hurt. I can't process it now... I didn't want to. Rain blinked twice before finally finding his own feet again.

We walked out of the room and down the hall that we came from before, and my eyes stayed trained on Adams' back. How could he betray us? How could he live a lie like that for so long? How could-

I forced myself to look away, blinking so tears wouldn't fall. Every memory, every journey we had together... fake.

Adam suddenly stopped in front of us, turning to face us. The guards around him held their guns forward to halt us.

"Take him back to his'er cell." He jerked his chin at Rain. "You two." He said, pointing at two of the guards. "Remain 'ere."

The guards nodded and moved to grab Rain. My brother went wild, pushing the guards away with his hands.

"You stay away from her, you traitor!" Rain spat at Adam's feet. Adam stared at him like he was a wild animal.

"Curse you! Curse your whole family! Curse the very phantasm that possesses you!" He snarled at Adam while the guards fought to keep him restrained.

"Rain please, this isn't helping. Remember where we stand." I said, trying to calm him down.

I didn't really want to stop him, I wouldn't mind watching Rain beat Adam to the ground, but I didn't want the guards to hurt him for his emotional actions.

He froze, his eyes threatening to burn Adam's soul. Adam said nothing, he simply tilted his head at the guards in a silent command to take him away.

"There is nowhere you can sleep that your dreams will not be haunted by me, Adam! I will kill you every night you dare to close our eyes!" Rain shouted as he was dragged away. Adam turned to me, ignoring Rain's shouts. I stared back, daring him with my eyes to break the new silence.

"Well?" I crossed my arms, narrowing my eyes on him. Finally, he looked away, sighing.

"Even if I'er chose to explain myself, yer would never understand."

"I don't care for your explanation. I can't believe you'd dare to say you have one, and I most certainly don't care to understand. I hate you." I said, surprisingly calm.

His eyes flashed with sudden sadness at my words, but I was too angry to think about his reaction. I meant my words, I hated him.

"I know that." He said quietly. "But I did what'er had to do, I'er almost didn't. Kept myself from givin' you to 'em so many times.... Even though I'er knew it was'a only way to ally ourselves with El-norsefall."

"So why?" I shouted while throwing my hands up in the air, annoyed at his little game. He wanted to talk, then I'd let him talk. So what?

He froze, anger flashing through his eyes. "Why?" He asked, laughing. "Because y'er didn't listen to me! I told y'er not to go to Vaymos, I warned you so many times!" He punched the wall with his fist and waved a hand accusingly at me, but I refused to flinch. "And then y'er, Clove. Yer had to go'n give y'er heart to him..." He spat out the word like it had a bad smell, and I knew immediately who he was talking about. "I'er asked myself why 'thousand times, but when I saw y'er with 'em that day, I knew why. Because no matter how much I wanted y'er, yer would'n never want me. I'er could never change 'way things were, so why bother? I'er was born a Union member and was stupid to think they'd ever let me go."

My breathing stopped.

What did he mean he wanted me?

He took in my expression and suddenly grabbed me and turned me so that my back was shoved up against the wall. His arm pressed against me, holding me in place as his face remained only a breath away from mine. I gasped at his sudden reaction. He'd never been physically aggressive with me, but he wasn't the man I knew, he never was.

"Yes, I'er love yer. Yes, I'er have always loved yer. That was why I'er lived that lie for so long... 'cause Rain was my brother, and y'er the one I'er wanted to spend the rest of my life with." His other hand went to my cheek, rubbing his thumb on my lower lip. "But I'er could never have you." His voice was hoarse, and he whispered the words as if they were forbidden.

Anger vibrated throughout his body, causing a cold shiver to run down my spine. I wanted to move away, I wanted to will my phantasm to blast him away, but I couldn't. My body refused to respond to my command.

"I'er let her go... for you. We had her, and I let her go." He whispered as he ran his lips against the side of my neck, making a cold shiver run down my spine. He was talking about Lucia. My jaw tightened at his touch, and at his words. I tried to move away out of disgust, but he held me firmly.

"Do not lie to me... You let her go for you!" My body shook in anger. "And to think I trusted you..." I murmured.

He lifted his head to look me in the eyes and stared as if he was searching for something, something I knew he would never find. I tried to shove him away with my hands, but he held me too tightly. Still, I continued to struggle. I didn't want him to touch me, his hands around me made me feel dirty. Adam let out a frustrated growl as he grabbed my hands roughly to pin them behind me, rendering me powerless as he stared down at me.

"You are right, you will never have me. I never want to see you again. If I do, I'll kill you." I promised to his face. Never before had

I felt such a strong urge to hurt someone, and Adam seemed to realize that because he immediately let go of me.

"Take her." He said to the remaining guards. This time, he didn't come with us.

I knew he was watching me while the guards dragged me away. I could feel his eyes on my back like a trail of fire, but I refused to look back even if it was the last time I would ever see him again. I should've been happy at the thought, but I wasn't.

The guards opened the cell and pushed me inside with such force that I tripped. Thankfully, Rain moved to catch me before I hit the ground.

"You okay?" He asked, checking me over. Somehow, I knew he was talking about more than just me tripping.

"I don't know." I admitted, keeping my eyes fixed on the ground. I finally gave up trying to stand on my shaking legs, and let my knees go limp. Rain held me, letting me fall to the floor slowly.

"Clove, look at me." He begged, but I couldn't obey him, I just stared at the ground. An ache formed in my chest. It felt like a knife, forcefully digging into my heart. I held my hand over my chest as if it could soothe the ache.

"Clove, please..."

Tears ran down my cheeks, and Rain tilted my chin upwards, forcing me to look at him. He cupped my face, wiping my tears away with his fingers. I heard Xorion's voice in my mind telling me my tears made me stronger, but I didn't feel stronger. I felt torn, and empty. Thinking about Xorion brought a new rush of tears to my eyes.

If I could only see you... just one last time. I would give almost anything, just to see you smile at me and tell me everything will be okay.

"I've never wished death as an option, Rain, truthfully. But right now, I welcome it." I whispered as I dropped my eyes to the ground once again. Rain shook me angrily.

"No! Do not say such things. You can't let him see you like this! Do you think he will stop when we are dead? No. You will not let him break you. You promised me this much." Rain said while stroking the top of my head. I wish it were that easy, but I didn't know how much more I could take.

Rain moved us to sit against the back of the room, facing the door. We knew it wouldn't be long now till they came to get us for their experiment. We didn't have to wait long. We heard their footsteps even before we saw them coming for us. Both of us sat up, surprised that it wasn't the scientists but rather the bane of our existence standing before us once again.

"Now, now children, why must you look so distraught?" Our father said with a cherry look about his face. Both of us cringed. We didn't need to make this situation worse with angry words.

"Nothing? Not another word for your father?"

"What's there to say? You only come here to torment us once again." Rain crossed his arms and slouched down into a comfortable position.

"Am I not allowed to have an alone conversation with my two children?" He placed his hands on his hips and let out a sigh. "Now if only Cronos were here. He was always a strong headed boy wasn't he? Took everything far too seriously." He shook his hand as if amused.

"We've nothing to say to you." I spat.

"And yet I have so much to say to you, daughter." His eyes looked over me with wonder. I don't know why he seemed so fascinated with me. "So much to know, so little time."

"Unless you're here to tell us what this experiment is, we have no need for conversation."

He smiled at Rain's comment. "You will find out soon, Rain. Very soon." He said as he walked away.

We watched him go before turning to look at each other and moving closer together, getting comfort from each other's warmth. I felt ashamed for the thought, but I was glad Rain was here with me. We should have been glad that they were taking their time, it gave us more time together, but with each passing hour, we both anxiously waited for their arrival. Fear overtook any rest Rain suggested we should get, but eventually, we slept against the wall.

It was Rain who shook me awake to the sound of more guards coming in. We remained seated while the door slid open. The same lead guard from earlier stood before us again.

"Time to go." He said, jerking his head to the side in a gesture for us to hurry up. We stared at him, contemplating whether we should let them drag us to our deaths. The guard sighed, walking forward and kneeling in front of us.

"Look, you really don't have an option here. I know you two don't deserve this, no one ever does, but there's nothing you can do to stop it." He sighed again, looking at the floor before looking up and giving us a wry smile. "Even if I could help you, I wouldn't. It's a game of survival here." The guard stood, even offering us a hand to help us up. We refused his help, and the guard dropped his hand with a short laugh. In the end, we finally stood up and followed the guards out. I swallowed, wanting to ask a question, but fearing the answer.

"What's this experiment for?" I finally asked, despite my fear. The guard raised a brow at me.

"Didn't think you'd want to know."

"She doesn't, but since we're the ones it'll be happening to, don't you think we should know?" Rain responded for me, sharing my same thoughts. The guard seemed to consider it before shrugging casually.

"The experiment is a machine that can remove phantasm cores from within the host and give its control to another."

I bit my own tongue to keep from gagging. I was wrong, I didn't want to die. I didn't wish for death, not like this.

The guard eyed us with a look of pity. "The Rizen created it. Though, it hasn't been tested yet, and certainly not on royals. It might not even work."

We gave a tight nod at his explanation. I tried to think of other things as we walked towards our death. Anything was a better nightmare than this.

The guard swiped his hand over a panel, and a huge wall-like door opened upwards revealing a large room with white tables and chairs. Chemicals in bottles were placed on the tables, and bubbling tanks were secured to the walls, wires pouring out of them and clinging to the ceiling. Scientists wearing white masks and coats stopped their work as they turned to stare at us. It was the most terrifying place I'd ever stepped foot into.

The guard let out a cough, and we turned to him with wide eyes as he indicated the room.

"Welcome to the labs."

32

— ◆ —

CHAPTER 31

M e and Rain stood frozen in place, taking in our new surroundings. The room looked like it was made just for torture. As we
stood staring, slowly accepting our fate, the guard called a rather
young-looking woman forward. She looked us up and down and
then indicated for us to follow her without saying a word. Reluctantly, we followed her to the back of the lab where four raised table-like
beds were.

"Lay down." She commanded us, her tone neutral without excitement or pity.

We could fight them, we could. Do as much damage as we could
before being forced into the experiment. I wanted to go down with
a fight, but I knew that whatever we did would affect the others they
had aboard this ship. Due to their minimal security watching us, I
guessed they knew that too. So, we obeyed without protest, laying
down on the two closest to each other.

"Restrain them." She ordered the guard, who immediately moved
to do the task.

He first went to Rain, tying each arm and foot to the bed. He then
picked up a circular device with a folded metal piece over it from
the side of the bed. The flowed-eyed guard tore Rain's shirt down

to expose his chest and placed the device on his bare skin while the other half of the device unfolded and was made to extend over his neck and clamp around it. The young woman picked up two small mechanisms that connected to the circular device before grabbing two more and attaching them to both his temples. Rain grunted uncomfortably.

I shivered as I watched them ready their machines. They seemed to be doing him first. I wished they'd done me first, then I wouldn't have to wait in anticipation, which was somehow so much worse. The woman took out a syringe and injected something into Rain's bicep.

He closed his eyes. "What's that for?" He asked, his voice quiet and oddly calm. The woman typed something into her computer before responding,

"Something that will keep you from passing out, we need you fully conscious for this experiment to work properly."

"Lovely." Rain said sarcastically, opening his eyes again. The guard smirked at Rain's comment, and then moved over to me to tie my restraints.

"Sorry about this, pretty." He murmured as he pulled down my shirt, tearing it down to reveal the top of my breasts before placing the cold circular device over my chest as he'd done for Rain.

I didn't speak or move; I just wanted this all to be over. Part of me still held out hope that none of this was real, but it was just a fantasy. I knew this was real.

"We'll do him first." The woman said as if it wasn't obvious. She placed a shiny object in the center of the circular device on top of Rain's chest.

"Just how bad is this going to hurt?" Rain mumbled, his breathing slightly increasing. The woman ignored him, busy typing something on the computer while other scientists whispered around her.

The guard leaned against the wall in between our two beds. "You're wearing restraints for a reason, royal." He remarked matter-of-factly.

I started counting my breaths, afraid that I'd stop breathing altogether. I wanted to be strong, for Rain, but I didn't know if it would be enough to just be strong. I turned my head to look at Rain as fear overtook me. I could feel my hands starting to sweat, my breathing increasing, beginning signs of a panic attack. Rain turned his head to me as if he could feel my fear and smiled at me as if nothing bad was about to happen at all.

"Just do me a favor will you? Don't count or anything, just do it." He said, closing his eyes and relaxing into the bed.

"Very well." The woman said, not even looking at him.

"Have to hand it to y'all, you're handling this better than I thought. Almost wish we could've been better acquainted." The guard said through a sigh.

Rain let out a small laugh. "Just another day in the life of a royal." Rain said dryly. He then eyed the guard closely. "You're better than this, don't let your life go to waste. You'll only ever be a disposable tool to him. Soon, you'll end up just like us."

"Thanks?" The guard shook his head. "You're right about that." The guard chuckled softly, looking to the ceiling almost desperately. "But what can any old tool do about it? Survival is our only option."

"It should not have to be an option, but dying knowing you have lived..." A small tear fell from my eye. "That is worth more than survival ever will." I whispered.

The guard stared at me for a long time, contemplating my words.

He swallowed and looked away. "You would have made a good Empress."

I didn't respond. The fact that he said 'would' made our fate feel all too real for me. Instead, I kept my eyes focused on Rain. The device on his chest lit up and started humming.

"The machine is secured, begin the process."

His entire body started vibrating, and he had a confused look on his face as his markings began to shimmer. They glowed so bright it illuminated the entire room, but then he started jerking as if in pain. He gasped out as his body jerked forward again, and bit his bottom lip and closed his eyes as if trying to hold back a scream.

Tears streamed down my face as I was forced to watch his agony. This was torture in itself. Pure and utter torture being strapped down and powerless to stop my brother's pain before me.

"Please stop!" I screamed at them, unable to remain silent any longer. I tried to break through the restraints, but it was specifically designed to hold us in place. "You'll kill him!" Subconsciously, I knew they wouldn't care that they would kill him. We were going to die anyway.

The markings around his eyes suddenly went completely dark, and I gasped in horror at the sight. Our markings could dim to a point they weren't quite as visible, but never dark. Never, ever, dark. Only the dead's markings were dark.

He let out a scream as if his limbs were being ripped off, his body jerking towards the ceiling as the machine sucked his phantasm straight from his core. His phantasm lit around his heart where the device sat as the center shiny object glowed with his light. Sweat poured from his forehead, and tears fell as he continued to jerk against the restraints.

Cursing at the scientists who watched with curious eyes at my brother's agony, I fought using every amount of strength I had left, trying to break free. I actually managed to loosen the restraint on my leg, but then the guard used his hands to hold me down, keeping me from moving.

"Quiet! You will not make things better for him this way."

I fought against him, wanting nothing more than to constrict his heart. They would pay for his agony; they would pay with blood.

The guard sighed and moved his hands to hold my shoulders down and force me to look at him. "He will live through the process, look!" He pointed to the computer screen next to Rain's bed.

I squinted my eyes, trying to read the screen. It was at ninety-eight percent. Rain threw his head back into the bed, mumbling curses as tears continued to stream down his cheeks, but his body had finally stopped jerking. Dread washed over me. I felt nothing from him, nothing at all. I always felt him, the presence of his phantasm, it was something everyone could feel. It was as if he disappeared, but he was right in front of me.

"Rain?" I whispered, but he didn't even look at me. He stared at the ceiling, his eyes vacant of any color or life.

The lights from the machine cut off, but the small shiny object placed in the circlet remained glowing Rain's blue phantasm color. The scientist pulled on some gloves and grabbed the object. She then proceeded to place it in the center of some kind of metal pendant. Another scientist checked Rain vitals. They checked his pulse, heart rate, and pupils.

"He's alive. Half-dead, but still technically alive." The scientist said, typing something into the computer.

I breathed out in relief; thankful he was still alive. We could escape this place. They would think our fight was already out from us and lower their guard. That was when we would strike back. We could reverse whatever they did. All I had to do was get hold of that pendant.

But all thoughts of hope were crushed in a simple eight-word sentence.

"Tell the Emperor we're ready for his presence."

"He's already on his way." The guard responded to the scientist, checking a communication device on his wrist.

She nodded, "Excellent." She continued her work while the rest of us, even the guard, appeared to wait miserably for his arrival. I shuddered as I heard the loud footsteps of Zaphon's boots on the ground when he entered the lab.

"I take it the experiment was successful?" He asked as he walked up to our beds. He eyed Rain with curious eyes, watching as he silently gasped for breath.

"Yes, Emperor." She said, handing him the pendant.

He smiled as he took it and placed it around his neck. He closed his eyes as his markings glowed in a light red light, the pendant now changing from Rain's blue light to his red light.

"His energy is powerful, more so than I ever dreamed of." He mumbled with a lopsided smile, as if he were drunk. "Is it true that my phantasm will become even more powerful now that I have taken my son's phantasm?"

"Yes, Emperor. If our reading is correct, you are now fully connected to his phantasm. It surrounds your core." The woman said proudly.

I felt sick to my stomach. This technology was wrong, it was downright evil. This experiment in itself was more than just sickening, it was madness.

"How is he responding to the process?" Zaphon asked, creating a small beam of phantasm between his fingers. He stared at it as if mesmerized.

"He is incredibly weaker. His senses have been dialed back significantly as well. I would like to test his capabilities. It seems like he will have to relearn how to do simple tasks once again due to his lack of phantasm. His body is unused to its own heaviness." The Woman mused, checking a tablet.

At her words, Rain groaned, slouching back into the bed. Zaphon smirked as he watched Rain's pain. It made me want to burn his face off. His eyes glinted with phantasm as he observed Rain from above.

"Rain, my boy. I'm grateful for the phantasm you have provided me with." Rain closed his eyes, but was still unable to move. I could see his muscles tighten as Zaphon gently removed the circular device from his chest, replacing it with his own hand.

"But unfortunately, I have no further use for you anymore."

My eyes widened in horror when I realized what he was about to do. Screaming and kicking, I begged him to stop, but my attempts did nothing as he shot Rain's heart with his phantasm.

"Rain, no! Get away from him, you monster!" I screamed over and over as I watched my brother's heart become constricted with his own phantasm. He couldn't even scream. "Please...." I sobbed uncontrollably. It was as if a string holding my heart together snapped as I watched Rain's body go limp as Zaphon lifted his hand from his chest, shaking his head.

"Imagine. If we made all those who opposed us this weak. We would be more than victorious." He turned to me and smiled. "We would be gods."

My body shook in pure hatred. I wanted to hurt him like he hurt me and my family. I would kill him. I would kill him painfully, and I would take pleasure in it.

There is no place you can run to escape me, father. My phantasm is a part of me, and I will use every last breath I have in me to destroy you. That is a promise.

"Prepare my daughter for the process. You can do your testing on her." He crossed his arms, and smirked at me. It only fueled the fire burning in my eyes. He flicked his wrist at Rain's body.

"Throw him out the airlock, we don't need any more useless bodies around here."

"May God have mercy on you Zaphon, because I will make you pay in the cruelest way, in a way that not even you can imagine. You will die by my phantasm, and by my phantasm alone!" I screamed at him.

He looked down at me as if amused. "You don't have it in you to do that, Cloverlyne. You're too much like your mother."

"You don't know me. I am your daughter, am I not? What else could I have possibly inherited from you?" I let myself smile. Thoughts of how I would kill him filled my mind. I wanted him to know I was completely serious about my threats. I wanted him to know I would make it hurt just as badly as he hurt me.

His mouth twitched into a frown as he considered me before narrowing his eyes and walking closer to me with his shoulders tense. I recognized his look; it was the same look he had before he killed my mother. For the first time in my life, I wasn't afraid of him. He was going to take everything from me anyways, but I wouldn't give him my fear. He didn't deserve to be feared, he was no god. He was just a man that would die like the rest of us. Surprisingly, the guard stopped him from his approach.

"Emperor, you are being called back to the bridge."

"Whatever it is can wait." He snarled, but the guard didn't even flinch.

"It seems urgent, Emperor."

Zaphon raised a brow at him, and for a second, I thought he might snap the guard's head right off for getting in his way. Instead, he just nodded his head.

"Make sure she remains alive." He ordered, and just like that, he left.

The guard looked down at me and nodded his head as if he were trying to tell me something. I tilted my head at him, but he purposely kept his eyes away from me.

What was happening on the bridge?

I wondered.

And why was the guard being so secretive all of a sudden?

The woman took out another small shiny object from a box, and placed it in the circular machine.

"Are systems active?" She asked, typing on her tablet and glancing at the machine, which was now glowing.

"System active and secure."

"Activate process." I closed my eyes.

This was it; this was the end. I wasn't a fool. Once my phantasm was gone, I needed to find a way to kill myself, otherwise I would be used by my father. It shouldn't be too difficult; they did say I would become significantly weaker.

I tensed, feeling a tugging on my phantasm as the machine forced me to call it to the surface. I resisted, but the pull was too strong. It felt like trying to stop an ocean from moving. My markings glowed in blue light, and my body starts vibrating like Rain's did. Rain... maybe he was still alive? Maybe they kept him alive somewhere. It wasn't like I saw his vitals; he could still be alive. A tear threatened to fall from my eye from the pain, but I forced myself not to cry. I couldn't do that now; I needed to be strong. Strong, for Rain. He deserved that much.

My body jerked upwards, and I gasped, my eyes only seeing blue electric light. I felt the machine tug at my core, trying to pull it from me, but my phantasm clung to me. I felt it running wild through my veins, fighting the machine's pull. Sweat poured from my face, and a sharp pain jabbed my heart, sending what felt like electric shocks throughout my body. I yelped as I fought the pull, and threw my head back against the bed, gasping for air. If I stopped breathing, I was sure I would die.

Suddenly, my phantasm was sucked from my veins, the light I saw was growing dim, just as the machine had done to Rain. I screamed in pain. It hurt worse than anything I had ever felt in my life. My heart felt like it was being ripped from my chest. My head, like it was being torn in half, and my muscles felt like liquid. I screamed out again, this time in terror. I could feel my core deep within my heart which pumped and channeled phantasm safely throughout my body, and I felt it crack.

No, I felt it shatter.

My phantasm surfaced and pulled from me in a way I'd never felt before. Just as I thought I couldn't take anymore of the pain, it ceased. Only the lingering ache remained. The light from my eyes withered away, and I noticed the room was darker. The device on my chest was no longer on, and the small shiny object inside the device glowed, but not nearly as bright as the first one.

I frowned, still feeling traces of my phantasm running through my veins. The scientists around me were typing on their computers, blocking me from seeing if the process was complete.

"It should've been able to finish before the malfunction." One of the scientists said, their tone confused.

Malfunction? Did that mean the process was not completed?

I pulled my eyebrows together, looking around the room for some clue. I was still restrained unfortunately, and I felt extremely weak. I moved my fingers, and then my toes, making sure I still could. So it was true. The process hadn't been completed.

"She must have previously tore her core already, which would make sense with the amount of phantasm the machine was about to surface from her. Perhaps it's a good thing the malfunction happened. The machine may not have been able to handle the overload." One of the scientists mused his thoughts out loud, earning a frown from the head female scientist.

"Not a malfunction." Another scientist said from the other side of the room.

"What?" The woman said as she gestured him over with her hand. He showed her his tablet.

"A power outage. They're happening all over the ship."

"What's the cause?" She asked while hurrying over to the main computer on the other side of the room. The scientists followed behind her.

"I will inquire about it." One said, and I heard him open the door to leave the room.

The guard from before walked over to my bed, and I watched him with wary eyes as he placed a finger over his lips, indicating for me to remain silent. I frowned as he slipped on a glove, grabbed the small device from the circular mechanism on my chest, and placed it into a box. He glanced around, and then placed the box in his pocket. Then, he began to tug at the restraints, removing them.

I glanced up at his face, trying to read him, but he remained focused on undoing my restraints. The scientist, preoccupied with the power outage, doesn't seem to notice him freeing me. Once my right arm was free, he leaned down and whispered in my ear.

"Blast them."

I didn't hesitate despite the pain as both me and the guard shot an arm towards the group of scientists along with a powerful blast of phantasm. All of them, unprepared for the attack, screamed, and fell to the ground. Whether they were simply unconscious or dead, I didn't know. Frankly, it didn't matter to me anymore. I wished I could blast the whole lot of them.

Using the remainder of my phantasm, I forced the rest of the restraints off my other arm and legs. I forced myself to sit up despite how groggy I felt, and gasped at how difficult it was. I could barely move, let alone stand.

"Let me help you." The guard said, offering a hand.

I slapped his hand away and held two fingers with phantasm crackling between them to his chest. He raised an eyebrow at me, and I let my eyes narrow hard on him.

"I'm not very keen on trusting anyone, so answer me this one question. Why?" I said through gritted teeth, trying to keep my strength up. He rolled his eyes.

"Look, pretty. Releasing you has already earned me a ticket to death, and this is ain't a self-righteous thing either." He said while holding his hands up in surrender. "I didn't do this for you, I did it for me. Everyone I ever cared for is either dead, or has been tortured to the point of never being sane again." He shrugged. "It's not like I have anything to lose. This ship is going down anyway."

"What do you mean?" I asked, lowering my fingers slightly, but not completely.

He pointed to the ceiling. "Feel that?"

I reached out with my phantasm senses and felt a slight vibration throughout the ship. I tilted my head at him, silently asking for an explanation.

He gave me an exasperated look. "The vibration? It's a ZENI. You know, space-hover?" He let out a laugh. "It's on the outside of our ship, and it's causing quite a few issues."

My eyes widened, and my mouth opened in a silent gasp. ZENI's were used by only one race, and that was the Anari of Ardiamus. Did that mean...? The guard nodded at the look of recognition on my face.

"It seems the Custodian Emperor has decided to pay us a little visit, with their lovely Anari allies."

I felt hope begin to bloom through me. I had a chance to escape, a chance to keep living. I slowly let the guard help me stand.

"Then let's go greet them."

33

CHAPTER 32

I leaned against the guard, my arm around his neck as we made our way through the hall of blaring alarms. The ship rumbled and shook every so often, signs we were being fired at by another ship. That was a good thing, of course, but I hoped we could get off this ship before possibly getting blown to pieces.

We tried our best to avoid other guards. Even if they were preoccupied with the battle to deal with us, we'd rather not just jump out in front of them. We moved as quickly as possible, but even with my flower-eyed guard's knowledge of the ship, it was difficult.

"It'd be easier, pretty, if you'd let me carry you." He huffed out, annoyed. We leaned against the wall while waiting for a few more guards to pass by. I shook my head. There was no chance I would let this man carry me. I was barely okay with him helping me walk.

"I don't understand why I still feel so weak." I mumbled, breathing heavily against his arm. He shrugged at my comment.

"They just tried to remove your core, give your phantasm a break will you? Thankfully, it'll replenish itself, but certainly not quickly enough to be useful for us."

"How come you kept the shiny ball?" I asked, nodding at his pocket where he'd placed the box. He patted it self-consciously while throwing me a smirk.

"Safety reasons."

I narrowed my eyes on him, looking suspiciously at his pocket. He chuckles softly before explaining.

"Your phantasm is a lot more powerful than mine. This little thing sucked pure phantasm right from your core, and we might have to use it if you want to get out of here." I cringed, but couldn't disagree with his reasoning. No matter how disgusting it sounded to me, he was right that we might as well use it. He peaked around the corner and cursed, quickly ducking before more guards saw him.

"This is no good. With this amount of guards we'll never get to the lower levels where your friends are before someone stops us." He shook his head to himself. Groaning, he took out the box with one hand, while ripping the top of his uniform open with the other. He clicked a small button on the box I hadn't noticed. The box opened, revealing small spike-like objects covering the edge of the box, while the shiny object glowed in the center. He slapped it to his chest with a grunt of pain. To my surprise, it stuck to him, blood seeping out from where the spikes stabbed him.

"What are you doing?" I asked as he mumbled unintelligible curses. He took my face in both his hands.

"Down this hall, make a left. There's a transport that takes you down to the cell's. You have a better chance of getting off this ship if you release your friends."

"What about you?" I warily glanced at the object on his chest that now glowed in a soft orange light. He sighed again.

"I told you, I'm a dead man anyways. I'm going to do what I should have done years ago. Blow this ship to pieces." My eyes widened in disbelief, but the look on his eyes was dead serious. It surprised me that he was willing to sacrifice himself so easily, but I think I understood him. He didn't want to be their tool anymore. He wanted to die free, he wanted a choice. He let go of my face and bowed to me. When he raised his head, I saw the fire deep inside him.

"Go."

"Wait!" I said, reaching out and holding his arm to keep him from leaving. He raised a brow at where my hand held him. "I don't even know your name."

He smiled, and placed his other hand over my shoulder. "I'm not looking to be remembered, pretty. I'd rather you not know who I was, just who I am right now." He looked off towards the opposite hall. "No one takes my own damned life but me. I want to die doing what I want, not by trying to survive. Now, thanks to you... I'll do just that." He gently shoved me against the wall as he lit his markings, his eyes glowing in a soft orange light. "Just know, In another life, I would have followed you to the ends of the universe." He stepped out from our cover, and threw a smile at me over his shoulder.

"Now go!" He commanded, and I obeyed. I moved as fast as I could using the wall to keep my steady. An explosion rocked the ship, and the circuits in the ceiling popped loudly causing the hall to go dark as my body slammed against the wall. I groaned out miserably. My phantasm was still in much lower amounts then I was used to, and it hurt terribly.

Down that hall, make a left. There will be a transport that takes you down.

The guard's voice rang in my ear as I gasped, clutching my chest. A sharp pain tingled there. I bit my lip to keep from crying out as I looked around my surroundings. I glared at the hall the guard at told me to go down, and push myself forward.

One step closer to home...

I turned down the hallway and stepped into the open before stopping dead in my tracks. Some kind of engineer held a tablet and stared at me with widened eyes.

I cursed at myself. I should've checked the hall before stepping into the open like that. Without caring about the pain, I shot one arm forward holding out two fingers. A small amount of phantasm sparks between my fingers as I narrowed my eyes on the engineer. His eyes widened and he dropped his tablet on the ground and held up his hands in surrender. I kept myself facing the guard as I moved slowly around him until my back was facing the other end of the hallway.

"Leave while you still can." The engineer backed away slowly, his eyes nervously looking at the sparks between my fingers. I scowled at him. "I've had about the worst day in Realmer history, if you don't leave this second I won't hesitate to watch your body crumble to the floor." At that, the engineer turned on his heels and made a break for it. I spun around and pushed my legs to move fast down the hallway despite my body screaming at me to stop. I refused my body's request until I reached the transport down. I figured that either the guards were too busy in the upper sections, or my flower-eyed guard somehow found a way to distract them. Either way, I was grateful my only run in was a single engineer. The transport opens and I enter it, hurriedly pressing the buttons to take me down. The transport closed, and I waited with my head leaned back against the wall.

Hopefully it wouldn't be too difficult to find any of our soldiers, and I prayed to also find Xorion.

If they are even still alive...

A small voice said in the back of my mind. I shook the thought from my head and punched the side of the transport.

"Ow..." I mumbled as I cradled my hand, but at least it distracted me from thinking negatively. The transport finally opened minutes later, and I hurried out. The lower levels were completely dark. I lit my markings so I could see where I was going. Definitely the lower levels of the ship, and it looked like a prison. Vaguely, I heard voices up ahead and slowly walked towards it. There was nowhere else for me to go anyways. I stepped as silently as possible, and dimmed my markings slightly.

"Who's there?" I asked hesitantly into the darkness. I heard the voice again, but can't make out what they're saying.

"Hello?" I asked more weakly, and stopped walking when I saw a small light up ahead.

"Who... there...?" I made out the two words, and though the voice was faint, I recognized it. I froze as they came closer. Their light was faint, and I knew they couldn't see me just as I couldn't really see them yet.

"Clove... is that you?" The hopeful voice asked, and I brightened my markings so they could see me. "By eternity, you're alive!" Before I could even say a word, he wrapped me in his arms. I didn't return his embrace. It didn't feel right to be embraced right now, on board an enemy ship. My mind could just be playing tricks on me. Maybe he wasn't even real? Maybe the warmth of his skin was just a figment of my imagination.

"Xorion...." I whispered, but held my arms at my sides, unable to move. He pulled me back, observing me. I looked into his face and saw tears forming in his eyes..

"Clove... what did they do to you?" A hint of anger clinged to his voice as he looked me over. I hadn't seen myself in awhile, I had no idea what kind of image I presented. Anger suddenly rose through me. I was alive, wasn't that enough for him? Did I have to act and look okay just so he wouldn't look at me in pity? He wrapped his arms around me again, mumbling something in his own language. He moved his hands to caress my face while his head buried my matted hair. I still didn't return his embrace. Instead, I trembled. He was making me feel things I didn't want to feel right now, things I couldn't feel right now. I needed to get off this ship. I used my hands to push him away. Hurt overtook his expression as well as confusion. I ignored his look. I recognized the two other soldiers from Rain's group that stood behind him. My eyes flickered to Xorion.

"We need to go. One of Elnosefall's guards is going to blow up this ship. The Anari and the Custodian Emperor are here to rescue us." They blinked at me, surprised. Without explaining further, I spun around and led them to the transport. We headed to the upper section of the ship, and I tried to think of where we could go to be rescued. As the doors to the transport opened the signs of a battle were seen. Smoke roamed the ship, and wires sparked from the walls.

"That explains what caused the malfunction in our cells." A soldier wondered out loud. I gave him a sideways glance, an idea forming in my mind. If we had a ship, maybe we could force one of the Elnorsefall pilots to help us to escape. Surely there were more like my flower-eyed guard?

"We must get to the hangar bay." I announce as I peek around a corner, making sure the hall is cleared. The others nodded.

"Agreed, but how do we get there?" One of the soldiers asked.

"I can get us there, I know the layout of this ship." The other soldier said much to our surprise. I raised a brow at him and he made a face. He shrugged,

"I used to live near an assembly that created these cruisers in East V'rasór before me and my brothers escaped. They're all the same. We were forced to work there as kids, suppose it was useful in the end." He explained quickly. I let him take the lead, and he looked both ways before we hurried down the hall behind him. Xorion kept in step beside me, glancing at me frequently, as if wanting to ask a question.

"What is it?" I finally asked, still jogging painfully because of the attempted experiment. It was nothing compared to the pain brewing in my heart. He eyed me carefully.

"What happened to Rain?" I stiffened at my brother's name, refusing to answer. Speaking about Rain would only... it would only shatter an already bleeding heart.

"What happened to Rava?" I asked instead. I could assume the answer.

"We think he chose to use the pill right before we were captured." Our new lead soldier said in a grim voice.

"Guess they didn't see the point of stopping the pill's effects for him, if they even bothered to bring him aboard at all. We never saw his body." The other soldier mumbled behind us. Xorion grabbed my shoulders, stopping me and spinning me around to face him. The two soldiers stopped moving seeing that we'd stopped. They leaned up against the wall and their eyes carried the same question. What happened to Rain?

"What are you saying, Clove?" His jaw tightened, and his eyes burned into mine, demanding an answer. I tried to jerk my arm out of his grip, but his arm held me too tight. I glared at him.

"We need to go." I said through gritted teeth. I hated him for demanding such a painful answer.

"Not until you answer me straight." He said placing one hand on the back of my head to hold my gaze.

"He will not be coming. Ever!" I yelled at him. He let go at me, shocked. I had never yelled at him before, but then he had never hurt me like this before. I shoved him back with my hands, still glaring at him. I felt tears form in my eyes, and I blinked to try and keep them from falling.

"Does that answer your question?" I asked bitterly. His face fell, and he stumbled back as if he'd just been slapped in the face.

"Clove... you can't mean that he is-" I refused to hear him finish his sentence. Spinning around I commanded the soldier to continue leading us to the hangar bay.

"Let's go. Now." They nodded at my order, and all of us ran while keeping our eyes alert for more guards.

As we ran down the hall, another blast hit the ship. We fumbled around, trying to keep ourselves steady as the ship continued to quiver with the explosions hitting it.

What in eternity is going on out there?

I thought while looking around as smoke and wires sparked from the walls next to us.

"Stay back!" The lead soldier commanded as he pressed himself into the wall despite the sparks.

"Looks like a squad is coming this way!"

"We have no time! Can we outrun them?" I whispered next to him trying to get a glimpse at how close the squad was.

"Oh, we'll make it, but they'll follow behind us." He pressed his head to the back of the wall before turning his head to me as if asking me what I wanted to do.

Stay hidden and risk dying on this ship when it explodes, or make a run for it to the hangar bay while being chased by guards?

There's really only one choice though. I'd rather risk our lives trying to escape than give up now when we were so close.

"We make a break for it." I decided, crouching beside him. He nodded at me, then to the others, letting them know our plan. He took a quick glance around the corner, sighed, and waved his hand.

"Now!" He shouted. We turned and ran down the exposed hall. As soon as they saw us in front of them, they fired their weapons at us. I shift my energy to be a shield behind us, but focusing on my phantasm caused my legs to give out from tiredness and I almost stumbled to the ground, but Xorion managed to grab me in time. He let out a curse, and picked me up so that my legs could wrap around his torso and my arms could hold his neck. Though I was still angry at him from earlier, I was grateful I didn't have to walk anymore and could just focus on the shield. I felt the guards' attack targeting my shield like a knife poking at my heart. Each time their phantasm or beams hit it, I had to stifle a cry of pain. My phantasm pulsed angrily from overuse. It felt more unnatural than usual, and I could feel my body burning from the side effects.

"Where almost there!" One of the soldiers said. "Just a bit farther!" I turned my head so I could see where Xorion was running towards, and saw that the door was firmly shut. The lead soldier let out an angry grunt when he noticed. We stopped in front of it, and Xorion put me down, holding me steady as I kept focusing on the shield. The soldier placed his hands on his head, his face full of worry.

"Do you know how to open it?" I asked, before crying out and slamming back into Xorion as the guards weapons made direct contact with my shield. The squad would be right upon us in a matter of minutes. The other soldier, seeing me struggling, raised his hands forward to help with the shield. I felt my body lighten with his help, but it wouldn't nearly be enough to keep the guards at bay.

"I- Yes. There are codes-" He stammered looking at the door in a nervous manner.

"Do you know the codes?" I cut him off, getting impatient. We needed to get out of this hallway, fast.

"They never gave us the codes, but-"

"Find a way around it then!" I yelled while turning around and pointing to the control panel on the side of the door. He flinched at my tone, but quickly moved to mess with the mechanisms inside. I turned to the other soldier, who visibly gulped as more shots were fired out the shield.

"My phantasm is much lower than it should be, this shield won't hold, even with your help. I need you to distract them from attacking this shield." He nodded at my words, and lit his markings in a bright peach light.

"Transfer some of your phantasm to me" Xorion demanded beside me. I raised a brow at him. There was no reason to give him any, he wouldn't be able to control it anyways and I would have to shrink my current shield.

"I have no weapons, nothing I can use to help defend from behind your shield." He stressed, looking at me as if doing this was the most obvious choice I had. Sighing, I shrunk the current shield and placed my hands over his to transfer a small amount to him. Surprisingly, it wasn't as difficult as I thought it would be to pour phantasm over his hands. Perhaps it was because my phantasm was more surfaced than usual?

"It'll only be surface energy, it will not enter you. I should warn you that controlling it will be difficult since it's not stable phantasm-" He waved his hand telling me to be silent.

"Believe me, I understand,"

"They're on us!" The soldier yelled, and before my shield could be overwhelmed by their phantasm, the soldier threw his phantasm at them like a wave, pushing them back. Xorion threw his arms forwards, and the unstable phantasm was thrown wildly around with no real target. It didn't do much other than distract, but it managed to keep them from directly targeting the center of my shield and paining me further. The other soldier held them off well, but with one glance at his sweaty face, I knew we won't be able to hold them off for much longer.

"How are you coming along, soldier?!" I managed to yell out to the soldier working on the panel.

"I need more time!"

"You have none!" Xorion yelled back at him. He threw his hands around, clearly frustrated that he couldn't control the phantasm I gave him.

All this just to die in the end?

I stared off at the angry guards attacking us and smiled sadly. On the bright side, I would be with Rain again, and everyone else who died before him.

"Wait, something's happening!" The soldier behind me said. His hands back away from the panel in a surrendering motion. I glanced at the panel. He was right, a bright green light began blinking from it.

"It's opening!" Xorion said, his voice relieved. My eyes widened. We might actually make it out of this alive!

"Well done, soldier!" I smiled at him, but frowned when he shook his head at me. He didn't look happy that the door was opening. If anything, he looked more worried than before.

"It wasn't me." He said in disbelief, staring at the door.

"What do you mean?" The other soldier asked, his tone darkening. The other soldier backed away from the door.

"It wasn't me who opened the door!"

"If it wasn't you who opened the door... then who did?" I asked. All of us took a step away from the door. The other soldier stopped attacking the guards and instead both soldiers added their phantasm to my shield. I winced at the direct hits from the guards' weapons and phantasm, but it didn't hurt as bad as before with both soldiers helping. We all watched as the door started to open, and a sick feeling churned my stomach. We watched as it fully opened. To our surprise, Anari knights stood before us with the symbol of Kingsemcore tattooed on their chests and on the side of their foreheads. One of the Anari knights threw some kind of ball aimed at the guards firing behind us. It hit the ground and an explosion threw the guards to the ground. Other Anari knights stepped out around us and guarded us with their own shields.

"Empress!" I froze when I heard the voice. It was Jamieson. He ran up to us from inside the hangar bay. Though, more surprising to me was the person running up to us from behind him.

"Jamieson... Rihaya." I whispered the words, astonished. I didn't think I would see her again, and after the revelation of Adam, I didn't know if I wanted to.

"Clove, it is good to see you're alive." She nodded to me with a smile. I didn't respond, unsure if she was the Rihaya I used to know. Perhaps all the rectifier crew were secretly working with Adam. She frowned when she saw the hesitation written on my face. She raised her hands in surrender.

"I understand what you're going through right now, Clove. We found out about him shortly after he left us on Eurkxo. Believe me when I say that if we find him, we'll have to flip a coin on who gets to end his sorry life." I stared at her for a moment, still processing her words, before giving her a curt nod.

"What's she talking about, Clove?" Xorion asked behind me, but I ignored him. I lifted my head to both Rihaya and Jamieson.

"I have been giving intel that this ship is about to blow itself up. We need to leave before the detonation happens." Jamieson widened his eyes, and Rihaya raised a brow, but both nodded. Rihaya yelled out to the knights behind us to get back to the ship. When their leader turned and questioned her, she told him what I told her. I watched as they both hurried off to warn the others to get back to the ship.

"Let's get off this horror ship." The soldier behind me said. Jamieson immediately turned to lead us to the ship they arrived in. I let out a breath I didn't even know I was holding.

"Yes, let's go."

34

CHAPTER 33

"I want an update on the situation. Now." I ordered one of the commanding knights of Kingsemcore who sat next to me on the transporting ship. He leaned forward, resting his arms on his knees.

"We are currently in the planet Guāsk's sector-"

"MioTamir's colony planet?" I interrupted with raised eyebrows. "Is it wise to engage in battle here?"

"Not really, but better here than MioTamir. Elnorsefall seems to have a base of operations on Māhera, one of Guāsk's moons. We arrived just in time, Elnorsefall sent warships from that moon to Eurkxo. It's our hope that with our combined forces, we can stop them."

I sucked in a breath. So, in exchange for us, Elnorsefall was going to help MioTamir win their quarrel with Eurkxo. Except they couldn't do that, it violated the rules of war.

"Elnorsefall can't... they can't attack Eurkxo, they have no reason to." I frowned at the knight, who nodded in response.

"No, they can't, but they can assist without directly attacking the planet."

It was a dirty move to surround the planet and give the Union weapons and supplies in the middle of battle, but no law of war forbade it.

"And what's the plan when we enter our mothership?" I asked, curious what Cronos was planning.

"The Elnorsefall warships have already begun their attack. The second we enter the mothership; we need to change our game from defense to offense. We have to win this battle."

So, it's a full-on battle then...

I nodded, telling the knight I was following along.

"How long until we enter the mothership?" Xorion leaned into the conversation, clinging to the safety restraints.

The knight jerked his chin upwards. "Right about now."

Just as he spoke, the sound of the docking bay doors opening could be heard. Our ship entered and landed safely with a loud thud. We unbind the restraints from ourselves and the exit when the back of the ship opens. The knight made a motion for us to follow as we stood from our seats. We followed him as he headed towards the bridge of the mothership where we met a Soaran who introduced himself as Commander Lyroik.

"Greetings Empress, and to all of you." He stood tall and bowed his head.

"Commander," I nodded back in respect.

"If I may get to the point..." he tilted his head.

"Please," I took a step forward since he seemed to want to talk to me only.

"Empress, I know you've just escaped hell, but unfortunately we're nowhere near out of this yet." He took a quick breath before continuing. "I would like you to help me command the Archann, my ship.

We may need your phantasm. As for your comrades, they will be sent to Med Bay."

"Of course," I said before I could think too much about it. He was right, I was more than exhausted and probably needed a trip to the Med Bay myself, but it was better for me to be doing something then to be left alone in my thoughts right now anyways.

"Morrigan will escort your friends there." He gestured to an armored woman near us. She walked over to us, and quickly bowed to me before addressing the two soldiers and Xorion who stood behind me.

"Please, follow." Her words were formal and direct.

I turned to look at my comrades one more time, and the two soldiers gave me a smile that showed their gratitude that we were alive. They bowed low to me, before turning to follow Morrigan. Xorion hovered a moment, staring at me as if unwilling to leave.

"Be safe, okay?" He said it as if it were a plea. I gave him a small smile that I hoped told him I would be fine.

"I will, please... be safe as well."

He flashed me a wry grin. "When am I ever not?"

I narrowed my eyes at him, but inwardly smiled. He leaned in, wanting to kiss me, but I stepped back. A flash of hurt crossed his face. I sighed and looked into his eyes. I hoped he saw the silent message.

Not here, not now. I care for you, I want you, but I can't right now.

He nodded, understanding, before turning and following the others. My heart clenched, there was always the possibility something could go wrong, and I would never see him again. I shook my head. I couldn't afford to think such thoughts when my heart was already so fragile. I'd have plenty of time to mourn later.

Sighing, I turned and followed Lyroik. He took me to the front of the bridge, letting me take a good look around first. It was bigger than the previous ship I'd been on, much bigger. It shouldn't really have surprised me though, but my eyes still widened at the site. This was a warship after all.

In the middle of the bridge was a platform, which was where me and Lyroik were to stand to command the ship. Lyroik moved to the side, and held his hand out while bowing, indicating for me to walk onto the platform.

I gulped. I'd never done this before. I'd never commanded a ship in a real-life scenario. Simulations I had practiced with, but this would be very different. I was glad I had a trained commander beside me, I knew he would be doing most of the commanding and I'd only assist.

I stepped forward, stepping onto the platform which was separated from the rest of the crew by a transparent half circular wall. A holographic handprint on it lit up as I fully stepped onto the platform. Hesitantly, I placed my hand on it. The holographic touch screen computer circled above and around me. It showed me our location, the location of our fleet, and the location of the enemy ships all at once. My eyes widened as I focused on the enemy ships. They were moving in fast.

Lyroik stepped up beside me and lit his markings which were a dark gray color. His phantasm flowed through the controls. Closing my eyes, I mimicked him and let my phantasm run through the controls as well. This was a phantasm-controlled ship. Its speed and precision would be entirely in me and Lyroik's control now that we were connected to it. As I opened my eyes, I fixed them on the new Elnorsefall warships heading towards our fleet. Past the transparent screen I noticed the crew had turned their attention to us with their heads bowed.

I turned to glance at Lyroik, who gave me a subtle nod. It was Soaran tradition for the highest-ranking individual on board to give a short prayer before battle. I breathed in softly, and as I breathed back out, I began the prayer.

"To our God, I pray these words. Be our protection, and our strength. Do not forsake us in this battle, but lead Natarah unto your will, and strike our opposing force. May we be forgiven for the souls we shall send to your afterlife."

"And when we die, let you guide us to your paradise." The crew responded in sync. They raised their heads in a new, proud confidence. Lyroik gave me another nod and I took a step forward and raised my voice.

"Full thrust forward. Let's finish this."

35

— ◆ —

CHAPTER 34

"Enemy is reading weapons." Someone on the lower screens informs me. I nodded,

"Inform us the moment they are in firing range." I hesitantly pressed one of the flashing lights on the control screen which switched me to co-contrals of the ship,

"Keep weapons steady." Lyroik said calmly next to me as he focused his attention on the main controls.

"They're in range!" Someone else said just as I saw the warning flash on my screen.

"Return fire!" Lyroik commandded, and I switched my screen to see where most of the damage was being inflicted. They were aiming for our main weapons systems.

"Avert the ship's position, they're aiming for main weapons." I said to the commander. He grunted and focused on helping to ease the ship's movement. I felt a bit strange not asking for permission to do something since this wasn't my ship, but a battle was no place for pleasantries, and I guessed if he had a problem with something I was doing he'd override me.

"They're moving into our blind spot!" Someone yelled, and I mumbled a curse at the information.

"Get in contact with the closest ship to us, tell them we need a distraction!" Lyroik said as he shifted power to shields, guarding our blind spot as much as we could. I followed his order, switching my controls to see who the closest ship of ours was. The Matias, a smaller, but faster warship. I opened communications, hoping they'd answer.

"This is the Archann to the Matias. Please come in."

"This is the Matias, what is your status, Archann?" The commander's voice was rough sounding, and in the background I heard the crew yelling out something to him.

"We need you to distract that incoming ship. It's heading into our blind spot and we can't shift our position, it's too fast."

"Know the design? It's the Nyx, one of their experimental ships. Its weapons are lethal in close proximity. Seems Elnorsefall's mixing Soaran tech with MioTamir tech. If I move us too close it'll destroy my ship." He raised his voice to emphasize his point, but I'm sure Lyroik was already aware of that.

"Noted. Keep at a distance, but pull their focus from us. We'll cover you." Lyroik chimed in beside me, leaving no more room for argument from the other commander.

The commander grunted, clearly not liking the idea, but didn't refuse.

"God be with you, Archann."

"And with our entire fleet." I said through a sigh, and switched off communications.

To Lyroik I say, "We're going to have to take that ship out."

"Concentrate all fire on the Nyx!" He told the crew in response to my concern. Our ship maneuvered around the Nyx while they were preoccupied with the Matias. No longer surrounded, I let my shoulders relax. Unfortunately, it didn't take long for another light to start flashing in warning.

"Commander! We are about to lose the Genosin! They are taking continual heavy damage!" A woman on one of the visual stations yelled out. I switched to the hologram that showed the fleet so both me and Lyroik could see. She was right, the Genosin's shields were at 10% and dropping quickly.

"Switch to engines. We need to help them." Lyroik said. I fed the engine station side of the control panel some of my phantasm, and the engine room immediately responded, giving us all they could.

"Switching power to engines, maximum thrust!"

Our best option was to block the inflicting damage by using our ship as a shield till they managed to escape. It seemed the Commander had the same idea, and managed to reach the Genosin just in time. The ship shook with every blast from the enemy ship, but we managed to protect the Genosin from a fatal end.

"This is Genosin contacting the Archann. Come in Archann." Their commander's voice said, attempting to contact us.

"This is the Archann, we read you. What is your status?" I responded immediately.

"The damage was critical, but we're alive. Thanks to you, Archann." Clear relief could be heard in the commander's voice, and I smiled in relief, thankful we were able to save them.

"To think I'm saving your sorry hide again Commander Fraya." Lyroik turned slightly to face my screen, cracking a smile.

"Commander Lyroik, I clearly remember it was you getting saved by me last time." The commander responded in an almost sultry tone. I raised a brow at Lyroik who smirked to himself at her words.

"You don't say? No matter, get out of here before you get your ship blown up and I have to pull you out of hell."

"I wouldn't mind that." The woman practically purred before switching off communications. Lyroik shook his head, smiling the entire time. I continued to stare at him until he finally caught my eye and let out a short cough.

"Long story, Empress." He said becoming serious once more. I nodded, but deep down, I was smiling. It was a nice way to ease the tension with a bit of joking. Maybe one day I'd learn to be more like them and not be so stiff and unsure. Both of them had spoken with a carefree confidence I didn't have yet.

"I'm picking up an energy spike from one of the enemy ships!" A young man managing another visual station informed us just as the information was sent to our screen. Lyroik immediately magnified it. Before either of us could properly analyze it, an ear piercing blast sounded, and the entire ship shook furiously.

"What was that!" I called out above the shouts of the crew. A bunch of warnings filled my screen, and I tried to click on them to answer my own question, but there were too many all at once.

"By eternity!" Someone from a station below said and another yelled out a stream of choice curses at the same time. It was then I finally noticed it. The ship that we'd been captured on was a ball of fire as a shockwave blew up smaller Elnorsefall ships surrounding it as well. The front and back were split, bursting into electric blue flames.

I let out a short laugh at the scene. It seemed my flowered-eyed guard wasn't kidding about destroying the ship. I only hoped that both Adam, and my father were still on the ship when it happened.

I turned to Lyroik and said,"Use this advantage, they are distracted!" He responded by sending his phantasm to main weapons once more, seeming to agree.

"Focas all blasts on the Nyx!" He commanded.

"They are returning fire!" Someone yelled out.

"Shields down to 40%!" Another said as the diagnostics were sent to my screen.

"Continue firing! We must take down that ship!" I said while holding onto the panel in front of me, bracing myself for the incoming attacks. If we lost shields, things were going to get really bad, really quickly.

"Archann, this is Commander Marrin of the Sapphira. Do you read?" I fought back the urge to ignore the incoming communication.

"A little busy, Commander!" I said through gritted teeth while gripping the controls on my panel due to another blast that shook the ship.

"A ship snuck through our defense! They're heading away from the fight!"

"Another experimental warship?" I asked, dreading the answer. Lyroik casted a wary look my way. He seemed to dread the answer too.

"Maybe, but this one's something else. It's bigger than the other ships out here. Know this, they're powering up for a phantasm-jump." Commander Farrin said, and though I knew he was trying to appear calm, I heard the worry in his tone. This ship was planning on leaving the battle. The question was, to where? And why?

"Wherever it's going, it can't be good. It must be stopped." He says, mirroring my thoughts out loud.

"Thank you for the report Commander, we'll do our best." I promised him, and switched off communications.

"What is our status of our fleet?" I asked Lyroik, knowing he was listening in. If we went after that ship, we wouldn't be able to finish this fight. Our fleet might not be able to spare us though.

"The Genosin has already pulled back. The Sapphira is with Marn 9, taking out those smaller battle vessels. They're steady so far. Coronet 6 is having a face off with some other experimental warship, and the Matias must have gone to help Marn 9." He said quickly, a frown coming over his face.

Marn 9 and Coronet 6? Those must be the names of the Anari vessels that were helping us.

I'd never gotten to properly see Anari warships. I wondered if they were as majestic looking as some said. I glanced at Lyroik, whose frown deepened as he turned to one of the stations and asked,

"Shields?"

"Down to 34%!" The woman managing the station said, sending up another diagnostic. A warning sounded again as the ship trembled with the Nyx's attacks. We needed to stop that other ship from leaving the scene, but the Nyx wouldn't just let us leave in the middle of a battle. What were we going to do? We didn't have much time left to catch up to them.

"Need a hand, Archann?"

I let out a breath I didn't know I was holding when I heard the sound of the Matias's commander over our communications.

"We were told to stop a ship that's attempting to leave the battle, but we're stuck with the Nyx." I explained as the commander let out a hum.

"Go! Me and the Sapphira will take down the Nyx." He said firmly. I raised a brow in surprise. Just before this he was worried the Nyx would take down his ship, but I suppose with the help of the Sapphira, and with the Nyx already having damage, he was ready to take them on.

"Goodluck, Matias." Lyroik said while looking over at my screen before I switched off communications.

"Target the enemy ship powering a phantasm-jump!" I informed all the stations. Me and Lyroik searched our screens for any signs of the incoming ship, but we saw nothing. I opened a visual screen hoping to see it, and it opened just in time to see a flash of light moving away from the fight.

Dear Natarah, it was fast!

I thought with widened eyes.

"Locking on target. Fire all weapons on their drive!" Lyroik commanded.

"Damage inflicted minimal! They're jumping through space!" Someone said, and I sucked in a panicked breath. Switching all our power to weapons, I did my best to maximize our inflicting damage.

"Keep firing!" I insisted, but it was already too late. There was a blinding flash of light, and the ship was gone. The speed was incredible. It made me want to scream in frustration, but I bit it back. Opening communications, I informed Commander Farrin of the unfortunate situation.

"This is the Archann to Commander Farrin. Please come in."

"Archann, were you able to neutralize the target?" He asked, his tone hopeful. I sighed,

"No, the ship was too fast for us to neutralize."

"Damn, I didn't think we would get so lucky." He paused for a moment. "At least we have the Nyx."

"You're able to take them down?" I asked, checking my screen again. The Matias, and the Sapphira were still surrounding it. If we focused our weapons on it as well, it would easily be finished.

"Soon." He sighed in relief. "Perhaps that ship was simply carrying something back to some Elnorsefall's base."

"We can only wonder what." I switched from communications to full thrust so we could help them finish off the Nyx.

"Ready weapons." Lyroik told the stations.

"Weapons ready, target locked." One of the stations replied.

"Fire!"

The Nyx, now being targeted by all three of our ships, was unable to save themselves no matter how fast they were. It only took a few minutes of direct attack for their ship to erupt in light. It burnt in electrical blue flames, and sent out a massive shock wave. Cheers sounded all throughout the bridge.

"Target has been neutralized!" Lyroik said, throwing a smile over his shoulder at me. I smiled back, but not as big. My mind wandered to the ship that got away. We would be hearing of what disaster they would cause soon. I hoped we'd be able to stop it. Another flash lights up the screen.

"Empress." A new voice said over communications. This one coming from within the ship.

"What is it?" I asked, curious.

"You are being summoned to the transmission room, the Emperor wishes to have a word."

Swallowing a sigh, I let them know I'd be right there. Lyroik nodded at me, letting me know he had everything under control. I went ahead and had someone from the non-essential stations escort me to this transmission room since I didn't know my way around this ship yet. She seemed happy about getting out of the bridge for a bit and led me into a transporter. While waiting for us to arrive at our stop, I noticed her fidgeting from side to side, as if nervous about something.

"If there's something you have to say, you have permission to speak." She slowly shook her head even before I finished my sentence, but then sighed as the doors to the transporter opened.

"Forgive me Empress, It's just- I think you should know that just before the Emperor asked for you, we were informed about a locked signal for V'rasór being sent from Eurkxo." My eyes widened, and without thinking, I broke into a sprint, leaving her behind. I stopped only to ask a few engineers for directions. A sickening feeling churned my stomach. What reason would Eurkxo contact V'rasór for? Was it a coincidence? Or was Elnorsefall going to break the laws of war and attack Eurkxo? Maybe they'd found some horrible loophole we failed to see.

As soon as I found the transmission room I quickly entered, placing my hand on the door panel. The room was dark, except for a flashing light on the table in the center of the room. I sucked in a breath. I almost didn't want to know what had happened, but I needed to know. Letting out that same breath, I pressed the flashing light. A hologram appeared, shaping into a person. Specifically, Cronos.

"Emperor Cronos." I bowed my head, respectfully acknowledging his presence. I waited for him to say something, anything, but he didn't. I lifted my head only to watch as his eyes pursued my clearly unpleasant appearance. His eyes lifted to mine and a deep-rooted anger was held in them before shifting to something that looked a lot like stricken grief.

God, I was glad he and Rain looked so different. His face was long and lean, and he shared our father's stoic looking eyes whereas Rain had our mother's softer features, and her large doe eyes. Comparing his features to my father gave me a sudden new strength. I needed to remember that face. I needed to focus on the threat.

"Na'la..." He said quietly. "I-"

I held my hand up, cutting off his speech.

"Not now, Cronos. We have more pressing matters to attend to than our own personal affairs."

His face tightened, and he opened his mouth as if to argue with me, but then chose to let out a sigh while simply nodding in agreement. Taking a deep breath in, I got straight to the point.

"A signal was sent from Eurkxo." I started, narrowing my eyes on him. He nodded,

"Yes, a signal was sent to us."

"Well?" I asked impatiently. I had this deep need to know, and an unpleasant coiling feeling wrapped around my heart. I didn't care that Eurkxo wasn't my birth planet. It was where part of me grew up, which made it home.

"It was a distress signal of sorts. The ship from the battle that escaped..." I sucked in a breath as he mentioned the ship.

So he'd heard about that already? What was the ship for? And why was he mentioning it in addition to a distress signal? Unless...

"The Elder's believe they plan to test their new weapon on them, handing over the weapon to the Myan's so they obey our war laws." He took a quick breath. "Cloverlyne, I know what Eukrxo means to you. From what the Elder's said, that weapon will turn the planet into a wasteland, unless we stop them."

"A wasteland?! They can't, they wouldn't dare! Eurkxo is a valuable asset to the Realms, the planet itself is rich with life, they-" My hand lifted to cover my mouth in horror. Where did they even get such technology? It wasn't as if we didn't have the knowledge to create such destructive weapons in the Realms, but it just wasn't done. No planet, no matter how great the evil one planet did to another, would ever create something destructive to the planet itself. The planet's were sacred, a gift from the Makers. As if reading my thoughts, Cronos answered my unspoken questions.

"They've been working with The Rizen... as you already know." A pained look came over him for a second before he lifted his chin, and cleared his throat. He hid his emotions so easily.

At least we had that in common...

"Whether or not the weapon will truly be used on Eurkxo has yet to be determined."

"But it's where they've jumped to, isn't it?" I tilted my head, wondering why he'd think they might not use it. This was Elnorsefall we were talking about, they'd do it in a heartbeat if it meant gaining more power.

He nodded his head again. "For now, yes. As for your next question which I already know you're about to ask me. Yes, we can make it there in time..." He trailed off, telling me there's more to it then he was letting on.

"Continue." I wished he'd just say it rather than me having to coax it out of him. It was as if he enjoyed this sickening anticipation.

"My spies informed us that Elnorsefall was given the location of the planets Eurkxo has set up trades with... outside of the Realms." He scrunched his face, clearly disapproving our methods of survival. "I know you may believe Elnorsefall would use this weapon on Eurkxo, but I don't. Eurkxo is part of the Realms, and we all are the Realms, despite our quarrels. Even Elnorsefall realizes this. That won't stop them from attempting to cripple them, and there are no laws against it, not for outsiders. Even if I am wrong, Cloverlyne, and I very much doubt that, Eurkxo must remain." He locked eyes with me, his face darkening. "Even if we have to sacrifice other worlds."

I blinked at him, processing his words. I knew what he was saying, even if I hated it. Despite Cronos insisting that they'd leave Eurkxo be, I know they wouldn't. If we jumped to protect Eurkxo, they'd use their weapons elsewhere. They'd take out our trading planets... E'arka, and Vaymos. I clenched my fists. There was only one person who could have given them the locations of both those planets. Adam. I really hoped Adam was still on that ship when it exploded. He knew too much to be alive. I really, really hoped he was dead.

"Wouldn't they just use it on all of them?" I asked, finally finding my voice. He shook his head while answering.

"Not according to what I've heard, they only have the power for one test, and it won't be Eurkxo." He said firmly, his tone final as if giving me a command. I sneered at his last words.

"Pretending to care about my home, are you?"

"We haven't the time for arguments, little sister. I already told you my opinion. Elnorsefall will not use it on them, but it's your choice who you choose to protect. You're the only available ship at the moment." He frowned at me, before sighing and looking away.

I whipped my head away from him, angry that he was putting this on my shoulders, but I already knew my decision. I had to save my home. I didn't doubt for a second Elnorsefall would do it, despite Cronos's opinion. I saw them for who they were, for who they all were. Monsters.

"The second Eurkxo is secure, we're heading straight to those two planets. I don't care that it's forbidden." I left no room for argument. Cronos would just have to deal with the consequences. He raised an eyebrow at me, but still bowed his head, submitting to my demand.

"As you wish, Empress."

His virtual form flickered, before it finally faded from view. For a while, I stood frozen. It was almost too much to process. Swallowing, I stepped away from the table towards the door and placed my hand on the panel to open it. Once the door opened, I noticed two soldiers standing outside the room. When they saw me, they immediately bowed.

I gave them a formal nod. "You." I said, jerking my chin at one of them.

"Yes, Empress?"

"Go to Commander Lyroik. Inform him that I'll be in engineering. He needs to prepare for a phantasm-jump."

Both their eyes widened. Phantom-jumps were dangerous, especially with bigger ships like this. The experimental Elnorsefall ship would have been specially made to channel phantasm throughout the ship and move it through space, but ours wasn't built for that. This ship was made for battle, and specifically with an engine made for evasive maneuvers, not jumping from world to world. It would have to be a manual phantasm-jump, like the one we used before when we first entered D'thaya. However, that was a much smaller ship. This jump would have to be much more powerful.

36

CHAPTER 35

"**A**re you sure about this, Empress?" Commander Lyroik said over the engine's room intercom.

I settled into the seat that would both secure me and connect my phantasm to the rest of the ship. My phantasm would be channeled through it, and I could pull us through space. I was sure about my decision, no matter how dangerous it was. I was not sure, however, that I'd be able to pull it off. Moving a ship as big as this was enough to burn me up from the inside out, which I wasn't thrilled about, but I didn't have a choice. We had to get to Eurkxo before Elnorsefall tried that weapon.

"I'm sure," I answered, hoping he wouldn't catch the lie. The engineers glanced at me nervously as they helped hook me up to the ship. It was a mess of wires and mechanisms. The mechanism attached to my chest specifically made me very uneasy. I tried to control my breathing as it lit up.

Fine. I would be fine.

Who was I kidding? I was terrified this would go wrong.

The feel of my phantasm being sucked from me as the cold metal pulled it straight from my core, as if it were being ripped from my chest...

I sucked in a breath. I really needed to stop thinking so much.

"Empress, please reconsider. We were informed about you being recently subjected to terrible experiments by-"

"No!" I shouted louder than I meant to. The engineers froze. Some carried clear pity in their eyes while others held an 'I told you so' look. I took a deep breath to calm my anger. The last thing I needed was to look unstable when the entire ship was about to be in my hands. This time I spoke in a calmer manner.

"No, Commander. I'm the only royal aboard, and I'm confident in my abilities. If I didn't believe I could do this, I wouldn't have volunteered." I said pointily, hoping I'd convinced him. I was lying, of course. I wasn't sure I could do it, and I still volunteered. He didn't respond right away, but after a few seconds of hesitation, he murmured an agreement.

"Everything's set, Empress." One of the engineers said. I took in a deep breath, and held it for a while, before releasing it.

"Take your positions."

"Increasing speed and starting countdown." A woman with bright orange hair said while sitting down at a control panel for the intercom, and strapping in. The other engineers followed her lead, sitting down and strapping on their safety restraints. The orange haired woman looked back to make sure everyone was seated, before turning back to her screen and starting the sequence.

"Phantasm-jump on 20, 19, 18..." I closed my eyes as she slowly counted down. I willed my phantasm through my body and opened myself up to the rest of the ship. I felt it being channeled, connecting me to every part of the ship. Maybe it would be easier than I thought? I let out a small puff of air. Even with my eyes closed I could see my phantasm shining in electric blue light.

"...15, 14, 13, 12, 11, 10..."

At least if something went wrong, no one would feel it even as their bodies would be ripped apart. Except me, of course. My phantasm would keep me alive as long as possible, even if my body burned up.

"...9, 8, 7, 6, 5, 4, 3, 2, 1, 0. NOW!" The orange haired woman yelled out. I pushed my phantasm throughout the ship, and felt it circle back to me, my body heating up in response. I willed my phantasm to move, to pull us forward.

My body jerked back into the chair, and I murmured a thank you to the safety restraints as I counted the seconds of pure agony. Doing a phantasm-jump was like swimming against a current, underwater. I could only hold it for so long.

Sweat poured down my face as I bit back a scream, feeling myself being pulled in so many directions. Not myself literally, but my phantasm, which was circling all throughout the ship, and pulling us forward by connecting with phantasm along our set path of space. Finally, I felt the agony end, and knew the machine connecting me to the ship had stopped. I pulled my phantasm back to me and tried to settle it. Biting back another cry of pain, I opened my eyes. The engineers were surrounding me, quickly removing the restraints. I sat for a few minutes even after I was free, gasping.

"Are... we...?" I stammered out in-between deep breaths. The orange haired woman nodded her head.

"We have successfully jumped into Eurkxo's sector, Empress." Forcing myself to stand while clutching my chest, I asked them to open communications.

"Commander, what's our status?" I used the wall of the engine room to keep myself steady while glaring at the engineers who kept glancing at me with uncertainty and whispering amongst themselves. How dare they whisper about me, like I was too weak to notice. I wasn't weak, I could handle it. I was handling it.

"Empress, you should be resting-"

"What. Is. Our. Status?" I paused after each word. The last thing I wanted was for someone to tell me to rest. I heard him murmur something, and guessed he was saying something to someone on his side.

"Empress, there's nothing here. No experimental Elnorsefall ship is here..."

"What?" I seethed out. Phantasm crackled between my fingers, and I felt my markings flickering in dim lights. That wasn't possible, they were here. Cronos told me himself they were here.

"They jumped away." He paused. "Before we even entered Eurkxo's sector."

I felt dizzy. The room spun around me, and I threw my head back against the wall. It hurt, but I didn't really care.

"No... they must have gone to E'arka or Vaymos! We have to jump again! We cannot-"

"Empress, you're in no condition to make another Phantasm-jump. I'm sorry, Empress. They mean to use your sympathy against you. We cannot fall into their trap."

"Do not lecture me on sympathy! They will turn E'arka into a wasteland!"

I thought of the little creatures. Of their lopsided smiles and hunched over figures. Ugly as they were, they were innocent. I had to protect them; I had to save them from Elnorsefall!

"Empress...." His voice was painfully quiet.

"What?" I said, ready to argue with him. My grip on the wall tightened. He was going to try to convince me not to take the ship there, but he wouldn't convince me.

"The trading ships that were sent to this planet from E'arka just relayed a message to our ships guarding the borders. They already have."

I felt the air rip from my lungs.

Already have...? E'arka... gone?

I gasped against the wall, before finally stilling. The information finally registered in my mind. E'arka was gone. Everyone on the planet was dead. I covered my mouth with both hands, trying not to throw-up. My whole body trembled, my knees going limp as I fell to the ground, shaking violently. My phantasm moved around me, making loud zapping sounds and the engineers gasped, hurrying away from me.

"Someone call a medic! Her phantasm is burning her up!"

The words somehow sounded far away, even though they were in the same room as me. Was it true? I thought something like that would hurt, not feel like this. This felt better, it felt right. Maybe... I could be stronger this way.

"No...no, no, no..." I murmured through trembles, hugging my knees. Tears fell from my eyes and ran down my cheeks.

They were gone. It was my fault. Billions of souls died in an instant, not even able to say goodbye. Just gone.

My veins were glowing in light, as well as my markings. It was not the usual calm, blinding light, but an ecstatic, wild one. The light filled the room, circling above and around me. My vision blurred, overtaken in brilliant blue light. I felt myself drifting, but I didn't care. I feel better now. I feel so much better.

"Do not...! She's.... burning...." I heard bits and pieces of voices screaming around me. Everything sounded so slow, so far away too. My body's senses felt like nothing compared to this. I felt through my phantasm. I felt everything around the ship, outside the ship, reaching into the cold ocean of space. I was running towards it; I wanted to be wrapped in it.

"Clove! Not... letting you go..."

My heart clenched at the sound of their voice.

That voice... I knew that voice. Who was it? Did I trust them? What-

I stilled myself, feeling their presence coming closer, and opened myself up to their soothing voice. Warm arms wrapped around my shoulders, and soft lips pressed against the back of my neck.

It didn't feel nice, it didn't feel nice at all. I didn't want warmth; I felt like I was burning in it. I wanted to go back to that cold feeling.

"Come back to me." The voice whispered in my ear. "Come back to me, my Clove."

"No... it hurts too much." I whispered.

Suddenly, I was angry. They were ruining everything! I was just starting to feel okay again, and now they wanted me to hurt all over again. I felt my lips moving into a scream, and I jerked against whoever was holding me.

"Let me go!" I screamed at the top of my lungs. My phantasm surrounded them, ready to constrict their heart to save myself, but I stopped. The cold feeling was back, pricking the side of my neck. Without thinking, I reached up to touch it. Metal... a needle? My eyelids drooped, and my phantasm gave out. Finally, I surrendered. Surrendered to complete darkness as my mind went blank.

37

EPILOGUE

My eyes fluttered open and I was momentarily blinded by the brightness which surrounded me. Blinking a couple of times, my eyes finally adjusted. I was in some kind of hospital room, though I didn't remember how I got there. A figure sat on the opposite end of the bed I was lying on. It was my brother, Cronos. He was facing the door, his eyes were dark and droopy, as if he hadn't slept in days.

"Follow the path of colors, a rare phenomenon after rainfall. Legends said if you followed it to the end you'd find a treasure. Some said it was on some unknown world in the forbidden region, others say it was on the first planet, but everyone claimed it was real. A magnificent treasure. All gone now, but the legend lives on. Remember? We always joked as children that we'd try and find it. Rain was the best pilot of the three of us, and I was the navigator. You..." He chuckled softly. "You were always the commander. Always telling us boys what to do." He let out a sigh. "I forgot about how much I missed those days..."

My face wrinkled, and I raised an eyebrow at him.

What in Natarah was he talking about?

He tilted his head back towards me and gasped. He stood up and hurried to my side of the bed, leaning into me.

"You're awake! I will tell the doctor immediately, stay here!" He said, holding his hands above me. I frowned up at him. As if I could go anywhere anyways. He turned to hurry away, but I reached out and grabbed his arm.

"Don't..." I managed to choke out, my throat felt sore and swollen. What had happened to me?

He turned back, considering me. Finally, he nodded and sat back down beside me.

"How are you feeling?" He rubbed the nape of his neck as if he were nervous. I stared at him through slightly narrowed eyes. This wasn't like him at all. He was always confident, serious, and cold. The way he was acting... it reminded me of-

Rain.

Tears clouded my eyes, and I quickly turned my body over to hide my tears.

"Ne'la, you're okay now. Everything is okay..." He soothed while using his other hand to rub my back. His gentleness only made me cry harder.

"Everyone is gone. Everyone!" I sobbed. "Rain... he-"

Cronos turned me back towards him and placed his finger over my lips, silencing me. "Shhh, ne'la. Be calm." He whispered. "I already know." He used his arms to lift my body up before wrapping his arms around me. I gasped. It had been years since I'd been hugged by him. Reluctantly, I return his embrace, letting my arms circle around his torso.

"We will get his phantasm back ne'la, and have a proper ceremony for him. I promise you that." He whispered, squeezing his arms around me. "But right now the only thing we can do is remember him for who he was. A warrior who fought so we could have more life." He pushed me back and reached his hands up to cup my face. "No matter what happens, from here until my death, I will not leave you. I will be here... for you."

I stared into his eyes, contemplating his words. Dear Natarah, did he sound sincere, but how could I trust him? I dropped my arms from around him and pushed him away.

"I don't believe that Cronos."

"Ne'la..." He sighed. "The reason-" He paused and looked down, before finally lifting his chin to look me in the eye. "The reason I didn't look back that day, the reason I sent you and Rain away."

I tried to shift away from him, my eyes stinging with tears as I remembered that day, but he held me firm. His hand rested on the back of my head, keeping me in place. Looking up at his face again, I was surprised to see his eyes filling with tears.

"It was because I couldn't let you see me so- so broken. I couldn't let you see my regret. If I'd turned back that day, I would've never let you leave, even if it meant putting you in danger."

"I never wanted your protection, Cronos. I just wanted us to be together." I whispered back as I blinked away more tears.

His other hand reached up to wipe the tears from my cheek before pulling our foreheads together. We both closed our eyes and rested in each other's presence. We only had each other now.

"I know that, now. Coming so close to losing you... I only have you now, and everyone will try to use you against me. I am afraid, sister. I-"

I opened my eyes and placed a finger against his lips.

"You can't be afraid to lose me, Cronos. Do not let me hold you back, nor let yourself hold me back. The Realms come first. Or else everything that happened... everyone who died, died for nothing, and I can't live with that." I grabbed his face and pulled him back as he locked eyes with me.

"I can't live with that." I stressed again, hoping he would understand how important it was to me.

He nodded, accepting my words. We embraced each other again, choosing to stay like that for a while before finally separating ourselves. I rubbed my forehead.

"What happened to me anyways? I don't remember much." I asked curiously. Everything that happened before coming to the hospital was a blur for me. I remembered a few things here and there, but I didn't think I was thinking straight then.

He sighed, "We almost lost you. Your body went into shock. Your phantasm- It was burning your mind. The only reason you made it is because... well, you can handle more than most. You're strong."

I raised an eyebrow at him.

He shrugs and says, "Always have been, ne'la."

I hummed in response.

"What was it you were talking about when I first woke up?" I tilted my head. He seemed to have been talking nonsense, but something about it felt familiar. His cheeks reddened in embarrassment, and he looked away.

"Oh that..." He looked back at me sheepishly. "The doctors said it would help if someone talked to you. So, me and your... fiancé? What's his name... Xorion? We took turns talking to you."

I watched him closely. It was so strange to see him like this. He seemed so much more relaxed than I was used to. It unnerved me a bit because I was used to keeping my guard up around him. He smiled brightly as if remembering a fond memory.

"Remember that old legend about the treasure that could be found by following a path of sky colors on the first planet? The treasure we always said we would find?"

I threw my head back and laughed. How did he remember that? It was so long ago. A story from an old book our mother used to read to us as children.

"You said you were going to steal mother's personal ship, and that Rain would fly it. We were going to be the first explorers of the Realms to find the first planet." I smiled at the memory. He grinned, and his arm jerked forward, mimicking a ship making a jump through space.

"Ah! I almost succeeded, remember? If it weren't for those annoying guards, we would have been halfway across the galaxy by the time they missed us."

"Your excuse, and I quote. 'Our mother, the Empress, left her handbag in the cockpit, and has asked us to retrieve it.'" I reminded him, and we both giggled. I shook my head, still giggling, "Dear Natarah, you were such a bad liar."

"Who was I to know mother didn't actually fly it? I was ten. Ten!" He insisted, pointing at me accusingly. I gently shoved his finger away, rolling my eyes playfully.

"I was six, and still a better liar than you! Remember all the pastries I got the guards to give us at Lucia's mother's birthday celebration?" He let out a whole-hearted laugh, throwing his head back and moaning at the memory.

"I still don't know how you managed that. Those were the best pasties I've ever tasted." We both laughed again, before finally falling silent. Cronos gave me a sad smile. "Remember what she always used to tell us?" I tilted my head, not knowing what he was talking about. She had said lots of things.

"She always said that part of being a leader is learning to accept your decisions and stick to them proudly even if they were a mistake. Because if you can't accept your choices, you don't deserve people's trust anyways."

I hung my head low at his words, thinking. Did I stick to my decisions? Yes. Was I proud of them? I didn't think I was. He rubbed my back up and down.

"Cloverlyne, I tried to force you to comply with my decisions, but you wouldn't listen to me."

I glanced at him and noticed a hardness in his expression. Did he blame me for Rain's death? He had every right to, I blamed myself.

How could I have been so stupid?

Even as I thought those words, I saw his expression soften, and I wondered if he was just putting on a front for me. Before a new round of tears could come over me, he continued.

"Even through everything that's happened, I am proud of you for not simply complying with me, otherwise you'll never grow. You gave D'thaya a chance. You showed Elnorsefall we wouldn't turn a blind eye. You showed them we'd fight back, and from now on you don't have to make those hard choices alone. I'm here with you."

"Thank you." I murmured while resting my head on his shoulder. "I'm happy we're together again. Don't try to keep me out of it ever again, or I'll rebel against you."

"Never again, I promise." He placed his arm over the front of my chest. I raised my arm up, and placed it against his, pressing into it. The symbol of respect for each other. We both finally pulled back, and I moved my legs to swing off the bed. At first, he tried to stop me, but with one glare, he changed his mind and helped me stand to my feet.

I glanced around the room. "Do you, um-"

"Know where your fiancé is?" He finished my question, his eyes sparkling with amusement. I blushed and nodded.

He jerked his hand towards one of the halls and pointed. "He's on the balcony, down that way. I'll take you there."

My mouth twitched in a smile. He still commanded rather than asked, but I guess I could ignore it this time. I wrapped my right arm around his shoulder and let him lead me to the balcony. It didn't take very long, we only had to turn through a corridor and there it was. Cronos used his other hand to push the painted glass doors open. The soft breeze of sea air filled my lungs, and the blue sun sparkled down on us. Xorion was facing away from us. His copper hair flew loosely down his shoulders, looking oily and unkempt. I mentally scolded him. How could he ignore his health on my account? But I couldn't really be mad at him, not really.

He must have heard us approaching because he turned towards us, his eyes widening in shock at seeing me. We stared at each other for some time, before his expression finally softened, and he took a bold step towards us. I smiled softly at him. Cronos looked between us a few times before letting out a short cough.

"I'll take my leave now." He nodded his head at Xorion, who took long strides to stand before us. Cronos guided my hand from his shoulder to rest on Xorion's arm,

"I'll see you soon, ne'la."

I nodded my head as he left us, but kept my eyes locked on Xorion. He raised his other hand to gently stroke my hair.

"You're okay..." He said as if he was trying to reassure himself.

"Yes, I'm okay."

"I thought... seeing you like that, I-" He murmured something quietly in his language, and kissed my forehead. It must have been his voice I'd heard as my phantasm was burning me up. I wasn't surprised.

"Xorion, I am here. I am fine." I reassured him, rubbing my hand up and down his forearm. He smiled, closing his eyes and relaxing into my touch. Only a few seconds later his eyes opened widely, a light in them as if he just remembered something.

"While you slept, we got word from Cedric and Lucia!" He said excitedly. I grasped his arm and let out a small gasp of excitement.

"Really? Are they well?" The news was like a drop of rain in the middle of the desert. I almost couldn't believe it.

"Yes, they are well! They'll be coming home soon." He hugged me close to him, nuzzling his nose into my hair. I pulled back a little and tilted my head up at him.

"Home?"

Why would he say home? Did he consider this planet his home now?

"Yes, home." He paused. "I think my planet will manage without me. I think I've found where I want to spend the rest of my life."

"Really? I thought influencers were rare. Are you sure your people will maintain order without you?" I fake a concerned look, gauging his reaction. It was priceless.

He froze, looking down at me in shock.

"How...?"

I rolled my eyes. He was a terrible liar too it seemed. Funny enough, I liked that about him. It made him more honest.

"I didn't, only suspected you. Your reaction right now gave you away."

He stared at me for some time, before throwing his head back and letting out a laugh. He wiped tears from his eyes from laughing so hard and said,

"You're correct, my Meirv. I was born as an Influencer on my planet, though my gifts were only used in emergencies. Surprisingly enough, my gift does not work in your galaxy. Your strange energy-phantasm, seems to mess with it."

I relaxed in his arms. I was relieved it didn't work here, or else it might cause a panic. It was a very controversial gift I wasn't ready to argue about. I'm glad it didn't matter anymore. Besides, I trusted him enough to have people's best interest at heart. Of that, I was sure.

"Clove, there's something I want to ask you." He moved a lock of hair out of my face to behind my ear, his tone becoming more serious.

"Yes?" I said, and wondered what he could possibly want to ask me about. Did something happen? He glanced around, and then back at me. I frowned at him. He was acting strangely and seemed nervous. I had hardly ever seen him nervous.

I was about to ask him what was wrong when he dropped to one knee, holding my much smaller hand in his. I gasped, shocked at his action.

Was he doing what I think he is?

"Clove, I know I have already asked this of you, but I'd like to do this according to your traditions. I know we haven't known each other very long but feel like I've spent a lifetime with you already. Being here in your galaxy has taught me something. Life comes and goes in a second, and I'm not going to waste that time." His hand squeezed mine. "Cloveryne Akkir Naviadah, will you marry me?" He said softly. With his other hand, he pulled out a beautiful gold ring from the pocket of his shirt.

My mouth parted, and I blinked away tears forming in my eyes.

"You're right." I whispered, my hand lifting to stroke his cheek. "We haven't known each other long. You understand my feelings about you and yet you stay by my side. You've witnessed countless deaths that follow my path, yet you stay by my side. You could have run. Maybe you should have." I said the last words quieter than the rest.

He'd seen me at my worst and yet he was willing to stay; despite knowing I didn't love him romantically. God above knew I cared for him deeply. Was this selfish of me? To tie him to my side forever? To use him without returning his love? Perhaps it was, but I never claimed to be a good person anyways. Right now, I didn't want to be. I wanted to be a little selfish.

"Xorion, warrior of Vaymos." I dropped to my knees and placed my other hand on his other cheek. "Yes, I will marry you." I tilted my head and placed a soft kiss over his lips. He let go of my hand and reached up to caress the back of my head, deepening the kiss. We separate for a moment, catching our breath. He smiled down at me and placed the ring on my finger.

I stared down at it, enjoying how it sparkled against the sun rays before looking up at him curiously.

"How did you even know this was our way?" His people's traditions were different then ours, I'm sure he wouldn't have known this was our way of proposing a marriage. I was happy to accept his traditions, but our engagement hadn't seemed all that real to me then. Now, it felt real. He smirked and shrugged knowingly.

"Your brother was helpful..."

I let out a short laugh at his explanation.

Cronos you sly creature...

I looked up to sigh at the heavens but gave a cry of fright instead. Above us, battleships fired weapons of light across the sky, scorching the sky in different colored light. The opposing ships were built in the signature style of Elnorsefall. Our skies were alight in battle, and I hadn't even known about it. If I listened closely, I could hear the sounds of the weapons being fired, but I'd been too distracted to realize. Elnorsefall had finally responded to our previous attack, by attacking our side of the planet.

"It's alright, Cronos says the city's shields are more than capable of holding back the explosions." Xorion soothed while running his hands up and down my lower back.

I sent him a quick glare. How could he say it was alright? I should be doing something to help, not sitting here watching.

"He didn't tell me..." I mumbled, suddenly very annoyed at my older brother. Didn't he tell me he wouldn't keep me out of it anymore?

"Meirv, just for now let's be happy that we live and can be here together. Tomorrow, we can show them the power they've given us with everything they've put us through." He hugged me tightly. I stared at the sky for a bit before finally sinking into his arms.

I sighed, "Okay...just for today." I whispered, burying my head in his neck. He put his fingers under my chin and lifted my head from his neck to kiss me again. This kiss was different from before, it felt like a promise.

"We will make them run, Clove. There won't be any corner of this galaxy or any galaxy that they can hide from our rage." He looked up, jerking his chin slightly at the scene above. "This is only the beginning of their end."

I looked up to the skies as well just as a ship burst into a million different colored flames. My arms tightened around him as we watched those same little flames dance across the sky. In a way, it was strangely beautiful.

"The beginning of the end to Elnorsefall."